– Classic –
AUSTRALIAN
SHORT
STORIES
& VERSE

SUMMIT
PRESS

Publisher's Note

Classic Australian Short Stories and *Classic Australian Verse*
were first published as separate editions in 2001. Both books are
now incorporated here as one volume.

PRESS

22 Summit Road
Noble Park Victoria 3174
Australia

This edition first published 2002

This compilation © Summit Press
Designer: Geoff Hocking
Cover design: Sonia Dixon
Formatting: Susannah Low

Printed in Australia by Griffin Press

National Library of Australia Cataloguing in Publication data
Classic Australian short stories and verse.
ISBN 1 86503 691 9.
1. Short stories, Australian. 2. Australian poetry. 3. Ballads, English – Australia. 4.
Folk songs, English – Australia. I. Pinkney, Maggie. II. Pinkney, Maggie, Classic
Australian stories. III. Pinkney, Maggie, Classic Australian verse.

A820.8

Contents

Introduction

T he convicts – and other early British settlers – saw Australia as a hostile, almost bizarre, land. It was not until the late 1800s, about a century after the arrival of the First Fleet, that a sense of national identity began to emerge. And this identity was largely forged by Australia's writers, poets and painters, most of whom, significantly, were born here. To them, Australia was home.

Two men who, above all others, provided Australians with a romantic view of themselves as rough-edged, laconic battlers were Henry Lawson and A.B. ('Banjo') Paterson. Lawson is acknowledged as the Australian master of the short story and Paterson of the bush ballad, although both men, of course, were prolific writers and poets.

The stories and poems in this collection have been chosen because of the light every one of them throws upon some aspect of life in early Australia.

Among the stories are Lawson's moving portrayals of the loneliness of a woman's life in the bush, including his classics, 'The Drover's Wife' and 'Water Them Geraniums'. Edward Dyson takes up the theme with his haunting 'The Conquering Bush', while Barbara Baynton's story, 'The Chosen Vessel', adds a touch of pure horror to the picture of the pioneer woman's experience.

Steele Rudd's much-loved 'Dad and Dave' stories depict the grinding poverty and hardship of life on a poor selection, but these tales are softened by his light-hearted approach. But possibly the most hilarious Australian short story ever written is Lawson's 'The Loaded Dog', which begins this anthology.

Charles Harpur and Henry Kendall, both Australian-born, were among the first poets to write of the Australian landscape with any affection. But it would be a later generation of poets whose verse helped us see our country clearly – in all its contrasts – forging a sense of nationhood.

Paterson single-handedly provided us with most of our best-loved and most essentially Australian poems: 'The Man from Snowy River', 'Clancy of the Overflow', 'The Geebung Polo Club' and our unofficial national anthem, 'Waltzing Matilda'. C. J. Dennis, Henry Lawson, Barcroft Boake and Dorothea Mackellar were among the many other poets who helped shape our growing national consciousness. Finally, we owe a great debt to the forgotten versifiers of our many rollicking ballads, which tell of the suffering of the convicts and the exploits of the bushrangers.

A vivid picture of a vanished Australia – peopled by rugged shearers, drovers, swaggies and poor selectors – emerges from this nostalgic anthology. It offers us a deeper understanding of our colonial past.

Maggie Pinkney, 2002

– Classic –
AUSTRALIAN
SHORT
STORIES

Compiled by Maggie Pinkney

Contents

The Loaded Dog

Henry Lawson

D AVE REGAN, JIM BENTLY, AND ANDY PAGE were sinking a shaft at Stony Creek in search of a rich gold quartz reef which was supposed to exist in the vicinity. There is always a rich quartz reef supposed to exist in the vicinity; the only questions are whether it is ten feet or hundreds beneath the surface, and in which direction. They had struck some pretty solid rock, also water which kept them baling. They used the old-fashioned blasting powder and time-fuse; they'd dip the cartridge in melted tallow to make it watertight, get the drill hole as dry as possible, drop in the cartridge with some dry dust, and wad and ram with stiff clay and broken brick. Then they'd light the fuse and get out of the hole and wait. The result was usually an ugly pot-hole in the bottom of the shaft and half a barrow-load of broken rock.

There was plenty of fish in the creek, fresh-water bream, cod, cat-fish, and tailers. The party were fond of fish, and Andy and Dave of fishing. Andy would fish for three hours at a stretch if encouraged by a 'nibble' or a 'bite' now and then – say once in twenty minutes. The butcher was always willing to give meat in exchange for fish when they caught more than they could eat; but now it was winter, and these fish wouldn't bite. However, the creek was low, just a chain of muddy waterholes, from the hole with a few bucketfuls in it to the sizable pool with an average depth of six or seven feet, and they could get fish by bailing out the smaller holes or muddying up the water in the larger ones till the fish rose to the surface. There was the cat-fish, with spikes growing out of the sides of its head, and if you got pricked you'd know it, as Dave said. Andy took off his boots, tucked up his trousers, and went into a hole one day to stir up the mud with his feet, and he knew it. Dave scooped one out with his hand and got pricked, and he knew it too; his arm swelled, and the pain throbbed up into his shoulder, and down into his stomach too, he said, like a toothache he had once, and kept him awake for two nights – only the toothache pain had a 'burred edge', Dave said.

Dave got an idea. 'Why not blow up the fish in the big waterhole with a cartridge?' he said. 'I'll try it.'

He thought the thing out and Andy Page worked it out. Andy usually put Dave's theories into practice if they were practicable, or bore the blame for the failure and chaffing of his mates if they weren't.

He made a cartridge about three times the size of those they used in the rock. Jim Bently said it was big enough to blow the bottom out of the river. The inner skin was of stout calico; Andy stuck the end of a six-foot piece of fuse well down in the powder and bound the mouth of the bag firmly to it with whipcord. The idea was to sink the cartridge in the water with the open end of the fuse attached to a float on the surface, ready for lighting. Andy dipped the cartridge in melted beeswax to make it watertight. 'We'll have to leave it some time before we light it,' said Dave, 'to give the fish time to get over their scare when we put it in, and come nosing around again; so we'll want it watertight.'

Round the cartridge Andy, at Dave's suggestion, bound a strip of sail canvas – that they had used for making water-bags – to increase the force of the explosion, and round that he pasted layers of stiff brown paper – on the plan of the sort of fireworks we called 'gun-crackers'. He let the paper dry in the sun, then he sewed a covering of two thicknesses of canvas over it, and bound the thing from end to end with stout fishing line. Dave's schemes were elaborate, and he often worked his inventions out to nothing. The cartridge was rigid and solid enough now – a formidable bomb; but Andy and Dave wanted to be sure. Andy sewed on another layer of canvas, dipped the cartridge in melted tallow, twisted a length of fencing-wire round it as an after-thought, dipped in it tallow again, and stood it carefully against a tent peg, where he'd know where to find it, and wound the fuse loosely round it. Then he went to the campfire to try some potatoes which were boiling in their jackets in a billy, and to see about frying some chops for dinner. Dave and Jim were at work in the claim that morning.

They had a big black young retriever dog – or rather an overgrown pup, a big, foolish, four-footed mate, who was always slobbering round them and lashing their legs with his heavy tail that swung round like a stock whip. Most of his head was usually a red, idiotic slobbering grin of appreciation of his own silliness. He seemed to take life, the world, his two-legged mates, and his own instinct as a huge joke. He'd retrieve anything; he carted back most of the camp rubbish that Andy threw away. They had a cat that died in hot weather, and Andy threw it a good distance away in the scrub; and early one morning the dog found the cat, after it had been dead a week or so, and carried it back to camp, and laid it just inside the tent flaps, where it could make its presence felt when the mates should rise and begin to sniff suspiciously in the sickly smothering atmosphere of the summer sunrise. He used to retrieve them when they went in swimming; he'd jump in after them, and scratch their naked bodies with his paws. They loved him for his good-heartedness and his foolishness, but when they wished to enjoy a swim they had to tie him up in camp.

He watched Andy with great interest all morning making the cartridge, and hindered him considerably, trying to help; but about noon he went off to the claim to see how Dave and Jim were getting on, and to come home to dinner with them. Andy saw them coming, and put a panful of mutton chops on the fire. Andy was cook today; Dave and Jim stood with their backs to the fire, as bushmen do in all weathers, waiting till dinner should be ready. The retriever went nosing round after something he seemed to have missed.

Andy's brain still worked on the cartridge; his eye was caught by the glare of an empty kerosene tin lying in the bushes, and it struck him that it wouldn't be a bad idea to sink the cartridge packed with clay, sand, or stones in the tin, to increase the force of the explosion. He may have been all out, from a scientificpoint of view, but the notion looked all right to him. Jim Bently, by the way, wasn't interested in their 'damned silliness'. Andy noticed an empty treacle tin – the sort with the little tin neck or spout soldered on to the top for the convenience of pouring out the treacle – and it struck him that this would have made the best kind of cartridge-case: he would only have had to pour in the powder, stick the fuse through the neck, and cork and seal it with beeswax. He was turning to suggest this to Dave, when Dave glanced over his shoulder to see how the chops were doing – and bolted. He explained afterwards that he thought he heard the pan spluttering extra, and looked to see if the chops were burning. Jim Bently looked behind and bolted after Dave. Andy stood stock-still, staring after them.

'Run, Andy! Run!' they shouted back at him. "Run! Look behind you, you fool!' Andy turned slowly and looked, and there, close behind him, was the retriever with the cartridge in his mouth – wedged into the broadest and silliest grin. And that wasn't all. The dog had come round the fire to Andy, and the loose end of the fuse had trailed and waggled over the burning sticks into the blaze; Andy had slit and nicked the firing end to the fuse well, and now it was hissing and spitting properly.

Andy's legs started with a jolt; his legs started before his brain did, and he made after Dave and Jim. And the dog followed Andy.

Dave and Jim were good runners – Jim the best – for a short distance; Andy was slow and heavy, but he had the strength and the wind and could last. The dog capered round him, delighted as a dog could be to find his mates, as he thought, on for a frolic. Dave and Jim kept shouting back, 'Don't foller us! Don't foller us, you coloured fool!' But Andy kept on, no matter how they dodged. They could never explain, any more than the dog, why they followed each other, but so they ran, Dave keeping in Jim's track in all its turnings, Andy after Dave, and the dog circling round

CLASSIC AUSTRALIAN SHORT STORIES —

Andy – the live fuse swishing in all directions and hissing and spluttering and stinking. Jim yelling at Dave not to follow him. Dave shouting to Andy to go in another direction – to 'spread out', and Andy roaring at the dog to go home. Then Andy's brain began to work, stimulated by the crisis; he tried to get a running kick at the dog, but the dog dodged; he snatched up sticks and stones and threw them at the dog and ran on again. The retriever saw that he'd made a mistake about Andy, and left him and bounded after Dave. Dave, who had the presence of mind to think that the fuse's time wasn't up yet, made a dive and a grab for the dog, caught him by the tail, and as he swung round snatched the cartridge out of his mouth and flung it as far as he could; the dog immediately bounded after it and retrieved it. Dave roared and cursed at the dog, who, seeing that Dave was offended, left him and went after Jim, who was well ahead. Jim swung to a sapling and went up it like a native bear; it was a young sapling, and Jim couldn't safely get more than ten or twelve feet from the ground. The dog laid the cartridge, as carefully as it were a kitten, at the foot of the sapling, and capered and leaped and whooped joyously round under Jim. The big pup reckoned that this was part of the lark – he was all right now – it was Jim who was out for a spree. The fuse sounded as if it were going a mile a minute. Jim tried to climb higher and the sapling bent and cracked. Jim fell on his feet and ran. The dog swooped on the cartridge and followed. It all took but a very few moments. Jim ran to a digger's hole, about ten feet deep, and dropped down into it – landing on soft mud – and was safe. The dog grinned sardonically down on him, over the edge, for a moment, as if he thought it would be a good lark to drop the cartridge down on Jim.

'Go away, Tommy,' Jim said feebly, 'go away.'

The dog bounded off after Dave, who was the only one in sight now; Andy had dropped behind a log, where he lay flat on his face, having suddenly remembered a picture of the Russo-Turkish war with a circle of Turks lying flat on their faces (as if they were ashamed) round a newly-arrived shell.

There was a small hotel or shanty on the creek, on the main road, not far from the claim. Dave was desperate; the time flew much faster in his stimulated imagination than it did in reality, so he made for the shanty. There were several casual bushmen on the verandah and in the bar; Dave rushed into the bar, banging the door behind him. 'My dog!' he gasped, in reply to the astonished publican, 'the blanky retriever – he's got a live cartridge in his mouth.'

The retriever, finding the front door shut against him, had bounded round and in by the back way, and now stood smiling in the doorway leading from the passage, the cartridge still in his mouth and the fuse spluttering. They burst out of that bar. Tommy bounded first after one and then after another, for, being a young dog, he tried to make friends with everybody.

The bushmen ran round corners, and some shut themselves in the stable. There was a new weatherboard and corrugated iron kitchen and wash-house on piles in the backyard, with some women washing clothes inside. Dave and the publican bundled in there and shut the door – the publican cursing Dave and calling him a crimson fool, in hurried tones, and wanting to know what the hell he came here for.

The retriever went in under the kitchen, amongst the piles, but, luckily for those inside, there was a vicious yellow mongrel cattle-dog sulking and nursing his nastiness under there – a sneaking, fighting, thieving canine, whom neighbours had tried for years to shoot or poison. Tommy saw his danger – he'd had experience from this dog – and started out across the yard, still sticking to the cartridge. Halfway across the yard the yellow dog caught him and nipped him. Tommy dropped the cartridge, gave one terrified yell, and took to the Bush. The yellow dog followed him to the fence and then ran back to see what he had dropped. Nearly a dozen other dogs came from round all the corners and under the buildings – spidery, thievish, cold-blooded kangaroo dogs, mongrel sheep- and cattle-dogs, vicious black and yellow dogs – that slip after you in the dark, nip your heels, and vanish without explaining – and yapping, yelping small fry. They kept at a respectable distance round the nasty yellow dog, for it was dangerous to go near him when he thought he had found something which might be good for a dog or cat. He sniffed at the cartridge twice and was just taking a third cautious sniff when --

It was very good blasting powder – a new brand that Dave had recently got up from Sydney; and the cartridge had been excellently well made. Andy was very patient and painstaking in all he did, and nearly as handy as the average sailor with needles, twine, canvas and rope.

Bushmen say that the kitchen jumped off its piles and on again. When the smoke and dust cleared away, the remains of the nasty yellow dog were lying against the paling fence of the yard looking as if he had been kicked into a fire by a horse and afterwards rolled in the dust under a barrow, and finally thrown against the fence from a distance. Several saddle horses, which had been 'hanging up' round the verandah, were galloping wildly down the road in clouds of dust, with broken bridle reins flying; and from a circle round the outskirts, every point of the compass in the scrub, came the yelping of dogs. Two of them went home to the place where they were born, thirty miles away, and reached it the same night and stayed there; it was not till towards evening that the rest came cautiously back to make inquiries. One was trying to walk on two legs, and most of 'em looked more or less singed; and a little, singed, stumpy-tailed dog, who had been in the habit of hopping the back half of him along on one leg, had reason to be glad he'd saved up the other leg all those years, for he needed it now. There was one old one-eyed cattle-dog round that shanty for years afterwards, who couldn't stand the smell of a gun being cleaned. He it was who had taken an interest, only second to that of the yellow dog, in the cartridge. Bushmen said that it was amusing to slip up on his blind side and stick a dirty ramrod under his nose; he wouldn't wait to bring his solitary eye to bear — he'd take to the bush and stay out all night.

For half an hour or so after the explosion there were several bushmen round behind the stable who crouched, doubled up, against the wall, or rolled gently on the dust, trying to laugh without shrieking. There were two white women in hysterics in the house, and a half-caste rushing aimlessly round with a dipper of cold water. The publican was holding his wife tight and begging her between squawks, to 'hold up for my sake, Mary, or I'll lam the life out of ye.'

Dave decided to apologise later on, 'when things had set-tled down a bit', and went back to camp. And the dog that had done it all, Tommy, the great idiotic mongrel retriever, came slobbering round Dave and lashing his legs with his tail, and trotted home after him, smiling his broadest, longest, and reddest smile of amiability, and apparently sat-isfied for one afternoon with the fun he'd had.

Andy chained up the dog securely, and cooked more chops, while Dave went to help Jim out of the hole.

And most of this is why, for years afterwards, lanky, easy-going bushmen, riding lazily past Dave's camp, would cry, in a lazy drawl and with just a hint of the nasal twang:

'Ello, Da-a-ave! How's the fishin' getting on, Da-a-ave?'

Dead Man's Lode

Edward Dyson

IT WAS BRIGHT WITHIN THE PILE-GETTERS' HUT; outside the night was wet and stormy, and the wind piped a deep, mournful organ tone in the gnarled and stunted gums on the hillside. The three young men had finished tea, and washed up and squared up – that is to say, Dayton had stowed the bread and butter and the remainder of the salt and beef in the kerosene box that served them as a larder, M'Gill had dipped the tin plates in hot water and wiped them carefully on a superannuated white shirt, and Woodhead had raised a tremendous dust under a pretence of sweeping out the hut with a broom extemporised from a bundle of scrub ferns; for it was the first principle of their association that every man should 'do his whack' in the matter of attendance of domestic duties.

'Too thunderin' wet to go down to the camp, an' too blessed windy to climb up to Scrubby's,' said Dayton, who was curing himself of an extraordinary habit of profanity for a wager, and found the task of filling in the blanks rather a trial. 'I s'pose cut-throat's our little dart,' he continued, producing an over-worked euchre pack.

M'Gill was fighting his way into a stubborn oilskin coat that crackled like tin armour.

'Not cut-throat tonight, boys,' he said. 'I'm going up the gully a spell.'

'Where bound, Mack?' queried Dayton, with quick suspicion. The young men had discovered a pretty girl at

Scrubby Scanlan's settlement, two miles off, and each thought he had an exclusive right to the friendship and hospitality of Scanlan and the smiles of his handsome, hard-working and very sensible eldest daughter.

M'Gill smiled.

'Not there, old man,' he said. 'I promised "The Identity" I'd give him a look in tonight.'

'Well, you ought!' with great derision. 'What d'ye want foolin' after that evil old beast? If he was well tomorrer he'd bang you on the head for half a quid. That's my straight say-so. I'll be sworn he shook our crosscut; an' here you are, dancin' attendance same as if he was clear white!'

'The poor devil is as harmless as a baby,' said M'Gill. 'Anyhow, I can't leave a sick man to take his chances in that miserable hole up there.'

Joe M'Gill went out amidst a rush of wind and rain, and left his mates to their game and the comfort of their warm, watertight hut.

'Off his bloomin' chump!' commented Dayton emphatically, slapping down the cards.

The philosophical Woodhead, who was smoking placidly, looked up and cut.

'Joe's all right,' he drawled. 'Always had a weakness for sick things. I've seen him take more trouble with a lame dog than most men would over a poor relation. Besides, the old man is real bad, and if Mack didn't give an eye to him I expect I would have to do it myself. I'm awfully soft-hearted that way, and I like to see other fellows looking after the poor and the sick – it saves me the trouble.'

Meanwhile M'Gill was boring his way through the storm towards a point of light showing fitfully amongst the thick, supple saplings that rolled like a sea in a gale. 'The Identity's' hut stood at the head of the gully, in the centre of a small clearing. It was sheltered on one side by the abrupt rise of Emu Hill, and exposed on the other (saving for the intervention of the leafy young peppermints, the growth of recent years) to the fierce winds that seemed to gather the rains into the narrow confines of the gully, and drive them pounding up its whole length, in eddying torrents, to be thrown back in tumbling yellow floods from the invulnerable side of Emu Hill.

Peter Shaw, variously known as 'The Identity', 'The Hermit', 'Blue Peter', and 'Old Shaw', was a veteran fossicker, a reticent, gruff man, whose almost complete isolation had recently been broken by the appearance in the locality of Brown's Patch of a few parties of sleeper-cutters and pile getters, driven thitherward by the approach of the railway to Bunyip.

Peter was living in the same chock-and-log hut at the head of Grasshopper Gully when the first selector settled in the district, and when the reputation of Brown's Patch as an alluvial field had already faded and been forgotten, and when the fact that the creek, and the hill, and the gully had once rattled and rung with the clatter of cradle and puddling-tub, pick and shovel, and windlass-barrel was unknown to all within the jurisdiction of the Bunyip Shire Council, with the exception of old Shaw. Even now Peter's settled neighbours were few and far between, and until the arrival of the timber getters his beloved seclusion was but rarely disturbed by man, woman or child. He lived, according to the common belief, on the vegetables he grew, eked out with the supplies he bought from Bunyip at long intervals – supplies bought with the price of the few 'weights' of gold won by fossicking patiently and laboriously up and down the creek and in the many little blind gullies running up into Emu Hill.

Of course 'The Identity' was talked about. Whenever two or more selectors were met together Peter's character and habits were sure, sooner or later, to come under discussion, and as he was one of the stock themes of the local fabulist, the history attached to him did not lack romantic interest. He was generally credited with having stolen everything that went missing in the district, and, amongst the women, at least, there was a profound belief that he and 'the old devil' were on excellent terms and exchanged visits frequently; but for all the attention Shaw gave these people they might have been merely stumps or stones by the way.

M'Gill pulled the catch of the old man's door, and entered without knocking. The remains of a big log were smouldering in the wide sod chimney, and a slush lamp, manufactured from a sardine tin, guttered on the bush table, filling the hut with a villainous smoke. On a narrow bunk, face downward, lay the half-clad figure of a man. 'The Identity' lifted himself up on his hands as the door clanged to, and turned a haggard face, surrounded by a scrub of iron-grey hair, towards the intruder. His eyes brightened as he recognised Joe.

'Good on you! Good on you!' he gasped, extending a shaky hand. 'I was hopin' you'd come.'

Joe threw open his oilskin and drew a couple of small parcels from his shirt.

'Here you are, old party,' he said: 'I've brought you some

stuff for beef tea, and a bottle of medicine.' Shaw took the bottle in his hand and examined it. It contained a patent medicine then very popular with bushmen as an infallible remedy for all the physical ills that man is heir to, from cuts to consumption.

'It's too late, my boy,' he said. 'I'm a done man: but a dose might ease me a bit if it's hot enough – gimme a dose.'

Joe poured out a quantity of the medicine into a pannikin, and held it towards him; but the sick man clutched his hand, and a sudden excitement lit up his deathly face as he whispered:

'Did you do the other thing what I told you?'

M'Gill nodded.

'Put your pegs in an' make your application for the lease all correct an' accordin' to law?'

'Yes, yes, just as you told me. Now drink.'

Shaw drainedoff his medicine, but retained his grip on Joe's arm.

'Certain you didn't let on to no one?' he asked, with a look half suspicious, half cunning in his eyes – 'no p'lice, no doctors – eh?'

'Not a soul; I always keep my word. But for all that I think you should have a doctor.'

'No, no, no!' cried the old man, with fierce energy; 'no doctors – no p'lice! I'm peggin' out – don't I know it? – an' I won't have doctors, damn 'em! Can't you let a man die his own way?'

'Right you are,' said Joe, soothingly. 'You'll buck up again, though, when you get outside a pint or two of this.'

M'Gill threw the wood in the fireplace together, and set

about preparing the beef tea, and Shaw, who had relapsed
into his former position, face downwards upon the bunk,
watched every movement with one alert eye. Presently he
spoke again.

'I said I'd tell you the whole yarn t'night, Joe.'

'Not tonight, Peter, you're not equal to it – wait until you
are stronger.'

'Stronger! stronger!' The fossicker had started up again
and was glaring angrily. 'Wait till I'm dead an' dumb, you
mean. No, it mus' be t'night. One of the chaps up at the
camp'll be knockin' together a coffin fer me t'morrer.'

M'Gill admitted to himself, as he looked into the brilliant,
deep-set eyes of the man, and saw the grisly configuration
of the skull standing out under the stark yellow skin of his
face, that nothing was more probable. Shaw looked a man
face to face with death, sustained only by the feverish
excitement that blazed in his restless eyes and manifested
itself in the uneasy motions of his wasted hands. The
young man offered him a pannikin of beef tea, but Peter
put it aside after trying a couple of mouthfuls.

'No, I can't take it, boy,' he said. 'I can't take nothin'. I
don't want nothin'; only to tell you all before I cave in. Sit
here on the edge of the bunk.

'Joe,' said 'The Identity', 'you come here to help me, an'
you've took a lot of trouble with me, 'cause you're a good
sort, an' can't help it, like; but you don't like me. I could
see you didn't like me – you suspicioned me from the first,
eh – didn't you?

This was quite true, but the young man returned no
answer. There had never been anything about Peter Shaw
to invite affection; in health he was sullen, covert, and

uncanny, and in sickness evil-tempered and childish in his wants, and, more particularly, in his fears.

'I knew it – I knew it!' he continued, 'but because you are a good sort, an' because I must out with this load here, here!' – he struck his breast feebly with his hand – 'I'm goin' to tell you somethin' that'll make a rich man of you, Joseph M'Gill.'

Clutching Joe's sleeve with his bony fingers, he went on with his story, speaking in quick undertones, with a sort of insane energy that sustained him to the end.

'I came to this district twenty odd years ago, my lad. Brown had just struck the surfacin' down the gully by the creek, an' we called the rush Brown's Patch. Two days after campin' I picked up my mate Harry Foote – Stumpy Foote we named him 'cause he was bumble-footed. He was a dog, a mean hound, but he didn't look it, an' he was a good miner. We went to work on the alluvial, an' did fairly, but we both had a great idea about a good reef in these hills. All the indications pointed to it, an' presently we slung the wash an' started prospectin'. We trenched, an' travelled, an' trenched fer weeks without strikin' an ounce of quartz, an' Stumpy got full of it: but I grew more certain about that lode, an' hung on. So we agreed that he'd go back to the alluvial again, an' I'd keep on peggin away after the reef, an' we'd be mates whatever turned up. Well, we kep' this up fer a long time, me trustin' Stumpy all the time, an' intendin' t' do the square thing by him when I lobbed on the lode, as I was sure I would. I worked like a fiend. I was mad fer gold then. I hadn't been out on'y a few years, an' strikin' it lucky meant everythin' t' me; meant – but no matter, that ain't anythin' t' do with the story. You wouldn't understand how I felt if I told you, an' I believe I don't understand meself now. Stumpy did poorly, or told me as much. I got barely enough as my share to pay tucker bills, but he kep' workin' away, sluicin' the surfacin' down along the creek – a patch he had hit on himself.

'One night I returned to the tent unexpected. Foote had told me the week afore that he was goin' to roll up his swag an' skip, an' I'd bin out on those hills beyond Scanlan's ever since. A light was burnin' inside, an' Stumpy didn't hear me till I'd thrown back the flap of the tent. He was leanin' over the table, an' he looked up at me sudden, an' his face went milky white. Well it might – I caught him in the act of sweepin' a pile of gold into a canvas bag. A pile – a heap – hundreds of ounces it looked t' me – hundreds of ounces in coarse nuggets an' rich specimens. The cur fumbled in his hurry to get it out of sight, an' spilled some of the finer stuff on the floor.

'I went mad at the sight of all that gold, an' at the thought of the dirty trick he'd served me. I didn't speak, but jes' grabbed him so, by the neck, an' dragged him outer the tent. I don't think I meant murder – I don't know what I meant, but there was a pick handle leanin' agen the sod chimbley, an' I took it in my right hand. He opened his mouth to yell, an' I hit him one – jes once – an' he went over like a wet shirt. I waited for him to get up, but he didn't move agen, an' when I come t' look at him he was dead. The paper-skulled, chicken-hearted cur was dead!

'I didn't funk – I didn't lose my head fer a second. I was never cooler in my life; my brain was clear, but I saw on'y one thing at a time – on'y one thing, and I acted on it. After dousin' the light in the tent, I took Stumpy up on my shoulder an' carried him over the hill to the slope furthest from the camp.

"'Twas a clear, moonlight night, bright enough t' read Bible print by, but the side of Emu Hill was well timbered, an' the saplin's was as thick as scrub, so I was not likely t' be seen. I dropped the body in a small clear space amongst a thick patch of scrub on that spur above the soda spring. There was a good depth of soft vegetable soil there – a beautiful quiet place fer a grave.

'Then I went back to the tent, careless like, case anyone should chance along; but the camp was a good step down the creek from our tent, an' I never met a soul. Stumpy had his swag ready for rollin' up – he meant to cut and leave me. I took up his things an' a pick an' shovel, an' trudged back t' the body. It lay sprawlin' in the shadder of the scrub, jest as I'd dropped it, one hand reachin' out into the light clawin' grass; but I on'y thought of my job, and I set t' work t' dig his grave at once.

'I worked quietly – the pick made no noise in that soft ground – but I worked hard. I meant t' bury him deep, an' bury him well. A neat hole I made him, seven by two, an' as plumb as a prospectin' shaft. As I dug an' shovelled – quite cool in my mind, fer all the body was spread out there behind me in the shadder – my thoughts went wanderin' over my bad luck, an' the idea that Stumpy had been on good gold, an' meant to rob me of my fair half, made me vicious, an' I belted in hard an' fast.

'I had her down 'bout three foot, an' reckoned that'd nearly do. I was squarin' up the end when my pick struck somethin' that made it ring. I dug away a bit around that somethin', a sudden excitement growin' in me, an' makin' me ferget I was diggin' a grave – a grave for a murdered man. Down in the west corner of the hole I saw the white gleam of quartz. Stoopin', I lit a match to examine it. By the Lord, Joe! I'd struck it – struck it thick an' rich!'

Old Peter's agitation became so intense at this stage that Joe was compelled to put his arms around his attenuated form, and hold him on the bunk.

'See that fire, boy?' he gasped, pointing an uncertain hand, and glaring as if in frenzy.

'Well, it was like that – the live embers, the glowin' red gold in it! Rich! It seemed all gold. I'd struck the cap of the reef, an' I went a'most mad with joy at the sight of the beautiful, beautiful gold. I was staggered back agen the other end of the hole, starin' at the reef. I was goin' to yell an' dance, thinkin' of nothin' but my lovely luck, when I half turned, an' caught a glimpse of Stumpy's white, dead face glowerin' at me in the moonlight, an' I funked fer the first time. The shadder had crep' back, leavin' jest his face showin', an' there it was, with a spark in each of its big eyes, mouthin' at me – grinnin' horribly!

'I went dead cold, my legs broke under me. All of a sudden I was dreadfully afraid. Then I thought: 'Pete, this is a hangin' match – Peter, they're after you. What's the good of a golden reef to a hanged man? I crawled out of the hole, wantin' to run, but its devilish eyes followed me. Oh! I crawled like a worm crazy with fear – sick with it! The findin' the gold there in his grave seemed a damned trick of his an' the devil's t' spite me – t' make me mad. I seemed t' know then, while the horror was on me, what it all meant – that I'd cursed myself fer ever – thet, good luck or bad luck, fer the future t'was all the same t' me.

'But I was strong enough t' bury him. I turned his face down, an' dragged the body along, an' flung it into the hole on top of the reef; and when it was out of sight, under a foot or so of dirt, I began t' feel stronger and braver, an' t' reason a bit. I would bury him beautifully there, I said to meself, an' wait, an' some time I would dig him up again and hide him far enough away, an' then I would work the reef, an' bye-an-bye go home to – to – go home a rich man!

'I did bury him, an' then crawled back t' the tent, an' tried t' sleep, but couldn't. At daylight I was back at the grave again; smoothin' it over with my fingers, rakin' dry leaves, an' grass, an' bark over it t' hide every trace, shiverin' in my boots all the time. They reckoned me a brave man once. I'd done some things that made men think me game. But I've been a cur ever since the night I killed my mate – a coward in the night an' in the day, before men and before devils.

'Durin' the day I managed to go down among the men an' make enquiries 'bout Stumpy. None of the chaps seemed surprised t' hear he was not around an' one or two hinted pretty straight that I wasn't likely to see him agen – thet he'd been doin' pretty well down the creek, an' had cleared with the gold to do me outer my share.

'Joe, I never dared t' touch Stumpy's grave from thet day t' this. For five years small parties was workin' down about the creek off an' on, an' I kep' tellin' myelf that when they'd all gone some day I'd shift Stumpy's bones. Then the Chows came fossickin' an' time went on, an' as it passed I grew more an' more of a coward. Once or twice there's bin prospectin' parties out here after the reef, an' I think I was stark crazy while they was about. The fear of them strikin' the lode used t' drive me wild, an' I grew t' hate every man who come near Emu Hill, an' gradually to loathe the sight of humin' bein's. I shifted up here t' be further from the grave, an' 'cause I'd got loony notions that Stumpy was walkin' about o' nights.

'There was on'y a hundred ounces or so in my mate's bag after all. It'd looked five times ez much t' me. It's buried in the ground jest under the head of my bunk. Onst I sold a few ounces of it at the township, but it was coarse stuff, an' the news got 'round an' the next thing I knew there was another small rush along the creek, an' diggers was pokin' about everywhere. That frightened me again. If the reef was struck Stumpy's bones would be found, an' they'd hang me, sure ez death. Half a dozen men lived at Wombat who'd remembered my mate's disappearance, an' there was things I'd buried with Stumpy that'd make his bones known. So I buried the gold, an' never tried t' sell another colour of it.

'Since then I've had scores of chances of shiftin' them bones, but I wasn't the man t' do it, an' then I begun t' find thet I didn't want to – thet I didn't want the gold – thet I didn't want any of the things thet I'd wanted like mad before. But I didn't go away. I was chained here, an' I always thought thet some day someone would find Stumpy, an' I would be wanted, an' all these years I've dreaded it, an' waited fer it, an' hated, an' suffered, an' here I am, an' there, out on the hill, are Stumpy's bones, an' the gold – the beautiful yellow gold! It's yours, Joe – all yours. I leave it to you! You know the spot. I planted that stunted bluegum, with the limb thet turns down to the ground, right on the top of the grave the mornin' after I buried him.

You'll find his bones in among the roots.'

'The Identity' sank back on his bed, cold and exhausted.

'You'll bury them bones decent, Joe!' he murmured in a voice that had suddenly grown faint.

'Yes, Peter,' replied M'Gill, in whose mind the story had created both amazement and doubt.

'An' you've got the lease, Joe, sure!'

'I've applied for it – the ground is secured.'

'Yes, yes, an' you'll stick by me while I last, eh – you won't go? An' no p'lice, mind – no p'lice!'

It was already daylight when Joe M'Gill awakened his mates stumbling into the hut.

'Old Shaw is dead,' he explained to the indignant Dayton. 'You might dress, Jack, and go and stay by him, for decency's sake, while I have a few hours' sleep. And, Woodhead, you must go to Bunyip and bring the police. They will have to take charge of the body.

M'Gill and his mates found the skeleton of Foote exactly as Peter Shaw had said they would, and the grinning skull rested upon the cap of the golden reef that was eventually known as 'Dead Man's Lode', and which, before twelve months went by, had enriched the three young men, and had yielded small fortunes to many besides.

Starting the Selection

Steele Rudd

I T'S TWENTY YEARS NOW since we settled on the Creek.
Twenty years! I remember well the day we came from
Stanthorpe, on Jerome's dray – eight of us, and all the
things – beds, tubs, a bucket, the two cedar chairs with
pine bottoms and backs that Dad put in them, some pint-
pots and old Crib. It was a scorching hot day, too – talk
about thirst! At every creek we came to we drank till it
stopped running.

Dad didn't travel up with us; he had gone some months
before, to put up the house and dig the water-hole. It was
a slabbed house, with shingled roof, and space enough for
two rooms, but the partition wasn't up. The floor was
earth, but Dad had a mixture of sand and fresh cow-dung
with which he used to keep it level. About once every
month he would put it on, and everyone had to keep out-
side that day till it was dry. There were no locks on the
doors. Pegs were put in them to keep them fast at night,
and the slabs were not very close together, for we could
easily see anybody coming on horseback by looking
through them. Joe and I used to play at counting the stars
through the cracks in the roof.

The day after we arrived Dad took Mother and us out to
see the paddock and the flat on the other side of the gully
that he was going to clear for cultivation. There was no
fence round the paddock, but he pointed out on a tree the
surveyor's marks showing the boundary of our ground. It

must have been fine land, the way Dad talked about it. There was very valuable timber on it, too, he said; and he showed us a place among some rocks on a ridge where he was sure gold would be found, but we weren't to say anything about it. Joe and I went back that evening and turned over every stone on the ridge, but we didn't find any gold.

No mistake, it was a real wilderness – nothing but trees, goannas, dead timber, and bears; and the nearest house, Dwyer's, was three miles away. I often wonder how the women stood it the first few years, and I can remember how Mother, when she was alone, used to sit on a log where the lane is now and cry for hours. Lonely! It *was* lonely.

Dad soon talked about clearing a couple of acres and putting in corn – all of us did, in fact – till the work commenced. It was a delightful topic before we started, but in two weeks the clusters of fires that illuminated the whooping bush in the night, and the crash upon crash of the big trees as they fell, had lost all their poetry.

We toiled and toiled clearing those four acres, where the haystacks are now standing, till every tree and sapling that had grown there was down. We thought then the worst was over – but how little we knew of clearing land! Dad was never tired of calculating and telling us how much the crop would fetch if the ground could only be got ready in time to put it in; so we laboured the harder.

With our combined male and female forces and the aid of a sapling lever we rolled the thundering big logs together in the face of hell's own fires; and when there were no logs to roll it was tramp, tramp the day through, gathering armfuls of sticks, while the clothes clung to our backs with a muddy perspiration. Sometimes Dan and Dave would sit in the shade beside the billy of water and gaze at the small patch that had taken so long to do, then they would turn hopelessly to what was before them and ask Dad (who would never take a spell) what was the use of ever getting such a place cleared. And when Dave wanted to know why Dad didn't take up a place on the plain, where there were no trees to grub and plenty of water, Dad would cough as if something was sticking in his throat, and then curse terribly the squatters and political jobbery. He would soon cool down, though, and get hopeful again.

'Look at the Dwyers,' he'd say. 'From ten acres of wheat they got seventy pounds last year, besides feed for the fowls. They've got corn in now, and there's only the two of them.'

It wasn't only burning off! Whenever there was a drought the waterhole was sure to run dry. Then we had to take turns to carry water from the springs – about two miles.

We had no draught horse, and even if we had had one there was neither water-cask, trolly, nor dray. So we humped it – and talk about a dray! By the time you returned, if you hadn't drained the bucket, in spite of the big drink you'd take before leaving the springs, more than half would certainly be spilt through the vessel bumping against your leg every time you stumbled in long grass. Somehow, none of us liked carrying water. We would sooner keep the fires going all day without dinner than do a trip to the springs.

One hot, thirsty day it was Joe's turn with the bucket, and he managed to get back without spilling very much. We were all pleased because there was enough left after the

tea had been made to give us all a drink. Dinner was near-
ly over. Dan had finished and was taking it easy on the sofa
when Joe said, 'I say, Dad, what's a nater-dog like?'

Dad told him. 'Yellow, sharp ears and bushy tail.'

'Those muster been some then that I seen – I don't know
'bout the bushy tail – all the hair had comed off.'

'Where'd y'see them, Joe?' we asked.

'Down the springs floating about – dead.'

Then everyone seemed to think hard and look at the tea.
I didn't want any more. Dan jumped off the sofa and went
outside; and Dad looked after Mother.

At last the four acres – except for the biggest ironbark-
trees and about fifty stumps – were pretty well cleared.
Then came a problem that couldn't be worked out on a
draught-board. I have already said that we hadn't any
draught-horses. Indeed, the only thing on the selection
like a horse was an old 'tuppy' mare that Dad used to
straddle. The date of her foaling went farther back than
Dad's, I believe, and she was shaped something like an
alderman. We found her one day in about eighteen inches
of mud, with both eyes picked out by the crows, and her
hide bearing evidence that a feathery tribe made a roost
of her carcass. Plainly, there was no chance of breaking
up the ground with her help. And we had no plough.
How, then, was the corn to be put in? That was the
question.

Dan and Dave sat outside in the corner of the chimney,
both scratching the ground with a chip and not saying any-
thing. Dad and Mother sat inside talking it over. Sometimes
Dad would get up and walk round the room shaking his
head, then he would kick old Crib for lying under the table.

At last Mother struck something which brightened him up, and he called Dave.

'Catch Topsy and –' he paused because he remembered the old mare was dead.

'Run over and ask Mr Dwyer to lend me three hoes.'

Dave went. Dwyer lent the hoes, and the problem was solved. That was how we started.

White-When-He's-Wanted

A.B. ('Banjo') Paterson

BUCKALONG WAS A BIG FREEHOLD of some 80,000 acres, belonging to an absentee syndicate, and therefore run in most niggardly style. There was a manager on £200 a year, Sandy McGregor to wit – a hard-headed old Scotchman known as 'four-eyed McGregor', because he wore spectacles. For assistants, he had half a dozen of us – jackaroos and colonial experiencers – who got nothing a year, and earned it. We had, in most instances, paid premiums to learn the noble art of squatting, which now appears to me hardly worth studying, for so much depends on luck that a man with a head as long as a horse's has little better chance than the fool just imported. Besides the manager and the jackaroo, there were a few boundary riders round the fences of the vast paddock. This constituted the whole station staff.

Buckalong was on one of the main routes by which stock were taken to market, or from the plains to the tablelands, and vice versa. Great mobs of travelling sheep constantly passed through the run, eating up the grass and vexing the soul of the manager. By law, sheep must travel six miles per day, and they must keep within half a mile of the road. Of course, we kept all the grass near the road eaten bare, to discourage travellers from coming that way. Such hapless wretches as did venture through Buckalong used to try hard to stray from the road and pick up a feed, but Old Sandy was always ready for them, and would have them dogged right through the run. This bred feuds, and bad language, and personal combats between us and the drovers, whom we looked upon as natural enemies. Then the men who came through with the mobs of cattle used to pull down the paddock fences at night, and slip the cattle in for refreshments, but old Sandy often turned out at 2 or 3 a.m. to catch a big mob of bullocks in the horse paddock, and then off they went to Buckalong pound. The drovers, as in duty bound, attributed the trespass to accident – broken rails, and so on – and sometimes they tried to rescue the cattle, which again bred strife and police court summonses.

Besides having a particular aversion to drovers, old McGregor had a general 'down' on the young 'colonials', whom he comprehensively described as a 'feckless, horse-dealin', horse-stealin', crawlin' lot o' wretches'. According to him, a colonial would sooner work a horse to death than work for a living, any day. He hated any man who wanted to sell him a horse. 'As ah walk the street,' he used to say,'the folk disna stawp me to buy claes nor shoon, an' wheerfore should they stawp me to buy horses? It's Mister McGregor, will ye purrchase a horrse? Let them wait till I ask them to come wi' theer horrses.'

Such being his views on horseflesh and drovers, we felt no little excitement when one Sunday, at dinner, the cook came in to say there was a 'drover chap outside wanted the boss to come and have a look at a horse'. McGregor simmered awhile, and muttered something about the 'Sawbath day'; but a last he went out, and we filed after him to see the fun.

The drover stood by the side of his horse, beneath the acacia trees in the yard. He had a big scar on his face, apparently the result of a collision with a tree; and seemed poverty-stricken enough to disarm hostility. Obviously, he was 'down on his luck'. He looked very thin and sickly, with clothes ragged and boots broken. Had it not been for that indefinable self-reliant look which drovers – the Ishmaels of the bush – always acquire, one might have taken him for a swagman. His horse was in much the same plight. A ragged, unkempt pony, pitifully poor and very footsore – at first sight, an absolute 'moke', but a second glance showed colossal round ribs, square hips, and a great length of rein, the rest beneath a wealth of loose hair. He looked like 'a good journey horse', possibly something better.

We gathered round while McGregor questioned the drover. The man was monosyllabic to a degree, as real bushmen generally are. It is only the rowdy and the town-bushy that is fluent of speech.

'Good morning,' said McGregor.

'Mornin', boss,' said the drover shortly.

'Is this the horrse ye have for sale?'

'Yes,'

'Aye,' and McGregor looked at the pony with a businesslike don't-think-much-of-him air; ran his hand lightly over the hard legs and opened the passive creature's mouth.

'H'm,' he said. Then he turned to the drover. 'Ye seem a bit oot o' luck. Ye're thin, like. What's been the matter?'

'Been sick with fever – Queensland fever. Just come through from the north. Been out on the Diamantina last.'

'Aye. I was there myself,' said McGregor. 'Have ye the fever on ye still?'

'Yes – goin' home to get rid of it.'

It should be explained that a man can only get Queensland fever in a malarial district, but he can carry it with him wherever he goes. If he stays, it will sap all his strength and pull him to pieces; if he moves to a better climate, the malady moves with him, leaving him only by degrees, and coming back at regular intervals to rack, shake, burn, and sweat its victim. Queensland fever will pull a man down from fifteen stone to nine stone faster, and with greater certainty, than any system of dosing yet invented. Gradually it wears itself out, often wearing its patient out at the same time. McGregor had been through the experience, and there was a slight change in his voice as he went on with the palaver.

'Where are ye makin' for the noo?

'Monaro – my people live in Monaro.'

'How will ye get to Monaro if ye sell the horrse?'

'Coach and rail. Too sick to care about ridin',' said the drover, while a wan smile flitted across his yellow-grey features. 'I've rode him far enough. I've rode that horse a thousand miles. I wouldn't sell him, only I'm a bit hard up. Sellin' him now to get the money to go home.'

'How old is he?'

'Seven.'

'Is he a good horse on a camp?' asked McGregor.

'No better camp horse in Queensland,' said the drover. 'You can chuck the reins on his neck, an' he'll cut out a beast by himself.'

McGregor's action in this matter puzzled us. We spent our time crawling after sheep, and a camp horse would be about as much use to us as side pockets to a pig. We had expected Sandy to rush the fellow off the place at once, and we couldn't understand how it was that he took so much interest in him. Perhaps the fever-racked drover and the old camp horse appealed to him in a way to us incomprehensible. We had never been on the Queensland cattle camps, nor shaken and shivered with the fever, nor lived the roving life of the overlanders. McGregor had done all this, and his heart (I can see it all now) went out to the man who brought the old days back to him.

'Ah, weel,' he said, 'we hae'na much use for a camp horse here, ye ken; wi'oot some of these lads wad like to try theer han' cuttin' oot the milkers' cawves frae their mithers.' And the old man laughed contemptuously, while we felt humbled and depraved in the eyes of the man from far back. 'An what'll ye be wantin' for him?' asked McGregor.

'Reckon he's worth fifteen notes,' said the drover.

This fairly staggered us. Our estimates had varied between thirty shillings and a fiver. We thought the negotiations would close abruptly, but McGregor, after a little more examination, agreed to give the price, provided the saddle and bridle, both grand specimens of ancient art, were given in. This was agreed to, and the drover was sent off to get his meals in the hut before leaving by the coach.

'The mon is verra hard up, and it's a sair thing that Queensland fever,' was the only remark that McGregor made. But we knew that there was a soft spot in his heart somewhere.

And so, next morning, the drover got a crisp-looking cheque and departed by coach. He said no word while the cheque was being written, but, as he was going away, the horse happened to be in the yard, and he went over to the old comrade that had carried him so many miles, and laid a hand on his neck. 'He ain't much to look at,' said the drover, speaking slowly and awkwardly, 'but he's white, when he's wanted.' And just before the coach rattled off, the man of few words lent down from the box and nodded impressively, and repeated, 'Yes, he's white when he's wanted.'

We didn't trouble to give the new horse a name. Station horses are generally called after the man from whom they are bought. 'Tom Devine,' 'the Regan mare', 'Black McCarthy', and 'Bay McArthy' were amongst the appellations of our horses at that time. As we didn't know the drover's name, we simply called the animal 'the new horse' until a still newer horse was one day acquired. Then, one of the hands being told to take the new horse, said, 'D'yer mean the new new horse or the *old* new horse?' 'No,' said the boss, 'not the new horse – that bay horse we bought from the drover. The one he said was white when he was wanted.'

And so, by degrees, the animal came to be referred to as the horse that's white when he's wanted, and at last settled down to the definite name of 'White-When-He's-Wanted.'

White-When-He's-Wanted didn't seem much of an acquisition. He was sent out to do slavery for Greenhide Billy, a boundary rider who plumed himself on having once been a cattle man. After a week's experience of 'White', Billy came into the homestead disgusted – the pony was so lazy that he had to build a fire under him to get him to move, and so rough that it would make a man's nose bleed to ride him more than a mile. 'The boss must have been off his head to give fifteen notes for such a cow.'

McGregor heard this complaint. 'Verra weel, Mr Billy,' said he, hotly, 'ye can just tak' one of the young horrses in yon paddock, an' if he bucks wi' ye, an' kills ye, it's yer ain fault. Ye're a cattle man – so ye say – dommed if ah believe it. Ah believe ye're a dairy farmin' body frae Illawarra. Ye don't know neither horrse nor cattle. Mony's the time ye never rode buckjumpers, Mr Billy,' and with this parting shot the old man turned into the house, and White-When-He's-Wanted came back to the head station.

For a while he was a sort of pariah. He used to yard the horses, fetch up the cows, and hunt travelling sheep through the run. He really was lazy and rough, and we all decided that Billy's opinion of him was correct, until the day came to make one of our periodical raids on the wild horses in the hills at the back of the run. Every now and again we formed parties to run in some of these animals, and, after nearly galloping to death half-a-dozen good horses, we would capture three or four brumbies, and bring them in triumph to the homestead. These we would break in, and by the time they had thrown half the crack riders on the station, broken all the bridles, rolled on all the saddles and kicked all the dogs, they would be marketable (and no great bargains) at about thirty shillings a head.

Yet there is no sport in the world to be mentioned in the same volume as 'running horses', and we were very keen on it. All the crack nags were got as fit as possible, and fed up beforehand, and on this particular occasion White-When-He's-Wanted, being in good trim, was given a week's hard feed and lent to a harum-scarum fellow from the upper Murray who happened to be working in a survey camp on the run. How he did open our eyes. He ran the mob from hill to hill, from range to range, across open country and back again to the hills, over flats and gullies, through hop scrub and stringybark ridges; and all the time White-When-He's-Wanted was on the wing of the mob, pulling double. The mares and foals dropped out, then the colts and young stockpulled up deadbeat, and only the seasoned veterans of the mob were left. Most of our horses caved in altogether; one or two were kept in the hunt by judicious nursing and shirking the work, but White-When-He's-Wanted was with the quarry from end to end of the run, doing double his share; and at the finish, when a chance offered to wheel them into the trap yard, he simply smothered them for pace and slowed them into the wings before they knew where they were. Such a capture had not fallen to our lot for many a day, and the fame of White-When-He's-Wanted was speedily noised abroad.

He was always fit for work, always hungry, always ready to lie down and roll, and always lazy. But when he heard the rush of the brumbies' feet in the scrub, he became frantic with excitement. He could race over the roughest ground without misplacing a hoof or altering his stride, and he could sail over fallen timber and across gullies like a kangaroo. Nearly every Sunday we were after the brumbies until they got as lean as greyhounds and as cunning as policemen. We were always ready to back White-When-He's-Wanted to run down single handed, any animal in the bush that we liked to put him after – wild horses, wild cattle, kangaroos, emus, dingoes, kangaroo rats – we barred nothing, for, if he couldn't beat them for pace, he would outlast them.

And then one day he disappeared from the paddock, and we never saw him again. We knew there were plenty of men in the district who would steal him, but, as we knew also that there were plenty more who would 'inform' for a pound or two, we were sure that it could not have been the local 'talent' who had taken him. We offered good rewards and set some of the right sort to work, but we heard nothing of him for about a year.

Then the surveyor's assistant turned up again after a trip to the interior. He told us the usual string of backblock lies, and then wound up by saying that out on the very fringe of settlement he had met an old acquaintance.

Who was that?'

'Why, that little bay horse that I rode after the brumbies that time. The one you called White-When-He's-Wanted.'

'The deuce you did! Are you sure? Who had him?'

'Sure? I'd swear to him anywhere. A little drover fellow had him. A little fellow, with a big scar across his forehead. Came from Monaro way, somewhere. He said he bought the horse from you for fifteen notes.'

And then there was a chorus about the thief getting seven years.

But he hasn't so far, and, as the Queen's warrant doesn't run much out west of Boulia, it is not at all likely that any of us will ever see the drover again, or will ever cross the back of 'White-When-He's-Wanted'.

The Drover's Wife

Henry Lawson

THE TWO-ROOMED HOUSE is built of round timber, slabs and stringy bark, and floored with split slabs. A big bark kitchen standing at one end is larger than the house itself, verandah included

Bush all round – bush with no horizon, for the country is flat. No ranges in the distance. The bush consists of stunted, rotten native apple trees. No undergrowth. Nothing to relieve the eye save the darker green of a few sheoaks which are sighing above the narrow, almost waterless creek. Nineteen miles to the nearest sign of civilisation – a shanty on the main road.

The drover, an ex-squatter, is away with sheep. His wife and children are left here alone.

Four ragged, dried–up-looking children are playing about the house. Suddenly one of them yells: 'Snake! Mother, here's a snake!'

The gaunt, sun-browned woman dashes from the kitchen, snatches her baby from the ground, holds it on her left hip, and reaches for a stick.

'Where is it?'

'Here! Gone to the wood-heap!' yells the eldest boy – a sharp-faced, excited urchin of eleven. 'Stop there, Mother! I'll have him. Stand back! I'll have the beggar!'

'Tommy, you come here, or you'll be bit! Come here at once when I tell you, you little wretch!'

The youngster comes reluctantly, carrying a stick bigger

than himself. Then he yells, triumphantly

'There it goes – under the house!' and darts away with club uplifted. At the same time the big, black, yellow-eyed dog-of-all-breeds, who has shown the wildest interest in the proceedings, breaks his chain and rushes after the snake. He is a moment late, however, and his nose reaches the crack in the slabs just as the end of its tail disappears. Almost at the same moment the boy's club comes down, and skins the aforesaid nose. Alligator takes small notice of this, and proceeds to undermine the building; but he is subdued after a struggle and chained up. They cannot afford to lose him.

The drover's wife makes the children stand together near the dog-house while she watches for the snake. She gets two small dishes of milk and sets them down near the wall to tempt it to come out; but an hour goes by and it does not show itself.

It is near sunset, and a thunderstorm is coming. The children must be brought inside. She will not take them into the house, for she knows the snake is there, and may at any moment come up through the cracks in the rough slab floor; so she carries several armfuls of firewood into the kitchen, and then takes the children there. The kitchen has no floor – or, rather, an earthen one – called a 'ground floor' in this part of the bush.

There is a large, roughly made table in the centre of the place. She brings the children in, and makes them get on this table. They are two boys and two girls – mere babies. She gives them some supper, and then, before it gets dark, she goes into the house, and snatches up some pillows and bedclothes – expecting to see or lay her hand on the snake any minute. She makes a bed on the kitchen table for the children, and sits down beside it to watch all night.

She has an eye on the corner, and a green sapling club laid in readiness on the dresser by her side, together with her sewing basket and a copy of the *Young Ladies' Journal*. She has brought the dog into the room.

Tommy turns in, under protest, but says he'll lie awake all night and smash that blinded snake.

His mother asks him how many times she has asked him not to swear.

He has his club with him under the bedclothes, and Jacky protests:

'Mummy! Tommy's skinnin' me alive wif his club. Make him take it out.'

Tommy: 'Shet up, you little – ! D'yer want to be bit with the snake?'

Jacky shuts up.

'If yer bit,' says Tommy, after a pause, 'you'll swell up, an' smell, an' turn red an' green an' blue all over till yer bust. Won't he, Mother?'

'Now then, don't frighten the child. Go to sleep,' she says.

The two younger children go to sleep, and now and then Jacky complains of being 'skeezed'. More room is made for him. Presently Tommy says: 'Mother! Listen to them (adjective) little possums. I'd like to screw their blanky necks.'

And Jacky protests drowsily:

'But they don't hurt us, the little blanks!'

Mother: 'There, I told you you'd teach Jacky to swear.' But the remark makes her smile. Jacky goes to sleep.

Presently Tommy asks:

'Mother! Do you think they'll ever extricate the (adjective) kangaroo?'

'Lord! How am I to know, child? Go to sleep.'

'Will you wake me if the snake comes out?'

'Yes. Go to sleep.'

Near midnight. The children are all asleep and she sits there still, sewing and reading by turns. From time to time she glances round the floor and wall-plate, and whenever she hears a noise she reaches for the stick. The thunderstorm comes on, and the wind, rushing through the cracks in the slab wall, threatens to blow out her candle. She places it on a sheltered part of the dresser and fixes up a newspaper to protect it. At every flash of lightning, thunder rolls, and the rain comes down in torrents.

Alligator lies at full length on the floor, with his eyes turned towards the partition. She knows by this that the snake is there. There are large cracks in that wall opening under the floor of the dwelling-house.

She is not a coward, but recent events have shaken her nerves. A little son of her brother-in-law was lately bitten by a snake, and died. Besides, she has not heard from her husband for six months, and is anxious about him.

He was a drover, and started squatting here when they married. The drought of 18— ruined him. He had to sacrifice the remnant of his flock and go droving again. He intends to move his family into the nearest town when he comes back, and, in the meantime, his brother, who keeps a shanty on the main road, comes over about once a month with provisions. The wife has still a couple of cows, one horse, and a few sheep. The brother-in-law kills one of the sheep occasionally, gives her what she needs of it, and takes the rest in return for other provisions.

She is used to being left alone. She once lived like this for eighteen months. As a girl she built the usual castles in the air, but all her girlish hopes and aspirations have long been dead. She finds all the excitement and recreation she needs in the *Young Ladies' Journal*, and, Heaven help her! takes a pleasure in the fashion-plates.

Her husband is an Australian, and so is she. He is careless, but a good enough husband. If he had the means he would take her to the city and keep her there like a princess. They are used to being apart, or at least she is. 'No use fretting,' she says. He may forget sometimes that he is married; but if he has a good cheque when he comes back he will give most of it to her. When he had money he took her to the city several times – hired a railway sleeping compartment, and put up at the best hotels. He also bought her a buggy, but they had to sacrifice that along with the rest.

The last two children were born in the bush – one while her husband was bringing a drunken doctor, by force, to attend to her. She was alone on this occasion, and very weak. She had been ill with a fever. She prayed to God to send her assistance. God sent Black Mary – the 'whitest' gin in all the land. Or, at least, God sent 'King Jimmy' first, and he sent Black Mary. He put his black face around the doorpost, took in the situation at a glance, and said cheerfully, 'All right, Missis – I bring my old woman, she down alonga creek.'

One of her children died while she was here alone. She rode nineteen miles for assistance, carrying the dead child.

It must be near one or two o'clock. The fire is burning low. Alligator lies with his head resting on his paws, and watches the wall. He is not a very beautiful dog to look at, and the light shows numerous old wounds where the hair will not grow. He is afraid of nothing on the face of the earth or under it. He will tackle a bullock as readily as he will tackle a flea. He hates all other dogs – except kangaroo-dogs – and has a marked dislike of friends or relations of the family. They seldom call, however. He sometimes makes friends with strangers. He hates snakes and has killed many, but he will be bitten some day and die; most snake-dogs end that way.

Now and then the bush woman lays down her work and watches, and listens, and thinks. She thinks about things in her own life, for there is little else to think about.

The rain will make the grass grow, and this reminds her how she fought a bush fire once while her husband was away. The grass was long, and very dry, and the fire threatened to burn her out. She put on an old pair of her husband's trousers and beat out the flames with a green bough, till great drops of sooty perspiration stood out on her forehead and ran in streaks down her blackened arms. The sight of their mother in trousers greatly amused Tommy, who worked like a little hero by her side, but the terrified baby howled lustily for his 'mummy'. The fire would have mastered her but for four excited bushmen who arrived in the nick of time. It was a mixed-up affair all round; When she went to take up the baby, he screamed and struggled convulsively, thinking it was a 'black man'; and Alligator, trusting more to the child's sense than his own instinct, charged furiously, and (being old and slightly deaf) did not in his excitement at first recognise his mistress's voice, but continued to hang on to the moleskins until choked off by Tommy with a saddle strap. The dog's sorrow for his blunder, and his anxiety to let it be known that it was all a mistake, was as evident as his ragged tail and a twelve-inch grin could make it. It was a glorious time for the boys; a day to look back to, and talk about, and laugh over for many years.

She thinks how she fought a flood during her husband's absence. She stood for hours in the drenching downpour, and dug an overflow gutter to save the dam across the creek. But she could not save it. There are things that a bush woman cannot do. Next morning the dam was broken, and her heart was nearly broken too, for she thought how her husband would feel when he came home and saw the result of years of labour swept away. She cried then.

She also fought the *pleuro-pneumonia* – dosed and bled the few remaining cattle, and wept again when her two best cows died

Again, she fought a mad bullock that besieged the house for a day. She made bullets and fired at him through the cracks in the slabs with an old shotgun. He was dead in the morning. She skinned him and got seventeen-and-sixpence for the hide.

She also fights crows and eagles that have designs on her chickens. Her plan of campaign is very original. The children cry 'Crows, Mother!' and she rushes out and aims a broomstick at the birds as though it were a gun, and says, 'Bung!' The crows leave in a hurry; they are cunning, but a woman's cunning is greater.

Occasionally a bushman in the horrors, or a villainous-looking sundowner, comes and nearly scares the life out of her. She generally tells the suspicious-looking stranger that her husband and two sons are at work below the dam, or over at the yard, for he always cunningly inquires for the boss.

Only last week a gallows-faced swagman – having satisfied himself that there were no men on the place – threw his swag down on the verandah, and demanded tucker. She gave him something to eat; then he expressed his intention of staying for the night. It was sundown then. She got a batten from the sofa, loosened the dog, and confronted the stranger, holding the batten in one hand and the dog's collar with the other. 'Now you go!' she said. He looked at her and at the dog, said, 'All right, mum,' in a cringing tone, and left. She was a determined-looking woman, and Alligator's yellow eyes glared unpleasantly – besides, the dog's chawing-up apparatus greatly resembled that of the reptile he was named after.

She has few pleasures to think of as she sits here alone by the fire, on guard against a snake. All days are much the same to her, but on Sunday afternoon she dresses herself, tidies the children, smartens up baby, and goes for a lonely walk along the bush-track, pushing an old perambulator in front of her. She does this every Sunday. She takes as much care to make herself and children look smart as she would if she were going to do the block in the city. There is nothing to see, however, and not a soul to meet. You might walk for twenty minutes along this track without being able to fix a point in your mind, unless you are a bushman. This is because of the everlasting, maddening sameness of the stunted trees – that monotony which makes a man long to break away and travel as far as trains can go, and sail as far as ships can sail – and further.

But this bushwoman is used to the loneliness of it. As a girl-wife she hated it, but now she would feel strange away from it.

She is glad when her husband returns, but she does not gush or make a fuss about it. She gets him something good to eat, and tidies up the children.

She seems contented with her lot. She loves her children, but has no time to show it. She seems harsh to them. Her surroundings are not favourable to the development of the 'womanly' or sentimental side of her nature.

It must be near morning now; but the clock is in the dwelling-house. Her candle is nearly done; she forgot that she was out of candles. Some more wood must be got to keep the fire up, and so she shuts the dog inside and hurries round to the wood-heap. The rain has cleared off. She seizes a stick, pulls it out, and – crash! the whole pile collapses.

Yesterday she bargained with a stray blackfellow to bring her some wood, and while he was at work she went in search of a missing cow. She was absent an hour or so, and the native black made good use of his time. On her return she was so astonished to see a good heap of wood by the chimney, that she gave him an extra fig of tobacco, and praised him for not being lazy. He thanked her, and left with a head erect and a chest well out. He was the last of his tribe and a King; but he built that wood-heap hollow.

She is hurt now, and tears spring to her eyes as she sits down again by the table. She takes up a handkerchief to wipe the tears away, but pokes her eyes with bare fingers instead. The handkerchief is full of holes, and she finds that she has put her thumb through one and her forefinger through another.

This makes her laugh, to the surprise of the dog. She has a keen, very keen, sense of the ridiculous; and some time or other she will amuse bushmen with the story.

She has been amused before like that. One day she sat down 'to have a good cry' as she said – and the old cat rubbed against her dress and 'cried too'. Then she had to laugh.

It must be near daylight. The room is very close and hot because of the fire. Alligator still watches the wall from time to time. Suddenly he becomes greatly interested; he draws himself a few inches nearer the partition, and a thrill runs through his body. The hair on the back of his neck begins to bristle, and the battle-light is in his yellow eyes. She knows what this means, and lays her hand on the stick. The lower end of one of the partition slabs has a large crack on both sides. An evil pair of small, bright, bead-like eyes glisten at one end of these holes. The snake – a black one – comes slowly out, about a foot, and moves its head up and down. The dog lies still, and the woman sits as one fascinated. The snake comes out a foot further. She lifts her stick, and the reptile, as though suddenly aware of danger, sticks his head in through the crack on the other side of the slab, and hurries to get his tail round after him. Alligator springs and his jaws come together with a snap. He misses, for his nose is large and the snake's body down in the angle formed by the slabs and the floor. He snaps again as the tail comes round. He has the snake now, and tugs it out eighteen inches. Thud, thud, comes the woman's club on the ground.

Alligator pulls again. Thud, thud, Alligator gives another pull and he has the snake out – a black brute, five feet long. The head rises to dart about, but the dog has the enemy close to the neck. He is a big, heavy dog, but quick as a terrier. He shakes the snake as though he felt the original curse in common with mankind. The eldest boy wakes up, seizes his stick, and tries to get out of bed, but his mother forces him back with a grip of iron. Thud, thud – the snake's back is broken in several places. Thud, thud – its head is crushed and Alligator's nose skinned again.

She lifts the mangled reptile on the point of her stick, carries it to the fire, and throws it in; then piles on the wood, and watches the snake burn. The boy and dog watch, too. She lays her hand on the dog's head, and all the fierce angry light dies out of his yellow eyes. The younger children are quieted, and presently go to sleep. The dirty-legged boy stands for a moment in his shirt, watching the fire. Presently he looks up at her, sees the tears in her eyes, and throwing his arms round her neck, exclaims:

'Mother, I won't never go drovin'; blast me if I do!'

And she hugs him to her worn-out breast and kisses him; and they sit thus together while the sickly daylight breaks over the bush.

Squeaker's Mate

Barbara Baynton

THE WOMAN CARRIED THE BAG with the axe and wedges; the man had the billy and clean tucker-bags; the cross-cut saw linked them. She was taller than the man, and the equability of her body, contrasting with his indolent slouch, accentuated the difference. 'Squeaker's mate', the men called her, and these agreed that she was the best long-haired mate that ever stepped in petticoats. The selectors' wives pretended to challenge her right to womanly garments, but if she knew what they said, it neither turned nor troubled Squeaker's mate.

Nine prospective posts and maybe sixteen rails – she calculated this yellow gum would yield. 'Come on,' she encouraged the man; 'let's tackle it.'

From the bag she took the axe, and ring-barked a preparatory circle, while he looked for a shady spot for the billy and tucker-bags.

'Come on.' She was waiting with the greased saw. He came. The saw rasped through a few inches, then he stopped and looked at the sun.

'It's nigh tucker-time,' he said, and when she dissented, he exclaimed with sudden energy, 'There's another bee! Wait, you go on with the axe, an' I'll track 'im.'

As they came, they had already followed one and located the nest. She could not see the bee he spoke of, though her grey eyes were as keen as a black's. However, she knew the man, and her tolerance was of the mysteries.

She drew on the saw, spat on her hands, and with the axe began weakening the inclining side of the tree.

Long and steadily and in secret the worm had been busy in the heart. Suddenly the axe blade sank softly, the tree's wounded edges closed on it like a vice. There was a 'settling' quiver on its top branches, which the woman heard and understood. The man, encouraged by the sounds of the axe, had returned with an armful of sticks for the billy. He shouted gleefully, 'It's fallen', look out.'

With a shivering groan the tree fell, and as she sprang aside, a thick, worm-eaten branch snapped at a joint and silently she went down under it.

'I tole yer to' look out,' he reminded her, as with a crowbar, and grunting earnestly, he forced it up. 'Now get out quick.'

She tried moving her arms and the upper part of her body. Do this; do that, he directed, but she made no movement after the first.

He was impatient, because for once he had actually to use his strength. His share of a heavy life usually consisted of a make-believe grunt, delivered at a critical moment. Yet he hardly cared to let it again fall on her, though he told her he would if she 'didn't shift'.

Near him lay a piece broken short; with his foot he drew it nearer, then gradually worked it into a position, till it acted as a stay to the lever.

He laid her on her back when he drew her out, and waited expecting some acknowledgement of his exertions, but she was silent, and as she did not notice that the axe she had tried to save lay with the fallen trunk across it, he told her. She cared almost tenderly for all their possessions and treated them as friends. But the half-buried broken axe did not affect her. He wondered a little, for only last week she had patiently chipped out the old broken head, and put in a new handle.

'Feel bad?' he inquired at length.

'Pipe,' she replied with slack lips.

Both pipes lay in the fork of a near tree. He took his, shook out the ashes, filled it, picked up a coal and puffed till it was alight – then he filled hers. Taking a small fire-stick he handed her the pipe. The hand she raised shook and closed in an uncertain hold, but she managed by a great effort to get it to her mouth. He lost patience with the swaying hand that tried to take the light.

'Quick,' he said, 'quick, that damn dog's at the tucker.'

He thrust it into her hand that dropped helplessly across her chest. The lighted stick, falling between her bare arm and dress, slowly roasted the flesh and smouldered the clothes.

He rescued their dinner, pelted his dog out of sight – hers was lying near her head – put on the billy, then came back to her.

The pipe had fallen from her lips; there was blood on the stem.

'Did yer jam yer tongue?' he asked.

She always ignored trifles, he knew, therefore he passed her silence.

He told her that her dress was on fire. She took no heed. He put it out and looked at the burnt arm, then with intent-ness at her.

Her eyes were turned unblinkingly to the heavens, her lips were grimly apart, and a strange greyness was upon her face, and the sweat-beads were mixing.

'Like a drink er tea? Asleep?'

He broke a green branch from the fallen tree and swished from his face the multitudes of flies that had descended with it.

In a heavy way he wondered why did she sweat, when she was not working? Why did she not keep the flies out of her mouth and eyes? She'd have bungy eyes, if she didn't. If she was asleep, why did she not close them?

But asleep or awake, as the billy began to boil, he left her, made the tea, and ate his dinner. His dog had disappeared, and as it did not come to his whistle, he threw the pieces to hers, that would not leave her head to reach them.

He whistled tunelessly his one air, beating his own time with a stick on the toe of his blucher, then looked overhead at the sun and calculated that she must have been lying like that for 'close upon an hour'. He noticed that the axe handle was broken in two places, and speculated a little as to whether she would again pick out the back-broken handle or burn it out in his method, which was less trouble, if it did spoil the temper of the blade. He examined the worm-dust in the stump and limbs of the newly-fallen tree; mounted it and looked round the plain. The sheep were straggling in a manner that meant walking work to round them, and he supposed he would have to yard them tonight, if she didn't liven up. He looked down at unenlivened her. This changed his 'chune' to call for his hiding dog.

'Come on, old feller,' he commanded her dog. 'Fetch 'em back.' He whistled further instructions, slapping his thigh and pointing to the sheep.

But a brace of wrinkles either side of the brute's closed mouth demonstrated determined disobedience. The dog would go if she told him, and by and by she would.

He lighted his pipe and killed half an hour smoking. With the frugality that hard graft begets, his mate limited both his and her own tobacco, so he must not smoke all afternoon. There was no work to shirk, so time began to drag. Then a 'goanner' crawling up a tree attracted him. He gathered various missiles and tried vainly to hit the seemingly grinning reptile. He came back and sneaked a fill of her tobacco, and while he was smoking, the white tilt of a cart caught his eye. He jumped up. 'There's Red Bob goin' t'our place fur th' 'oney,' he said. 'I'll go and weigh it an' get the gonz' (money).'

He ran for the cart, and kept looking back as if fearing she would follow and thwart him.

Red Bob the dealer was, in a business way, greatly concerned when he found that Squeaker's mate was ''avin' a sleep out there 'cos a tree fell on her'. She was the best honey-strainer and boiler that he dealt with. She was straight and square too. There was no water in her honey whether boiled or merely strained, and in every kerosene-tin the weight of the honey was to an ounce as she said. Besides he was suspicious and diffident of paying the indecently eager Squeaker before he saw the woman. So reluctantly Squeaker led to where she lay. With many fierce oaths Red Bob sent her lawful protector for help, and compassionately poured a little from his flask down her throat, then swished away the flies from her till help came.

Together these men stripped a sheet of bark, and laying her with pathetic tenderness upon it, carried her to her hut.

Squeaker followed in the rear with the billy and tucker.

Red Bob took his horse from the cart, and went to town for the doctor. Late that night at the back of the old hut (there were two) he and others who had heard that she was hurt, squatted with unlighted pipes in their mouths, waiting to hear the doctor's verdict. After he had given it and gone, they discussed in whispers, and with a look seen only on bush faces, the hard luck of that woman who alone had hard-grafted with the best of them for every acre and hoof on that selection. Squeaker would go through it in no time. Why she had allowed it to be taken up in his name, when the money had been her own, was also for them among the mysteries.

Him they called 'a nole woman', not because he was hanging round the honey-tins, but after man's fashion to eliminate all virtue. They beckoned him, and explaining his mate's injury, cautioned him to keep from her the knowledge that she would be forever a cripple.

'Jus' the same, now, then fur 'im,' pointing to Red Bob, 't' pay me, I'll 'ev to to t' town.'

They told him in whispers what they thought of him, and with a cowardly look to where she lay, but without a word of parting, like shadows these men made for their homes.

Next day the women came. Squeaker's mate was not a favourite with them – a woman with no leisure for yarning was not likely to be. After the first day they left her severely alone, their pleas to their husbands, her uncompromising independence. It is in the ordering of things that by degrees most husbands accept their wives' views of other women.

The flour bespattering Squeaker's now neglected clothes

spoke eloquently of his clumsy efforts at damper making. The women gave him many a feed, agreeing that it must be miserable for him.

If it were miserable and lonely for his mate, she did not complain; for her the long, long days would give place to longer nights – those nights with the pregnant bush silence suddenly cleft by a bush voice. However, she was not fanciful, and being a bush scholar knew 'twas a dingo when a long whine came from the scrub on the skirts of which lay the axe under the worm-eaten tree. That quivering wail from the billabong lying murkily mystic towards the East was only the cry of the fearing curlew.

Always her dog – wakeful and watchful as she – patiently waiting for her to be up and about again. That would be soon, she told her complaining mate.

'Yer won't. Yer back's broke,' said Squeaker laconically. 'That's wot's wrong er yer; injoory t' th' spine. Doctor says that means back's broke, and yer won't never walk no more. No good not t' tell yer, cos I can't be doin' everything.'

A wild look came on her face, and she tried to sit up.

'Erh,' said he, 'see! Yer carnt, yer jes' ther same as a snake w'en ees back's broke, on'y yer don't bite yerself like a snake does w'en 'e carnt crawl. Yer did bite yer tongue w'en yer fell.'

She gasped, and he could hear her heart beating when she let her head fall back a few moments; though she wiped her forehead with the back of her hand, and still said that was the doctor's mistake. But day after day she tested her strength, and whatever the result, was silent, though white witnesses, halo-wise, gradually circled her brown and temples.

"Tisn't as if yer was agoin' t' get better t'morrer, the doctor says yer won't never work no more, an' I can't be cookin' an' workin; an' doin' everythin'!'

He muttered something about 'selling out', but she firmly refused to think of such a monstrous proposal.

He went into town one Saturday afternoon soon after, and did not return till Monday.

Her supplies, a billy of tea and scraps of salt beef and damper (her dog got the beef), gave out the first day, though that was as nothing to her compared with the bleat of the penned sheep, for it was summer and droughty, and her dog could not unpen them.

Of them and her dog only she spoke when he returned. He d—d him, and d—d her, and told her to 'double up yer old broke back an' bite yerself'. He threw things about, made a long-range feint of kicking her threatening dog, than sat outside in the shade of the old hut, nursing his head till he slept.

She, for many reasons, had when necessary made these trips into town, walking both ways, leading a pack-horse for supplies. She never failed to indulge him in a half pint – a pipe was her luxury.

The sheep waited till next day; so did she.

For a few days he worked a little in her sight; not much – he never did. It was she who always lifted the heavy end of the log, and carried the tools; he – the billy and tucker.

She wearily watched him idling his time; reminded him that the wire lying near the fence would rust, one could run the wire through easily, and when she got up in a day or so, she would help strain and fasten it. At first he pretended he had done it, later said he wasn't goin' t' go wirin' or nothin' else by 'imself if every other man on the place did.

She spoke of many other things that could be done by one, reserving the great till she was well. Sometimes he whistled while she spoke, often swore, generally went out, and when this was inconvenient, dull as he was, he found the 'Go and bite yerself like a snake', would instantly silence her.

At last the work worry ceased to exercise her, and for night to bring him home was a rare thing.

Her dog rounded and yarded the sheep when the sun went down and there was no sign of him, and together they kept watch on their movements till dawn. She was mindful not to speak of this care to him, knowing he would have left it for them to do constantly, and she noticed that what little interest he seemed to share went to the sheep. Why, was soon demonstrated.

Through the cracks her ever watchful eyes one day saw the dust rise out of the plain. Nearer it came till she saw him and a man on horseback rounding and drivng the sheep into the yard, and later both left in charge of a little mob. Their 'Baa-baas' to her were cries for help; many had been pets. So he was selling her sheep to the town butchers.

In the middle of the next week he came from town with a fresh horse, new saddle and bridle. He wore a flash red shirt, and round his neck a silk handerchief. On the next occasion she smelt scent, and though he did not try to display the dandy meerschaum, she saw it, and heard the squeak of new boots, not bluchers. However he was kinder to her this time, offering a fill of his cut tobacco; he had long ceased to keep her supplied. Several of the men who sometimes took a passing look in, would have made up her loss had they known, but no word of complaint passed her lips.

She looked at Squeaker as he filled his pipe from his pouch, but he would not meet her eyes, and, seemingly dreading something, slipped out.

She heard him hammering in the old hut at the back which served for tools and other things which sunlight and rain did not hurt. Quite briskly he went in and out. She could see him through the cracks carrying a narrow strip of bark, and understood he was making a bunk. When it was finished he had a smoke, then came to her and fidgetted about; he said this hut was too cold, and that she would never get well in it. She did not feel cold, but submitting to his mood, allowed him to make a fire that would roast a sheep. He took off his hat, and, fanning himself, said he was roastin', wasn't she? She was.

He offered to carry her into the other; he would put a new roof on it in a day or two, and it would be better than this one, and she would be up in no time. He stood to say this where she could not see him.

His eagerness tripped him.

There were months to run before all the Government conditions of residence, etc., in connection with the selection, would be fulfilled; still she thought perhaps he was trying to sell out, and she would not go.

He was away four days that time, and when he returned he slept in the new bunk.

She compromised. Would he put a bunk there for himself, keep out of town, and not sell the place? He promised instantly with additions.

'Try could yer crawl yerself?' he coaxed, looking at her bulk.

Her nostrils quivered with her suppressed breathing, and her lips tightened, but she did not attempt to move.

It was evident some great purpose actuated him. After attempts to carry and drag her, he rolled her on the sheet of bark that had brought her home, and laboriously drew her round.

She asked for a drink; he placed her billy and tin pint besides the bunk, and left her, gasping and dazed, to her sympathetic dog.

She saw him run up and yard his horse, and though she called him, he would not answer or come.

When he rode swiftly towards the town, her dog leaped on the bunk, and joined a refrain to her lamentation, but the cat took to the bush.

He came back at dusk next day in a spring cart – not alone – he had another mate. She saw her though he came a roundabout way, trying to keep in front of the new hut.

There were noises of moving many things from the cart to the hut. Finally he came to a crack near where she lay, and whispered the promise of many good things to her if she kept quiet, and that he would set her hut afire if she didn't. She was quiet, he need not have feared, for that time she was past it, she was stunned.

The released horse came stumbling round to the old hut, and thrust its head in the door in a domesticated fashion. Her dog promptly resented this straggler mistaking their hut for a stable. And the dog's angry dissent, together with the shod clatter of the rapidly disappearing intruder, seemed to have a disturbing effect on the pair in the new hut. The settling sounds suddenly ceased, and the cripple heard the stranger close the door, despite Squeaker's assurances that the woman in the old hut could not move from her bunk to save her life, and that her dog would not leave her.

Food, more and better, was placed near her – but, dumb and motionless, she lay with her face turned to the wall, and her dog growled menacingly at the stranger. The new woman was uneasy, and told Squeaker what people might say and do if she died.

He, scared at the 'do', went into the bush and waited.

She went to the door, not the crack, the face was turned that way, and said she had come to cook and take care of her.

The disabled woman, turning her head slowly, looked steadily at her. She was not much to look at. Her red hair hung in an uncurled bang over her forehead, the lower part of her face had robbed the upper, and her figure evinced imminent motherhood, though it is doubtful if the barren woman, noting this, knew by calculation the paternity was not Squeaker's. She was not learned in these matters, though she understood all about a ewe and lamb.

One circumstance was apparent – ah! bitterest of all bitterness to women – she was younger.

The thick hair that fell from the brow of the woman on the bunk was white now.

Bread and butter the woman brought. The cripple looked at it, at her dog, at the woman. Bread and butter for a dog! but the stranger did not understand till she saw it offered to the dog. The bread and butter was not for the dog. She brought meat.

All next day the man kept hidden. The cripple saw his dog, and knew he was about.

But there was an end of this pretence when at dusk he came back with a show of haste, and a finger of his right hand bound and ostentatiously prominent. The old mate, who knew this snake-bite trick from its inception, maybe, realised how useless were the terrified stranger's efforts to rouse the snoring man after an empty pint bottle had been flung on the outside heap.

However, what the sick woman thought was not definite, for she kept silent always. Neither was it clear how much she ate, and how much she gave to her dog, though the new mate said to Squeaker one day that she believed that the dog would not take a bit more than its share.

The cripple's silence told on the stranger, especially when alone. She would rather have abuse. Eagerly she counted the days past and to pass. Then back to the town. She told no word of that hope to Squeaker, he had no place in her plans for the future. So if he spoke of what they would do by and by when his time would be up, and he able to sell out, she listened in an uninterested silence.

She did tell him she was afraid of 'her', and after the first day would not go within reach, but every morning made a billy of tea, which with bread and beef Squeaker carried to her.

The rubbish heap was adorned, for the first time, with jam and fish tins from the table in the new hut. It seemed to be understood that neither woman nor dog in the old hut required them.

Squeaker's dog sniffed and barked joyfully around them till his licking efforts to bottom a salmon tin sent him careering in a muzzled frenzy, that caused the younger woman's thick lips to part grinningly till he came too close.

The remaining sheep were regularly yarded. His old mate heard him whistle as he did it. Squeaker began to work about a little burning-off. So that now, added to the other bush voices, was the call from some untimely falling giant. There is no sound so human as that from the riven souls of these tree people, or the trembling sighs of their upright neighbours whose hands in time will meet over the victim's fallen body.

There was no bunk on the side of the hut to which her eyes turned, but her dog filled that space, and the flash that passed between this back-broken woman and her dog might have been the spirit of these slain tree folk, it was so wondrous ghostly. Still, at times, the practical in her would be dominant, for in a mind so free of fancies, backed by bodily strength, hope died slowly, and forgetful of self she would almost call to Squeaker her fears that certain bees' nests were in danger.

He went into town one day and returned, as he had promised, long before sundown, and next day a clothes-line bridged the space between two trees near the back of the old hut; and – an equally rare occurrence – Squeaker placed his shoulders across the yoke that his old mate had fashioned for herself, with two kerosene tins attached, and brought them filled with water from the distant creek; but both only partly filled the tub, a new purchase. With utter disregard of the heat and Squeaker's sweating brow, his new mate said, even after another trip, two more now for the blue water. Under her commands he brought them, though sullenly, perhaps contrasting the old mate's methods with the new.

His old mate had periodically carried their washing to the

creek, and his mole-skins had been as white as snow without the aid of blue.

Towards noon, on the clothes-line many strange garments fluttered, suggestive of a taunt to the barren woman. When the sun went down she could have seen the assiduous Squeaker lower the new prop-sticks and considerately stoop to gather the pegs his inconsiderate new mate had dropped. However, after one load of water next morning, on hearing her estimate that three more would put her own things through, Squeaker struck. Nothing he could urge would induce the stranger to trudge to the creek, where thirst-slaked snakes lay waiting for someone to bite. She sulked and pretended to pack up, till a bright idea struck Squeaker. He fastened a cask on a sledge and, harnessing the new horse, hitched him to it, and, under the approving eyes of his new mate, led off to the creek, though, when she went inside, he bestrode the spiritless brute.

He had various mishaps, any one of which would have served as an excuse to his old mate, but even babes soon know on whom to impose. With an energy new to him he persevered and filled the cask, but the old horse repudiated such a burden even under Squeaker's unmerciful welts. Almost half was sorrowfully baled out, and under a rain of whacks the horse shifted a few paces, but the cask tilted and the thirsty earth got its contents. All Squeaker's adjectives over his wasted labour were as unavailing as the cure for spilt milk.

It took skill and patience to rig the cask again. He partly filled it, and, just as success seemed probable, the rusty wire fastening the cask to the sledge snapped with the strain, and springing free, coiled affectionately round the terrified horse's hocks. Despite the sledge (the cask had soon been disposed of) that old town horse's pace was his record. Hours after, on the plain that met the horizon, loomed two specks: the distance between them might be gauged, for the larger was Squeaker.

Anticipating a plentiful supply and lacking in bush caution, the new mate used the half-bucket of water to boil the salt mutton. Towards noon she laid this joint and bread on the rough table, then watched anxiously in the wrong direction for Squeaker.

She had drained the new tea-pot earlier, but she placed the spout to her thirsty mouth again.

She continued looking for him for hours.

Had he sneaked to town, thinking she had not used that water, or not caring whether or no? She did not trust him; another had left her. Besides she judged Squeaker by his treatment of the woman who was lying in there with wide-open eyes. Anyhow no use to cry with only that silent woman to hear her.

Had she drunk all hers?

She tried to see at long range through the cracks, but the hanging bed-clothes hid the billy. She went to the door, and, avoiding the bunk looked at the billy.

It was half full.

Instinctively she knew that the eyes of the woman were upon her. She turned away, and hoped and waited for thirsty minutes that seemed hours.

Desperation drove her back to the door. Dared she? No, she couldn't.

Getting a long forked propstick, she tried to reach it from the door, but the dog sprang at the stick. She dropped it and ran.

A scraggy growth fringed the edge of the plain. There was the creek. How far? she wondered. Oh, very far, she knew, and besides there were only a few holes where water was, and the snakes; for Squeaker, with a desire to shine in her eyes, was continually telling her of snakes – vicious and many – that he daily did battle with.

She recalled the evening he came from hiding in the scrub with a string round one finger, and said a snake had bitten him. He had drunk the pint of brandy she had brought for her sickness, and then slept till morning. True, although next day he had to dig for the string round the swollen blue finger, he was not worse than the many she had seen at the Shearer's Rest suffering a recovery. There was no brandy to cure her if she was bitten.

She cried a little in self-pity, then withdrew her eyes, that were getting red, from the outlying creek, and went again to the door. She of the bunk lay with closed eyes.

Was she asleep? The stranger's heart leapt, yet she was hardly in earnest as she tip-toed billy-wards. The dog, crouching with head between two paws, eyed her steadily, but showed no opposition. She made dumb show. 'I want to be friends with you, and won't hurt her.' Abruptly she looked at her, then at the dog. He was motionless and emotionless. Besides if that dog – certainly watching her – wanted to bite her (her dry mouth opened) it could get her any time.

She rated this dog's intelligence almost human, from many of its actions in omission and commission in connection with this woman.

She regretted the pole, no dog would stand that.

Two more steps.

Now just one more; then, by bending and stretching her arm, she would reach it. Could she now? She tried to encourage herself by remembering how close the first day she had been to the woman, and how delicious the first few mouthfuls would be – swallowing dry mouthfuls.

The thought of those sunken eyes suddenly opening made her heart bound. Oh! she must breathe – deep, loud breaths. Her throat clicked noisily. Looking back fearfully, she went swiftly out.

She did not look for Squeaker this time, she had given him up.

While she waited for her breath to steady, to her relief and surprise the dog came out. She made a rush to the new hut, but he passed seemingly oblivious of her, and, bounding across the plain, began rounding the sheep. Then he must know Squeaker had gone to town.

Stay! Her heart beat violently; was it because she on the bunk slept and did not want him?

She waited till her heart quieted, and again crept to the door.

The head of the woman on the bunk had fallen towards the wall in deep sleep; it was turned from the billy, to which she must creep so softly.

Slower, from caution and deadly earnestness, she entered.

She was not so advanced as before, and felt fairly secure, for the woman's eyes were still turned to the wall, and so tightly closed she could not possibly see where she was.

She would bend right down, and try and reach it from where she was.

She bent.

It was so swift and sudden, that she had not time to

scream when those bony fingers had gripped the hand that she prematurely reached for the billy. She was frozen with horror for a moment, then her screams were piercing. Panting with victory, the prostrate one held her with a hold that the other did not attempt to free herself from.

Down, down she drew her.

Her lips had drawn back from her teeth, and her breath almost scorched the face that she held so close for the staring eyes to gloat over. Her exultation was so great that she could only gloat and gasp, and hold with a tension that had stopped the victim's circulation.

As a wounded, robbed tigress might hold and look, she held and looked.

Neither heard the swift steps of the man, and if the tigress saw him enter, she was not daunted. 'Take me from her,' shrieked the terrified one. 'Quick, take me from her,' she repeated.

He hastily fastened the door and said something that the shrieks drowned, then picked up the pole. It fell with a thud across the arms which the tightening sinews had turned into steel. Once, twice, thrice. Then the one that got the fullest force bent; that side of the victim was free.

The pole had snapped. Another blow with a broken end freed the other side.

Still shrieking 'Take me from her, take me from her,' she beat on the closed door till Squeaker opened it.

Then he had to face and reckon with his old mate's maddened dog, that the closed door had baffled.

The dog suffered the shrieking woman to pass, but though Squeaker, in bitten agony, broke the stick across the dog, he was forced to give the savage brute best.

'Call 'im orf, Mary, 'e's eatin' me,' he implored. 'Oh, corl 'im orf.'

But with stony face the woman lay motionless.

'Sool 'im on t' 'er.' He indicated his new mate, who, as though all the plain led to the desired town, still ran in unreasoning terror.

'It's orl 'er doin', ' he pleaded, springing on the bunk beside his old mate. But when, to rouse her sympathy, he would have laid his hand on her, the dog's teeth fastened in it and pulled him back.

Dave's Snakebite

Steele Rudd

O NE HOT DAY, as we were finishing dinner, a sheriff's bailiff rode up to the door. Norah saw him first. She was dressed up ready to go over to Mrs Anderson's to tea. Sometimes young Harrison had tea at Anderson's – Thursdays, usually. This was Thursday; and Norah was starting early, because it was 'a good step of a way'. She reported the visitor. Dad left the table, munching some bread, and went out to him. Mother looked out of the door; Sal went to the window; little Bill and Tom peeped through a crack; Dave remained at his dinner; and Joe knavishly seized the opportunity of exploring the table for leavings, finally seating himself in Dad's place, and commencing where Dad had left off.

'Jury-summons,' said the meek bailiff, extracting a paper from his breast-pocket, and reading, 'Murtagh Joseph Rudd, selector, Shingle Hut ... Correct?'

Dad nodded assent.

'Got any water?'

There wasn't a drop in the cask, so Dad came in and asked Mother if there was any tea left. She pulled a long, solemn, Sunday-school face, and looked at Joe, who was holding the teapot upside-down, shaking the tea-leaves into his cup.

'Tea, Dad?' he chuckled – 'by golly!'

Dad didn't think it worth while going out to the bailiff again. He sent Joe.

'Not any at all?'

'Nothink,' said Joe.

'H'm! Nulla bona, eh?' And the Law smiled at its own joke and went off thirsty.

Thus it was that Dad came to be away one day when his great presence of mind and ability as a bush doctor was most required at Shingle Hut.

Dave took Dad's place at the plough. One of the horses – a colt that Dad bought with the money he got for helping with Anderson's crop – had only just been broken. He was bad at starting. When touched with the rein he would stand and wait until the old furrow-horse put in a few steps; then plunge to get ahead of him, and if a chain or a swingle-tree or something else didn't break, and Dave kept the plough in, he ripped and tore along in style, bearing in and bearing out, and knocking the old horse about till that much-enduring animal became as cranky as himself, and the pace terrible. Down would go the plough-handles, and, with one tremendous pull on the reins, Dave would haul them back on to their rumps. Then he would rush up and kick the colt on the root of the tail; and if that didn't make him put his leg over the chains and kick till he ran a hook into his heel and lamed himself, or broke something, it caused him to rear up and fall back on the plough and snort and strain and struggle till there was not a stitch left on him but the winkers.

Now, if Dave was noted for one thing more than another it was for his silence. He scarcely ever took the trouble to speak. He hated to be asked a question, and mostly answered by nodding his head. Yet, though he never seemed to practise, he could, when his blood was fairly up, swear with distinction and effect. On this occasion he swore through the whole afternoon without repeating himself.

Towards evening Joe took the reins and began to drive. He hadn't gone once around when, just as the horses approached a big dead tree that had been left standing in the cultivation, he planted his left foot heavily upon a Bathurst-burr that had been cut and left lying. It clung to him. He hopped along on one leg, trying to kick it off; still it clung to him. He fell down. The horses and the tree got mixed up, and everything was confusion.

Dave abused Joe remorselessly. 'Go on! Clear out' he howled, waving in the air a fistful of grass and weeds which he had pulled from the nose of the plough. 'Clear out of this altogether! – you're only a damn nuisance.'

Joe's eyes rested on the fistful of grass. They lit up suddenly.

'L-l-look out, Dave,' he stuttered; 'y'-y' got a s-s-snake.'

Dave dropped the grass promptly. A deaf-adder crawled out of it. Joe killed it. Dave looked closely at his hand, which was all scratches and scars. He looked at it again; then he sat on the beam of the plough, pale and miserable-looking.

'D-d-did it bite y', Dave?' No answer.

Joe saw a chance to distinguish himself, and took it. He ran home, glad to be the bearer of the news, and told Mother that 'Dave's got bit by a adder – a sudden-death adder – right on top o' th' finger.'

How Mother screamed! 'My God! whatever shall we do? Run quick,' she said, 'and bring Mr Maloney. Dear! oh dear! oh dear!'

Joe had not calculated on this injunction. He dropped his head and said sullenly:

'Wot, walk all the way over there?'

Before he could say another word a tin-dish left a dinge on the back of his skull that will accompany him to his grave if he lives to be a thousand.

'You wretch, you! Why don't you run when I tell you?'

Joe sprang in the air like a shot wallaby.

'I'll not go *at all* now – y' see!' he answered, starting to cry. Then Sal put on her hat and ran for Maloney.

Meanwhile Dave took the horses out, walked inside, and threw himself on the sofa without uttering a word. He felt ill.

Mother was in a paroxysm of fright. She threw her arms about frantically and cried for someone to come. At last she sat down and tried to think what she could do. She thought of the very thing, and ran for the carving-knife, which she handed to Dave with shut eyes. He motioned her with a disdainful movement of the elbow to take it away.

Would Maloney never come! He was coming, hat in hand, and running for dear life across the potato-paddock. Behind him was his man. Behind his man – Sal, out of breath. Behind her, Mrs Maloney and the children.

'Phwat's th' thrubble?' cried Maloney. 'Bit be a dif-adher? O, be the tares of war!'

Then he asked Dave numerous questions as to how it happened, which Joe answered with promptitude and pride. Dave simply shrugged his shoulders and turned his face to the wall. Nothing was to be got out of *him*.

Maloney held a short consultation with himself. Then – 'Hould up yer hand!' he said, bending over Dave with a knife. Dave thrust out his arm violently, knocked the instrument to the other side of the room, and kicked wickedly.

'The pison's wurrkin',' whispered Maloney quite loud.

'Oh, my gracious!' groaned Mother.

'The poor crathur,' said Mrs Maloney.

There was a pause.

'Phwhat finger's bit?' asked Maloney. Joe thought it was the littlest one of the lot.

He approached the sofa again, knife in hand.

'Show me yer finger,' he said to Dave.

For the first time Dave spoke. He said:

'Damn ye' – what the devil do y' want? Clear out and lea' me 'lone.'

Maloney hesitated. There was a long silence. Dave commenced breathing heavily.

'It's maikin' 'm slape,' whispered Maloney, glancing over his shoulder at the women.

'Don't let him! Don't let him!' Mother wailed.

'Salvation to 's all!' muttered Mrs Maloney, piously crossing herself.

Maloney put away the knife and beckoned to his man, who was looking on from the door. They both took a firm hold of Dave and stood him upon his feet. He looked hard and contemptuously at Maloney for some seconds. Then with gravity and deliberation Dave said: 'Now wot 'n th' *devil* are y' up t'? Are y' *mad*?'

'Walk 'm along, Jaimes – walk 'm along,' was all Maloney had to say. And out into the yard they marched him. How Dave did struggle to get away! – swearing and cursing Maloney for a cranky Irishman till he foamed at the mouth, all of which the other put down to snake-poison. Round and round the yard and up and down it they trotted him till long after dark, until there wasn't a struggle left in him.

They placed him on the sofa again, Maloney keeping him awake with a strap. How Dave ground his teeth and kicked and swore whenever he felt that strap! And they sat and watched him.

It was late in the night when Dad came from town. He staggered in with the neck of a bottle showing out of his pocket. In his hand was a piece of paper wrapped round the end of some yards of sausage. The dog outside carried the other end.

'An' 'e ishn't dead?' Dad said after hearing what had befallen Dave. 'Don' b'leevsh id – wuzhn't bit. Di 'fore shun'own ifsh desh ad'er bish 'm.'

'Bit!' Dave said bitterly, turning round to the surprise of everyone. 'I never said I was bit. No one said I was – only those snivelling idiots and that pumpkin-headed Irish pig there.'

Maloney lowered his jaw and opened his eyes.

'Zhackly. Did'n' I *(hic)* shayzo, 'Loney? Did'n' I, eh, ol' wom'n!' Dad mumbled, and dropped his chin on his chest.

Maloney began to take another view of the matter. He put a leading question to Joe.

'He *muster* been bit,' Joe answered, ''cuz he had the d-death-adder in his hand.'

More silence.

'Mush die 'fore shun'own,' Dad murmured.

Maloney was thinking hard. At last he spoke. 'Bridgy!' he cried, 'where's th' childer?' Mrs Maloney gathered them up.

Just then Dad seemed to be dreaming. He swayed about. His head hung lower, and he muttered: 'Shen'l'm'n, yoush disharged wish shanksh y'cun'ry.'

The Maloneys left.

Dave is still alive and well, and silent as ever; and if any one question is more intolerable and irritating to him than another, it is to be asked if he remembers the time he was bitten by a deaf-adder.

Send Round the Hat

Henry Lawson

Now this is the creed from the Book of the Bush –
Should be simple and plain to a dunce:
'If a man's in a hole you must pass round the hat –
Were he jail-bird or gentleman once.'

'IS IT ANY HARM TO WAKE YER?'

It was about nine o'clock in the morning, and, though it was Sunday morning, it was no harm to wake me; but the shearer had mistaken me for a deaf jackeroo, who was staying at the shanty and was something like me, and had good-naturedly shouted almost at the top of his voice, and he woke the whole shanty. Anyway he woke three or four others who were sleeping on beds and stretchers, and one on a shake-down on the floor, in the same room. It had been a wet night, and the shanty was full of shearers from Big Billabong Shed which had cut out the day before. My roommates had been drinking and gambling overnight, and they swore luridly at the intruder for disturbing them.

He was six-foot-three or thereabout. He was loosely built, bony, sandy-complexioned and grey-eyed. He wore a good-humoured grin at most times, as I noticed later on; he was of a type of bushman that I always liked – the sort that seem to get more good-natured the longer they grow, yet are hard knuckled and would accommodate a man who wanted to fight, or thrash a bully in a good-natured way.

The sort that like to carry somebody's baby round, and cut wood, carry water and do little things for overworked married bushmen. He wore a saddle-tweed sac suit two sizes too small for him, and his face, neck, great hands and bony wrists were covered with sunblotches and freckles.

'I hope I ain't disturbin' yer,' he shouted, as he bent over my bunk, 'but there's a cove – '

'You needn't shout!' I interrupted, 'I'm not deaf.'

'Oh – I beg you pardon!' he shouted. 'I didn't know I was yellin'. I thought you was the deaf feller.'

'Oh, that's all right,' I said. 'What's the trouble?'

'Wait till them other chaps is done swearin' and I'll tell yer,' he said. He spoke with a quiet, good-natured drawl, with something of the nasal twang, but tone and drawl distinctly Australian – altogether apart from that of the Americans.

'Oh, spit it out for Christ's sake, Long-'un,' yelled One-eyed Bogan, who had been the worst swearer in a rough shed, and he fell back on his bunk as if his previous remarks had exhausted him.

'It's that there sick jackaroo that was pickin'-up at Big Billabong,' said the Giraffe. 'He had to knock off the first week, an' he's been here ever since. They're sendin' him away to the hospital in Sydney by the speeshall train. They're just goin' to take him up in the wagonette to the railway-station, an' I thought I might as well go round with the hat an' get him a few bob. He's got a missus and kids in Sydney.'

'Yer always goin' round with yer gory hat!' growled Bogan. 'Yer'd blanky well take it round in hell.'

'That's what he's doing, Bogan,' muttered Gentleman

Once, on the shake-down, with his face to the wall.

The hat was a genuine cabbage-tree, one of the sort that 'last a lifetime'. It was well coloured, almost black in fact with weather and old age, and it had a new strap around the base of the crown. I looked into it and saw a dirty pound note and some silver. I dropped in half a crown, which was more than I could spare, for I had only been a green-hand at Big Billabong.

'Thank yer!' he said. 'Now then, you fellers!'

'I wish you'd keep your hat on your head, and your money in your pockets and your sympathy somewhere else,' growled Jack Moonlight as he raised himself painfully on his elbow and felt under his pillow for two half-crowns. 'Here,' he said, 'here's two half-casers. Chuck 'em in and let me sleep for God's sake!'

Gentleman Once, the gambler, rolled round on his shake-down, bringing his good-looking dissipated face from the wall. He had turned in in his clothes and, with considerable exertion, he shoved his hand down into the pocket of his trousers, which were a tight fit. He brought up a roll of pound notes and could find no silver.

'Here,' he said to the Giraffe, 'I might as well lay a quid. I'll chance it anyhow. Chuck it in.'

'You've got rats this morning, Gentleman Once,' growled the Bogan. 'It ain't a blanky horse-race.'

'P'raps I have,' said Gentleman Once, and he turned to the wall again with his head on his arm.

'Now, Bogan, yer might as well chuck in somethin', said the Giraffe.

'What's the matter with the — jackeroo?' asked the Bogan, tugging his trousers under his mattress.

Moonlight said something in a low tone.

'The — he has!' said Bogan. 'Well I pity the —! Here, I'll chuck in half a — quid!' and he dropped half a sovereign into the hat.

The fourth man, who was known to his face as 'Barcoo-Rot', and behind his back as 'The Mean Man', had been drinking all night, and not even Bogan's stump-splitting adjectives could rouse him. So Bogan got out of bed, and calling on us (as blanky female cattle) to witness what he was about to do, he rolled the drunkard over, prospected his pockets till he made up five shillings (or a 'caser' in bush language) and 'chucked' them into the hat.

And Barcoo-Rot is probably unconscious to this day that he was ever connected with an act of charity.

The Giraffe struck the deaf jackaroo in the next room. I heard the chaps cursing Long-'un for waking them, and Deaf-'un for being, as they thought at first, the indirect cause of the disturbance. I heard the Giraffe and his hat being condemned in other rooms and cursed along the verandah where more shearers were sleeping; and after a while I turned out.

The Giraffe was carefully fixing a mattress and pillows on the floor of a wagonette, and presently a man, who looked like a corpse, was carried out and lifted into the trap.

As the wagonette started, the shanty-keeper – a fat, soulless-looking man – put his hand in his pocket and dropped a quid into the hat which was still going round, in the hands of the Giraffe's mate, little Teddy Thompson, who was as far below medium height as the Giraffe was above it.

The Giraffe took the horse's head and led him along on

the most level parts of the road towards the railway-station, and two or three chaps went along to help get the sick man into the train.

The shearing season was over in that district, but I got a job of house-painting which was my trade, at the Great Western Hotel (a two-storey brick place), and I stayed in Bourke for a couple of months.

The Giraffe was a Victorian native from Bendigo. He was well known in Bourke and to many shearers who came through the great dry scrubs from hundreds of miles round. He was stake holder, drunkard's banker, peace-maker where possible, referee or second to oblige the chaps when a fight was on, big brother or uncle to most of the children in town, final court of appeal when the youngsters had a dispute over a foot-race at the school picnic, referee at their fights, and he was the stranger's friend.

'The feller as knows can battle around for himself,' he'd say. 'But I always like to do what I can for a hard-up stranger cove. I was a green-hand jackaroo once meself, and I know what it is.'

'You're always bothering about other people, Giraffe,' said Tom Hall, the Shearers' Union secretary, who was only a couple of inches shorter than the Giraffe. 'There's nothing in it, you can take it from me – I ought to know.'

'Well, what's a feller to do?' said the Giraffe. 'I'm only hangin' around here till shearin' starts agen, an' a cove might as well be doin' something. Besides, it ain't as if I was like a cove that had old people or a wife an' kids to look after.

I ain't got no responsibilities. A feller can't be doin' noth-in'. Besides, I like to lend a helpin' hand when I can.'

'Well, all I've got to say,' said Tom, most of whose screw went in borrowed quids, etc.; 'all I've got to say is that you'll get no thanks, and you might blanky well starve in the end.'

'There ain't no fear of me starvin' so long as I've got me hands about me; and I ain't a cove as wants thanks,' said the Giraffe.

He was always helping someone or something. Now it was a bit of a 'dance' that we was getting' up for the girls; again it was Mrs Smith, the woman whose husban' was drowned in the flood in the Bogan River lars' Christmas, or that there poor woman down by the Billabong – her hus-band cleared out and left her with a lot o' kids. Or Bill Something, the bullocky, who was run over by his own wagon, while he was drunk, and got his leg broke.

Towards the end of his spree One-eyed Bogan broke loose and smashed nearly all the windows of the Carriers' Arms, and next morning he was fined heavily at the police court. About dinner-time I encountered the Giraffe and his hat, with two half-crowns in it for a start.

'I'm sorry to trouble yer,' he said. 'but One-eyed Bogan carn't pay his fine, an' I thought we'd fix it up for him. He ain't half a bad sort of feller when he ain't drinkin'. It's only when he gets too much booze in him.'

After shearing, the hat usually started round with the Giraffe's own dirty crumpled note in the bottom of it as a send-off, later on it was half a sovereign; till in the end he would borrow a 'few bob' – which he always repaid after next shearing – 'just to start the thing goin'.'

There were several yarns about him and his hat. 'Twas said that the hat had belonged to his father, whom he resembled in every respect, and it had been going round for so many years that the crown was worn as thin as paper by the quids, half-quids, casers, half-casers, bobs and tanners or sprats – to say nothing of the scrums – that had been chucked into it in its time and shaken up.

They say that when a new Governor visited Bourke the Giraffe happened to be standing on the platform close to the exit, grinning good-humouredly, and the local toady nudged him urgently and said in an awful whisper, 'Take off your hat! Why don't you take off your hat?'

'Why?' drawled the Giraffe, 'he ain't hard up, is he?'

And they fondly cherish an anecdote to the effect that, when the One-Man-One-Vote Bill was passed (or Payment of Members, or when the first Labor Party went in – I forget on which occasion they said it was) the Giraffe was carried away by the general enthusiasm, got a few beers in him, 'chucked' a quid into his hat, and sent it round. The boys contributed by force of habit, and contributed largely, because of the victory and the beer. And when the hat came back to the Giraffe, he stood holding it in front of him with both hands and stared blankly into if for a while. Then it dawned on him.

'Blowed if I haven't bin an' gone an' took up a bloomin' collection for meself!' he said.

He was almost a teetotaller, but he stood his shout in reason. He mostly drank ginger-beer.

'I ain't a feller that boozes, but I ain't got nothin' agen chaps enjoyin' themselves, as long as they don't go too far.'

It was common for a man on the spree to say to him:

'Here! here's five quid. Look after if for me, Giraffe, will yer, till I get off the booze.'

His real name was Bob Brothers, and his bush names, Long-'un, The Giraffe, Send-around-the-hat, Chuck-in-a-bob and Ginger-ale.

Some years before, camels and Afghan drivers had been imported to the Bourke district; the camels did very well in the dry country, they went right across the country and carried everything from sardines to flooring-boards. And the teamsters loved the Afghans nearly as much as Sydney furniture makers love the cheap Chinese in the same line. They loved 'em even as union shearers on strike love blacklegs brought up-country to take their places.

Now the Giraffe was a good, straight unionist, but in cases of sickness or trouble he was apt to forget his unionism, as all bushmen are, at all times (and for all time), to forget their creed. So, one evening, the Giraffe blundered into the Carriers' Arms – of all places in the world – when it was full of teamsters; he had his hat in his hand and some small silver and coppers in it.

'I say, you fellers, there's a poor Afghan in the camp down there along the – '

A big, brawny bullock-driver took him firmly by the shoulders, or rather by the elbows, and ran him out before any damage was done. The Giraffe took it as he took most things, good humouredly; but, about dusk, he was seen slipping down towards the Afghan camp with a billy of soup.

'I believe,' remarked Tom Hall, 'that when the Giraffe goes to heaven – and he's the only one of us, as far as I can see, that has a ghost of a show – I believe that when he goes to heaven, the first thing he'll do will be to take his infernal hat round amongst the angels – getting up a collection for this damned world that he left behind.'

'Well, I don't think there's so much to his credit, after all,' said Jack Mitchell, shearer. 'You see, the Giraffe is ambitious; he likes public life, and that accounts for him shoving himself forward with his collections. As for bothering about people in trouble, that's only common curiosity; he's one of those chaps that are always shoving their noses into other people's troubles. And as for looking after sick men – why! there's nothing the Giraffe likes better than pottering round a sick man, and watching him and studying him. He's awfully interested in sick men, and they're pretty scarce out here. I tell you there's nothing he likes better – except, maybe, it's pottering round a corpse. I believe he'd ride forty miles to help and sympathise and potter round a funeral. The fact of the matter is that the Giraffe is only enjoying himself with other people's troubles – that's all it is. It's only vulgar curiosity and selfishness. I set it down to his ignorance; the way he was brought up.'

A few days after the Afghan incident the Giraffe and his hat had a run of luck. A German, one of a party who were building a new wooden bridge over the Big Billabong, was helping unload some girders from a truck at the railway-station when a big log slipped on the skids and his leg was smashed badly. They carried him to the Carriers' Arms, which was the nearest hotel, and into a bedroom behind the bar, and sent for the doctor. The Giraffe was in evidence as usual.

'It vas not that at all,' said German Charlie, when they asked him if he was in much pain. 'It vas not that at all. I

don't care a damn for der bain; but dis is der tird year –
and I vas going home dis year – after der gontract – und
der gontract yoost commence!'

That was the burden of his song all through, between his
groans.

There were a good few chaps sitting quietly about the bar
and verandah when the doctor arrived. The Giraffe was sit-
ting at the end of the counter, on which he had laid his hat
while he wiped his face, neck, and forehead with a big
speckled sweat-rag. It was a very hot day.

The doctor, a good-hearted young Australian, was heard
saying something. Then German Charlie, in a voice that
rung with pain:

'Make that leg right, doctor – quick! Dis is der tird plud-
dy year – und I must go home!'

The doctor asked him if he was in great pain.

'Neffer mind der pluddy bain, doctor! Neffer mind der
pluddy bain! Dot vas nossing. Make dat leg vell quick, doc-
tor. Dis vas der last contract, and I vas going home dis
year.' Then the words jerked out of him by physical agony:
'Der girl vas vaiting dree year, and – by Got! I must go
home.'

The publican – Watty Braithwaite, known as Watty
Broadweight, or, more familiarly, Watty Bothways – turned
over the Giraffe's hat in a tired, bored sort of way, dropped
a quid into it, and nodded resignedly at the Giraffe.

The Giraffe caught up the hint and the hat with alacri-
city. The hat went all round town, so to speak; and as soon
as his leg was firm enough not to come loose on the road
German Charlie went home.

It was well known that I contributed to the Sydney

Bulletin and several other papers. The Giraffe's bump of reverence was very large, and swelled especially for sick men and poets. He treated me with much more respect than is due from a bushman to a man, and with an odd sort of extra gentleness I sometimes fancied. But one day he rather surprised me.

'I'm sorry to trouble yer,' he said in a shamefaced way. 'I don't know as you go in for sportin', but One-eyed Bogan an' Barcoo-Rot is going to have a bit of a scrap down the Billybong this evenin, an' – '

'A bit of a what?' I asked.

'A bit of a fight to a finish,' he said apologetically. 'An' the chaps is tryin' to fix up a fiver to put some life into the thing. There's bad blood between One-eyed Bogan and Barcoo-Rot, an' it won't do them any harm to have it out.'

It was a great fight, I remember. There must have been a couple of score blood-soaked handkerchiefs (or sweat-rags) buried in a hole on the field of battle, and the Giraffe was busy the rest of the evening helping to patch up the principals. Later on he took up a small collection for the loser, who happened to be Barcoo-Rot in spite of the advantage of an eye.

The Salvation Army lassie, who went round with the *War Cry*, nearly always sold the Giraffe three copies.

A newchum parson, who wanted a subscription to build or enlarge a chapel, or something, sought the assistance of the Giraffe's influence with his mates.

'Well,' said the Giraffe, 'I ain't a churchgoer meself. I ain't what you might call a religious cove, but I'll be glad to do what I can to help yer. I don't suppose I can do much. I ain't been to church since I was a kiddy.'

The parson was shocked, but later on he learned to appreciate the Giraffe and his mates, and to love Australia for the bushman's sake, and it was he who told me the above anecdote.

The Giraffe helped fix some stalls for a Catholic Church bazaar, and some of the chaps chaffed him about it in the union office.

'You'll be taking up a collection for a joss-house down in the Chinamen's camp next,' said Tom Hall in conclusion.

'Well, I ain't got nothing agen the Roming Carflicks,' said the Giraffe. 'An' Father O'Donovan's a very decent sort of cove. He stuck up for the unions all right in the strike anyway.' ('He wouldn't be Irish if he wasn't,' someone commented.) 'I carried swags once for six months with a feller that was a Carflick, an' he was a very straight feller. And a girl I knowed turned Carflick to marry a chap that had got her into trouble, an' she was always jes the same to me after as she was before. Besides, I like to help everything that's goin' on.'

Tom Hall and one or two others went out hurriedly to have a drink. But we all loved the Giraffe.

He was very innocent and very humorous, especially when he meant to be most serious and philosophical.

'Some of them bush girls is regular tomboys,' he said to me solemnly one day. 'Some of them is too cheeky altogether. I remember once I was stoppin' at a place – they was sort of relations o' mine – an' they put me to sleep in a room off the verander, where there was a glass door an' no blinds. An' the first mornin' the girls – they was sort o' cousins o' mine – they come gigglin' and foolin' round outside the door on the verander, an' kep' me in bed till nearly ten o'clock. I had to put me trowsis on under the bed-clothes in the end. But I got back on them next night,' he reflected.

'How did you do that, Bob,' I asked.

'Why, I went to bed in my trowsis!'

One day I was on a plank, painting the ceiling of the bar of the Great Western Hotel. I was anxious to get the job finished. The work had been kept back most of the day by chaps handing up long beers to me, and drawing my attention to the alleged fact that I was putting on the paint wrong side out. I was slapping it on over the last few boards when:

'I'm very sorry to trouble yer: I always seem to be troublin' yer; but there's that there woman and them girls – '

I looked down – about the first time I had looked down on him – and there was the Giraffe, with his hat brim-up on the plank and about two half-crowns in it.

'Oh, that's all right, Bob,' I said, and I dropped in half a crown.

There were shearers in the bar, and presently there was some barracking. It appeared that that there woman and them girls were strange women, in the local as well as the Biblical sense of the word, who had come from Sydney at the end of the shearing season, and had taken a cottage on the edge of the scrub on the outskirts of the town. There had been trouble this week in connection with a row at their establishment, and they had been fined, warned off by the police, and turned out by their landlord.

'This is a bit too red-hot, Giraffe,' said one of the shear-ers. 'Them —s has made enough out of us coves. They've got plenty of stuff, don't you fret. Let 'em go to — ! I'm blanked if I give a sprat.'

'They ain't got their fares to Sydney,' said the Giraffe. 'An' what's more, the little 'un is sick, an' two of them has kids in Sydney.'

'How the — do you know?'

'Why one of 'em come to me an' told me all about it.'

There was an involuntary guffaw.

'Look here, Bob,' said Billy Woods, the rouseabouts' sec-retary, kindly. 'Don't make a fool of yourself. You'll have all the chaps laughing at you. Those girls are only working you for all you're worth. I suppose one of 'em came crying and whining to you. Don't you bother about 'em. You don't know 'em; they can pump water at a moment's notice. You haven't had any experience with women yet, Bob.'

'She didn't come whinin' and cryin' to me,' said the Giraffe, dropping his twanging drawl a little. 'She looked me straight in the face an' told me all about it.'

'I say, Giraffe,' said Box-o'-Tricks, 'what have you been doin'? You've been down there on the nod. I'm surprised at yer, Giraffe.'

'An' he pretends to be so gory soft an' innocent, too,' growled the Bogan. 'We know all about you, Giraffe.'

'Look here, Giraffe,' said Mitchell the shearer. 'I'd never have thought it of you. We all thought you were the only virgin youth west of the river; I always thought you were a moral young man. You mustn't think that because your conscience is pricking you everyone else's is.'

'I ain't had nothing to do with them,' said the Giraffe,

drawling again. 'I ain't a cove that goes in for that sort of thing. But other chaps has, and I think they might as well help 'em out of their fix.'

'They're a rotten crowd,' said Billy Woods. 'You don't know them, Bob. Don't bother about them – they're not worth it. Put your money in your pocket. You'll find a better use for it before next shearing.'

'Better shout, Giraffe,' said Box-o'Tricks.

Now in spite of the Giraffe's softness he was the hardest man in Bourke to move when he'd decided on what he thought was 'the fair thing to do'. Another peculiarity of his was that on occasion, such for instance as 'sayin' a few words' at a strike meeting, he would straighten himself, drop the twang, and rope in his drawl, so to speak.

'Well, look here, you chaps,' he said now. 'I don't know anything about them women. I s'pose they're bad, but I don't suppose they're worse than men has made them. All I know is that there's four women turned out, without any stuff, and every woman in Bourke, an' the law agen 'em. An' the fact that they is women is agenst 'em most of all. You don't expect 'em to hump their swags to Sydney! Why, only I ain't got the stuff I wouldn't trouble yer. I'd pay their fares meself. Look,' he said, lowering his voice, 'there they are now, an' one of the girls is cryin'. Don't let 'em see you lookin'.'

I dropped softly from the plank and peeped out with the rest.

They stood by the fence on the opposite side of the street, a bit up towards the railway-station, with their portmanteaux and bundles at their feet. One girl leant with her arms on the fence rail and her face buried in them, another was trying to comfort her. The third girl and the woman stood facing our way. The woman was good-looking; she had a hard face, but it might have been made hard. The third girl seemed half defiant, half inclined to cry. Presently she went to the other side of the girl who was crying on the fence and put her arm round her shoulder. The woman suddenly turned her back on us and stood looking away over the paddocks.

The hat went round. Billy Woods was first, then Box-o'-Tricks, and then Mitchell.

Billy contributed with eloquent silence. 'I was only jokin', Giraffe,' said Box-o'-Tricks, dredging his pockets for a couple of shillings. It was some time after the shearing, and most of the chaps were hard up.

'Ah, well,' sighed Mitchell. 'There's no help for it. If the Giraffe would take up a collection to import some decent girls to this God-forgotten place there might be some sense in it … It's bad enough for the Giraffe to undermine our religious prejudices, and tempt us to take a morbid interest in sick Chows and Afghans, and blacklegs and widows; but when he starts mixing us up with strange women it's time to buck.' And he prospected his pockets and contributed two shillings, some odd pennies, and a pinch of tobacco dust.

'I don't mind helping the girls, but I'm damned if I'll give a penny to the old —, ' said Tom Hall.

'Well, she was a girl once herself,' drawled the Giraffe.

The Giraffe went round to the other pubs and to the union offices, and when he returned he seemed satisfied with the plate, but troubled by something else.

'I don't know what to do for them for tonight,' he said.

'None of the pubs or any boardin'-houses will hear of them, an' there ain't no empty houses, an' the women is all agen 'em.'

'Not all,' said Alice, the big, handsome barmaid from Sydney. 'Come here, Bob.' She gave the Giraffe half a sovereign and a look for which some of us would have paid him ten pounds – had we the money, and had the look been transferable.

'Wait a minute, Bob,' she said, and went in to speak to the landlord.

'There's an empty bedroom at the end of the store in the yard,' she said when she came back. 'They can camp there for tonight if they behave themselves. You'd better tell 'em, Bob.'

'Thank yer, Alice,' said the Giraffe.

Next day, after work, the Giraffe and I drifted together and down by the river in the cool of the evening, and sat on the edge of the steep, drought-parched bank.

'I heard you saw your lady friends off this morning, Bob,' I said, and was sorry I said it, even before he answered.

'Oh, they ain't no friends of mine,' he said. 'Only four poor devils of women. I thought they mightn't like to stand waitin' with the crowd on the platform, so I jest offered to get their tickets an' told 'em to wait round at the back of the station till the bell rung. An' what do yer think they did, Harry?' he went on with an exasperatingly unintelligent grin. 'Why, they wanted to kiss me.'

'Did they?'

'Yes. An' they would have done it, too, if I hadn't been so long. Why, I'm blessed if they didn't kiss me hands.'

'You don't say so.'

'God's truth. Somehow I didn't like to go on the platform

with them after that; besides, they was cryin', and I can't stand women cryin'. But some of the chaps put them into an empty carriage.' He thought a moment and then:

'There's some terrible good-hearted fellers in the world,' he reflected.

I thought so too.

'Bob,' I said, 'you're a single man. Why don't you get married and settle down?'

'Well,' he said, 'I ain't got no wife and kids, that's a fact. But it ain't my fault.'

He may have been right about the wife. But I thought of the look that Alice had given him.

'Girls seem to like me right enough,' he said, 'but it don't go no further than that. The trouble is that I'm so long, and I always seem to get shook after little girls. At least there was one little girl in Bendigo that I was properly gone on.'

'And wouldn't she have you?'

'Well, it seems not.'

'Did you ask her?'

'Oh, yes, I asked her right enough.'

'Well, and what did she say?'

'She said it would be redicilus for her to be seen trottin' alongside of a chimbly like me.'

'Perhaps she didn't mean that. There are any amount of little women who like tall men.'

'I thought of that too – afterwards. P'raps she didn't mean it that way. I s'pose the fact of the matter was that she didn't cotton on to me, and wanted to let me down easy. She didn't want to hurt me feelin's, if yer understand – she was a very good-hearted little girl. There's some terrible tall fellers where I come from, and I know two as married little girls.'

He seemed a hopeless case.

'Sometimes,' he said, 'sometimes I wish that I wasn't so blessed long.'

'There's that there deaf jackaroo,' he reflected presently. 'He's something in the same fix about girls as I am. He's too deaf and I'm too long.'

'How do you make that out?' I asked. 'He's got three girls, to my knowledge, and as for being deaf, why he gasses more than any man in the town, and knows more of what's going on than old Mother Brindle the washer-woman.'

'Well, look at that now!' said the Giraffe, slowly. 'Who'd have thought it? He never told me he had three girls, an' as for hearin' news, I always tell him anything that's goin' on that I think he doesn't catch. He told me his trouble was that whenever he went out with a girl people could hear what they was sayin' – at least they could hear what she was sayin' to him, an' draw their own conclusions, he said. He said he went out one night with a girl, and some of the chaps foxed 'em an' heard her saying "don't" to him, an' put it all round town.'

'What did she say "don't" for?' I asked.

'He didn't tell me that, but I s'pose he was kissin' her or huggin' her or something.'

'Bob,' I said presently, 'didn't you try the little girl in Bendigo a second time?'

'No,' he said. 'What was the use? She was a good little girl, and I wasn't goin' to go botherin' her. I ain't the sort of cove that goes hangin' round where he isn't wanted. But somehow I couldn't stay about Bendigo after she gave me the hint, so I thought I'd come over an' have a knock around on this side for a year or two.'

'And you never wrote her?'

'No. What was the use of goin' pesterin' her with letters? I know what trouble letters give me when I have to answer one. She'd have only had to tell me the straight truth in a letter an' it wouldn't have done me any good. But I've pretty well got over it by this time.'

A few days later I went to Sydney. The Giraffe was the last I shook hands with from the carriage window, and he slipped something in a piece of paper into my hand.

'I hope yer won't be offended,' he drawled, 'but some of the chaps thought you mightn't be too flush of stuff – you've been shoutin' a good deal; so they put a quid or two together. They thought it might help yer to have a bit of a fly round in Sydney.'

I was back in Bourke before next shearing. On the evening of my arrival I ran against the Giraffe; he seemed strangely shaken over something, but he kept his hat on his head.

'Would yer mind takin' a stroll as fur as the Billerbong?' he said. 'I got something I'd like to tell yer.'

'I've just got a letter,' he said. 'A letter from that little girl at Bendigo. It seems it was all a mistake. I'd like yer to read it. Somehow I feel as if I want to talk to a feller, and I'd rather talk to you than any of them other chaps.'

It was a good letter, from a big-hearted little girl. She had been breaking her heart for the great ass all these months. It seemed that he had left Bendigo without saying good-bye to her.

'Somehow I couldn't bring meself to it,' he said, when I

taxed him with it. She had never been able to get his address until last week; then she got it from a Bourke man who had gone south. She called him 'an awful long fool', which he was, without the slightest doubt, and she implored him to write, and to come back to her.

And as I sit here writing by lamplight at midday, in the midst of a great city of social sham, of hopeless, squalid poverty, of ignorant selfishness, cultured or brutish, and of noble and heroic endeavour frowned down or callously neglected, I am almost aware of a sudden burst of sunshine in the room, and a long form leaning over my chair, and:

'Excuse me for troublin' yer; I'm always troublin' yer, but there's that there poor woman ... '

And I wish I could immortalise him.

Romance of Bullocktown

Marcus Clarke

Mr John Hardy, the schoolmaster, was regarded with some degree of awe by the Bullocktown folks. As a general rule, Bullocktown stood in awe of nothing under or over heaven, believing utterly in the eternal fitness of things, and the propriety of its own existence. But Mr John Hardy was a human being of a type so unfamiliar to Bullocktown, that for once in its life the township unwillingly did reverence.

The new schoolmaster was a tall, gaunt, angular man, with a mop of black hair, large bony hands, and black melancholy eyes. He arrived by the night coach with no more property than a small bag sufficed to carry, and asked Flash Harry if the schoolmaster's house was anywhere near. Harry pointed with his whip to the little hut which, embowered in creepers, stood on the hill, and the new-comer at once tramped away to it, ignoring with provoking complacency the great business of 'liquoring up' which was the commercial pursuit of Bullocktown.

Nor was he more sociable next day. Maggie Burns, who was 'keeping' the schoolhouse, deposed that Mr Hardy had asked her for a light, opened his bag, produced a small book, and read till daylight. At daylight he had gone for a walk and returned laden with plants and ferns, just in time to open school. School being over, he went for another walk, and did not come back till 10 o'clock. This process of self-abstraction from the joys of Bullocktown was at first resented. It was the custom that every stranger should be made free of the place – receive the liberty of the city, so to speak – by at least one glorious bout of brandy. Intoxication in Bullocktown had become elevated to an art, and, as with other delights of a sensual character, connoisseurs studied to protract its enjoyment as long as possible. Rumours were afloat that Mr Hardy was a scholar of eminence, a man of much erudition, whom 'circumstances' had compelled to accept the appointment of a common schoolmaster. A report filtered through the common layers of society, as such reports mysteriously do filter, that Mr Hardy had been a man well known in Melbourne, and that his name was not really Hardy, but something else. Now, Bullocktown, the best-hearted place in the universe, was ready to receive this unfortunate victim of unknown circumstances with open arms – was ready to clasp him to its manly bosom, and to initiate him into all the art and mystery of its profession of drinking.For the proper reception of such a stranger, Bullocktown was prepared to risk a present of insensibility and a future of trembling delirium. Had it been possible to set the kennels running with red wine, and have the fountain square spouting particular sherries, Bullocktown would have done it; but it was quite impossible for there were no kennels, no fountain, no square, and no red wine or sherries (worth mentioning), in Bullocktown. There was no lack of brandy, however: Hennessy, Otard, and 'Three Star' were all at command, and brandy would have flowed like water had the stranger wished it. It is not to be wondered at, therefore, that when Mr Hardy declared that 'he did not drink,' Bullocktown considered itself slighted.

A sort of consultation was held at Coppinger's as to the course to be pursued with this extremely unsociable schoolmaster. Fighting Fitz said that not only had Mr Hardy refused to drink with him, but that he had mildly but decidedly withdrawn from his company. Archy Cameron said that if he got 'Good day,' it was as much as he did get; for all that his three children were regular attendants at the schoolhouse; and Coppinger topped the chorus of complaints by relating that Mr Hardy had not only declined to partake of the gentle stimulant afforded by brandy and bitters at 9 a.m., but that he had expressed himself astonished at the inordinate consumption of grog by the men, women and children of the district.

'He flew into a tearing rage,' said Coppinger, 'and declared that drink was the curse of the country. I don't say that it isn't, boys, but I'm d—d if I'll allow any man to say so in my bar!'

So it was agreed that Mr Hardy should be sent to Coventry. Strange to say, he did not seem to mind the decision in the least; in fact, his punishment seemed rather to amuse him.

One creature in the township, however, did not partake of the general feeling. Rose Melliship, the daughter of old Melliship, of the Sawpits, openly said that the conduct of Bullocktown was 'mean and ridiculous'. Now, had anyone but Rose said this, Bullocktown, with its Widow Grip at the head of it, would have arisen like one woman, and torn her to pieces; but Rose was privileged. It was known in Bullocktown that old Melliship had 'married a lady,' and this fact constituted the pale, quiet girl the constitutional sovereign of the little State. Nothing that Rose Melliship did could be anything but right; anything she said was received with the respect due to a Queen's speech ere yet Prime Ministers had acquired the art of writing. Rose Melliship herself did not disdain this humble homage. Whatever her parentage may have been, it was certain she owned a large share of that grace and intelligence which are presumed to belong entirely to the aristocracy. Rose Melliship, taught at a common school, with a few books, with no companions of similar tastes to her own, grown to womanhood among vulgar sights and sounds, was – well, let me put it plainly at once – the one woman for whom John Hardy felt he had all his life been seeking.

I do not know how their courtship began – I fancy at some accidental meeting, at which a word or two on either side gave token to each of sympathy with the other; but no one ever knew. They met, talked, and parted. Rose, with feminine instinct of such things, knew the middle-aged man loved her, though he had never expressed to her his love as lovers in books were wont to express it. He was often absent-minded, always sad, sometimes impatient.

'You have some great trouble,' said Rose once to him. 'Tell it to me; I will try and comfort you.'

But he angrily put by the question, and she said no more.

There was not much love-making at these interviews. It was enough for her to listen, to know that her thoughts were understood, that those speculations which she had imagined tremblingly were hers only, were common to many; that there was by her side a strong soul upon which she could lean and rest.

It seemed enough for him to have her near him, a tender-eyed woman, with soft voice, and bright perceptions, who comprehended without explanation, and read his griefs before he could utter them. It was to both of them, as though their souls, long divided, had mysteriously met. There was harmony between them.

Yet they had been many months acquainted before John Hardy spoke of marriage.

Old Melliship had a shrewd notion of the progress of affairs, and desired, in his worldly wisdom – which is, we know, so much superior to anything else in this world – to bring the schoolmaster to book. He told Rose he was going to send her to Melbourne on a visit to her uncle, the cooper. Rose told this to Hardy, and Hardy called on Melliship next day to try and dissuade him.

'You had better leave your daughter here, Mr Melliship. She is just at an age when she should remain at home; and – we are reading French together.'

'Look ye here, Mr Hardy,' returned old Melliship, 'I think you read French a great deal too much together, that's a fact.'

'Sir,' stammered Hardy.

'Oh, I don't think you mean no harm. You are a gentleman, I believe, and I can trust my girl anywhere; but – she'd better go to town for a bit.'

John Hardy slept less than ever that night, if Mrs Burns is to be believed. According to her account, he walked up and down his schoolroom, as one in violent agitation, for some hours, and then dashed out of the house, hatless, into the bush. When the school opened, however, he was at his place, as quiet, though perhaps paler than usual, and after school he walked straight to the Sawpits.

'I have come to ask you to marry me, Rose.'

She blushed a little – a very little – and looked away across the hills without answering.

'Do you love me enough to do so?' he asked after a pause.

'I was thinking,' said she, frankly turning her head; and then – giving him both her hands – 'Yes, I do. I will marry you.'

It was his turn to look away and to keep silence. By-and-by he spoke in a laboriously controlled voice. 'I have no fortune to offer you, no hopes of future grandeur to hold out to you. If we marry we must live here, or in some place like this, poor and obscure, until we die. Are you content?'

'Yes, dear. I am content.'

He turned – suddenly and passionately – catching her in his arms, and devouring her face with his great eyes.

'Rose, do you love me enough, knowing me only as you do, to keep faith for me, to think always well of me, to remember that whatever happens – whatever has happened – I loved you, and will love you always?'

For reply she gently unwound his arms, and took his hot hands in her cool ones.

'There is some mystery in your life. If you choose to tell it to me, tell it. But I do not seek to know, saving that I may comfort you. It is idle to promise that we will always love. How can we tell? I love you now, and you only, dear, of all men on earth. What does it matter to me what you have done, or may do?'

There was no passion in the tones, though, perhaps a taste of high-flown sentiment might not have seemed misplaced in a reply to such a wild appeal as his; but the simple truthfulness of the grave, sweet voice soothed and convinced the questioner.

'You are a woman who would meet death for one you loved, my Rose!'

'Death is the least of human ills,' said Rose, smiling at him, 'if your philosophy is to be believed. Ah, my love, my love, you need not doubt me.'

The township was more indignant than ever when it heard that 'that d—d Hardy' was going to marry their pride and darling. Not only did the township receive a blow in the tenderest portion of its corporeal anatomy by old Melliship daring to give away his darling daughter at all, but it was highly offended by the fact that old Melliship had done this deed *propria motu*, and without duly lubricating that machine he called his mind, with brandy. The affair would appear to have been decided without even a 'nobbler'. In a township where the advent of a calf was the subject of alcoholic rejoicing, such a proceeding was simply monstrous. Moreover, by thus artfully placing himself under the protection of the township's pet, 'that d—d Hardy' had escaped the usual penalty decreed by the jovial fellows at Coppinger's for bridegrooms. Had the schoolmaster married anyone else, the whole battery of Bullocktown wit and humour would have been turned against him. In accordance with the time-honoured practice, his door would have been nailed up, his chimney choked, his water-tank filled with the bodies of defunct township cats, and his wood-head carted into the bush. A band of merry boys would have exploded in his back yard, and have banged kerosene tins beneath his wedding window. The jovial dogs might even have gone so far as to burn him in effigy – as they did Boss Corkison, of Quartzborough, at the back of the Church. But it was impossible that these jests should be indulged in when Rose Melliship, 'whose mother was a lady', was to be the subject of them. So, with a sigh, Bullocktown saw the wedding morning of the schoolmaster arrive, and gave up all projects of midnight merriment.

The little Church by the river bank was crowded, and when Rose came out with her husband the cheers deafened her. Tears stood in her eyes. How ungenerous she had been to despise these people. They had good hearts and loved her.

As the thought crossed her mind she looked up to John Hardy to compare him proudly with the others, and was astonished at his paleness. His mouth was firmly shut, but the lips quivered, and from time to time the muscles of the face relaxed as though weary with the strain upon them. It was evident that the schoolmaster suffered strong emotion.

The Quartzborough and Seven Creeks coach, which passed through Bullocktown at noonday, made its appearance in a cloud of red dust from over the hill and swung heavily towards the Church. Flash Harry, seeing the lock mass of buggies, carts and horsemen which hung upon the tail of the bridal party, checked his unicorn team, and waved a hasty order to clear the way.

Fighting Fitz, spurring his buck-jumping ginger-coloured nag beside the wheel, urged a parley.

'Curse ye man,' cried Harry, savagely, 'let me pass. Are they married?'

'Yes,' says Fitz, 'as fast as old Spottleboy can do it.'

'God help him then! I'll break every bone in his body.'

'Whose?'

'His!' returned Flash Harry, pointing to the bridegroom. 'Let me pass I tell ye, man; we don't want a scene here.'

But it was too late. The scene was over. There was no box-passenger on the coach that day, but it seemed that the bulging leathern curtains concealed something that looked like a bundle of parti-coloured clothes, surmounted by a horse's tail. This object lying, groaning feeble oaths, at the very feet of the advancing pair, Coppinger caught hold of it, and dragging it upwards, discovered a being with tangled hair and dirty hands, and bloated lips murmuring blasphemy – a being that was obscene, drunk, and a woman.

The party paused, disgusted at this hideous intrusion into their midst, and Flash Harry felt constrained to say, 'Come, get in again, mum, get in; I knew that nobbler at the Cross Reefs would set yer off. Get in.'

But the bemuzzled poor wretch, striking some frowsy hair out of her eyes, made reply by suddenly plunging at the bridegroom.

'What's all this, John?' said she, supported by Coppinger. 'Don't ye know me?'

The face and attitude of the miserable schoolmaster answered more decidedly than words.

He had loosed hold of the bride's arm, and stood apart, haggard, wild, despairing. Presently he raised his head, and taking a step forward, indicated with a gesture the drunken woman, and said, with a deliberate accent of disgust and despair on each syllable – 'This is my wife.'

Old Melliship clenched his fist, and stepped out to fell the man to the earth, but his daughter laid her light touch upon his arm and, restraining him by that single gesture, stood motionless, tearless, speechless – looking at the hideous thing which had come to blight her life. The drunken woman, her intellects roused by the dramatic force of the scene, suddenly seemed to comprehend her husband's offence, and breaking from Coppinger, rushed forward to pour forth a torrent of blasphemous reproach, until exhausted with her own violence, she fell prone before them all upon the Church steps, a spectacle to shudder at and to pity. Her husband raised her from the ground and placed her inside the porch. Then, averting his face, he seemed to wait until he should be left alone with her, and so standing, became conscious of a hand whose electric touch thrilled him. It was Rose. 'How you must have suffered,' she said, and kissed the hand she held.

There is much delicacy in the minds of the poor, and those who are forced to live face to face with nature. The rovers of the bush and the sea are seldom vulgar, for in the forests and on the ocean, are no meannesses, no vulgarities. Bullocktown felt that at a moment like this it was an intruder. Flash Harry flogged his horses, Fitz struck spurs to his pony, Coppinger made for his buggy, and in a few seconds the space in front of the church was empty.

You are a d—d villain,' said old Melliship. 'What could make you come into a quiet place like this to break my lass's heart?'

'I intended no wrong, sir; believe me. She will understand me, if you do not. But I was weak. You do not know, perhaps, what it is to have a drunken wife. Pray God you never may. Pray God you may never know what it is to come home, and find the mother of your children – oh, my God! – how can I picture what I have suffered! Night after night, sir – for my business took me out – have I found her there,' – pointing with both hands to the floor – 'drunk, drunk, drunk! I have been rich; she has made me poor. I have had a good name; she has dragged it through the dirt. I have had children; she let them die. I have been much to blame – of course, where is there a case of wrong in which one only is blameworthy? But I am passionate; have tastes incompatible with dirt and shame; am cursed with too keen a memory, too feeble hope. I despaired.'

The girl had drawn closer to him, and now was almost on his heart. Yet her father did not chide her. In the frightful incongruity of all things around them, it seemed natural only that she should be there.

'At last I left her. I had money, which I assigned for her. I thought I would seek peace in some harmless way of life, in some quiet place like this. I came here, and – and, for the first time met a woman whom I could love. Do not frown, sir. I do not think you understand your daughter nor me! That I have done wrong, I admit. I was weak, weary, suffering, alone; and love is very sweet to those who can taste it first in middle age. I thought myself so far removed from chance discovery that no shame could come to your daughter by my act; and my way of thought led me to see for her no sin where there was no shame. Enough – I have been punished. Good-bye my Rose; this is the calamity I feared.'

The old man made in silence for the door. Turning then for his daughter, he saw her clinging to John Hardy's breast, and heard her last farewell to him. 'Good-bye, my love, my love! When first I knew you, I used to think it no desert in me to love a man so worthy, and have wished, in foolish dreaming, you might do some terrible act for which all the world would spurn you, and so make my love of value. Good-bye, my – .You must go back – you must! Good-bye. Nay, I have nothing to forgive, nor you to regret. Time may cripple us with sorrow, or with suffering, but it cannot change our loves – cannot, at least, destroy the memory, that we have known each other. Good-bye!'

So she left him, and his last look of her showed him a sweet face, smiling, sad hope, and streaming with silent tears.

The next morning he returned to Melbourne and fate, with his unhappy wife.

'But did they meet again, and does she love him still?' Ah, these are questions always asked.

Water them Geraniums

Henry Lawson

1. A Lonely Track

THE TIME MARY AND I SHIFTED OUT into the Bush from Gulgong to 'settle on the land' at Lahey's Creek.

I'd sold the two tip-drays that I used for tank-sinking and dam-making, and I took the traps out in the waggon on top of a small load of rations and horse-feed that I was taking to a sheep-station out that way. Mary drove out in the spring-cart. You remember we left little Jim with his aunt in Gulgong till we got settled down. I'd sent James (Mary's brother) out the day before, on horseback, with two or three cows and some heifers and steers and calves we had, and I'd told him to clean up a bit, and make the hut as bright and cheerful as possible before Mary came.

We hadn't much in the way of furniture. There was the four-poster cedar bedstead that I bought before we were married, and Mary was rather proud of it: it had 'turned' posts and joints that bolted together. There was a plain hardwood table, that Mary called her 'ironing-table', upside down on top of the load, with the bedding and blankets between the legs; there were four of those common black kitchen-chairs – with apples painted on the hard-board backs – that we used for the parlour; there was a cheap batten sofa with arms at the ends and turned rails between the uprights of the arms (we were a little proud of the turned rails); and there was the camp-oven, and the three-legged pot, and pans and buckets, stuck about the load and hanging under the tail-board of the waggon.

There was the little Wilcox and Gibb's sewing-machine – my present to Mary when we were married (and what a present, looking back to it!). There was a cheap little rocking-chair, and a looking-glass and some pictures that were presents form Mary's friends and sister. She had her mantel-shelf ornaments and crockery and knick-knacks packed away, in the linen and old clothes, in a big tub made of half a cask, and a box that had been Jim's cradle. The live stock was a cat in one box, and in another an old rooster, and three hens that formed cliques, two against one, turn about, as three of the same sex will do all over the world. I had my old cattle-dog, and of course a pup on the load – I always had a pup that I gave away, or sold and didn't get paid for, or had 'touched' (stolen) as soon as it was old enough. James had his three spidery, sneaking, thieving, cold-blooded kangaroo-dogs with him. I was taking out three months' provisions in the way of ration-sugar, tea, flour, and potatoes, etc.

I started early, and Mary caught up to me at Ryan's Crossing on Sandy Creek, where we boiled the billy and had some dinner.

Mary bustled about the camp and admired the scenery and talked too much, for her, and was extra cheerful, and kept her face turned from me as much as possible. I soon saw what was the matter. She'd been crying to herself coming along the road. I thought it was all on account of leaving little Jim behind for the first time. She told me that she couldn't make up her mind till the last moment to leave him and that, a mile or two along the road, she'd have turned back for him, only that she knew her sister would laugh at her. She was always terribly anxious about the children.

We cheered each other up, and Mary drove with me the rest of the way to the creek, along the lonely branch track, across native apple-tree flats. It was a dreary, hopeless track. There was no horizon, nothing but the rough ashen trunks of the gnarled and stunted trees in all directions, little or no undergrowth, and the ground, save for the coarse, brownish tufts of dead grass, as bare as the road, for it was a dry season: there had been no rain for months, and I wondered what I should do with the cattle if there wasn't more grass on the creek.

In this sort of country a stranger might travel for miles without seeming to have moved, for all the difference there is in the scenery. The new tracks were 'blazed' – that is, slices of bark cut off from both sides of trees, within sight of each other, in a line, to mark the track until the horses and wheelmarks made it plain. A smart Bushman, with a sharp tomahawk, can blaze a track as he rides. But a Bushman a little used to the country soon picks out differences amongst the trees, half unconsciously as it were, and so finds his way about.

Mary and I didn't talk much along this track – we couldn't have heard each other very well, anyway, for the 'clock-clock' of the waggon and the rattle of the cart over the hard lumpy ground. And I suppose we both began to feel pretty dismal as the shadows lengthened. I'd noticed lately that Mary and I had got out of the habit of talking to each other – noticed it in a vague sort of way that irritated me (as vague things will irritate one) when I thought of it. But then I thought, 'It won't last long – I'll make life brighter for her by-and-by.'

As we went along – and the track seemed endless- I got brooding, of course, back into the past. And I feel now, when it's too late, that Mary must have been thinking that way too. I thought of my early boyhood, of the hard life of 'grubbin'' and 'milkin'' and 'fencin'' and 'ploughin'' and 'ring-barkin'' etc., and all for nothing. The few months at the little bark-school, with a teacher who couldn't spell. The cursed ambition or craving that tortured my soul as a boy – ambition or craving for – I didn't know what for!' For something better and brighter, anyhow. And I made the life harder by reading at night.

It all passed before me as I followed on in the waggon, behind Mary in the spring-cart. I thought of these old things more than I thought of her. She had tried to help me to better things. And I tried too – I had the energy of half-a-dozen men when I saw a road clear before me, but shied at the first check. Then I brooded, or dreamed of making a home – that one might call a home – for Mary – some day. Ah, well!

And what was Mary thinking about, along the lonely, changeless miles? I never thought of that. Of her kind, careless, gentleman father, perhaps. Of her girlhood. Of her homes – not the huts and camps she lived in with me. Of our future? – she used to plan a lot, and talk a good deal of our future – but not lately. These things didn't strike me at the time – I was so deep in my own brooding. Did she think now – did she begin to feel now that she had made a great mistake and thrown away her life, but must make the best of it? This might have roused me, had I thought of it. But whenever I thought Mary was getting indifferent towards me, I'd think, 'I'll soon win her back. We'll be sweethearts again – when things brighten up a bit.'

It's an awful thing to me, now I look back to it, to think how far apart we had grown, what strangers we were to each other. It seems, now, as though we had been sweethearts long years before, and had parted, and had never really met since.

The sun was going down when Mary called out – 'There's our place, Joe!'

She hadn't seen it before, and somehow it came new and with a shock to me, who had been out here several times. Ahead, through the trees to the right, was a dark green clump of she-oaks standing out of the creek, darker for the dead grey grass and blue-grey bush on the barren ridge in the background. Across the creek (it was only a deep, narrow gutter – a water-course with a chain of water-holes after rain), across on the other bank, stood the hut, on a narrow flat between the spur and the creek, and a little higher than this side. The land was much better than on our old selection, and there was good soil along the creek on both sides: I expected a rush of selectors out here soon. A few acres round the hut were cleared and fenced in by a light two-rail fence of timber split from logs and saplings. The man who took up this selection left it because his wife died there.

It was a small oblong hut built of split slabs, and he had roofed it with shingles which he split in spare times. There was no verandah, but I built one later on. At the end of the house was a big slab-and-bark shed, bigger than the hut itself, with a kitchen, a skillion for tools, harness, and horse-feed, and a spare bedroom partitioned off with sheets of bark and old chaff-bags. The house itself was floored roughly, with cracks between the boards; there were cracks between the slabs all round – though he'd nailed strips of tin, from old kerosene-tins, over some of them; the partitioned-off bedroom was lined with old chaff-bags with newspapers pasted over them for wall-paper. There was no ceiling, calico or otherwise, and we could see the round pine rafters and battens, and the under ends of the shingles. But ceilings make a hut hot and harbour insects and reptiles – snakes sometimes. There was one small glass window in the 'dining-room' with three panes and a sheet of greased paper, and the rest were rough wooden shutters. There was a pretty good cow-yard and calf-pen, and – that was about all. There was no dam or tank (I made one later on); there was a water-cask, with the hoops falling off and the staves gaping, at the corner of the house, and spouting, made of lengths of bent tin, ran around under the eaves. Water from a new shingle roof is wine-red for a year or two, and water from a stringy-bark roof is like tan-water for years. In dry weather the selector had got his house water from a cask sunk in the gravel at the bottom of the deepest water-hole in the creek. And the longer the drought lasted, the farther he had to go down the creek for his water, with a cask on a cart, and take his cows to drink, if he had any. Four, five, six or seven miles – even ten miles to water is nothing in some places.

James hadn't found himself called upon to do more than milk old 'Sport' (the grandmother cow of our mob), pen the calf at night, make a fire in the kitchen, and sweep out the house with a bough. He helped me unharness and water and feed the horses, and then started to get the furniture off the waggon and into the house. James wasn't lazy – so long as one thing didn't last too long; but he was too uncomfortably practical and matter-of-fact for me. Mary and I had some tea in the kitchen. The kitchen was permanently furnished with a table of split slabs, adzed smooth on top, and supported by four stakes driven into the ground, a three-legged stool and a block of wood, and two long stools made of half-round slabs (sapling trunks split in halves) with auger-holes bored in the round side and sticks stuck into them for legs. The floor was of clay; the chimney of slabs and tin; the fireplace was about eight feet wide, lined with clay, and with a blackened pole across, with sooty chains and wire hooks on it for the pots.

Mary didn't seem able to eat. She sat on the three-legged stool near the fire, though it was warm weather, and kept her face turned from me. Mary was still pretty, but not the little dumpling she had been: she was thinner now. She had big dark hazel eyes that shone a little too much when she was pleased or excited. I thought at times that there was something very German about her expression; also something aristocratic about the turn of her nose, which nipped in at the nostrils when she spoke. There was nothing aristocratic about me. Mary was German in figure and walk. I used sometimes to call her 'little Dutchy' and 'Pigeon Toes'. She had a will of her own, as shown sometimes by the obstinate knit in her forehead between the eyes.

Mary sat still by the fire, and presently I saw her chin tremble.

'What is it, Mary?'

She turned her face farther from me. I felt tired, disappointed and irritated – suffering from a reaction.

'Now, what is it, Mary?' I asked, 'I'm sick of this sort of thing. Haven't you got everything you wanted? You've had your own way. What's the matter with you now?'

'You know very well, Joe.'

'But I don't know,' I said. I knew too well.

She said nothing.

'Look here, Mary,' I said, putting my hand on her shoulder, 'don't go on like that; tell me what's the matter?'

'It's only this,' she said suddenly, 'I can't stand this life here; it will kill me!'

I had a pannikin of tea in my hand, and I banged it down on the table.

'This is more than a man can stand!' I shouted. 'You know very well that it was you that dragged me out here. You ran me on to this! Why weren't you content to stay in Gulgong?'

'And what sort of a place was Gulgong, Joe?' asked Mary quietly.

(I thought even then in a flash what sort of a place Gulgong was. A wretched remnant of a town on an abandoned goldfield. One street, each side of the dusty main road; three or four one-storey square brick cottages with hip roofs of galvanised iron that glared in the heat – four rooms and a passage – the police-station, bank-manager and schoolmaster's cottages, etc. Half-a-dozen tumbledown weather-board shanties – the three pubs, the two stores, and the post-office. The town tailing off into weatherboard boxes with tin tops, and old bark huts – relics of the digging days – propped up by many rotting poles. The men, when at home, mostly asleep or droning over their pipes or hanging about the verandah posts of the pubs, saying, ' 'Ullo, Bill!' or ' 'Ullo, Jim!' – or sometimes drunk. The women, mostly hags, who blackened each other's and girls' characters with their tongues, and criticised the aristocracy's washing hung out on the line: 'And the colour of the clothes! Does that woman wash her clothes at all? Or only soak 'em and hang 'em out?' – that was Gulgong.)

'Well, why didn't you come to Sydney, as I wanted you to?' I asked Mary.

'You know very well, Joe,' said Mary quietly.

(I knew very well, but the knowledge only maddened me. I had had an idea of getting a billet in one of the big wool-stores – I was a fair wool expert – but Mary was afraid of the drink. I could keep well away from it so long as I worked hard in the Bush. I had gone to Sydney twice since I met Mary, once before we were married, and she forgave me when I came back; and once afterwards. I got a billet there then, and was going to send for her in a month. After eight weeks she raised the money somehow and came to Sydney and brought me home. I got pretty low down that time.)

'But, Mary,' I said, 'it would have been different this time. You would have been with me. I can take a glass now or leave it alone.'

'As long as you take a glass there is danger,' she said.

'Well, what did you want to advise me to come out here for, if you can't stand it? Why didn't you stay where you were?' I asked.

'Well,' she said, 'why weren't you more decided?'

I'd sat down, but I jumped to my feet then.

'Good God!' I shouted, 'this is more than any man can stand. I'll chuck it all up! I'm damned well sick and tired of the whole thing.'

'So am I, Joe,' said Mary wearily.

We quarrelled badly then – that first hour in our new home. I know now whose fault it was.

I got my hat and went out and started to walk down the creek. I didn't feel bitter against Mary – I had spoken too cruelly to her to feel that way. Looking back, I could see plainly that if I had taken her advice all through, instead of now and again, things would have been all right with me. I had come away and left her crying in the dust, and James telling her, in a brotherly way, that it was all her fault. The trouble was that I never liked to 'give in' or go half-way to make it up – not half-way – it was all the way or nothing with our natures.

'If I don't make a stand now,' I'd say, 'I'll never be a master. I gave up the reins when I got married, and I'll have to get them back again.'

What women some men are! But the time came, and not many years after, when I stood by the bed where Mary lay, white and still; and, amongst other things, I kept saying, 'I'll give in, Mary – I'll give in,' and then I'd laugh. They thought that I was raving mad, and took me from the room. But that time was to come.

As I walked down the creek track in the moonlight the question rang in my ears again, as it had done when I first caught sight of the house that evening –

'Why did I bring her here?'

I was not fit to 'go on the land'. The place was only fit

for some stolid German, or Scotsman, or even Englishman and his wife, who had no ambition but to bullock and make a farm of the place. I had only drifted here through carelessness, brooding, and discontent.

I walked on and on till I was more than half-way to out neighbours – a wretched selector's family, about four miles down the creek – and I thought I'd go on to the house and see if they had any fresh meat.

A mile or two farther I saw the loom of the bark hut they lived in, on a patchy clearing in the scrub, and heard the voice of the selector's wife – I had seen her several times: she was a gaunt, haggard Bushwoman, and, I suppose, the reason why she hadn't gone mad through hardship and loneliness was that she hadn't either the brains or the memory to go farther than she could see through the trunks of the 'apple-trees'.

'You, An-nay!' (Annie.)

'Ye-es' (from somewhere in the gloom).

'Didn't I tell yer to water them geraniums!'

'Well, didn't I?'

'Don't tell lies or I'll break yer young back!'

'I did, I tell yer – the water won't soak inter the ashes.'

Geraniums were the only flowers I saw grow in the drought out there. I remembered this woman had a few dirty grey-green leaves behind some sticks against the bark wall near the door; and in spite of the sticks the fowls used to get in and scratch beds under the geraniums, and scratch dust over them, I suppose; and greasy dish-water, when fresh water was scarce – till you might as well try to water a dish of fat.

Then the woman's voice again –

'You, Tom-may!' (Tommy.)

'Y-e-e-s!' a shrill shriek from across the creek.

'Didn't I tell you to ride up to them new people and see if they want any meat or anythink?' in one long screech.

'Well – I karnt find the horse.'

'Well-find-it-first-think-in-the-morning and. And-don't-forgit-to-tell-Mrs-Wi'son-that-mother'll-be-up-as-soon-as-she-can.'

I didn't feel like going to the woman's house that night. I felt – and the thought came like a whip-stroke on my heart – that this was what Mary would come to if I left her here.

I turned and started to walk home, fast. I'd made up my mind I'd take Mary back to Gulgong in the morning – I forgot about the load I had to take take to the sheep station. I'd say, 'Look here, Girlie' (that's what I used to call her), 'we'll leave this wretched life; we'll leave the bush for ever! We'll go to Sydney, and I'll be a man and work my way up.' And I'd sell the waggon, horses and all, and go.

When I got back to the hut it was lighted up. Mary had the only kerosene lamp, a slush lamp, and two tallow candles going. She had got both rooms washed out – to James's disgust, for he had to move the furniture and boxes about. She had a lot of things unpacked on the table; she had laid clean newspapers on the mantel-shelf – a slab on two pegs over the fireplace – and put the little wooden clock in the centre and some ornaments on each side, and was tacking a strip of vandyked American oil-cloth round the rough edge of the slab.

'How does that look, Joe? We'll soon get things ship-shape.'

I kissed her, but she had her mouth full of tacks. I went out in the kitchen, drank a pint of cold tea, and sat down.

Somehow I didn't feel satisfied with the way things had gone.

II. 'Past Carin''

Next morning things looked a lot brighter. Things always look brighter in the morning – more so in the Australian Bush, I should think, than in most other places. It is when the sun goes down on the dark bed of the lonely Bush, and the sunset flashes like a sea of fire and then fades, and then glows out again, like a bank of coals, and then burns away to ashes – it is then that old things come home to one. And strange, new-old things too, that haunt and depress you terribly, and that you can't understand. I often think how, at sunset, the past must come home to new-chum black-sheep, sent out to Australia and drifted into the Bush. I used to think that they couldn't have much brains, or the loneliness would drive them mad.

I'd decided to let James take the team for a trip or two. He could drive alright; he was a better business man, and no doubt would manage better than me – as long as the novelty lasted; and I'd stay at home for a week or so, till Mary got used to the place, or I could get a girl from some-where to come and stay with her. The first weeks or few months of loneliness are the worst, as a rule, I believed, as they say the first weeks in jail are – I was never there. I know it's so with tramping or hard graft: the first day or two are twice as hard as any of the rest. But, for my part, I could never get used to loneliness and dullness; the last days used to be the worst with me: then I'd have to make a move, or drink. When you've been too much and too long alone in a lonely place, you begin to do queer things and think queer thoughts – provided you have any imagination at all. You'll sometimes sit of an evening and watch the lonely track, by the hour, for a horseman or a cart or someone that's never likely to come that way – someone, or a stranger, that you can't and don't really expect to see. I think most men who have been alone in the Bush for any length of time – and married couples too – are more or less mad. With married couples it is generally the husband who is painfully shy and awkward when strangers come. The woman seems to stand the loneliness better, and can hold her own with strangers, as a rule.

It's only afterwards, and looking back, that you see how queer you got. Shepherds and boundary-riders, who are alone for months, must have their periodical spree, at the nearest shanty, else they'd go raving mad. Drink is the only break in the awful monotony, and the yearly or half-yearly spree is the only thing they've got to look forward to; it keeps their minds fixed on something definite ahead.

But Mary kept her head pretty well through the first months of loneliness. *Weeks*, rather, I should say, for it wasn't as bad as it might have been farther up-country; there was generally some one came of a Sunday afternoon – a spring-cart with a couple of women, or maybe a family – or a lanky sky Bush native or two on lanky shy horses. On a quiet Sunday, after I'd brought Jim home, Mary would dress him and herself – just the same as if we were in town – and make me get up on one end and put on a collar and take her and Jim for a walk along the creek. She said she wanted to keep me civilised. She tried to make a gentleman of me for years, but gave it up gradually.

Well. It was the first morning on the creek: I was greasing the waggon-wheels, and James out after the horse, and Mary hanging out clothes, in an old print dress and a big ugly white hood, when I heard her being hailed as 'Hi, missus!' from the front slip-rails.

It was a boy on horseback. He was a light-haired, very much freckled boy of fourteen or fifteen, with a small head, but with limbs, especially his bare sun-blotched shanks, that might have belonged to a grown man. He had a good face and frank grey eyes. An old, nearly black cabbage-tree hat rested on the butts of his ears, turning them out at right angles from his head, and rather dirty sprouts they were. He wore a dirty torn Crimean shirt; and a pair of man's moleskin trousers rolled up above the knees, with the wide waistband gathered under a greenhide belt. I noticed, later on, that, even when he wore trousers short enough for him, he always rolled 'em up above the knees when on horseback, for some reason of his own: to suggest leggings, perhaps, for he had them rolled up in all weathers, and he wouldn't have bothered to save them from the sweat of the horse, even if that horse ever sweated.

He was seated astride a three-bushel bag thrown across the ridge-pole of a big grey horse, with a coffin-shaped head, and built astern something after the style of a roughly put up hip-roofed box-bark humpy. His colour was like old box-bark, too, a dirty bluish-grey; and, one time, when I saw his rump looming out of the scrub, I really thought it was some old shepherd's hut that I hadn't noticed there before. When he cantered it was like the hump starting off on its corner-posts.

'Are you Mrs Wilson?' asked the boy.

'Yes,' said Mary.

'Well, Mother told me to ride acrost and see if you wanted anything. We killed lar' night, and I've fetched a piece er cow.'

'Piece of *what?*' asked Mary.

He grinned, and handed a sugar-bag across the rail with something heavy in the bottom of it, that nearly jerked Mary's arm out when she took it. It was a piece of beef, that looked as if it had been cut off with a wood-axe, but it was fresh and clean.

'Oh, I'm so glad!' cried Mary. She was always impulsive, save to me sometimes. 'I was just wondering where we were going to get any fresh meat. How kind of your mother! Tell her I'm very much obliged to her indeed.' And she felt behind her for a poor little purse she had. 'And now – how much did your mother say it would be?'

The boy blinked at her, and scratched his head.

'How much will it be?' he repeated, puzzled. 'Oh – how much does it weigh I-s'pose-yer-mean. Well, it ain't been weighed at all – we ain't got no scales. A butcher does all that sort of think. We just kills it, and cooks it, and eats it – and goes by guess. What won't keep we salts down in the cask. I reckon it weighs about a ton by the weight of it if yer wanter know. Mother thought that if she sent any more it would go bad before you could scoff it. I can't see –.'

'Yes, yes,' said Mary, getting confused. 'But what I want to know is, how do you manage when you sell it?'

He glared at her, and scratched his head. 'Sell it? Why, we only goes halves in a steer with someone, or sells steers to the butcher – or maybe some meat to a party of fencers or surveyors, or tank-sinkers, or them sorter people –.'

'Yes, yes; but what I want to know is, how much am I send to your mother for this?'

'How much what?'

'Money, of course, you stupid boy,' said Mary. 'You seem a very stupid boy.'

Then he saw what she was driving at. He began to fling his heels convulsively against the sides of his horse, jerking this body backward and forward at the same time, as if to wind up and start some clockwork machinery inside the horse, that made it go, and seemed to need repairing or oiling.

'We ain't that sorter people, missus,' he said. 'We don't sell meat to new people that come to settle here.' Then jerking his thumb contemptuously towards the ridges, 'Go over ter Wall's if yer wanter buy meat; they sell meat ter strangers.' (Wall was the big squatter over the ridges.)

'Oh!' said Mary, 'I'm so sorry. Thank your mother for me. She *is* kind.'

'Oh, that's nothink. She said to tell yer she'll be up as soon as she can. She'd have come up yesterday evening – she thought yer'd feel lonely comin' new to a place like this – but she couldn't git up.'

The machinery inside the old horse showed signs of starting. You almost heard the wooden joints creak as he lurched forward; like an old propped-up humpy when the rotting props give way; but at the sound of Mary's voice he settled back on his foundations again. It must have been a very poor selection that couldn't afford a better spare horse than that.

'Reach me that lump er wood, will yer, missus?' said the boy, and he pointed to one of my 'spreads' (for the team-

135

chains) that lay inside the fence. 'I'll fling it back agin over the fence when I git this ole cow started.'

'But wait a minute – I've forgotten your mother's name,' said Mary.

He grabbed at his thatch impatiently. 'Me mother – oh! – the old woman's name's Mrs Spicer. (Git up, karnt yer!)' He twisted himself round, and brought the stretcher down on one of the horse's 'points' (and he had many) with a crack that must have jarred his wrist.

'Do you go to school?' asked Mary. There was a three-days-a-week school over the ridges at Wall's station.

'No!' he jerked out, keeping his legs going. 'Me – why I'm going on fur fifteen. The last teacher at Wall's finished me. I'm going to Queensland next month drovin'.' (The Queensland border was over three hundred miles away.)

'Finished you? How?' asked Mary.

'Me edgercation, of course! How do yer expect me to start this horse when yer keep talkin'?'

He split the 'spread' over the horse's point, threw the pieces over the fence, and was off, his elbows and legs flinging wildly, and the old saw-tool lumbering along the road like an old working bullock trying a canter. That horse wasn't a trotter.

And next month he *did* start for Queensland. He was a younger son and a surplus boy on a wretched, poverty-stricken selection; and as there was 'northin' doin' in the district, his father (in a burst of fatherly kindness, I suppose) made him a present of the old horse and a new pair of Blucher boots, and I gave him an old saddle and a coat, and he started for the Never-Never Country.

And I'll bet he got there. But I'm doubtful if the old horse did.

Mary gave the boy five shillings, and I don't think he had anything more except a clean shirt and an extra pair of white cotton socks.

'Spicer's farm' was a big bark humpy on a patchy clearing in the native apple-tree scrub. The clearing was fenced in by a light 'dog-legged' fence (a fence of sapling poles resting on forks and X-shaped uprights) and the dusty ground round the house was almost entirely covered with cattle-dung. There was no attempt at cultivation when I came to live on the creek; but there were old furrow-marks amongst the stumps of another shapeless patch in the scrub near the hut. There was a wretched sapling cow-yard and calf-pen, and a cow-bail with one sheet of bark over it for shelter. There was no dairy to be seen, and I suppose the milk was set in one of the two skillion rooms, or lean-tos behind the hut – the other was 'the boys' bedroom'. The Spicers kept a few cows and steers, and had thirty or forty sheep. Mrs Spicer used to drive down the creek once a week, in her rickety old spring-cart, to Cobborah, with butter and eggs. The hut was nearly as bare inside as it was out – just a frame of 'round-timber' (sapling poles) covered with bark. The furniture was permanent (unless you rooted it up), like in our kitchen: a rough slab table on stakes driven into the ground, and seats made in the same way. Mary told me afterwards that the beds in the bag-and-bark partitioned-off room ('mother's bedroom') were simply poles laid side by side on cross-pieces supported by stakes driven into the ground, with straw mattresses and some worn-put bedclothes. Mrs Spicer had an old patchwork

137

quilt, in rags, and the remains of a white one, and Mary said it was pitiful to see how these things would be spread over the beds – to hide them as much as possible – when she went down there. A packing-case, with something like an old print skirt draped round it, and a cracked looking-glass (without a frame) on top, was the dressing-table. There were a couple of gin-cases for a wardrobe. The boys' beds were three-bushel bags stretched between poles fastened to uprights. The floor was the original surface, tramped hard, worn uneven with much sweeping, and with puddles in rainy weather where the roof leaked. Mrs Spicer used to stand old tins, dishes, and buckets under as many of the leaks as she could. The saucepans, kettles, and boilers were old kerosene-tins and billies. They used kerosene-tins, too, cut longways in halves, for setting the milk in. The plates and cups were of tin; there were two or three cups without saucers, and a crockery plate or two – also two mugs, cracked and without handles, one with 'For a Good Boy' and the other with 'For a Good Girl' on it; but all these were kept on the mantel-shelf for ornament and for company. They were the only ornaments in the house, save a little wooden clock that hadn't gone for years. Mrs Spicer had a superstition that she had 'some things packed away from the children'.

The pictures were cut from old copies of the *Illustrated Sydney News* and pasted on to the bark. I remember this, because I remember, long ago, the Spencers, who were our neighbours when I was a boy, had the walls of their bedroom covered with illustrations of the American Civil War, cut from illustrated London papers, and I used to 'sneak' into 'mother's bedroom' with Fred Spencer whenever we got the chance, and gloat over the prints. I gave him a blade of a pocket-knife once, for taking me in there.

I saw very little of Spicer. He was a big, dark, dark-haired and whiskered man. I had an idea that he wasn't a selector at all, only a 'dummy' for the squatter of the Cobborah run. You see, selectors were allowed to take up land on runs, or pastoral leases. The squatters kept them off as much as possible, by all manner of dodges and paltry persecution. The squatter would get as much freehold as he could afford, 'select' as much land as the law allowed one man to take up, and then employ dummies (dummy selectors) to take up bits of land that he fancied about his run, and hold them for him.

Spicer seemed gloomy and unsociable. He was seldom at home. He was generally supposed to be away shearin', or fencin', or workin' on somebody's station. It turned out that the last six months he was away it was on the evidence of a cask of beef and a hide with the brand cut out, found in his camp on a fencing contract up-country, and which he and his mates couldn't account for satisfactorily, while the squatter could. Then the family lived mostly on bread and honey, or bread and treacle, or bread and dripping, and tea. Every ounce of butter and every egg was needed for the market, to keep them in flour, tea and sugar. Mary found that out, but couldn't help them much – except by 'stuffing' the children with bread and meat or bread and jam whenever they came up to our place – for Mrs Spicer was proud with the pride that lies down in the end and turns its face to the wall and dies.

Once, when Mary asked Annie, the eldest girl at home, if she was hungry, she denied it – but she looked it. A ragged mite she had with her explained things. The little fellow said –

'Mother told Annie not to say we was hungry if yer asked; but if yer give us anythink to eat, we was to take it an' say thenk yer, Mrs Wilson.'

'I wouldn't 'a' told yer a lie; but I thought Jimmy would split on me, Mrs Wilson,' said Annie. 'Thenk yer, Mrs Wilson.'

She was not a big woman. She was gaunt and flat-chested, and her face was 'burnt to a brick', as they say out there. She had brown eyes, nearly red, and a little wild-looking at times, and a sharp face – ground sharp by hardship – the cheeks drawn in. She had an expression like – well, like a woman who had been very curious and suspicious at one time, and wanted to know everybody's business and hear everything, and had lost all her curiosity, without losing the expression or the quick suspicious movements of the head. I don't suppose you understand. I can't explain it any other way. She was not more than forty.

I remember the first morning I saw her. I was going up the creek to look at the selection for the first time, and called at the hut to see if she had a bit of fresh mutton, as I had none and was sick of 'corned beef'.

'Yes – of – course,' she said, in a sharp nasty tone, as if to say 'Is there anything more you want while the shop's open?' I'd met just the same sort of woman years before while I was carrying swag between the shearing-sheds in the awful scrubs out west of the Darling river, so I didn't turn on my heels and walk away. I waited for her to speak again.

'Come – inside,' she said, 'and sit down. I see you've got the waggon outside. I s'pose your name's Wilson, ain't it?

You're thinkin' about takin' on Harry Marshfield's selection up the creek, so I heard. Wait till I fry you a chop and boil the billy.'

Her voice sounded, more than anything else, like a voice coming out of a phonograph – I heard one in Sydney the other day – and not like a voice coming out of her. But sometimes when she got outside her everyday life on this selection she spoke in a sort of – in a sort of lost groping-in-the dark kind of voice.

She didn't talk much this time – just spoke in a mechanical way of the drought, and the hard times, 'an' butter 'n' eggs bein' down, an' her husban' an' eldest son bein' away, an' that makin' it so hard for her.'

I don't know how many children she had. I never got a chance to count them, for they were nearly all small, and shy as piccaninnies, and used to run and hide when anybody came. They were mostly nearly as black as piccaninnies too. She must have averaged a baby a year for years – and God only knows how she got over her confinements! Once, they said, she only had a black gin with her. She had an elder boy and girl, but she seldom spoke of them. The girl, 'Liza', was 'in service in Sydney'. I'm afraid I knew what that meant. The elder son was 'away'. He had been a bit of a favourite round there, it seemed.

Someone might ask her, 'How's your son Jack, Mrs Spicer?' or, 'Heard of Jack lately? and where is he now?'

'Oh, he's somewheres up country,' she'd say in the 'groping' voice, or 'He's drovin' in Queenslan'', or 'Shearin' on the Darlin' the last time I heard from him.' 'We ain't had a line from him since – let's see – since Chris'mas 'fore last.'

And she'd turn her haggard eyes in a helpless, hopeless

sort of way towards the west – towards 'up-country' and 'Out-Back'.

The eldest girl at home was nine or ten, with a little old face and lines across her forehead; she had an older expression than her mother. Tommy went to Queensland, as I told you. The eldest son at home, Bill (older than Tommy), was 'a bit wild'.

I've passed the place in smothering hot mornings in December, when the droppings about the cow-yard had crumpled to dust that rose in the warm, sickly, sunrise wind, and seen that woman at work in the cow-yard, 'bailing-up' and leg-roping cows, milking, or hauling at a rope round the neck of a half-grown calf that was too strong for her (and she was as tough as fencing-wire), or humping great buckets of sour milk to the pigs or the 'poddies' (hand-fed calves) in the pen. I'd get off the horse and give her a hand sometimes with a young steer, or a cranky old cow that wouldn't 'bail-up' and threatened her with the horns.

She'd say –

'Thenk yer, Mr Wilson. Do yer think we're ever goin' to have any rain?'

I've ridden past the place on bitter black rainy mornings in June or July, and seen her trudging about the yard – that was ankle-deep in black liquid filth – with an old pair of Blucher boots on, and an old coat of her husband's, or maybe a three-bushel bag over her shoulders. I've seen her climbing on the roof by means of the water-cask at the corner, and trying to stop a leak by shoving a piece of tin in under the bark. And when I'd fixed the leak –

'Thenk yer, Mr Wilson. This drop of rain's a blessin'! Come in and have a dry at the fire and I'll make yer a cup of tea.' And, if I was in a hurry, 'Come in, man alive! Come in! and dry yerself a bit till the rain holds up. Yer can't go home like this! Yer'll git yer death o' cold.'

I've even seen her, in the terrible drought, climbing she-oaks and apple-trees by a makeshift ladder, and awkwardly lopping off boughs to feed the starving cattle.

'Jist tryin' ter keep the milkers alive till the rain comes.'

They said that when the pleuro-pneumonia was in the district and amongst her cattle she bled and physicked them herself, and fed those that were down with slices of half-ripe pumpkins (from a crop that had failed).

'An', one day,' she told Mary, 'there was a big barren heifer (that we called Queen Elizabeth) that was down with the ploorer. She'd been down for four days and hadn't moved, when one mornin' I dumped some wheaten chaff – we had a few bags that Spicer brought home – I dumped it in front of her nose, an' – would yer b'lieve me, Mrs Wilson? – she stumbled onter her feet an' chased me all the way to the house! I had to pick up me skirts an' run! Wasn't it redic'lus?'

They had a sense of the ridiculous, most of those poor sun-dried Bushwomen. I fancy that helped save them from madness.

'We lost nearly all our milkers,' she told Mary, 'I remember one day Tommy came running to the house and screamed: "Marther! there's another milker down with the ploorer!" Jist as if it was great news. Well, Mrs Wilson, I was dead-beat, an' I giv' in. I jist sat down to have a good cry, and felt for my han'kerchief – it was a rag of a han'kerchief an' me thumb through the other, and poked me fingers into me eyes, instead of wipin' them. Then I had to laugh.'

There's a story that once, when the Bush, or rather grass, fires were out all along the creek on Spicer's side, Wall's station hands were up above our place, trying to keep the fire back from the boundary, and towards evening one of the men happened to think of the Spicers: they saw smoke down that way. Spicer was away from home, and they had a small crop of wheat, nearly ripe, on the selection.

'My God! that poor devil of a woman will be burnt out, if she ain't already!' shouted young Billy Wall. 'Come along, three or four of you chaps' – (it was shearing-time, and there were plenty of men on the station).

They raced down the creek to Spicer's, and were just in time to save the wheat. She had her sleeves tucked up, and was beating out the burning grass with a bough. She'd been at it for an hour, and was as black as a gin, they said. She only said when they'd turned the fire: 'Thenk yer! Wait an' I'll make some tea.'

After tea the first Sunday she came to see us, Mary asked –

'Don't you feel lonely, Mrs Spicer, when your husband goes away?'

'Well – no, Mrs Wilson,' she said in the groping sort of voice. 'I uster, once. I remember, when we lived on the Cudgeegong River – we lived in a brick house then – the first time Spicer had to go away from home I nearly fretted my eyes out. And he was only goin' shearin' for a month. I muster bin a fool; but then we were only jist married a little while. He's been away droving' in Queenslan' as long as eighteen months at a time since then. But' (her voice

seemed to grope in the dark more than ever) 'I don't mind,
- I somehow seem to have got past carin'. Besides –
besides, Spicer was a very different man then to what he is
now. He's got so moody and gloomy at home, he hardly
ever speaks.'

Mary sat silent for a minute thinking. Then Mrs Spicer
roused herself –

'Oh, I don't know what I'm talkin' about! You mustn't
take any notice of me, Mrs Wilson, I don't often go on like
this. I do believe I'm gittin' a bit ratty at times. It must be
the heat and the dullness.'

But once or twice afterwards she referred to a time 'when
Spicer was a different man to what he was now'.

I walked home with her a piece along the creek. She said
nothing for a long time, and seemed to be thinking in a
puzzled way. Then she said suddenly –

'What-did-you-bring-her-here-for? She's only a girl.'

'I beg pardon, Mrs Spicer?'

'Oh, I don't know what I'm talkin' about! I b'lieve I'm git-
tin' ratty. You mustn't take any notice of me, Mr Wilson.

She wasn't much company for Mary; and often, when she
had a child with her, she'd start taking notice of the baby
while Mary was talking, which used to exasperate Mary.
But poor Mrs Spicer couldn't help it, and she seemed to
hear all the same. Her great trouble was that she 'couldn't
git no reg'lar schoolin' for the children'.

'I learns 'em at home as much as I can. But I don't git a
minute to call me own; and' I'm ginerally that dead-beat at
night that I'm fit for nothink.'

Mary had some of the children up now and then later on,
and taught them a little. When she first offered to do so,

Mrs Spicer laid hold of the handiest youngster and said –

'There – do you hear that? Mrs Wilson is goin' to teach yer, and it's more that yer deserve!' (the youngster had been 'cryin'' over something). 'Now, go an' say "Thenk yer, Mrs Wilson" and if yer ain't good, and don't do as she tells yer, I'll break every bone in yer young body!'

The poor little devil stammered something, and escaped.

The children were sent by turns over to Wall's to Sunday-school. When Tommy was at home he had a new pair of elastic-sided boots, and there was no end of rows about them in the family – for the mother made him lend them to his sister Annie, to go to Sunday-school in, in her turn. There were only about three pairs of any-way decent boots in the family, and these were saved for great occasions. The children were always as clean and tidy as possible when they came to our place.

And I think the saddest and most pathetic sight on the face of God's earth is the children of very poor people made to appear well: the broken wornout boots polished or greased, the blackened (inked) pieces of string for laces; the clean patched pinafores over the wretched threadbare frocks. Behind the little row of children hand-in-hand – and no matter where they are – I always see the worn face of the mother.

Towards the end of the first year on the selection our little girl came. I'd sent Mary to Gulgong for four months that time, and when she came back with the baby Mrs Spicer used to come up pretty often. She came up several times when Mary was ill, to lend a hand. She wouldn't sit down and condole with Mary, or waste time asking questions, or talking about the time when she was ill herself. She'd take off her hat – a shapeless little lump of black straw she wore for visiting – give her hair a quick brush back with the palms of her hands, roll up her sleeves, and set to work to 'tidy up'. She seemed to take most pleasure in sorting out our children's clothes, and dressing them. Perhaps she used to dress her own like that in the days when Spicer was a different man from what he was now. She seemed interested in the fashion-plates of some women's journals we had, and used to study them with an interest that puzzled me, for she was not likely to go in for fashion. She never talked of her early girlhood; but Mary, from some things she noticed, was inclined to think that Mrs Spicer had been fairly well brought up. For instance, Dr Balanfantie, from Cudgeegong, came out to see Wall's wife, and drove up the creek to our place on his way back to see how Mary and the baby were getting on. Mary got out some crockery and some table-napkins that she had packed away for occasions like this; and she said that the way Mrs Spicer handled the things, and helped set the table (though she did it in a mechanical sort of way), convinced her that she had been used to table-napkins at one time in her life.

Sometimes, after a long pause in the conversation, Mrs Spicer would say suddenly –

'Oh, don't think I'll come up next week, Mrs Wilson.'

'Why, Mrs Spicer?'

'Because the visits doesn't do me any good. I git the dismals afterwards.'

'Why, Mrs Spicer? What on earth do you mean?'

'Oh, I-don't-know-what-I'm-talking-about. You mustn't take any notice of me.' And she'd put on her hat, kiss the children – and Mary too, sometimes, as if she mistook her for a child – and go.

Mary thought her a little mad at times. But I seemed to understand.

Once, when Mrs Spicer was sick, Mary went down to her, and down again next day. As she was coming away the second time, Mrs Spicer said –

'I wish you wouldn't come down any more till I'm on me feet, Mrs Wilson. The children can do for me.'

'Why, Mrs Spicer?'

'Well, the place is in such a muck, and it hurts me.'

We were the aristocrats of Lahey's Creek. Whenever we drove down on Sunday afternoon to see Mrs Spicer, and as soon as we got near enough for them to hear the rattle of the cart, we'd see the children running to the house as fast as they could split, and hear them screaming –

'Oh, Marther! Here comes Mr and Mrs Wilson in their spring-cart.'

And we'd see her bustle round, and two or three fowls fly out the front door, and she' lay hold of a broom (made of a bound bunch of 'broom-stuff' – coarse reedy grass or bush from the ridges – with a stick stuck in it) and flick out the floor, with a flick or two round in front of the door perhaps. The floor nearly always needed at least one flick of the broom on account of the fowls. Or she'd catch a youngster and scrub his face with a wet end of a cloudy towel, or twist the towel round her finger and dig out the ears – as if she was anxious to have him hear every word that was going to be said.

No matter what state the house would be in she'd always say, 'I was just expectin' yer, Mrs Wilson.' And she was original in that, anyway.

She had an old patched and darned white table-cloth that she used to spread on the table when we were there, as a matter of course ('The others is in the wash, so you must excuse this, Mrs Wilson'), but I saw by the eyes of the children that the cloth was rather a wonderful thing to them. 'I must really git some more knives an' forks next time I'm in Cobborah,' she'd say. 'The children break an' lose 'em till I'm ashamed to ask Christians ter sit down ter the table.'

She had many Bush yarns, some of them very funny, some of them rather ghastly, but all interesting, and with a grim sort of humour about them. But the effect was often spoilt by her screaming at the children to 'Drive out them fowl, karnt yer,' or 'Take yer maulies outer the sugar,' or 'Don't touch Mrs Wilson's baby with them dirty maulies,' or 'Don't stand starin' at Mrs Wilson with yer mouth an' ears in that vulgar way.'

Poor woman! she seemed everlastingly nagging at the children. It was a habit, but they didn't seem to mind. Most Bushwomen get the nagging habit. I remember one, who had the prettiest, dearest, sweetest, most willing, and affectionate little girl I think I ever saw, and she nagged that child from daylight till dark – and after it. Taking it all round, I think that the nagging habit in a mother is often worse on ordinary children, and more deadly on sensitive youngsters, than the drinking habit in a father.

One of the yarns Mrs Spicer told us was about a squatter she knew who used to go wrong in his head every now and again, and try to commit suicide. Once, when the stationhand, who was watching him, had his eye off him for a minute, he hanged himself to a beam in the stable.

The men ran in and found him hanging and kicking. 'They let him hang for a while,' said Mrs Spicer, 'till he went black in the face and stopped kicking. Then they cut him down and threw a bucket of water over him.'

'Why! what on earth did they let the man hang for?' asked Mary.

'To give him a good bellyful of it: they thought it would cure him of tryin' to hang himself again.'

'Well, that's the coolest thing I ever heard of,' said Mary.

'That's jist what the magistrate said, Mrs Wilson,' said Mrs Spicer.

'One morning,' said Mrs Spicer, 'Spicer had gone off on his horse somewhere, and I was alone with the children, when a man came to the door and said –

'"For God's sake, woman, give me a drink!"

'Lord only knows where he came from! He was dressed like a new chum – his clothes was good, but he looked as if he'd been sleepin' in them in the Bush for a month. He was very shaky. I had some coffee that mornin', so I gave him some in a pint pot; he drank it, and then he stood on his head till he tumbled over, and then he stood up on his feet and said, ' "Thenk yer, mum."

'I was so surprised that I didn't know what to say, so I just said, "Would you like some more coffee?"

'"Yes, thenk yer," he said – "about two quarts."

'I nearly filled the pint pot, and he drank it and stood on his head as long as he could, and when he got right end up he said, "Thank yer, mum – it's a fine day," and then he walked off. He had two saddle-straps in his hands.'

'Why, what did he stand on his head for?' asked Mary.

'To wash it up and down, I suppose, to get twice as much

taste of the coffee. He had no hat. I sent Tommy across to Wall's to tell them that there was a man wanderin' about the Bush in the horrors of drink, and to get someone to ride for the police. But they was too late, for he hanged himself that night.'

'O Lord!' cried Mary.

'Yes, right close to here, jist down the creek where the track to Wall's branches off. Tommy found him while he was out after the cows. Hangin' to the branch of a tree with the two saddle-straps.'

Mary stared at her, speechless.

'Tommy came home yellin' with fright. I sent him over to Wall's at once. After breakfast, the minute my eyes was off them, the children slipped away and went down there. They came back screamin' at the tops of their voices. I did give it to them. I reckon they won't want ter see a dead body again in a hurry. Every time I'd mention it they'd huddle together, or ketch hold of me skirts and howl.

'"Yer'll go agen when I tell yer not to," I'd say.

'"Oh no, mother," they'd howl.

'"Yer wanted ter see a man hangin'," I said.

'"Oh, don't, mother! Don't talk about it."

'"Yer wouldn't be satisfied till yer see it," I'd say; "yer had to see it or burst. Yer satisfied now, ain't yer?"

'"Oh, don't, mother!"

'"Yer run all the way there, I s'pose?"

'"Don't, mother!"

'"But yer run faster back, didn't yer?"

'"Oh, don't mother."'

'But,' said Mrs Spicer, in conclusion, 'I'd been down to see it myself before they was up.'

'And ain't you afraid to live alone here, after all these horrible things?' asked Mary.

'Well, no; I don't mind. I seem to have got past carin' for anythink now. I felt it a little when Tommy went away – the first time I felt anythink for years. But I'm over that now.'

'Haven't you got any friends in the district, Mrs Spicer?'

'Oh yes. There's me married sister near Cobborah, and a married brother near Dubbo; he's got a station. They wanted to take me an' the children between them, or take some of the younger children. but I couldn't bring my mind to break up the home. I want to keep the children together as much as possible. There's enough of them gone, God knows. But it's a comfort to know that there's some one to see to them if anythink happens to me.'

One day – I was on my way home with the team that day – Annie Spicer came runing up the creek in terrible trouble.

'Oh, Mrs Wilson! something terrible's happened at home! A trooper' (mounted policeman – they called them 'mounted troopers' out there), 'a trooper's come and took Billy!' Billy was the eldest at home.

'What?'

'It's true, Mrs Wilson.'

'What for? What did the policeman say?'

'He – he – he said, "I – I'm very sorry, Mrs Spicer; but – I – I want William."'

It turned out that William was wanted on account of a

WATER THEM GERANIUMS

horse missed from Wall's station and sold down-country.

'An' mother took on awful,' sobbed Annie; 'an' now she'll only sit stock-still an' stare in front of her, and won't take no notice of any of us. Oh! it's awful, Mrs Wilson. The policeman said he'd tell Aunt Emma' (Mrs Spicer's sister at Cobborah), 'and send her out. But I had to come to you, an' I've run all the way.'

James put the horse to the cart and drove Mary down.

Mary told me all about it when I came home.

'I found her just as Annie said; but she broke down and cried in my arms. Oh, Joe! it was awful! She didn't cry like a woman. I heard a man at Haviland cry at his brother's funeral, and it was just like that. She came round a bit after a while. Her sister's with her now ... Oh, Joe! you must take me away from the Bush.'

Later on Mary said –

'How the oaks are sighing tonight, Joe!'

Next morning I rode across to Wall's station and tackled the old man; but he was a hard man, and wouldn't listen to me – in fact, he ordered me off the station. I was a selector, and that was enough for him. but young Billy Wall rode after me.

'Look here, Joe!' he said. 'it's a blanky shame. All for the sake of a horse! And as if that poor devil of a woman hasn't got enough to put up with already! I wouldn't do it for twenty horses. I'll tackle the boss, and if he won't listen to me, I'll walk off the run for the last time, if I have to carry my swag.'

Billy Wall managed it. The charge was withdrawn, and we got young Billy Spicer off up-country.

But poor Mrs Spicer was never the same after that. She

seldom came up to our place unless Mary dragged her, so to speak; and then she would talk of nothing but her last trouble, till her visits were painful to look forward to.

'If it only could have been kep' quiet – for the sake of the other children; they are all I think of now. I tried to bring 'em all up decent, but I s'pose it was my fault, somehow. It's the disgrace that's killin' me – I can't bear it.'

I was at home one Sunday with Mary and a jolly bush-girl named Maggie Charlsworth, who rode over sometimes from Wall's station (I must tell you about her some other time; James was 'shook after her') and we got talking about Mrs Spicer. Maggie was very warm about old Wall.

'I expected Mrs Spicer up today,' said Mary. 'She seems better lately.'

'Why!' cried Maggie Charlsworth, 'if that ain't Annie coming running up along the creek. Something's the matter!'

We all jumped up and ran out.

'What is it, Annie?' cried Mary.

'Oh, Mrs Wilson! Mother's asleep, and we can't wake her!'

'What?'

'It's – it's the truth, Mrs Wilson.'

'How long has she been asleep?'

'Since lars' night.'

'My God! cried Mary, *since last night?*'

'No, Mrs Wilson, not all the time; she woke wonst, about daylight this mornin'. She called me and said she didn't feel well, and I'd have to manage the milkin'.'

'Was that all she said ?'

'No. She said not to go for you; and she said to feed the pigs and calves; and she said to be sure and water them geraniums.'

Mary wanted to go, but I wouldn't let her. James and I saddled our horses and rode down the creek.

Mrs Spicer looked very little different from what she did when I last saw her alive. It was some time before we could believe that she was dead. But she was 'past carin'' right enough.

Baptising Bartholomew

Steele Rudd

THE BABY, TWELVE MONTHS OLD, was to be christened, and Mother decided to give a party. She had been thinking about the party for some time, but the decision was contemporaneous with the arrival of a certain mysterious parcel.We were preparing for the christening. Dad and Dave drawing water; Joe raking husks and corn-cobs into a heap at the door and burning them; Little Bill collecting the pumpkins and pie-melons strewn about the yard. Mother and Sal were busy inside. Mother stood on a box. Sal spread newspapers on the table and smeared them over with paste, then handed them cautiously to Mother, who fixed them on the wall. The baby crawled on the floor.

'Not that way,' said Mother. 'That's upside down. Give them to me straight, 'cause your father sometimes likes to read them when they're up.'

They chatted about the christening.

'Indeed, then, she won't be asked,' Sal said. 'Not if she goes down on her knees, the skinny little – '

'Min', min', mind, girl!' Mother screeched, and Sal dropped the newspaper she was about to hand up, and, jumping a stool, caught the baby by the skirt-tail just as it was about to wobble into the fire.

'My goodness! You little rat!' The baby laughed playfully and struggled to get out of her arms. Sal placed it at the opposite side of the room and the decorating continued.

'I can remember a time, then,' Mother said, 'when they hadn't so much to be flash about, when the old woman and that eldest girl, Johanna, used to go about in their bare feet and dresses on – dear me – that I wouldn't *give* away!'

'Not Johanna, Mother?'

'Yes, Johanna. You wouldn't remember it, of course. Norah was the baby then.'

'You little wretch!' And Sal rushed for the baby and pulled it from the fire once more. She dumped it down in a different corner, and returned to the paste. The baby made eagerly for the fire again, but when halfway across the room it stopped, rested its cheek on the floor and fell asleep – and it on the verge of being christened Bartholomew – until Dad came in and took it up.

Mother went into her bedroom and came out with a flaring red sash flying over her greasy gown, and asked Dad if he liked it. Dad looked at the ribbon, then out of the window and chuckled.

'What d'y' think of me?'

'Think of y'?' And Dad grinned.

Mother looked fondly at the ribbon. She was very satisfied with herself. She was a true woman, was Mother. She tripped into the room again and came out with some yards of print, and asked Dad what he thought of that. Mother was fond of dress.

'Dear me, woman,' Dad said, 'what's going to happen?'

'But how do you like it?' – letting it hang like a skirt.

Dad grinned more.

'Is it a nice pattern?'

Dad still grinned.

'Does it suit me?'

Dad looked out the window and saw Joe knock down little Bill with a pumpkin. He ran out.

'Men haven't a bit of taste,' Mother said to Sal, folding the print, 'except just for what – '

Joe rushed in at the front door and out the back one – ''cept for what's to go in their stomachs. All they think about's an old – ' Dad rushed in at the front door and out the back one – 'old horse or something. And then they think – ' Joe rushed in again at the front door, but dived under the sofa – 'think every old screw is a race-horse – ' Dad rushed in again a the front door and out at the back one. 'My word, if he finds you there, me shaver, y'll catch it.'

Joe grinned and breathed hard.

Mother put the print away and mounted the box again. Then Mrs Flannigan, a glib-tongued old gossip, the mother of sixteen shy selector children, dropped in, and they drank tea together and talked about christenings and matches and marriages and babies and bad times and bad husbands until dark – until Mrs Flannigan thought her husband would be wanting his supper and went home.

Joe talked of the christening at school. For a time nobody paid any attention to him; but as days passed and one and another went home to find that mother and father and bigger brothers and sisters had been asked, the interest grew, and a revulsion of feeling in favour of Joe set in. First Nell Anderson suddenly evinced a desire for his society – previously she would weep if made to stand next him in class. Then the Murphys and Browns and young Roberts surrounded him, and Reuben Burton put his string bridle on him and wouldn't ride any other horse in a race, till at last

Joe became the idol of the institution. They all fawned on him and followed him about – all but the two Caseys. They were isolated, and seemed to feel their position keenly.

Joe was besieged with questions and answered them all with head-shake and snuffling of one nostril. He disclosed the arrangements and gave melting descriptions of the pies and puddings Mother was preparing. How they danced and called him 'Joseph'! The two Caseys stood off in silence, and in fancy saw those pies and puddings – a pleasant contemplation till Nell Anderson pointed to them and asked Joe if they were invited.

'Nah,' Joe said, 'n-n-none of 'em is.'

'Ain't their mother?'

'N-nah, we d-don't want 'em,' and he snuffled some more. Then the two Caseys stole away to the rear of the school, where they sat and nursed their chagrin in lugubrious silence, and caught flies mechanically, and looked down at their dusty bare feet over which the ants crawled, until the teacher thumped the end of the little building with a huge paling and school went in.

The day came, and we all rose early and got ready. The parson, who had to ride twenty-five miles to be present, came about midday. His clothes were dusty, and he looked tired. Mother and Sal wondered if they should offer him something to eat or let him wait until the guests arrived and all sat down to the big spread. They called Dad and Dave into the little tumbledown kitchen to discuss the matter. Dad said he didn't care what they did, but Dave settled it. He said, 'Get the chap a feed.'

Joe sat on the sofa beside the parson's tall hat and eyed it in wonder. Joe had never seen so much respectability before. The parson ate with his back to Joe, while Mother and Sal flew busily about. Joe cautiously put out his hand to feel the beaver. Mother saw him and frowned. Joe withdrew his hand and stared at the rafters.

'Delicious tea,' said the parson, and Mother served him more.

Joe's hand stole out to the hat again. Dave, standing outside near the front door, noticed him and grinned. That emboldened Joe, and he lifted the hat and placed his head inside it and grinned out at Dave. Mother frowned more, but Joe couldn't see her. She hurried out. Then from the back of the house Dad's voice thundered, 'Joe!' Joe removed the beaver and obeyed the call. Harsh, angry whispers came from the door, then sounds of a scuffle, and an empty bucket flew after Joe as he raced across the yard towards the haystack.

Soon the guests began to arrive. The Maloneys and the Todds and the Taits and the Thomsons and others, with children and dogs, came in spring-carts and drays from Back Creek. The Watsons and the Whites and old Holmes and Judy Jubb, from Prosperity Peak, appeared on horseback. Judy, in the middle of the yard, stepped out of a torn and tattered old riding habit, with traces of the cow-yard about it, and displayed a pair of big boots and 'railway' stockings and a nice while muslin dress with red bows and geraniums and a lot of frills and things on it. Judy was very genteel.

The Sylvesters – nice people who had come from Brisbane with new ideas and settled near us, people who couldn't leg-rope a cow, who were going to make a big thing out of fowls, who were for ever asking Dad if jew-lizards were snakes – came on foot with their baby in a little painted cart. A large black dog, well groomed and in new harness, without reins, pulled the cart along.

We had never seen a dog pulling a cart before, neither had our dog. He rushed off to meet the Sylvesters, but stopped halfway and curled his tail over his back and growled and threw earth about with his legs. The Sylvesters' dog stood also, and curled his tail over his harness. Mrs Sylvester patted him and said, 'Carlo, Carlo, you naughty boy!'

Our dog suddenly made off. The Sylvesters' dog pursued him. He tore along the fence at coursing speed, making a great noise with the cart until he turned a corner, where it upset and left the baby. But he didn't catch our dog. And Paddy Maloney and Steve Burton and young Wilkie galloped up through the paddock shouting and whipping their horses and carried away the clothes-line stretched between two trees.

The house soon filled – there was just room for big Mrs McDoolan to squeeze in. She came on foot, puffing and blowing, and drank the glass of holy water that stood on the table with bull-frogs careering round in it. She shook hands with everybody she knew, and with everybody she didn't know, and kissed the baby. There was no pride about Mrs McDoolan.

The ceremony was about to commence. Joe and the young Todds and the young Taits, who, with the tomahawk and some dogs – about twenty-six dogs – had been up the paddock hunting kangaroo rats, returned with a live jew-lizard. They squatted round the door guarding the trophy.

Dad and Mother, with the baby in a dress of rebellious hues, stood up and faced the parson. All became silent and expectant. The parson whispered something to Mother, and she placed the baby in Dad's great arms. The band of hunters at the door giggled, and the jew-lizard tried to escape. Dad, his hair and beard grown very long, stared at the parson with a look of wild, weird reverence about him.

'In the name of the Father,' the parson drawled, dipping his fingers into the water and letting it drip on to the baby's face, 'I baptise thee, Barthol – '

Interruption.

The jew-lizard escaped and, with open mouth and head up, raced across the floor. Had it been a boa-constrictor or bunyip the women couldn't have squealed with more enthusiasm. It made straight for Judy Jubb. But Judy Jubb had been chased by a jew-lizard before. She drew back her skirts, also her leg, and kicked the vermin in the chest and lifted it to the rafters. It fell behind the sofa and settled on Todd's bull-dog that was planted there. Bully seized it and shook it vigorously and threw it against Mrs McDoolan, and seized it again and shook it more, shook it until our dog and a pack of others rushed in. 'T' the devil!' said Dad indignantly, aiming heavy kicks at the brutes. 'The child! Gimme the child!' Mother shrieked, pulling at Dad. 'Out w' y'!' said Anderson, letting fly his foot. 'Down, Bully!' shouted Todd, and between them all they kicked the dogs right through the door, then heaved the lizard after them.

But the ceremony was soon over, and everybody was radiant with joy, everybody but Bartholomew. He had been asleep until the parson dropped the water on his face, when he woke suddenly. He glared at the strange assemblage a moment, then whined and cried hard. Mother shushed him and danced him up and down, saying, 'Did they frigh–ten 'im?' Mrs McDoolan took him and shushed him and jumped him about and said, 'There now, there now.'

But Bartholomew resented it all and squealed till it seemed that some part of him must burst. Mrs Todd and Mrs Anderson and Judy Jubb each had a go at him. 'Must have the wind,' murmured Mrs Ryan feelingly, and Mrs Johnson agreed with her by nodding her head. Mother took him again and showed him the dog, but he didn't care for dogs. Then Sal ran out with him and put him on the gee-gee, the parson's old moke that stood buried in thought at the fence, and he was quiet.

A long table erected in the barn was laden with provisions, and Dad invited the company to come along and make a start. They crowded in and stared about. Green boughs and corn-cobs hung on the walls, some bags of shelled corn stood in one corner, and from a beam dangled a set of useless old cart harnesses that Dad used to lend to anyone wanting to borrow. Dad and Paddy Maloney took up the carving. Dad stood at one end of the table, Paddy at the other. Both brandished long knives. Dad proceeded silently, Paddy with joyous volubility. 'Fowl or pig?' he shouted, and rattled the knife, and piled the provender on their plates, and told them to 'back in their carts' when they wanted more; and he called the minister 'Boss'. Paddy was in his element.

It was a magnificent feast and went off most successfully. It went off until only the ruins remained. Then the party returned to the house and danced. Through the afternoon and far into the night, the concertina screeched its cracked refrain, while the forms of weary females, with muffled infants in their arms, hovered about the drays in the yard, and dog-tired men, soaked to the knees with dew-wet grass, bailing and blocking horses in a paddock corner, took strange, shadowy shape. It wasn't until all was bright and the sun seemed near that the last dray rolled heavily away from the christening of Bartholomew.

The Conquering Bush

Edward Dyson

NED 'PICKED UP' HIS WIFE IN SYDNEY. He had come down for a spell in town, and to relieve himself of the distress of riches – to melt the cheque accumulated slowly in toil and loneliness on a big station in the North. He was a stockrider, a slow, still man naturally, but easily moved by drink. When he first reached town he seemed to have with him some kind of atmosphere of silence and desolation that surrounded him during the long months back there on the run. Ned was about thirty-four, and looked forty. He was tall and raw-boned, and that air of settled melancholy, which is the certain result of a solitary bush life, suggested some romantic sorrow to Mrs Black's sentimental daughter.

Darton, taught wisdom by experience, had on this occasion taken lodgings in a suburban private house. Mrs Black's home was very small, but her daughter was her only child, and they found room for a 'gentleman boarder'.

Janet Black was a pleasant-faced, happy-hearted girl of twenty. She liked the new boarder from the start, she acknowledged to herself afterwards, but when by some fortunate chance he happened to be on hand to drag a half-blind and half-witted old woman from beneath the very hoofs of a runaway horse, somewhat at the risk of his own neck, she was enraptured, and in the enthusiasm of the moment she kissed the hand of the abashed hero, and left a tear glittering on the hard brown knuckles.

This was a week after Ned Darton's arrival in Sydney.

Ned went straight to his room and sat perfectly still, and with even more than his usual gravity watched the tear fade away from the back of his hand. Either Janet's little demonstration of artless feeling had awakened suggestions of some glorious possibility in Ned's heart, or he desired to exercise economy for a change; he suddenly became very judicious in the selection of his drinks, and only took enough whisky to dispel his native moodiness and taciturnity and make him rather a pleasant acquisition to Mrs Black's limited family circle.

When Ned Darton returned to his pastoral duties in the murmuring wilds, he took Janet Black with him as his wife. That was their honeymoon.

Darton did not pause to consider the possible results of the change he was introducing into the life of his bride – few men would. Janet was vivacious, and her heart yearned towards humanity. She was bright, cheerful, and impressionable. The bush is sad, heavy, despairing; delightful for a month, perhaps, but terrible for a year.

As she travelled towards her new home the young wife was effervescent with joy, aglow with health, childishly jubilant over numberless plans and projects; she returned to Sydney before the expiration of a year, a stranger to her mother in appearance and in spirit. She seemed taller now, her cheeks were thin, and her face had a new expression. She brought with her some of the brooding desolation of the bush – even in the turmoil of the city she seemed lost in the immensity of the wilderness. She answered her mother's every question without a smile. She had nothing to complain of; Ned was a very good husband and very kind. She found the bush lonesome at first, but soon got used to it, and she didn't mind now. She was quite sure she was used to it, and she never objected to returning.

A baby was born, and Mrs Darton went back with her husband to their hut by the creek on the great run, to the companionship of bears, birds, 'possums, kangaroos and the eternal trees. She hugged her baby to her breast, and rejoiced that her little mite would give her something more to do and something to think of that would keep the awful ring of the myriad locusts out of her ears.

Man and wife settled down to their choking existence again as before, without comment. Ned was used to the bush – he had lived in it all his life – and though its influence was powerful upon him he knew it not. He was necessarily away from home a good deal, and when at home he was not companionable, in the sense that city dwellers know. Two bushmen will sit together by the fire for hours, smoking and mute, enjoying each other's society; 'in mute discourse' two bushmen will ride for twenty miles through the most desolate or fruitful region. People who have lived in crowds want talk, laughter, and song. Ned loved his wife, but he neither talked, laughed nor sang.

Summer came. The babe at Mrs Darton's breast looked out on the world of trees with wide, unblinking, solemn eyes, and never smiled.

'Ned,' said Janet, one bright, moonlit night, 'do you know that 'possum in the big blue gum is crazy?' She has two joeys, and she has gone mad.'

Janet spent a lot of her time sitting in the shade of the hut on a candle-box, gazing into her baby's large, still eyes, listening to the noises of the bush, and the babe too seemed to listen, and the mother fancied their senses blended, and they both would some day hear something awful above the crooning of the insects and the chattering of the parrots. Sometimes she would start out of these humours with a shriek, feeling that the relentless trees which had been bending over and pressing down so long were crushing her at last beneath their weight.

Presently she became satisfied that the laughing jackasses were mad. She had long suspected it. Why else would they flock together in the dim evening and fill the bush with their crazy laughter? Why else should they sit so grave and still at other times, thinking and grieving?

Yes, she was soon convinced that the animals and birds, even the insects that surrounded her, were mad, hopelessly mad, all of them. The country was now burnt brown, and the hills ached in the great heat, and the ghostly mirage floated in the hollows. In the day-time the birds and beasts merely chummered and muttered querulously from the deepest shades, but in the dusk of evening they raved and shrieked, and filled the ominous bush with mad laughter and fantastic wailings.

It was at this time that Darton became impressed by the peculiar manner of his wife, and a great awe stole over him as he watched her gazing into her baby's eyes with that strange look of frightened conjecture. He suddenly became very communicative; he talked a lot, and laughed, and strove to be merry, with an indefinable chill in his heart. He failed to interest his wife; she was absorbed in a terrible thought. The bush was peopled with mad things – the wide wilderness of trees, and the dull, dead grass, and the cowering hills instilled into every living thing that came under the influence of their ineffable gloom a madness of melancholy. The bears were mad, the 'possums, the shrieking cockatoos, the dull grey laughing jackasses with their devilish cackling, and the ugly yellow-throated lizards that panted at her from the rocks – all were mad. How, then, could her babe hope to escape the influence of the mighty bush and the great white plains beyond, with their heavy atmosphere of despair pressing down upon his defenceless head? Would he not presently escape from her arms, and turn and hiss at her from the grass like a vicious snake; or climb the trees, and, like a bear, cling in day-long torpor from a limb; or, worst of all, join the grey birds on the big dead gum, and mock at her sorrow with empty, joyless laughter?

These were the fears that oppressed Janet as she watched her sad, silent baby at her breast. They grew upon her and strengthened day by day, and one afternoon they became an agonising conviction. She had been alone with the dumb child for two days and she sat beside the hut door and watched the evening shadows thicken, with a shadow in her eyes that was more terrible than the blackest night, and when a solitary mopoke began calling from Bald Hill, and the jackasses set up a weird chorus of laughter, she rose, and clasping her baby tighter to her breast, and leaning over it to shield it from the surrounding evils, she hurried towards the creek.

Janet was not in the hut when Ned returned home half an hour later. Attracted by the howling of his dog, he hastened to the waterhole under the great rock, and there in the shallow water he found the bodies of his wife and child and the dull grey birds were laughing insanely overhead.

The Union Buries Its Dead

Henry Lawson

WHILE OUT BOATING ONE SUNDAY AFTERNOON on a billabong across the river, we saw a young man on horseback driving some horses along the bank. He said it was a fine day, and asked if the water was deep there. The joker of our party said it was deep enough to drown him, and he laughed and rode further up. We didn't take much notice of him.

Next day a funeral gathered at a corner pub and asked each other to have a drink while waiting for the hearse. They passed away some of the time dancing jigs to a piano in the bar parlour. They passed away the rest of the time sky-larking and fighting.

The defunct was a young union labourer, about twenty-five, who had been drowned the previous day while trying to swim some horses across a billabong in the Darling.

He was almost a stranger in town, and the fact of his having been a union man accounted for the funeral. The police found some union papers in his swag, and called at the General Labourers' Union Office for information about him. That's how we knew. The secretary had very little information to give. The departed was a 'Roman', and the majority of the town was otherwise – but unionism is stronger than creed. Drink, however, is stronger than unionism; and, when the hearse presently arrived, more than two-thirds of the funeral were unable to follow. They were too drunk.

The procession numbered fifteen, fourteen souls following the broken shell of a soul. Perhaps not one of the fourteen possessed a soul any more than the corpse did − but that doesn't matter.

Four or five of the funeral, who were boarders at the pub, borrowed a trap which the landlord used to carry passengers to and from the railway station. They were strangers to us who were on foot, and we to them. We were all strangers to the corpse.

A horseman, who looked like a drover just returned from a big trip, dropped into our dusty wake and followed us a few hundred yards, dragging his pack-horse behind him, but a friend made wild and demonstrative signals from a hotel verandah − hooking at the air in front with his right hand and jabbing his left thumb over his shoulder in the direction of the bar − so the drover hauled off and didn't catch up to us any more. He was a stranger to the entire show.

We walked in twos. There were three twos. It was very hot and dusty; the heat rushed in fierce dazzling rays across every iron roof and light-coloured wall that was turned to the sun. One or two pubs closed respectfully until we got past. They closed their bar doors and the patrons went in and out through some side or back entrance for a few minutes. Bushmen seldom grumble at an inconvenience of this sort, when it is caused by a funeral. They have too much respect for the dead.

On the way to the cemetery we passed three shearers sitting on the shady side of a fence. One was drunk − very drunk. The other two covered their right ears with their hats, out of respect for the departed − whoever he might have been – and one of them kicked the drunk and muttered something to him.

He straightened himself up, stared, and reached helplessly for his hat, which he shoved off and then on again. Then he made a great effort to pull himself together – and succeeded. He stood up, braced his back against the fence, knocked off his hat, and remorsefully placed his foot on it – to keep it off his head until the funeral passed.

A tall, sentimental drover, who walked by my side, cynically quoted Byronic verses suitable to the occasion – to death – and asked with pathetic humour whether we thought the dead man's ticket would be recognised 'over yonder'. It was a GLU ticket, and the general opinion was that it would be recognised.

Presently my friend said, 'You remember when we were in the boat yesterday, we saw a man driving some horses along the bank?'

'Yes.'

'Well, that's him.'

I thought awhile.

'I didn't take any particular notice of him,' I said. ' He said something, didn't he?'

'Yes; said it was a fine day. You'd have taken more notice if you'd known that he was doomed to die in the hour, and that those were the last words he would say to any man in this world.'

'To be sure,' said a full voice from the rear. 'If ye'd known that, ye'd have prolonged the conversation.'

We plodded on across the railway line and along the hot, dusty road which ran to the cemetery, some of us talking about the accident, and lying about the narrow escapes we had had ourselves. Presently some one said:

'There's the Devil.'

I looked up and saw a priest standing in the shade of the tree by the cemetery gate.

The hearse was drawn up and the tail-boards were opened. The funeral extinguished its right ear with its hat as four men lifted the coffin out and laid it over the grave. The priest – a pale, quiet young fellow – stood under the shade of a sapling which grew at the head of the grave. He took off his hat, dropped it carelessly on the ground, and proceeded to business. I noticed that one or two heathens winced slightly when the holy water was sprinkled on the coffin. The drops quickly evaporated, and the little round black spots they left were soon dusted over; but the spots showed, by contrast, the cheapness and shabbiness of the cloth with which the coffin was covered. It seemed black before; now it looked a dusky grey.

Just here man's ignorance and vanity made a farce of the funeral. A big, bull-necked publican, with heavy, blotchy features, and a supremely ignorant expression, picked up the priest's straw hat and held it about twelve inches above the head of his reverence during the whole of the service. The father, be it remembered, was standing in the shade. A few shoved their hats on and off uneasily, struggling between their disgust for the living and their respect for the dead. The hat had a conical crown and a brim sloping down all round like a sunshade, and the publican held it with his great red claw spread over the crown. To do the priest justice, perhaps he didn't notice the incident. A stage priest or parson in the same position might have said, 'Put that hat down, my friend; is not the memory of our departed brother worth more than my complexion?' A wattlebark layman might have expressed himself in stronger language, none the less to the point. But my priest seemed unconscious of what was going on. Besides, the publican was a great and important pillar of the Church. He couldn't, as an ignorant and conceited ass, lose such a good opportunity of asserting his faithfulness and importance to his Church.

The grave looked very narrow under the coffin, and I drew a breath of relief when the box slid easily down. I saw a coffin get stuck once, at Rookwood, and it had to be yanked out with difficulty, and laid on the sods at the feet of the heart-broken relations, who howled dismally while the grave-digger widened the hole. But they don't cut contracts so fine out in the West. Our grave-digger was not altogether bowelless, and, out of respect for the human quality described as 'feelin's', he scraped up some light and dusty soil and threw it down to deaden the fall of the clay lumps on the coffin. He also tried to steer the first few shovelfuls gently down against the end of the grave with the back of the shovel turned outwards, but the hard, dry Darling River clods rebounded and knocked all the same. It didn't matter much – nothing does. The fall of lumps of clay on a stranger's coffin doesn't sound any different from the fall of the same things on an ordinary wooden box – at least I didn't notice anything awesome or unusual in the sound; but, perhaps, one of us – the most sensitive – might have been impressed by being reminded of a burial long ago, when the thump of every sod jolted his heart.

I have left out the wattle – because it wasn't there. I have also neglected to mention the heart-broken old mate, with his grizzled head bowed and great pearly drops streaming

down his rugged cheeks. He was absent – he was proba-
bly 'Out Back'. For similar reasons I have omitted reference
to the suspicious moisture in the eyes of a bearded ruffian
named Bill. Bill failed to turn up, and the only moisture
was that which was induced by the heat. I have left out the
'sad Australian sunset' because the sun was not going
down at the time. The burial took place at exactly mid-day.

The dead bushman's name was Jim, apparently; but they
found no portraits, nor locks of hair, nor any love letters,
nor anything of that kind in his swag – not even a refer-
ence to his mother; only some papers relating to union
matters. Most of us didn't know the name till we saw it on
the coffin; we knew him as 'that poor chap that got
drowned yesterday'.

'So his name's James Tyson,' said my drover acquain-
tance, looking at the plate.

'Why! Didn't you know that before?' I asked.

'No; but I knew he was a union man.'

It turned out, afterwards, that JT wasn't his real name –
only 'the name he went by'.

Anyhow he was buried by it, and most of the 'Great
Australian Dailies' have mentioned in their brevity columns
that a young man names James John Tyson was drowned
by a billabong of the Darling last Sunday.

We did hear, later on, what his real name was; but if we
ever chance to read in the 'Missing Friends Column,' we
shall not be able to give any information to heart-broken
Mother or Sister or Wife, not to any one who could let him
hear something to his advantage – for we have already for-
gotten the name.

The Chosen Vessel

Barbara Baynton

S HE LAID THE STICK AND HER BABY on the grass while she
untied the rope that tethered the calf. The length of
the rope separated them. The cow was near the calf,
and both were lying down. Feed along the creek was plen-
tiful, and every day she found a fresh place to tether it,
since tether it she must, for if she did not, it would stray
with the cow on the plain. She had plenty of time to go
after it, but then there was her baby; and if the cow turned
on her out on the plain, and she was with her baby, – she
had been a town girl and was afraid of the cow, but she
didn't want the cow to know it. She used to run at first
when it bellowed in protest against the penning up of its
calf. This satisfied the cow, also the calf, but the woman's
husband was angry, and called her – the noun was cur. It
was he who forced her to run and meet the advancing cow,
brandishing a stick, and uttering threatening words till the
enemy turned and ran. 'That's the way!' the man said,
laughing at her white face. In many things he was worse
than the cow, and she wondered if the same rule would
apply to the man, but she was not one to provoke skir-
mishes even with the cow.

It was early for the calf to go to 'bed' – nearly an hour
earlier than usual; but she had felt so restless all day. Partly
because it was Monday, and the end of the week that
would bring her and the baby the companionship of his
father, was so far off. He was a shearer, and had gone to

his shed before daylight that morning. Fifteen miles as the crow flies separated them.

There was a track in front of the house, for it had once been a wine shanty, and a few travellers passed along at intervals. She was not afraid of horsemen; but swagmen, going to, or worse coming from the dismal, drunken little township, a day's journey beyond, terrified her. One had called at the house today and asked for tucker.

That was why she had penned up the calf so early. She feared more from the look of his eyes, and the gleam of his teeth, as he watched her newly awakened baby beat its fists upon her covered breasts, than from the knife that was sheathed in the belt at his waist.

She had given him bread and meat. Her husband she told him was sick. She always said that when she was alone and a swagman came; and she had gone in from the kitchen to the bedroom and asked questions and replied to them in the best man's voice she could assume. Then he had asked her to go into the kitchen to boil his billy, but instead she gave him tea, and he drank it on the wood heap. He had walked round and round the house, and there were cracks in some places, and after the last time he had asked for tobacco. She had none to give him, and he had grinned, because there was a broken clay pipe near the wood heap where he stood, and if there were a man inside, there ought to have been tobacco. Then he asked for money, but women in the bush never have money.

At last he had gone, and she, watching through the cracks, saw him when about a quarter of a mile away, turn and look back at the house. He had stood so for some moments with a pretence of fixing his swag, and then, apparently satisfied, moved to the left towards the creek. The creek made a bow round the house, and when he came to the bend she lost sight of him, Hours after, watching intently for signs of smoke, she saw the man's dog chasing some sheep that had gone to the creek for water, and saw it slink back suddenly, as if it had been called by some one.

More than once she thought of taking her baby and going to her husband. But in the past, when she had dared to speak of the dangers to which her loneliness exposed her, he had taunted and sneered at her. 'Needn't flatter yerself,' he had told her, 'nobody 'ud want ter run away with yew.'

Long before nightfall she placed food on the kitchen table, and beside it laid the big brooch that had been her mother's. It was the only thing of value she had. And she left the kitchen door wide open.

The doors inside she securely fastened. Beside the bolt in the back one she drove in the steel and scissors; against it she piled the table and the stools. Underneath the lock of the front door she forced the handle of the spade, and the blade between the cracks in the flooring boards. Then the prop-stick, cut into lengths, held the top, as the spade held the middle. The windows were little more than portholes; she had little to fear through them.

She ate a few mouthfuls of food and drank a cup of milk. But she lighted no fire, and when night came, no candle, but crept with her baby to bed.

What woke her? The wonder was that she had slept – she had not meant to. But she was young, very young. Perhaps the shrinkage of the galvanized roof – hardly though, since that was so usual. Yet something had set her heart beating wildly; but she lay quite still, only she put her arm over her baby. Then she had both round it, and she prayed, 'Little baby, little baby, don't wake!'

The moon's rays shone on the front of the house, and she saw one of the open cracks, quite close to where she lay, darken with a shadow. Then a protesting growl reached her; and she could fancy she heard the man turn hastily. She plainly heard the thud of something striking the dog's ribs, and the long flying strides of the animal as it howled and ran. Still watching, she saw the shadow darken every crack along the wall. She knew by the sounds that the man was trying every standpoint that might help him to see in; but how much he saw she could not tell. She thought of many things she might do to deceive him into the idea that she was not alone. But the sound of her voice would only wake baby, and she dreaded that as though it were the only danger that threatened her. So she prayed, 'Little baby, don't wake, don't cry!'

Stealthily the man crept about. She knew he had his boots off, because of the vibration that his feet caused walking along the verandah to gauge the width of the little window in her room, and the resistance of the front door.

Then he went to the other end, and the uncertainty of what he was doing became unendurable. She had felt safer, far safer, while he was close, and she could watch and listen. She felt she must watch, but the great fear of wakening her baby again assailed her. She suddenly recalled that one of the slabs on that side of the house had shrunk in length as well as in width, and had once fallen out. It was held in position only by a wedge of wood underneath. What if he should discover that? The uncertainty increased her terror. She prayed as she gently raised herself with her little one in her arms, held tightly to her breast.

She thought of the knife, and shielded its body with her hands and arms. Even the little feet she covered with its white gown and the baby never murmured – it liked to be held so. Noiselessly she crossed to the other side, and stood where she could see him and hear, but not be seen. He was trying every slab, and was very near to that with the wedge under it. Then she saw him find it; and heard the sound of the knife as bit by bit he began to cut away the wooden support.

She waited motionless, with her baby pressed tightly to her, though she knew that in another few minutes this man with cruel eyes, lascivious mouth, and gleaming knife, would enter. One side of the slab tilted; he had only to cut away the remaining little end, when the slab, unless he held it, would fall outside.

She heard his jerked breathing as it kept time with the cuts of the knife, and the brush of his clothes as he rubbed the wall in his movements, for she was so still and quiet that she did not even tremble. She knew when he ceased, and wondered why, being so well concealed; for he could not see her, and would not fear if he did, yet she heard him move cautiously away. Perhaps he expected the slab to fall – his motive puzzled her, and she moved even closer, and bent her body the better to listen. Ah! what sound was that?' 'Listen! Listen!' she bade her heart – her heart that had kept so still, but now bounded with tumultuous throbs that dulled her ears. Nearer and nearer came the sounds, till the welcome thud of a horse's hoof rang out clearly.

'O God! O God! O God!' she panted, for they were very

close before she could make sure. She rushed to the door, and with her baby in her arms tore frantically at its bolts and bars.

Out she darted at last, and running madly along, saw the horseman beyond her in the distance. She called to him in Christ's Name, in her babe's name, still flying like the wind with the speed that deadly peril gives. But the distance grew greater and greater between them, and when she reached the creek her prayers turned to wild shrieks, for there crouched the man she feared, with outstretched arms that caught her as she fell.

She knew he was offering terms if she ceased to struggle and cry for help, though louder and louder did she cry for it, but it was only when the man's hand gripped her throat, that the cry of 'Murder!' came from her lips. And when she ceased, the startled curlews took up the awful sound, and flew wailing 'Murder! Murder!' over the horseman's head.

'By God!' said the boundary rider. 'It's been a dingo right enough! Eight killed up here, and there's more down in the creek – a ewe and a lamb, I'll bet: and the lamb's alive!' He shut out the sky with his hand, and watched the crows that were circling round and round, nearing the earth one moment, and the next shooting skywards. By that he knew the lamb must be alive; even a dingo will spare a lamb sometimes.

Yes, the lamb was alive, and after the manner of lambs of its kind did not know its mother when the light came. It had sucked the still warm breasts, and laid its little head on her bosom, and slept till the morn. Then, when it looked at the swollen disfigured face, it wept and would have crept away but for the hand that still clutched its little gown. Sleep was nodding its golden head and swaying its small body, and the crows were so close, to the mother's wide open eyes, when the boundary rider galloped down.

'Jesus Christ!' he said, covering his eyes. He told afterwards how the little child held out its arms to him, and how he was forced to cut its gown that the dead hand held.

It was election time, and as usual the priest had selected a candidate. His choice was so obviously in the interests of the squatter, that Peter Hennessy's reason, for once in his life, had over-ridden superstition, and he had dared promise his vote to another. Yet he was uneasy, and every time he woke in the night (and it was often), he heard the murmur of his mother's voice. It came through the partition, or under the door. If through the partition, he knew she was praying in her bed; but when the sounds came under the door, she was on her knees before the little Altar in the corner that enshrined the statue of the Blessed Virgin and Child.

'Mary, Mother of Christ! save my son! Save him!' prayed she in the dairy as she strained and set the evening's milking. 'Sweet Mary! for the love of Christ, save him!' The grief in her old face made the morning meal so bitter, that to avoid her he came late to his dinner. It made him so cowardly, that he could not say goodbye to her, and when night fell on the eve of the election day, he rode off secretly.

He had thirty miles to ride to the township to record his vote. He cantered briskly along the great stretch of plain that had nothing but stunted cotton bush to play shadow to the full moon, which glorified a sky of earliest spring. The bruised incense of the flowering clover rose up to him, and the glory of the night appealed vaguely to his imagination, but he was preoccupied with his present act of revolt.

Vividly he saw his mother's agony when she would find him gone. Even at that moment, he felt sure she was praying.

'Mary! Mother of Christ!' He repeated the invocation, half unconsciously, when suddenly to him, out of the stillness, came Christ's Name – called loudly in despairing accents.

'For Christ's sake! Christ's sake! Christ's sake!' called the voice. Good Catholic that he had been, he crossed himself before he dared to look back. Gliding across a ghostly patch of pipe-clay he saw a white-robed figure with a babe clasped to her bosom.

All the superstitious awe of his race and religion swayed his brain. The moonlight on the gleaming clay was a 'heavenly light' to him, and he knew the white figure not for flesh and blood, but for the Virgin and Child of his mother's prayers. Then, good Catholic that once more he was, he put spurs to his horse's sides and galloped madly away.

His mother's prayers were answered, for Hennessey was the first to record his vote – for the priest's candidate. Then he sought the priest at home, but found that he was out rallying the voters. Still under the influence of his blessed vision, Hennessey would not go near the public houses, but wandered about the outskirts of the town for hours, keeping apart from the towns-people, and fasting as penance. He was subdued and mildly ecstatic, feeling as a repentant chastened child, who awaits only the kiss of peace.

And at last, as he stood in the graveyard crossing himself with reverent awe, he heard in the gathering twilight the roar of many voices crying the name of the victor at the election. It was well with the priest.

Again Hennessey sought him. He was at home, the housekeeper said, and led him into the dimly lighted study. His seat was immediately opposite a large picture, and as the housekeeper turned up the lamp, once more the face of the Madonna and Child looked down on him, but this time silently, peacefully. The half-parted lips of the Virgin were smiling with compassionate tenderness; her eyes seemed to beam with the forgiveness of an earthly mother for her erring but beloved child.

He fell on his knees in adoration. Transfixed, the wondering priest stood, for mingled with the adoration, 'My Lord and my God!' was the exaltation. 'And hast Thou chosen me?'

'What is it, Peter?' said the priest.

'Father,' he answered reverently; and with loosened tongue he poured forth the story of his vision.

'Great God!' shouted the priest, 'and you did not stop to save her! Do you not know? Have you not heard?'

Many miles further down the creek a man kept throwing an old cap into a water-hole. The dog would bring it out and lay it on the opposite side to where the man stood, but would not allow the man to catch him, though it was only to wash the blood of the sheep from his mouth and throat, for the sight of blood made the man tremble. But the dog was also guilty.

'And Women Must Weep'

'For men must work'

Henry Handel Richardson

She was ready at last, the last bow tied, the last strengthening pin in place, and they said to her – Auntie Char and Miss Bidddons – to sit down and rest while Auntie Cha 'climbed into her own togs': 'Or you'll be tired before the evening begins.' But she could not bring herself to sit, for fear of crushing her dress – it was so light, so airy. How glad she felt now that she had chosen muslin, and not silk as Auntie Cha had tried to persuade her. The gossamer-like stuff seemed to float around her as she moved, and the cut of the dress made her look so tall and so different from everyday that she hardly recognised herself in the glass; the girl reflected there – in palest blue, with a wreath of cornflowers in her hair – might have been a stranger. Never had she thought she was so pretty ... nor had Auntie and Miss Biddons either; though all they said was: 'Well, Dolly, you'll *do*,' and: 'Yes, I think she will be a credit to you.' Something hot and stinging came up her throat at this: a kind of gratitude for her pinky-white skin, her big blue eyes and fair curly hair, and pity for those girls who hadn't got them. Or an Auntie Cha either, to dress them and see that everything was 'just so'.

Instead of sitting, she stood very stiff and straight at the window, pretending to watch for the cab, her long white gloves hanging loose over one arm so as not to soil them.

But her heart was beating pit-a-pat. For this was her first real grown-up ball. It was to be held in a public hall, and Auntie Cha, where she was staying, had bought tickets and was taking her.

True, Miss Biddons rather spoilt things at the end by saying: 'Now mind you don't forget your steps in the waltz. One, two, together; four, five, six.' And in the wagonette, with her dress filling one seat, Auntie Cha's the other, Auntie said: 'Now, Dolly, remember not to look too *serious*. Or you'll frighten the gentlemen off.'

She was only doing it now because of her dress: cabs were so cramped, the seats so narrow.

Alas! in getting out a little accident happened. She caught the bottom of one of her flounces – the skirt was made of nothing else – on the iron step, and ripped off the selvedge. Auntie Cha said: 'My *dear*, how clumsy!' She could have cried with vexation.

The woman who took their cloaks hunted everywhere, but could only find black cotton; so the torn selvedge – there was nearly half a yard of it – had just to be cut off. This left a raw edge, and when they went into the hall and walked across the enormous floor, with people sitting all round, staring, it seemed to Dolly as if every one had their eyes fixed on it. Auntie Cha sat down in the front row of chairs beside a lady-friend; but she slid into a chair behind.

The first dance was already over, and they were hardly seated before partners began to be taken for the second. Shyly she mustered the assembly. In the cloakroom, she had expected the woman to exclaim: 'What a sweet pretty frock!' when she handled it. (When all she did say was: 'This sort of stuff's bound to fray.') And now Dolly saw that the hall was full of *lovely* dresses, some much, much prettier than hers, which suddenly began to seem rather too plain, even a little dowdy; perhaps after all it would have been better to have chosen silk.

She wondered if Aunt Cha thought so too. For Auntie suddenly turned and looked at her, quite hard, and then said snappily: 'Come, come, child, you mustn't tuck yourself away like that, or the gentlemen will think you don't want to dance.' So she had to come out and sit in the front; and show that she had a programme, by holding it open on her lap.

When other ladies were being requested for the third time, and still nobody had asked to be introduced, Auntie began making signs and beckoning with her head to the Master of Ceremonies – a funny little fat man with a bright red beard. He waddled across the floor, and Auntie whispered to him … behind her fan. (But she heard. And heard him answer: 'Wants a partner? Why, certainly.') And then he went away and they could see him offering her to several gentlemen. Some pointed to the ladies they were sitting with or standing in front of; some showed their programmes were full. One or two turned their heads and looked at her. But it was no good. So he came back and said: 'Will the little lady do *me* the favour?' and she had to look glad and say: 'With pleasure,' and get up and dance with him. Perhaps she was a little slow about it … at any rate Auntie Cha made great round eyes at her. But she felt sure every one would know why he was asking her. It was the lancers, too, and he swung her off her feet at the corners, and was comic when he set to partners – putting one hand on his hip and the other over his head, as if he were dancing the hornpipe – and the rest of the set laughed. She was glad when it was over and she could go back to her place.

Auntie Cha's lady-friend had a son, and he was beckoned to next and there was more whispering. But he was engaged to be married, and of course preferred to dance with his fiancée. When he came and bowed – to oblige his mother – he looked quite grumpy, and didn't trouble to say all of 'May I have the pleasure?' but just 'The pleasure?' While she had to say 'Certainly,' and pretend to be very pleased, though she didn't feel it, and really didn't want much to dance with him, knowing he didn't, and that it was only out of charity. Besides, all the time they went round he was explaining things to the other girl with his eyes … making faces over her head. She saw him quite plainly.

After he had brought her back – and Auntie had to talked to him again – he went to a gentleman who hadn't danced at all yet, but just stood looking on. And this one needed a lot of persuasion. He was ugly, and lanky, and as soon as they stood up, said quite rudely: 'I'm no earthly good at this kind of thing, you know.' And he wasn't. He trod on her foot and put her out of step, and they got into the most dreadful muddle, right out in the middle of the floor. It was a waltz, and remembering what Miss Biddons had said, she got more and more nervous, and then went wrong herself and had to say: 'I beg your pardon,' to which he said: 'Granted.' She saw them in a mirror as they passed, and her face was red as red.

It didn't get cool again either, for she had to go on sitting out, and she felt sure he was spreading it that *she* couldn't dance. She didn't know whether Auntie Cha had seen her mistakes, but now Auntie sort of went for her. 'It's no use, Dolly, if you don't do your share. For goodness sake, try and look more agreeable!'

So after this, in the intervals between the dances, she sat with a stiff little smile gummed to her lips. And, did any likely-looking partner approach the corner where they were, this widened till she felt what it was really saying was: 'Here I am! Oh, *please* take *me*!'

She had several false hopes. Men, looking so splendid in their white shirt fronts, would walk across the floor and seem to be coming … and then it was always not her. Their eyes wouldn't stay on her. There she sat, with her false little smile, and her eyes fixed on them; but theirs always got away … flitted past … moved on. Once she felt quite sure. Ever such a handsome young man looked at her as if he was making straight for her. She stretched her lips, showing all her teeth (they were very good) and for an instant his eyes seemed to linger … really take her in, in her pretty blue dress and the cornflowers. And then at the last minute they ran away – and it wasn't her at all, but a girl sitting three seats further on; one who wasn't even pretty, or her dress either. But her own dress was beginning to get quite tashy, from the way she squeezed her hot hands down in her lap.

Quite the worst part of all was having to go on sitting in the front row, pretending you were enjoying yourself. It was so hard to know what to do with your eyes. There was nothing but the floor for them to look at – if you watched the other couples dancing they would think you were envying them. At first she made a show of studying her programme; but you couldn't go on staring at a programme for ever: and presently her shame at its emptiness grew till she could bear it no longer, and, seizing a moment when people were dancing, she slipped it down the front of her dress. Now she could say she'd lost it, if anyone asked to see it. But they didn't; they went on dancing with other girls. Oh, these men, who walked round and chose just who they fancied and left who they didn't ... how she hated them! It wasn't fair ... it wasn't fair. And when there was a 'leap-year dance' where the ladies invited the gentlemen, and Auntie Cha tried to push her up and make her go and said: 'Now then, Dolly, here's your chance!' she shook her head hard and dug herself deeper into her seat. She wasn't going to ask them when they never asked her. So she said her head ached and she'd rather not. And to this she clung, sitting the while wishing with her whole heart that her dress was black and her hair grey, like Auntie Cha's. Nobody expected Auntie Cha to dance, or thought it shameful if she didn't; she could do and be just as she liked. Yes, to-night she wished she was old ... an old, old woman. Or that she was safe at home in bed ... this dreadful evening, to which she had once counted the days, behind her. Even, as the night wore on, that she was dead.

At supper she sat with Auntie and the other lady, and the son and girl came too. There were lovely cakes and things, but she could not eat them. Her throat was so dry that a sandwich stuck in it and nearly choked her. Perhaps the son felt a little sorry for her (or else his mother had whispered again), for afterwards he said something to the girl, and then asked her to dance. They stood up together; but it wasn't a success. Her legs seemed to have forgotten how to jump, heavy as lead they were ... as heavy as she felt inside … and she couldn't think of a thing to say. So now he would put her down as stupid as well.

Her only other partner was a boy younger than she was – almost a schoolboy – who she heard them say was 'making a positive nuisance of himself'. This was to a very pretty girl called the 'belle of the ball'. And he didn't seem to mind how badly he danced (with her), for he couldn't take his eyes off this other girl; but went on staring at her all the time, and very fiercely, because she was talking and laughing with somebody else. Besides, he hopped like a grasshopper, and didn't wear gloves, and his hands were hot and sticky. She hadn't come there to dance with little boys.

They left before anybody else; there was nothing to stay for. And the drive home in the wagonette, which had to be fetched, they were so early, was dreadful; Auntie Cha just sat and pressed her lips and didn't say a word. She herself kept her face turned the other way, because her mouth was jumping in and out as if it might have to cry.

At the sound of the wheels Miss Biddons came running to the front door with questions and exclamations, dreadfully curious to know why they were back so soon. Dolly fled to her own little room and turned the key in the lock. She wanted only to be quite alone … where nobody could see her … where nobody would ever see her again. But the walls were thin, and as she tore off the wreath and ripped open her dress, now crushed to nothing from so much sitting, and threw them from her anywhere, anyhow, she could hear the two voices going on, Auntie Cha's telling and telling, and winding up at last, quite out loud with: 'Well, I don't know what it was, but the plain truth is, she didn't *take* !'

Oh, the shame of it! ... the sting and the shame. Her first ball, and not to have 'taken', to have failed to 'attract the gentlemen' – this was a slur that would rest on her all her life. And yet ... and yet ... in spite of everything, a small voice that wouldn't be silenced kept on saying: 'It wasn't my fault ... it wasn't my fault!' (Or at least not except for the one silly mistake in the steps of the waltz.) She had tried her hardest, done everything she was told to do: had dressed up to please and look pretty, sat in the front row offering her programme, smiled when she didn't feel a bit like smiling ... and almost more than anything she thought she hated the memory of that smile (it was like trying to make people buy something they didn't think worth while.) For really, truly, right deep down in her, she hadn't wanted 'the gentlemen' any more than they'd wanted her: she had only had to pretend to. And they showed only too plainly they didn't, by choosing other girls, who were not even pretty, and dancing with them, and laughing and talking and enjoying them. And now, the many slights and humiliations of the evening crowding upon her, the long repressed tears broke through; and with the blanket pulled up over her head, her face driven deep into the pillow, she cried till she could cry no more.

When the Wolf was at the Door

Steele Rudd

THERE HAD BEEN A LONG STRETCH of dry weather, and we were cleaning out the waterhole. Dad was down the hole shovelling up the dirt; Joe squatted on the brink catching flies and letting them go again without their wings, a favourite amusement of his; while Dan and Dave cut a drain to turn the water that ran off the ridge into the hole – when it rained. Dad was feeling dry, and told Joe to fetch him a drink.

Joe said, 'See first if this cove can fly with only one wing.' Then he went, but returned and said, 'There's no water in the bucket – Mother used the last drop to boil the punkins,' and renewed the flycatching. Dad tried to spit, and was going to say something when Mother, half-way between the house and the waterhole, cried out the grasspaddock was all on fire. 'So it is, Dad,' said Joe, slowly but surely dragging the head off a fly with a finger and thumb.

Dad scrambled out of the hole and looked. 'God God!' was all he said. How he ran! All of us rushed after him except Joe – he couldn't run very well, because the day before he had ridden fifteen miles on a poor horse, bareback. When near the fire Dad stopped running to break a green bush. He hit upon a tough one. Dad was in a hurry. The bush wasn't. Dad swore and tugged with all his might. Then the bush broke and Dad fell heavily on his back and swore again.

To save the cockatoo-fence that was round the cultivation was what was troubling Dad.

Right and left we fought the fire with boughs. Hot! It was hellish hot! Whenever there was a lull in the wind we worked. Like a windmill! Dad's bough moved – and how he rushed for another when that was used up! Once we had the fire almost under control, but the wind rose again, and away went the flames higher and faster than ever.

'It's no use,' said Dad at last, placing his hand on his head and throwing down his bough. We did the same, then stood and watched the fence go. After supper we went out again and saw it still burning. Joe asked Dad if he didn't think it was a splendid sight. Dad didn't answer him; he didn't seem conversational that night.

We decided to put the fence up again. Dan had sharpened the axe with a broken file, and he and Dad were about to start when Mother asked them what was to be done about flour. She said she had shaken the bag to get enough to make scones for that morning's breakfast, and unless some was got somewhere there would be no bread for dinner.

Dad reflected, while Dan felt the edge on the axe with his thumb.

Dad said, 'Won't Mrs Dwyer let you have a dishful until we get some?'

'No,' Mother answered, 'I can't ask her until we send back what we owe them.'

Dad reflected again. 'The Andersons, then?' he said.

Mother shook her head and asked what good there was in sending to them when they, only that morning, had sent to her for some.

'Well, we must do the best we can at present,' Dad answered, 'and I'll go to the store this evening and see what is to be done.'

Putting the fence up again, in the hurry that Dad was in, was the very devil! He felled the saplings – and such saplings – *trees* many of them were – while we, all of a muck of sweat, dragged them into line. Dad worked like a horse himself and expected us to do the same. 'Never mind staring about you,' he'd say, if he caught us looking at the sun to see if it were coming dinner-time. 'There's no time to lose if we want to get the fence up and crop in.'

Dan worked nearly as hard as Dad until he dropped the butt-end of a heavy sapling on his foot, which made him hop about on one leg and say that he was sick and tired of the dashed fence. Then he argued with Dad, and declared that it would be far better to put a wire fence up at once, and be done with it, instead of wasting time over a thing that would only be burnt down again. 'How long,' he said, 'will it take to get the posts? Not a week,' and he hit the ground disgustedly with a piece of stick he had in his hand.

'Confound it!' Dad said. 'Haven't you got any sense, boy? What earthly use would a wire fence be without any wire in it?'

Then we knocked off and went to dinner.

No one appeared in any humour to talk at the table. Mother sat silently at the end and poured out the tea while Dad, at the head, served the pumpkin and divided what cold meat there was. Mother wouldn't have any meat – one of us would have to go without if she had taken any.

I don't know if it was on account of Dan's arguing with him, or if it was because there was no bread for dinner, that

Dad was in a bad temper. Anyway, he swore at Joe for coming to the table with dirty hands. Joe cried and said that he couldn't wash them when Dave, as soon as he had washed his, had thrown the water out. Then Dad scowled at Dave, and Joe passed his plate along for more pumpkin.

Dinner was almost over when Dan, still looking hungry, grinned and asked Dave if he wasn't going to have some bread. Whereupon Dad jumped up in a tearing passion, 'Damn your insolence!' he said to Dan. 'Make a jest of it, would you?'

'Who's jestin'?' Dan answered and grinned again.

'Go!' said Dad furiously, pointing to the door. 'Leave my roof, you thankless dog!'

Dan went that night.

It was only when Dad promised faithfully to reduce his account within two months that the storekeeper let us have another bag of flour on credit. And what a change that bag of flour wrought! How cheerful the place became all at once! And how enthusiastically Dad spoke of the farm and the prospects of the coming season!

Four months had gone by. The fence had been up some time and ten acres of wheat had been put in; but there had been no rain, and not a grain had come up, or was likely to.

Nothing had been heard of Dan since his departure. Dad spoke about him to Mother. 'The scamp,' he said, 'to leave me just when I wanted help. After all the years I've slaved to feed him and clothe him, see what thanks I get! But, mark my word, he'll be glad to come back yet.' But Mother would never say anything against Dan.

The weather continued dry. The wheat didn't come up, and Dad became despondent again.

The storekeeper called every week and reminded Dad of his promise. 'I would give it to you willingly,' Dad would say, 'if I had it, Mr Rice, but what can I do? You *can't* knock blood out of a stone.'

We ran short of tea and Dad thought to buy more with the money Anderson owed him for some fencing he had done. But when he asked for it, Anderson was very sorry he hadn't got it just then, but promised to let him have it as soon as he could sell his chaff. When Mother heard Anderson couldn't pay she *did* cry, and said there wasn't a bit of sugar in the house, or enough cotton to mend the children's bits of clothes.

We couldn't very well go without tea, so Dad showed Mother how to make a new kind. He roasted a slice of bread on the fire till it was like a black coal, then poured the boiling water over it and let it draw well. Dad said it had a capital flavour – he liked it.

Dave's only pair of pants were pretty well worn off him; Joe hadn't a decent coat for Sunday; Dad himself wore a pair of boots with the soles tied on with wire; and Mother fell sick. Dad did all he could – waited on her, and talked hopefully of the fortune which would come to us some day – but once, when talking to Dave, he broke down, and said he didn't, in the name of the Almighty God, know what he would do. Dave couldn't say anything - he moped about, too, and home somehow didn't seem like home at all.

When Mother was sick and Dad's time was mostly taken up nursing her, when there was hardly anything in the house, when in fact the wolf was at the very door, Dan came home with a pocket full of money and a swag full of greasy clothes. How Dad shook him by the hand and welcomed him back! And how Dan talked of tallies, belly-wool, and ringers, and implored Dad, over and over again, to go shearing or rolling up, or branding – anything rather than work and starve on the selection.

But Dad stayed on the farm.

Going Blind

Henry Lawson

I MET HIM IN THE FULL AND PLENTY DINING ROOMS It was a cheap place in the city, with good beds upstairs let at one shilling per night – 'Board and residence for respectable single men, fifteen shillings per week'. I was a respectable single man then. I boarded and resided there. I boarded at a greasy little table in the greasy little corner under the fluffy little staircase in the hot and greasy little dining-room or restaurant downstairs. They called it dining-rooms, but it was only one room, and there wasn't half enough room in it to work your elbows when the seven little tables and forty-nine chairs were occupied. There was not room for an ordinary-sized steward to pass up and down between the tables; but our waiter was not an ordinary-sized man – he was a living skeleton in miniature. We handed the soup, and the 'roast beef one' and 'roast lamb one', 'corn beef and cabbage one', 'veal and pickled pork one' – or two, or three, as the case may be – and the tea and coffee, and the various kinds of pudding – we handed over each other, and dodged the drops as well as we could. The very hot and very greasy little kitchen was adjacent, and it contained the bath-room and other conveniences, behind screens of whitewashed boards.

I resided upstairs in a room where there were five beds and one wash-stand; one candle-stick, with a very short bit of soft yellow candle in it; the back of a hair-brush, with about a dozen bristles in it; and half a comb – the big tooth end – with nine and a half teeth at irregular distances apart.

He was a typical bushman, not one of those tall, straight, wiry, brown men of the West, but from the old Selection Districts, where many drovers came from, and of the old bush school; one of those slight, active little fellows whom we used to see in cabbage-tree hats, Crimean shirts, strapped trousers, and elastic-side boots – 'larstins', they called them. They could dance well, sing indifferently, and mostly through their noses, the old bush songs; play the concertina horribly; and ride like – like – well, they *could* ride.

He seemed as if he had forgotten to grow old and die out with this old colonial school to which he belonged. They *had* careless and forgetful ways about them. His name was Jack Gunther, he said, and he'd come to Sydney to try to get something done to his eyes. He had a portmanteau, a carpet bag, some things in a three-bushel bag, and a tin box. I sat beside him on his bed, and struck up an acquaintance, and he told me all about it. First he asked me would I mind shifting round to the other side, as he was rather deaf in that ear. He'd been kicked on the side of the head by a horse, he said, and had been a little dull o' hearing on that side ever since.

He was as good as blind. 'I can see the people near me,' he said, 'but I can't make out their faces. I can just make out the pavement and the houses close at hand, and all the rest is a sort of white blur.' He looked up: 'That ceiling is kind of white, ain't it? And this,' tapping the wall and putting his nose close to it, 'is a sort of green, ain't it:' The ceiling might have been whiter. The prevalent tints of the wall-paper had originally been blue and red, but it was mostly green enough now – a damp, rotten green; but I was ready to swear that the ceiling was snow and that the walls were as green as grass if it would have made him feel more comfortable. His sight began to get bad about six years before, he said; he didn't take much notice of it at first, and then he saw a quack, who made his eyes worse. He had already the manner of the blind – the touch in every finger, and even the gentleness in his speech. He had a boy down with him – a 'sorter cousin of his' – and the boy saw him round. 'I'll have to be sending that youngster back,' he said. 'I think I'll send him home next week. He'll be picking up and learning too much down here.'

I happened to know the district he came from, and we would sit by the hour and talk about the country, and chaps by the name of this and chaps by the name of that – drovers mostly, whom we had met or had heard of. He asked me if I'd ever heard of a chap by the name of Joe Scott – a big, sandy-complexioned chap, who might be droving; he was his brother, or, at least, his half-brother, but he hadn't heard of him for years; he'd last heard of him at Blackall, in Queensland; he might have gone overland to Western Australia with Tyson's cattle to the new country.

We talked about grubbing and fencing and digging and droving and shearing – all about the bush – and it all came back to me as we talked. 'I can see it all now,' he said once, in an abstracted tone, seeming to fix his helpless eyes on the wall opposite. But he didn't see the dirty blind wall, nor the dingy window, nor the skimpy little bed, nor the greasy wash-stand: he saw the dark blue ridges in the sunlight, the grassy sidings and flats, the creek with clumps of she-oak here and there, the course of the willow-fringed river below, the distant peaks and ranges fading away into a lighter azure; the granite ridge in the middle distance, and the rocky rises, the stringy-bark and the apple-tree flats, the shrubs, and the sunlit plains – and all. I could see it too – plainer than I ever did.

He had done a bit of fencing in his time, and we got talking about timber. He didn't believe in having fencing-posts with big butts; he reckoned it was a mistake. 'You see,' he said, 'the top of the butt catches the rain water and make the post rot quicker. I'd back posts without any butt at all to last as long or longer than posts with 'em – that's if the post is well put up and well rammed.' He had supplied fencing stuff, and fenced by contract, and – well, you can get more posts without butts out of a tree than posts with them. He also objected to charring the butts. He said it only made work, and wasted time – the butts lasted longer without being charred.

I asked him if he'd ever got stringy-bark palings or shingles out of mountain ash, and he smiled a smile that did my heart good to see, and said he had. He had also got them out of various other kinds of trees.

We talked about soil and grass, and gold-digging, and many other things which came back to one like a revelation as we yarned.

He had been to the hospital several times. 'The doctors don't say they can cure me,' he said; 'they say they might be able to improve my sight and hearing, but it would take a long time – anyway, the treatment would improve my general health. They know what's the matter with my eyes,' and he explained it as well as he could. 'I wish I'd seen a good doctor when my eyes first began to get weak; but young chaps are always careless over things. It's harder to get cured of anything when you're done growing.'

He was always hopeful and cheerful. 'If the worst comes to the worst,' he said, 'there's things I can do where I come from. I might do a bit o' wool-sorting, for instance. I'm a pretty fair expert. Or else when they're weeding out I could help. I'd just have to sit down and they'd bring the sheep to me, and I'd feel the wool and tell them what it was – being blind improves the feeling, you know.'

He had a packet of portraits, but he couldn't make them out very well now. They were sort of blurred to him, but I described them, and he told me who they were. 'That's a girl o' mine,' he said, with reference to one – a jolly, good-looking bush girl. 'I got a letter from her yesterday. I managed to scribble something, but I'll get you, if you don't mind, to write something more I want to put in on another piece of paper, and address an envelope for me.'

Darkness fell quickly upon him now – or, rather, the 'sort of white blur' increased and closed in. But his hearing was better, he said, and he was glad of that and still cheerful. I thought it natural that his hearing should improve as he went blind.

One day he said that he did not think he would bother going to the hospital any more. He reckoned he'd get back to where he was known. He'd stayed down too long already, and the 'stuff' wouldn't stand it. He was expecting a letter that didn't come. I was away for a couple of days, and when I came back he had been shifted out of the room, and had a bed in an angle of the landing on top of the staircase, with people brushing against him and stumbling over his things all day on their way up and down. I felt indignant, thinking that – the house being full – the boss had taken advantage of the bushman's helplessness and good nature to put him there. But he said that he was quite comfortable. 'I can get a whiff of air here,' he said.

Going in next day I thought for a moment that I had dropped suddenly back into the past and into a bush dance, for there was a concertina going upstairs. He was sitting on the bed, with his legs crossed, and a new cheap concertina on his knee, and his eyes turned to the patch of ceiling as if it were a piece of music and he could read it. 'I'm trying to knock a few tunes into my head,' he said, with a brave smile, 'in case the worst comes to the worst.' He tried to be cheerful, but seemed worried and anxious. The letter hadn't come. I thought of the many blind musicians in Sydney, and I thought of the bushman's chance, standing at a corner swanking a cheap concertina, and I felt very sorry for him.

I went out with a vague idea of seeing someone about the matter, and getting something done for the bushman – of bringing a little influence to his assistance; but I suddenly remembered that my clothes were worn out, my hat in a shocking state, my boots burst, and that I owed for a week's board and lodging, and was likely to be thrown out at any moment myself; and so I was not in a position to go where there was influence.

When I went back to the restaurant there was a long, gaunt, sandy-complexioned bushman sitting by Jack's side. Jack introduced him as his brother, who had returned unexpectedly to his native district, and had followed him to Sydney. The brother was rather short with me at first, and seemed to regard the restaurant people – all of us, in fact

– in the light of spielers, who wouldn't hesitate to take advantage of Jack's blindness if he left him a moment; and he looked ready to knock down the first man who stumbled across Jack, or over his luggage – but that soon wore off. Jack was going to stay with Joe at the Coffee Palace for a few weeks, and then go up country, he told me. He was excited and happy. His brother's manner towards him was as if Jack had just lost his wife, or boy, or someone very dear to him. He would not allow him to do anything for himself, nor try to – not even lace up his boots. He seemed to think that he was thoroughly helpless, and when I saw him pack up Jack's things, and help him at the table, and fix his tie and collar with his great muscular hands, which trembled all the time with grief and gentleness, and make Jack sit down on the bed whilst he got a cab and carried the traps down to it, and take him downstairs as if he were made of thin glass, and settle the landlord – then I knew Jack was all right.

We had a drink together – Joe, Jack, the cabman and I. Joe was very careful to hand Jack the glass, and Jack made a joke about it for Joe's benefit. He swore he could see a glass yet, and Joe laughed, but looked extra troubled the next moment.

I felt their grips on my hand for five minutes after we parted.

A Visit to Scrubby Creek

Eward Dyson

THE MEN AT THE MINE WERE ANXIOUS to have me visit our magnificent property. The battery and water-wheel were erected, there were fifty tons of stone in the hopper, and we only needed water and the blessing of Providence to start crushing out big weekly dividends. I know now that there has never been a time within the memory of man when Scrubby Gully did not want water, and that Scrubby Gully is the one place on earth to which a discriminating man would betake himself if he wished to avoid all the blessings of Providence forever. But that is beside the matter.

I was carefully instructed by letter to take the train to Kanan, coach it to the Rabbit Trap, take horse from Whalan's to the Cross Roads, ask someone at Old Poley's on the hill to direct me to Sheep's Eye; from there strike west on foot, keeping Bugle Point on my right, and 'Chin Whiskers' would meet me at The Crossing. There was no accommodation at the mine for city visitors; but I was given to understand Mr Larry Jeans would be happy to accommodate me at his homestead over the spur.

Casual references to Mr Jeans in the correspondence gave me the impression that Jeans was an affluent gentleman of luxurious tastes and a hospitable disposition, and that a harmless eccentricity led him to follow agricultural and pastoral pursuits in the vicinity of Scrubby Gully instead of wasting his time in voluptuous ease in the city.

'Chin Whiskers' met me at The Crossing. 'Chin Whiskers' was a meditative giant who exhausted his mental and physical energies chewing tobacco, and who bore about his person interesting and obvious evidence of the length and severity of the local drought – he was in fact, the drought incarnate. The Crossing was a mere indication of a track across a yellow rock-strewn indentation between two hills, which indentation, 'Chin Whiskers' informed me, was 'The Creek'. That did not surprise me, because I knew that every second country township and district in Australia has a somewhat similar indentation which it always calls 'The Creek'. Sometimes 'The Creek' has moist places in it, sometimes it is quite damp for almost a dozen miles, but more often it is as hard and dry as a brick-kiln. When the indentation is really wet along its whole length it is invariably called 'The River'.

I found the mine: it was a simple horizontal hole bored in a hill. The battery was there, and the water-wheel. The water-wheel stood disconsolate beside the dust-strewn creek, and looked as much at home as a water-wheel might be expected to look in the centre of the sandy wastes of the Sahara. The working shareholders were unaffectedly glad to see me. They were sapless and drought-stricken, but they assured me, with great enthusiasm, that they lived in momentary expectation of a tremendous downfall. Leen had been mending the roof of his hut, he said, in readiness for the heavy rains which were due before morning. He examined the sky critically, and expressed a belief that I would be detained on Scrubby Gully a couple of weeks or so in consequence of the floods.

This spirit of unreasonable hopefulness and trust seemed

to be shared by Cody, and Ellis and MacMahon. I alone was dubious. The journey up had worn me out; the dry desolation all around and the flagrant unprofitableness of our spec. sickened me; but Jeans still remained – the prodigal Jeans, with his spacious homestead and profuse hospitality. I was heartily grateful for Jeans. We met in due course. As I talked with Leen, a man came wearily down the hill, towing a meagre horse, which in turn was towing a log. This man delivered his log, unslung his animal, and approached us, heroically lugging behind him the miserable apology for a horse – a morbid brute manifestly without a hope or ambition left in life, and conveying mysteriously to the observer a knowledge of its fixed and unshakable determination to lie down and die the moment its owner's attention was otherwise directed. But the proprietor seemed fully alive to the situation, and never allowed his thoughts to stray entirely from the horse, but was continually jerking its head up, and addressing towards it reproaches, expostulations, and curses – curses that had lost all their vigour and dignity. This man was Jeans, and if I had not seen his horse I would have said that Jeans was the most hopelessly heart-broken and utterly used-up animal breathing on the face of the earth. He was about forty, grey, hollow-cheeked, hollow-chested, bent, and apathetic with the dreadful apathy that comes of wasted effort, vain toil, and blasted hopes. Jeans had a face that had forgotten how to smile and never scowled – a face that took no exercise, but remained set in the one wooden expression of joyless, passionless indifference to whatever fate could offer henceforth and forever. My last hope exploded at the sight of him.

Mr Larry Jeans said I was welcome to camp in the spare room 'up to' his place, and added dully that 'proberly' his missus could scrape up grub enough for me 'fer a day'r two'. 'Proberly' did not sound very encouraging, but I had no option, and being dead-beat, accepted the hospitality offered, and followed Mr Jeans. Larry laboriously hauled his melancholy horse over a couple of low stony rises, and then we tackled the scrag end of the range, across which led a vague track that wound in and out amongst a forest of great rocks, and presented all the difficulties and dangers of mountaineering without its compensations. Jeans struggled on with dull patience, and in silence, saving when it was necessary to divert the old horse from his morbid thoughts, and when he briefly answered my questions. I gathered from him that the men at the mine had been expecting rain for four months.

'And what do you think of the chances?' I asked.

'Oh, me, I never expect nothin'. Sometimes things happen. I don't expect 'em, though.'

'Things happen – what, for instance?'

'Well, dry spells.'

I elicited that pleuro happened, and rabbits, and fires, and 'this here new-fangled fever'. But whatever happened Jeans never fluctuated; he had struck an average of misery, and was bogged in the moral slough. It seemed as if his sensibilities above a certain capacity had been worn out by over-work, and refused to feel more than a fixed degree of trouble, so that whatever might come on top of his present woes, be it fever, or fire, or death, the man remained in his normal condition of grim apathy and spiritless obedience to fate.

The 'homestead' stood upon the flat timbered country beyond the rise. It was just what Jeans's homestead might have been expected to be – a low structure of bark and slabs, with a chimney at one end, and a door in the middle between two canvas 'windows'. It stood in a small clearing; just beyond the house stood the skeleton of a shed, upon which, it being sundown, roosted a few gaunt fowls; a lank cow with one horn was deeply meditating by the front door. There were signs of bold raids upon the stubborn bush, pathetic ventures; and great butts lay about in evidence of much weary, unprofitable work. A dog-leg fence, starting at no particular point, straddled along in front of the house, and finished nowhere, a hundred yards off. Not a new fence either, but an old one, with much dry grass matted amongst the logs – that was the pathos of it. There had been a brave attempt at a garden, too; but the few fruit trees that stood had been stripped of the bark, and then hens had made dust-baths in all the beds. In this dust an army of children were wallowing – half-clad, bare-footed, dirt-encrusted children, but all hale and boisterous.

At the door we were met by Mrs Larry Jeans, and after introducing me as 'him from the city', the master laboured away, dragging his shuffling horse, and leaving me in the centre of a wondering circle of youngsters of all sorts and sizes, from two dusty mites not yet properly balanced on their crooked little legs to a shock-headed lubberly boy of thirteen, curiously embossed with large tan freckles, and a tall, gawky girl of the same age in preposterously short skirts, whom my presence afflicted with a most painful bashfulness. A peculiarity about Jeans's children that struck me was the fact that they seemed to run in sets; there was

CLASSIC AUSTRALIAN SHORT STORIES —

a pair even for the sticky baby deftly hooked under its
mother's left arm, judging by the petulant wailing to be
heard within.

The Jeans's homestead consisted of two compartments. I
looked about in vain for the 'spare room', and concluded
it must be either the capacious fire-place or the skeleton
shed on which the hens were roosting. The principal arti-
cle of kitchen furniture was a long plank table built into the
floor; between it and the wall was a bush-made form, also
a fixture. A few crazy three-legged stools, a safe manufac-
tured from a zinc-lined case, and an odd assortment of
crockery and tin cups, saucers and plates piled on slab
shelves in one corner, completed the list of 'fixings'.

Mrs Larry Jeans was a short, bony, homely woman, very
like her husband – strangely, pathetically, like in face and
demeanour; similarly bowed with labour, and with the
same air of hopelessness and of accepting the toils and pri-
vations of their miserable existence as an inevitable lot. She
was always working, and always had worked; her hands
were hard and contorted in evidence of it, and her cheek
was as brown and dry as husks from labouring in the sun.

We had tea and bread and boiled onions and corned beef
for tea that evening – a minimum of beef and a maximum
of onions. The last onion crop had been a comparative suc-
cess somewhere within half a day's journey to Scrubby
Gully. Tea served to introduce more children; they dangled
over the arms of the unhappy mother, hung to her skirts,
sprawled about her feet, squabbled in the corners, and
overran the house. Jeans helped to feed the brood in his
slow, patient way, and after tea he helped to pack away the
younger in little bundles – here, there, and everywhere –

where they slept peacefully, but in great apparent peril, whilst the bigger kids charged around the room and roared, and fought, and raised a very real pandemonium of their own. Every now and again Mrs Jeans would lift her tired head from her sewing or her insatiable twins, and say weakly, 'Now, you Jinny, behave.' Or Larry would remark dispassionately, 'Hi, you, Billy!' But otherwise the youngsters raged unchecked, their broken-spirited parents seeming to regard the noise and worry of them as the lightest trial in a world of struggling and trouble.

I asked Jeans how many children he thought he had. He didn't seem certain, but after due deliberation said there might be thirteen in all. He had probably lost count, for I am certain I tallied fifteen – seven sets and one odd one.

When the washing-up was done, and half of the family were bedded down, Larry dragged a tangle of old harness from the corner of the room, and sat for two hours painfully piecing it up with cord, and his wife sat opposite him, silent and blank of face, mending one set of rags with another – I perched upon a stool watching the pair, studying one face after the other, irritated by the length of the sheep-like immobility of both, thinking it would be a relief if Jeans would suddenly break out and do something desperate, something to show that he had not, in spite of appearances, got beyond the possibility of sanguinary revolt, but he worked on steadily, uncomplainingly, till the boy with the unique freckles came hurrying in with the intelligence that the old horse was 'havin' a fit'r somethin'.' Jeans did not swear. He said, 'Is he but?' and put aside his harness, and went out, like a man for whom life has no surprises.

The selector was over an hour struggling with his hypochondriac horse, while I exchanged fragments of conversation with Mrs Jeans, and went upon various mental excursions after that spare room. It appeared that the Jeanses had neighbours. There was another family settled seven miles up the gully, but Mrs Jeans informed me that the Dicksons, being quiet and sort of down-hearted, were not very good company, consequently she and Jeans rarely visited them. I was indulging in a mental prospect of the jubilation at a reunion of the down-hearted Dicksons and the gay and frivolous Jeanses when Larry returned from his struggle with the horse. He resumed his work upon the harness without any complaint. His remark that 'Them skewball horses is alwis onreasonable' was not spoken in a carping spirit; it was given as conveying valuable information to a stranger.

At eleven o'clock my host 's'posed that p'raps maybe' I was ready to turn in. I was, and we went forth together in quest of the spare room. The room in question proved to be a hastily-constructed lean-to on the far corner of the house, at the back. Inside, one wall was six feet high and the other was merely a tree-butt. My bunk was against the butt, and between the bunk and the roof were about eighteen inches of space. That bunk had not been run up for a fat man. After establishing me in the spare room Jeans turned to go.

'Best bar the door with a log, case o' the cow,' he said. 'If she comes bumpin' round in the night, don't mind. She walks in her sleep moonlit nights.'

It only needed this to convince me that I was usurping the customary domicile of the meditative cow. The room had been carefully furbished up and deeply carpeted with scrub ferns. But the cow was not to be denied.

Weary as I was, I got little sleep that night. I had fallen off comfortably about half an hour after turning in, when I was awakened again by some commotion in the house. Half a dozen of the children were blubbering, and I could hear the heavy tread of Larry, and the equally heavy tread of his wife, moving about the house. Presently both passed by the lean-to, and away in the direction of the range. For another half-hour or so there was silence, and then the one-horned cow came along and tried my door. Failing to open it, she tried the walls and the roof, but could not break her way in, so she camped under the lee of the structure, and lowed dismally at intervals till daybreak.

When I arose a scantily attired small boy generously provided me with a pint pannikin three-parts full of water. The water was for my morning bath, and the small boy was careful to warn me not to throw it away when I was through with it. This youngster told me that 'Dad an' Mum, and Jimmy' had been out all night hunting Steve. Steve, I gathered, was the one enterprising child in the household, and was in the habit of going alone upon voyages of exploration along the range, where, being a very little fellow, he usually lost himself, and provided his parents with a night's entertainment searching for him in the barren gorges and about the boulder-strewn spurs of the range. How it happened that he was not missed till nearly midnight on this occasion I cannot say, unless the father and mother were really as ignorant of the extent and character of their family as they appeared to be.

Mrs Jeans was the first to return, and she brought Steve

with her. The dear child had not been lost, after all. Incensed by some indignity that had been put upon him during the afternoon, he had 'run away from home', he said, and slept all night in a wombat's hole about two hundred yards from the house. There his mother found him, returning from her long, weary search. The incident did not appear to have affected her in any way; she looked as tired and heart-sick as on the previous evening, but not more so.

'You know we lost one little one there' – she extended her hand towards the low, rambling, repellent hills – 'an' found him dead a week after.'

Larry returned half an hour later, and his apathy under the circumstances was simply appalling.

We had fried onions and bread and tea for breakfast, and immediately after the meal was over Larry, who I imagined would be going to bed for a few hours, appeared in front of the house leading his deplorable horse. He was bound for the mine, he said. I put in that day exploring the tunnel, examining the immovable mill, hunting for specimens in the quartz-tip, and listening to Leen's cheerful weather prophecies; and Jeans and his soured quadruped dragged logs to the mine from a patch of timber about a mile off, which patch the men alluded to largely as The Gum Forest.

Returning to the homestead at sundown we found the children fighting in the dust and the one-horned cow meditating at the door as on the previous evening. I fancied I detected in the eye of the cow a look of pathetic reproach as I passed her. Tea that evening consisted mainly of roast onions. Jeans felt called upon to apologise because the boys had been unable to trap a rabbit for my benefit.

'Now'n agen, after a rainy spell, we're 'most afraid the

rabbits is a-goin' to eat us, an' then when we'd like a rabbit-stoo there ain't a rabbit to be found within twenty mile,' said the settler impassively. 'When there is rabbits, there ain't onions,' he added as a further contribution to the curiosities of natural history.

The second night at Scrubby Gully was painfully like the first: Mrs Jeans stitched, Mr Jeans laboured over his tangle of harness, and the brood rolled and tumbled about the room, raising much dust and creating a deafening noise, to which Larry and Mary his wife gave little heed. When a section of the family had been parcelled up and put to sleep, I was tempted to ask Jeans why he continued to live in that unhallowed, out-of-the-way corner, and to waste his energies upon a parched and blasted holding instead of settling somewhere within reach of a market and beyond the blight of tangible and visible despair that hung over Scrubby Gully and its vicinity.

'Dunno,' said Jeans, without interest, ''pears to me t' be pretty much as bad in other places. Evans is the same, so's Calder.'

I did not know either Evans or Calder, but I pitied them from the bottom of my heart. Jeans admitted that he had given up hope of getting the timber off his land, though he 'suspected' he might be able to handle it somehow 'when the boys grew up'. He further admitted that he didn't know 'as the land was good for anythin' much' when it was cleared but his pessimism was proof against all arguments, and I went sadly to bunk, leaving the man and his wife working with slow, animal perseverance, apparently unconscious of the fact that they had not slept a wink for over thirty hours.

The cow raided my room shortly after midnight. She managed to break down the door this time, but as her intentions were peaceful, and as it was preferable rather to have her for a room-mate than to be kept awake by her pathetic complaints, I made no attempt to evict her, and we both passed an easy night.

I was up early next morning, but Mr and Mrs Jeans were before me. They were standing together down by the aimless dog-leg fence, and the hypochondriacal horse lay between them. I walked across, suspecting further 'unreasonableness' on the part of the horse. The animal was dead.

'Old man, how'll you manage to haul those logs in now?' As Mrs Jeans said this I fancied I saw flicker in her face for a moment a look of spiritual agony, a hint of revolt that might manifest itself in tears and bitter complainings, but it passed in the instant. Jeans merely shook his head, and answered something indicative of the complete destruction of faith in 'them skewbald horses'.

We had bread and onions for breakfast.

When I last saw Jeans, as I was leaving Scrubby Gully that day, he was coming down the hill from the direction of the gum forest, struggling in the blinding heat, with a rope over his shoulder, towing a nine-foot sluice log.

We had a letter from Leen yesterday; he says the working shareholders are hurrying to get the sluice fixed over the wheel, and he (Leen) anticipates a heavy downfall of rain during the night.

The Oracle at the Races

A.B. ('Banjo') Paterson

NO TRAM EVER GOES TO RANDWICK RACES without him; he is always fat, hairy, and assertive; he is generally one of a party, and he takes the centre of the stage all the time – pays the fares, adjusts the change, chaffs the conductor, crushes the thin, apologetic stranger next to him into a pulp, and talks to the whole compartment freely, as if they had asked for his opinion.

He knows all the trainers and owners, apparently – rather, he takes care to give the impression that he does. He slowly and pompously hauls out his race book, and one of his satellites opens the ball by saying, in a deferential way, 'What do you like for the 'urdles, Charley?'

The Oracle looks at the book, and breathes heavily; no one else ventures to speak. 'Well,' he says, at last, 'of course there's only one in it – if he's wanted. But that's it – will they spin him? I don't think they will. They's only a lot o' cuddies any'ow.'

No one likes to expose his own ignorance by asking which horse he refers to as being able to win; and he goes on to deal out some more wisdom in a loud voice: 'Billy K— told me' (he probably hardly knows Billy K— by sight). 'Billy K— told me that that bay 'orse ran the best mile an' a half ever done on Randwick yesterday; but I don't give him a chance, for all that; that's the worst of these trainers. They don't know when their horses are well – half of 'em.'

Then a voice comes from behind him. It is the voice of the Thin Man, who is crushed out of sight by the bulk of the Oracle.

'I think,' says the Thin Man, 'that that horse of Flannery's ought to run well in the handicap.'

The Oracle can't stand this sort of thing at all. He gives a snort, and wheels his bulk half-round, and looks at the speaker. Then he turns back to the compartment full of people, and says, 'No 'ope.'

The Thin Man makes a last effort. 'Well, they backed him last night, anyhow.'

'Who backed 'im?' says the Oracle.

'In Tattersall's,' says the Thin Man.

'I'm sure,' says the Oracle; and the Thin Man collapses.

On arrival at the course, the Oracle is in great form. Attended by his string of satellites, he plods from stall to stall, staring at the horses. The horses' names are printed in big letters on the stalls but the Oracle doesn't let that stop his display of knowledge.

' 'Ere's Blue Fire,' he says, stopping at that animal's stall, and swinging his race book. 'Good old Blue Fire,' he goes on loudly as a little court of people collect, 'Jimmy B— ' (mentioning a popular jockey) 'told me he couldn't have lost on Saturday week if he had only been ridden different. I had a good stake on him, too, that day. Lor', the races that has been chucked away on this horse. They will not ride him right.'

Then a trainer, who is standing by, civilly interposes. 'This isn't Blue Fire,' he says. 'Blue Fire's out walking about. This is a two-year-old filly that's in the stall – '

'Well, I can see that, can't I?' says the Oracle, crushingly.

'You don't suppose I thought Blue Fire was a mare, did you?' and he moves off hurriedly, scenting danger.

'I don't know what you thought,' mutters the trainer to himself, as the Oracle retires. 'Seems to me doubtful whether you have the necessary apparatus for thinking – ' But the Oracle goes on his way with undiminished splendour.

'Now, look here, you chaps,' he says to his followers at last. 'You wait here. I want to go and see a few of the talent, and it don't do to have a crowd with you. There's Jimmy M— over there now' (pointing to a leading trainer). 'I'll get hold of him in a minute. He couldn't tell me anything with so many about. Just you wait here.'

Let us now behold the Oracle in search of information. He has at various times unofficially met several trainers – has ridden with them in trams, and has exchanged remarks with them about the weather; but somehow in the saddling paddock they don't seem anxious to give away the good things that their patrons have paid for the preparation of, and he is not by way of getting any tips. He crushes into a crowd that has gathered round the favourite's stall, and overhears one hard-faced racing man say to another,. 'What do you like?' and the other answers, 'Well, either this or Royal Scot. I think I'll put a bit on Royal Scot.' This is enough for the Oracle. He doesn't know either of the men from Adam, or either of the horses from the great original pachyderm, but the information will do to go on with. He rejoins his followers, and looks very mysterious. 'Well did you hear anything?' they say.

The Oracle talks low and confidentially.

'The crowd that have got the favourite tell me they're not afraid of anything but Royal Scot,' he says. 'I think we'd better put a bit on both.'

'What did the Royal Scot crowd say?' asks an admirer deferentially.

'Oh, they're going to try and win. I saw the stable commissioner, and he told me they were going to put a hundred on him. Of course, you needn't say I told you, 'cause I promised him I wouldn't tell.' And the satellites beam with admiration of the Oracle, and think what a privilege it is to go to the races with such a knowing man.

They contribute their mites to a general fund, some putting in a pound, others half a sovereign, and the Oracle takes it into the ring to invest, half on the favourite, and half on Royal Scot. He finds that the favourite is at two to one and Royal Scot at threes, eight to one being given against anything else. As he ploughs through the ring, a whisperer (one of those broken-down followers of the turf who get their living in various mysterious ways, but partly by giving 'tips' to backers) pulls his sleeve.

"What are you backing?' he says. 'Favourite and Royal Scot,' says the Oracle.

'Put a pound on Bendemeer,' says the tipster. 'It's a certainty. Meet me here if it comes off, and I'll tell you something for the next race. Don't miss it now. Get on quick!'

The Oracle is humble enough before the hanger-on of the turf, and as a bookmaker roars 'Ten to one Bendemeer', the Oracle suddenly fishes out a sovereign of his own – and he hasn't money to spare for all his knowingness – and puts it on Bendemeer. His friends' money he puts on the favourite and Royal Scot, as arranged. Then they go all round to watch the race.

The horses are at the post; a distant cluster of crowded

animals, with little dots of colour on their backs. Green, blue, yellow, purple, French grey, and old gold; they change about in a bewildering manner, and though the Oracle has a (cheap) pair of glasses, he can't make out where Bendemeer has got to. Royal Scot and the favourite he has lost interest in, and he secretly hopes that they will be left at the post or break their necks; but he does not confide his sentiments to his companions. They're off! The long line of colours across the track becomes a shapeless clump, and then draws out into a long string. 'What's that in the front?' yells someone by the rails. 'Oh, that thing of Hart's,' says someone else. But the Oracle hears them not; he is looking in the mass of colour for a purple cap and grey jacket, with black armbands. He cannot see it any-where, and the confused and confusing mass swings round the turn into the straight.

Then there is a babel of voices, and suddenly a shout of 'Bendemeer! Bendemeer!' and the Oracle, without knowing which is Bendemeer, takes up the cry feverishly. 'Bendemeer! Bendemeer!' he yells, waggling his glasses about, trying to see where the animal is.

'Where's Royal Scot, Charley? Where's Royal Scot?' screams one of his friends in agony. ' 'Ow's he doin'?

'No 'ope!' says the Oracle, with fiendish glee. 'Bendemeer! Bendemeer!'

The horses are at the Leger stand now, whips are out, and three horses seem to be nearly abreast – in fact, to the Oracle there seem to be a dozen nearly abreast. Then a big chestnut seems to stick his head in front of the others, and a small man at the Oracle's side emits a deafening series of yells right by the Oracle's ear:

'Go on, Jimmy! Rub it into him! Belt him! It's a cake-walk! A cake-walk!' and the big chestnut, in a dogged sort of way, seems to stick his body clear of his opponents, and passes the post a winner by a length. The Oracle doesn't know what has won, but fumbles with his book. The number on the saddlecloth catches his eye. No. 7; and he looks hurriedly down the page. No. 7 – Royal Scot. Second is no. 24 – Bendemeer. Favourite nowhere.

Hardly has he realised it, before his friends are cheering and clapping him on the back. "By George, Charley, it takes you to pick 'em.'

'Come and 'ave a wet?'

'You 'ad a quid in, didn't you, Charley?' The Oracle feels very sick at having missed the winner, but he dies game. 'Yes, rather; I had a quid on,' he says. 'And' (here he nerves himself to smile) 'I had a saver on the second, too.'

His comrades gasp with astonishment. 'D'ye'r hear that, eh? Charley backed first and second. That's pickin' 'em, if you like.' They have a wet, and pour fulsome adulation on the Oracle when he collects their money.

After the Oracle has collected the winnings for his friends he meets the Whisperer.

'It didn't win?' he says to the Whisperer in enquiring tones.

'Didn't win! says the Whisperer who has determined to brazen the matter out. 'How could he win? Did you see the way he was ridden? That horse was stiffened just after I seen you, and he never tried a yard. Did you see the way he was pulled and hauled about at the turn? It'd make a man sick. What was the stipendiary stewards doing, I wonder?'

This fills the Oracle with a new idea. All that he remembers of the race at the turn was a jumble of colours, a kaleidoscope of horses, and of riders hanging out on the horses' necks. But it wouldn't do for the Oracle to admit that he didn't see everything, and didn't know everything; so he plunges in boldly.

'O' course, I saw it,' he says. 'A blind man could see it. They ought to rub him out.'

'Course they ought,' says the Whisperer. 'But look here, put two quid on Telltale; you'll get it all back!'

The Oracle does put on 'two quid', and doesn't get it all back. Neither does he see any more of this race than he did of the last one; in fact, he cheers wildly when the wrong horse is coming in; but when the public begins to hoot, he hoots as loudly as anybody – louder if anything – and all the way home in the tram he lays down the law about stiff running, and wants to know what the stipendiaries are doing. If you go into any barber's shop, you can hear him at it, and he flourishes in suburban railway carriages; but he has a tremendous local reputation, having picked the first and second in the handicap, and it would be a bold man who would venture to question the Oracle's knowledge of racing and of all matters relating to it.

A Dreamer

Barbara Baynton

A SWIRL OF WET LEAVES from the night-hidden trees decorating the little station, beat against the closed doors of the carriages. The porter hurried along holding his blear-eyed lantern to the different windows, and calling the name of the township in language peculiar to porters. There was only one ticket to collect.

Passengers from far-up country towns have importance from their rarity. He turned his lantern full on this one, as he took her ticket. She looked at him too, and listened to the sound of his voice, as he spoke to the guard. Once she had known every hand at the station. The porter knew everyone in the district. This traveller was a stranger to him.

If her letter had been received, someone would have been waiting with a buggy. She passed through the station. She saw nothing but an ownerless dog, huddled, wet and shivering, in a corner. More for sound she turned to look up the straggling street of the township. Among the she-oaks, bordering the river she knew so well, the wind made ghostly music, unheeded by the sleeping town. There was no other sound, and she turned to the dog with a feeling of kinship. But perhaps the porter had a message! She went back to the platform. He was locking the office door, but paused as though expecting her to speak.

'Wet night!' he said at length, breaking the silence.

Her question resolved itself into a request for the time, though this she already knew. She hastily left him.

She drew her cloak tightly round her. The wind made her umbrella useless for shelter. Wind and rain and darkness lay before her on the walk of three bush miles to her mother's home. Still it was the home of her girlhood, and she knew every inch of the way.

As she passed along the sleeping street, she saw no sign of life till near the end. A light burned in a small shop, and the sound of swift tapping came to her. They work late tonight, she thought, and, remembering their gruesome task, hesitated, half-minded to ask these night workers, for whom they laboured. Was it someone she had known? The long dark walk – she could not – and hastened to lose the sound.

The zigzag course of the railway brought the train again near to her, and this wayfarer stood and watched it tunnelling in the teeth of the wind. Whoof! whoof! its steaming breath hissed at her. She saw the rain spitting viciously at its red mouth. Its speed, as it passed, made her realise the tedious difficulties of her journey, and she quickened her pace. There was the silent tenseness that precedes a storm. From the branch of a tree overhead she heard a watchful mother-bird's warning call, and the twitter of the disturbed nestlings. The tender care of this bird-mother awoke memories of her childhood. What mattered the lonely darkness, when it led to Mother. Her forebodings fled, and she faced the old track unheedingly, and ever and ever she smiled, as she foretasted their meeting.

'Daughter!'

'Mother!'

She could feel loving arms around her, and a mother's sacred kisses. She thrilled, and in her impatience ran, but the wind was angry and took her breath. Then the child near her heart stirred for the first time. The instincts of motherhood awakened in her. Her elated body quivered, she fell on her knees, lifted her hands, and turned her face to God. A vivid flash of lightning flamed above her head. It dulled her rapture. The lightning was very near.

She went on, then paused. Was she on the right track? Back, near the bird's nest, were two roads. One led to home, the other was the old bullock-dray road, that the railway had almost usurped. When she should have been careful in her choice, she had been absorbed. It was a long way back to the cross roads, and she dug in her mind for landmarks. Foremost she recalled the 'Bendy Tree,' then the 'Sisters,' whose entwined arms talked, when the wind was from the south. The apple trees on the creek – split flat, where the cows and calves were always to be found. The wrong track, being nearer the river, had clumps of she-oaks and groups of pines in places. An angled line of lightning illuminated everything, but the violence of the thunder distracted her.

She stood in uncertainty, near-sighted, with all the horror of the unknown that this infirmity could bring. Irresolute, she waited for another flash. It served to convince her she was wrong. Through the bush she turned.

The sky seemed to crack with the lightning; the thunder's suddenness shook her. Among some tall pines she stood awed, while the storm raged.

Then again that indefinite fear struck at her. Restlessly she pushed on till she stumbled, and, with hands out-stretched, met some object that moved beneath them as she fell. The lightning showed a group of terrified cattle. Tripping and falling, she ran, she knew not where, but keeping her eyes turned towards the cattle. Aimlessly she pushed on, and unconsciously retraced her steps.

She struck the track she was on when her first doubt came. If this were the right way, the wheel ruts would show. She groped, but the rain had levelled them. There was nothing to guide her. Suddenly she remembered that the little clump of pines, where the cattle were, lay between the two roads. She had gathered mistletoe berries there in the old days.

She believed, she hoped, she prayed, that she was right. If so, a little further on, she would come to the 'Bendy Tree.' There long ago a runaway horse had crushed its drunken rider against the bent, distorted trunk. She could recall how in her young years that tree had ever had a weird fascination for her.

She saw its crooked body in the lightning's glare. She was on the right track, yet dreaded to go on. Her childhood's fear came back. In a transient flash she thought she saw a horseman galloping furiously towards her. She placed both her hands protectively over her heart, and waited. In the dark interval, above the shriek of the wind, she thought she heard a cry, then crash came the thunder, drowning her call of warning. In the next flash she saw nothing but the tree. 'Oh, God, protect me!' she prayed, and diverging with a shrinking heart passed on.

The road dipped to the creek. Louder and louder came the roar of its flooded waters. Even Little Dog-trap Gully was proudly foaming itself hoarse. It emptied below where she must cross. But there were others, that swelled it above.

CLASSIC AUSTRALIAN SHORT STORIES —

The noise of the rushing creek was borne to her by the wind, still fierce, though the rain had lessened. Perhaps there would be someone to meet her at the bank! Last time she had come, the night had been fine, and though she had been met at the station by a neighbour's son, Mother had come to the creek with a lantern and waited for her. She looked eagerly, but there was no light.

The creek was a banker, but the track led to a plank, which lashed to the willows on either bank, was usually above flood-level. A churning sound showed that the water was over the plank, and she must wade along it. She turned to the sullen sky. There was no gleam of light, save in her resolute white face.

Her mouth grew tender, as she thought of the husband she loved, and of their child. She must dare! She thought of the grey-haired mother, who was waiting on the other side. This dwarfed every tie that had parted them. There was atonement in these dificulties and dangers.

Again her face turned heavenward! 'Bless, pardon, protect and guide, strengthen and comfort!' Her mother's prayer.

Malignantly the wind fought her, driving her back, or snapping the brittle stems from her skinned hands. The water was knee-deep now, and every step more hazardous.

She held with her teeth to a thin limb, while she unfastened her hat and gave it to the greedy wind. From the cloak, a greater danger, she could not in her haste free herself; her numbed fingers had lost their cunning.

Soon the water would be deeper, and the support from the branches less secure. Even if they did reach across, she could not hope for much support from their wind-driven fragile ends.

Still she would not go back. Though the roar of that rushing water was making her giddy, though the deafening wind fought her for every inch, she would not turn back.

Long ago she should have come to her old mother, and her heart gave a bound of savage rapture in thus giving the sweat of her body for the sin of her soul.

Midway the current strengthened. Perhaps if she, deprived of the willows, were swept down, her clothes would keep her afloat. She took firm hold and drew a deep breath to call her child-cry 'Mother!'

The water was deeper and swifter, and from the sparsity of the branches she knew she was nearing the middle. The wind unopposed by the willows was more powerful. Strain as she would, she could reach only the tips of the opposite trees, not hold them.

Despair shook her. With one hand she gripped those that had served her so far, and cautiously drew as many as she could grasp with the other. The wind savagely snapped them, and they lashed her unprotected face. Round and round her bare neck they coiled their stripped fingers. Her mother had planted these willows, and she herself had watched them grow. How could they be so hostile to her!

The creek deepened with every moment she waited. But more dreadful than the giddying water was the distracting noise of the mighty wind, nurtured by the hollows.

The frail twigs of the opposite tree snapped again and again in her hands. She must release her hold of those behind her. If she could make two steps independently, the thick branches would then be her stay.

'Will you?' yelled the wind. A sudden gust caught her, and, hurling her backwards, swept her down the stream with her cloak for a sail.

She battled instinctively, and her first thought was of the letter-kiss she had left for the husband she loved. Was it to be his last?

She clutched a floating branch, and was swept down with it. Vainly she fought for either bank. She opened her lips to call. The wind made a funnel of her mouth and throat, and a wave of muddy water choked her cry. She struggled desperately, but after a few mouthfuls she ceased. The weird cry from the 'Bendy Tree' pierced and conquered the deep-throated wind. Then a sweet dream voice whispered 'Little woman!'

Soft, strong arms carried her on. Weakness aroused the melting idea that all had been a mistake, and she had been fighting with her friends. The wind even crooned a lullaby. Above the angry water her face rose untroubled.

A giant tree's fallen body said, 'Thus far!' and in vain the athletic furious water rushed and strove to throw her over the barrier. Driven back, it tried to take her with it. But a jagged arm of the tree snagged her cloak and held her.

Bruised and half conscious she was left to her deliverer, and the back-broken water crept tamed under its old foe. The hammer of hope awoke her heart. Along the friendly back of the tree she crawled, and among its bared roots rested. But it was only to get her breath, for this was Mother's side.

She breasted the rise. Then every horror was of the past and forgotten, for there in the hollow was home.

And there was the light shining its welcome to her.

She quickened her pace, but did not run – motherhood is instinct in woman. The rain had come again, and the wind buffeted her. To breathe was a battle, yet she went on swiftly, for at the sight of the light her nameless fear had left her.

She would tell her mother how she had heard her call in the night, and Mother would smile her grave smile and stroke her wet hair, call her 'Little woman! My little woman!' and tell her she had been dreaming, just dreaming. Ah, but Mother herself was a dreamer!

The gate was swollen with rain and difficult to open. It has been opened by Mother last time. But plainly her letter had not reached home. Perhaps the bad weather had delayed the mail boy.

There was light. She was not daunted when the bark of the old dog brought no one to the door. It might not be heard inside, for there was such a torrent of water falling somewhere close. Mechanically her mind located it. The tank near the house, fed by the spout, was running over, cutting channels through the flowerbeds, and flooding the paths. Why had not Mother diverted the spout to the other tank!

Something indefinite held her. Her mind went back to the many times long ago when she had kept alive the light while Mother fixed the spout to save the water that the dry summer months made precious. It was not like Mother, for such carelessness meant carrying from the creek.

Suddenly she grew cold and her heart trembled. After she had seen Mother, she would come out and fix it, but just now she could not wait.

She tapped gently, and called, 'Mother!'

While she waited she tried to make friends with the dog. Her heart smote her, in that there had been so long an interval since she saw her old home, that the dog had forgotten her voice.

Her teeth chattered as she again tapped softly. The sudden light dazzled her when a stranger opened the door for her. Steadying herself by the wall, with wild eyes she looked around. Another strange woman stood by the fire, and a child slept on the couch. The child's mother raised it, and the other led the now panting creature to the child's bed. Not a word was spoken, and the movements of these women were like those who fear to wake a sleeper.

Something warm was held to her lips, for through it all she was conscious of everything, even the numbing horror in her eyes met answering awe in theirs.

In the light the dog knew her and gave her welcome. But she had none for him now.

When she rose one of the women lighted a candle. She noticed how, if the blazing wood cracked, the women started nervously, how the disturbed child pointed to her bruised face, and whispered softly to its mother, how she who lighted the candle did not strike the match but held it to the fire, and how the light bearer lead the way noiselessly.

She reached her mother's room. Aloft the woman held the candle and turned away her head.

The daughter parted the curtains, and the light fell on the face of the sleeper who would dream no dreams that night.

That There Dog o' Mine

Henry Lawson

MACQUARIE THE SHEARER had met with an accident. To tell the truth, he had been in a drunken row at a wayside shanty, from which he had escaped with three fractured ribs, a cracked head, and various minor abrasions. His dog, Tally, had been a sober but savage participator in the drunken row, and had escaped with a broken leg. Macquarie afterwards shouldered his swag and staggered and struggled along the track ten miles to the Union-Town Hospital. Lord knows how he did it. He didn't exactly know himself. Tally limped behind all the way, on three legs.

The doctors examined the man's injuries and were surprised at his endurance. Even doctors are surprised sometimes – though they don't always show it. Of course they would take him in, but they objected to Tally. Dogs were not allowed on the premises.

'You will have to turn that dog out,' they said to the shearer, as he sat on the edge of a bed.

Macquarie said nothing.

'We cannot allow dogs about the place, my man,' said the doctor in a louder tone, thinking the man was deaf.

'Tie him up in the yard then.'

'No. He must go out. Dogs are not permitted on the grounds.'

Macquarie rose slowly to his feet, shut his agony behind his set teeth, painfully buttoned his shirt over his hairy chest, took up his waistcoat, and staggered to the corner where the swag lay.

'What are you going to do?' they asked.

'You ain't going to let my dog stop?'

'No. It's against the rules. There are no dogs allowed on the premises.'

He stooped and lifted his swag, but the pain was too great, and he leaned back against the wall.

'Come, come now! man alive!' exclaimed the doctor, impatiently, 'You must be mad. You know you are not in a fit state to go out. Let the wardsman help you undress.'

'No!' said Macquarie. 'No. If you won't take my dog in you don't take me. He's got a broken leg and wants fixing up just – just as much as – as I do. If I'm good enough to come in, he's good enough – and – and better.'

He paused awhile, breathing painfully, and then went on.

'That – that there old dog of mine has follered me faithful and true, these twelve long hard and hungry years. He's about – the only thing that ever cared whether I lived or fell and rotted on the cursed track.'

He rested again; then he continued; 'That – that there dog was pupped on the track,' he said with a sad sort of smile. 'I carried him for months in a billy can and afterwards on my swag when he was knocked up ... And the old slut – his mother – she'd foller along quite contented – sniff the billy now and again – just to see he was all right ... She follered me for God knows how many years. She follered me till she was blind – and for a year after. She follered my till she could crawl along through the dust no longer, and – and then I killed her, because I couldn't leave her behind alive!'

He rested again.

'And this here old dog,' he continued, touching Tally's upturned nose with his knotted finger, 'this here old dog has follered me for – for ten years; through floods and droughts, through fair times and – and hard – mostly hard; and kept me from going mad when I had no mate nor money on the lonely track; and watched over me for weeks when I was drunk – drugged and poisoned at the cursed shanties; and saved my life more'n once, and got kicks and curses very often for thanks; and forgave me for it all; and – and fought for me. He was the only living thing that stood up for me against that crawling push of curs when they set onter me at the shanty back yonder – and he left his mark on some of 'em too; and – and so did I.'

He took another spell.

Then he drew his breath, shut his teeth hard, shouldered his swag, stepped into the doorway, and faced round again.

The dog limped out of the corner and looked up anxiously.

'That there dog,' said Macquarie to the Hospital staff in general, 'is a better dog than I'm a man – or you too, it seems – and a better Christian. He's been a better mate to me than I ever was to any man – or any man to me. He's watched over me; kep' me from getting robbed many a time; fought for me; saved my life and took drunken kicks and curses for thanks – and forgave me. He's been a true, straight, honest, and faithful mate to me – and I ain't going to desert him now. I ain't going to kick him out in the road with a broken leg. I – Oh, my God! my back!'

He groaned and lurched forward, but they caught him, slipped off the swag, and laid him on a bed.

Half an hour later the shearer was comfortably fixed up. 'Where's my dog?' he asked, when he came to himself.

'Oh, the dog's all right,' said the nurse rather impatiently. 'Don't bother. The doctor's setting his leg out in the yard.'

The Parson and the Scone

Steele Rudd

IT WAS DINNER-TIME. And weren't we hungry! – particularly Joe! He was kept from school that day to fork up hay – work hard enough for a man – too hard for some men – but in many things Joe was more than a man's equal. Eating was one of them. We were all silent. Joe ate ravenously. The meat and pumpkin disappeared, and the pile of hot scones grew rapidly less. Joe regarded it with anxiety. He stole sly glances at Dad and at Dave and made a mental calculation. He fixed his eyes longingly on the one remaining scone, and ate faster and faster ... Still silence. Joe glanced again at Dad.

The dogs outside barked. Those inside, lying full-stretch beneath the table, instantly darted up and rushed out. One of them carried off little Bill – who was standing at the table with his legs spread out and a pint of tea in his hand – as far as the door on its back, and there scraped him off and spilled tea over him. Dad spoke. He said, 'Damn the dogs!' Then he rose and looked out the window. We all rose – all except Joe. Joe reached for the last scone.

A horseman dismounted at the slip-rails.

'Some stranger,' Dad muttered, turning to re-seat himself.

'Why, it's – it's the minister!' Sal cried, 'The minister that married Kate!'

Dad nearly fell over. 'Good God!' was all he said, and

stared hopelessly at Mother. The minister – for sure enough it was the Rev. Daniel Macpherson – was coming in. There was commotion. Dave finished his tea at a gulp, put on his hat, and left by the back-door. Dad would have followed, but hesitated, and so was lost. Mother was restless – 'on pins and needles'.

'And there ain't a bite to offer him,' she cried, dancing hysterically about the table. 'Not a bite; nor a plate, nor a knife, nor a fork to eat it with!' There was humour in Mother at times. It came from the father's side. He was a dentist.

Only Joe was unconcerned. He was employed on the last scone. He commenced it slowly. He wished it to last till night. His mouth opened and received it fondly. He buried his teeth in it and lingered lovingly over it. Mother' eyes happened to rest on him. Her face brightened. She flew at Joe and cried: 'Give me that scone! Put it back on the table this minute!"

Joe became concerned. He was about to protest. Mother seized him by the hair (which hadn't been cut since Dan went shearing) and hissed: 'Put – it – back – sir!' Joe put it back.

The minister came in. Dad said he was pleased to see him – poor Dad! – and enquired if he had had dinner. The parson had not, but said he didn't want any, and implored Mother not to put herself about on his account. He only required a cup of tea – nothing else whatever. Mother was delighted, and got the tea gladly. Still she was not satisfied. She would be hospitable. She said: "Why won't you try a scone with it, Mr Macpherson?' And the parson said he would – 'Just one'.

Mother passed the rescued scone along, and awkwardly apologised for the absence of plates. She explained that the Andersons were threshing their wheat, and had borrowed all our crockery and cutlery – everybody's, in fact, in the neighbourhood – for the use of the men. Such was the custom round our way. But the minister didn't mind. On the contrary, he commended everybody for fellowship and good-feeling, and felt sure that the district would be rewarded.

It took the Rev. Macpherson no time to polish off the scone. When the last of it was disappearing Mother became uneasy again. So did Dad. He stared through the window at the parson's sleepy-looking horse, fastened to the fence. Dad wished to heaven it would break away, or drop dead, or do anything to provide him with an excuse to run out. But it was a faithful steed. It stood there leaning on its forehead against a post. There was a brief silence.

Then the minister joked about his appetite – at which only Joe could afford to smile – and asked, 'May I trouble you for just another scone?'

Mother muttered something like 'Yes, of course' and went out to the kitchen just as if there had been some there. Dad was very uncomfortable. He patted the floor with the flat of his foot and wondered what would happen next. Nothing happened for a good while. The minister sipped and sipped his tea till none was left ...

Dad said: 'I'll see what's keeping her,' and rose – glad if ever man was glad – to get away. He found Mother seated on the ironbark table in the kitchen. They didn't speak. They looked at each other sympathisingly.

"Well?' Dad whispered at last, 'What are you going to do?'

Mother shook her head. She didn't know.

'Tell him straight there ain't any, an' be done with it,' was Dad's cheerful advice. Mother several times approached the door, but hesitated and returned again.

'What are you afraid of?' Dad would ask, 'He won't *eat y.*' Finally she went in.

Then Dad tiptoed to the door and listened. He was listening eagerly when a lump of earth – a piece of the cultivation paddock – fell dangerously near his feet. It broke and scattered round him, and rattled inside against the papered wall. Dad jumped round. A row of jackasses on a tree nearby laughed merrily. Dad looked up. They stopped. Another one laughed clearly from the edge of the tall corn. Dad turned his head. It was Dave. Dad joined him, and they watched the parson mount his horse and ride away.

Dad drew a deep and grateful breath. 'Thank God!' he said.

A Double Buggy at Lahey's Creek

Henry Lawson

I ~ Spuds and a Woman's Obstinacy

EVER SINCE WE WERE MARRIED it had been Mary's great ambition to have a buggy. The house or furniture didn't matter so much – out there in the Bush where we were – but, where there were no railways or coaches, and the roads were long and mostly hot and dusty, a buggy was the great thing. I had a few pounds when we were married, and was going to get one then; but new buggies went high, and another party got hold of a second-hand one that I'd had my eye on, so Mary thought it over and at last she said, 'Never mind the buggy, Joe; get a sewing-machine and I'll be satisfied. I'll want the machine more than the buggy, for a while. Wait till we're better off.'

After that, whenever I took a contract – to put up a fence or wool-shed, or sink a dam or something – Mary would say, 'You ought to knock a buggy out of this job, Joe;' but something always turned up – bad weather or sickness. Once I cut my foot with the adze and was laid up; and, another time, a dam I was making was washed away by a flood before I finished it. Then Mary would say, 'Ah well – never mind, Joe. Wait till we are better off.' But she felt it hard the time I built a wool-shed and didn't get paid for it, for we'd as good as settled about another second-hand buggy then.

I always had a fancy for carpentering, and was handy with tools. I made a spring-cart – body and wheels – in spare time, out of colonial hardwood, and got Little the blacksmith to do the ironwork; I painted the cart myself. It wasn't much lighter than one of the tip-trays I had, but it was a spring-cart, and Mary pretended to be satisfied with it: anyway, I didn't hear any more of the buggy for a while.

I sold that cart for fourteen pounds, to a Chinese gardener who wanted a strong cart to carry his vegetables round through the Bush. It was just before our youngster came; I told Mary that I wanted the money in case of extra expense – and she didn't fret much at losing the cart. But the fact was that I was going to make another try for a buggy, as a present for Mary when the child was born. I thought of getting the turnout, while she was laid up, keeping it dark from her till she was on her feet again, and then showing her the buggy standing in the shed. But she had a bad time, and I had to have the doctor regularly, and get a proper nurse, and a lot of things extra; so the buggy idea was knocked on the head. I was set on it, too; I'd thought of how when Mary was up and getting strong, I'd say one morning, 'Go round and have a look in the shed, Mary; I've got a few fowls for you,' or something like that – and follow her round to watch her eyes when she saw the buggy. I never told Mary about that – it wouldn't have done any good.

Later on I got some good timber – mostly scraps that were given to me – and made a light body for a spring-car. Galletly, the coach builder at Cudgegong, had got a dozen pairs of American hickory wheels up from Sydney, for light spring-carts, and he let me have a pair for cost price and carriage. I got him to iron the cart, and he put it through the paint-shop for nothing. He sent it out, too, at the tail of Tom Tarrant's big van – to increase the surprise. We were swell then for a while; I heard no more of a buggy until after we'd settled at Lahey's Creek for a couple of years.

I told you how I went into the carrying line, and took up a selection at Lahey's Creek – for a run for the horses and to grow a bit of feed – and shifted Mary and little Jim out there from Gulgong, with Mary's young scamp of a brother to keep them company while I was on the road. The first year I did well enough carrying, but I never cared for it – it was too slow; and, besides, I was always anxious when I was away from home. The game was right enough for a single man – or a married one whose wife had got the nagging habit (as many Bushwomen have – God help 'em), and who wanted peace and quietness sometimes. Besides, other small carriers started (seeing me getting on); Tom Tarrant, the coach builder at Cudgegong, had another heavy spring-van built, and put it on the road, and he took a lot of the light stuff.

The second year I made a rise – out of 'spuds', of all things in the world. It was Mary's idea. Down at the lower end of our selection – Mary called it 'the run' – was a small shallow watercourse called Snake's Creek, dry most of the year, except for a muddy waterhole or two; and, just above the junction, where it ran into Lahey's Creek, was a low piece of good black-soil flat, on our side – about three acres. The flat was fairly clear when I came to the selection – save for a few logs that had been washed up there in some big 'old man' flood, way back in blackfellows' times; and one day when I had a spell at home, I got the horses trace-chains and dragged the logs together – those that wouldn't split for fencing timber – and burnt them off. I had a notion to get the flat ploughed and make a lucerne-paddock of it. There was a good waterhole, under a clump of she-oak in the bend, and Mary used to take her stools and tubs and boiler down there in the spring-cart in hot weather, and wash the clothes under the shade of the trees – it was cooler, and saved carrying water to the house. And one evening after she'd done the washing she said to me; 'Look here, Joe; the farmers out here never seem to get a new idea: they don't seem to me ever to try and find out beforehand what the market is going to be like – they just go on farming the same old way, and putting in the same old crops year after year. They sow wheat, and, if it comes on anything like the thing, they reap and thresh it; if it doesn't they mow it for hay – and some of 'em don't have the brains to do that in time. Now I was looking at that bit of flat you cleared, and it struck me that it wouldn't be a half-bad idea to get a bag of seed potatoes, and have the land ploughed – old Corny George would do it cheap – and get them put in at once. Potatoes have been dear all round for the last couple of years.'

I told her she was talking nonsense, that the ground was no good for potatoes, and the whole district was too dry. 'Everybody I know has tried it, one time or another, and made nothing of it,' I said.

'All the more reason why you should try it, Joe,' said Mary. 'Just try one crop. It might rain for weeks, and then you'll be sorry you didn't take my advice.'

'But I tell you the ground is not potato ground,' I said.

'How do you know? You haven't sown any there yet,'

'But I've turned up the surface and looked at it. It's not rich enough, and too dry, I tell you. You need swampy, boggy ground for potatoes. Do you think I don't know land when I see it?'

'But you haven't tried to grow potatoes there yet, Joe. How do you know – '

I didn't listen any more. Mary was obstinate when she got an idea into her head. It was no use arguing with her. All the time I'd been talking she'd just knit her forehead and go on thinking straight ahead, on the track she'd started – just as if I wasn't there – and it used to make me mad. She'd keep driving at me till I took her advice or lost my temper – I did both at the same time, mostly.

I took my pipe and went out to smoke and cool down.

A couple of days after the potato breeze, I started with the team down to Cudgegong for a load of fencing-wire I had to bring out; and after I'd kissed Mary good-bye, she said, 'Look here, Joe, if you bring out a bag of seed potatoes, James and I will slice them, and old Corny George down the creek would bring his plough up in the dray, and plough the ground for very little. We could put the potatoes in ourselves if the ground were only ploughed.'

I thought she'd forgotten all about it. There was not time to argue – I'd be sure to lose my temper, and then I'd either have to waste an hour comforting Mary, or go off in a 'huff', as the women call it, and be miserable for the trip. So I said I'd see about it. She gave me another hug and a kiss. 'Don't forget, Joe,' she said as I started. 'Think it over on the road.' I reckon she had the best of it that time.

About five miles along, just as I turned into the main road, I heard someone galloping after me, and I saw young

James on his hack. I got a start, for I thought that some-
thing was wrong at home. I remembered the first day I left
Mary on the creek, for the first five or six miles I was half
a dozen times on the point of turning back – only I thought
she'd laugh at me.

'What is it, James?' I shouted, before he came up – but I
saw he was grinning.

'Mary says to tell you not to forget to bring a hoe out with
you.'

'You clear off home!' I said, 'or I'll lay the whip about
your young hide; and don't come riding after me again as
if the run was on fire.'

'Well, you needn't get shirty with me!' he said. 'I don't
want to have anything to do with a hoe.' And he rode off.

I *did* get to thinking about those potatoes, though I had-
n't meant to. I knew of an independent man in that district
who'd made his money out of a crop of potatoes; but that
was away back in the roaring fifties – fifty-four – when
spuds went up to twenty-eight shillings a hundredweight
(in Sydney), on account of the gold rush. We might get
good rain now, and, anyway, it wouldn't cost much to put
potatoes in. If they came on well, it would be a few pounds
in my pocket; if the crop was a failure, I'd have a better
show with Mary next time she was struck by an idea out-
side housekeeping, and have something to grumble about
when I felt grumpy.

I got a couple of bags of potatoes – we could use those
that were left over; and I got a small iron plough and har-
row that Little the blacksmith had lying in his yard and let
me have cheap – only a pound more than I told Mary I
gave for them. When I took advice I generally made the

mistake of taking more than was offered, or adding notions of my own. It was vanity, I suppose. If the crop came on well I could claim the plough-and-harrow part of the idea anyway. (It didn't strike me that if the crop failed Mary would have the plough and harrow against me, for old Corny would plough the ground for ten or fifteen shillings). Anyway, I'd want a plough and harrow later on, and I might as well get it now; it would give James something to do.

I came out by the western road, by Guntawang, and up the creek home; and the first thing I saw was old Corny George ploughing the flat. And Mary was down on the bank superintending. She'd got James with the trace-chains and the spare horses, and had made him clear off every stick and bush where another furrow might be squeezed in. Old Corny looked pretty grumpy on it – he'd broken all his ploughshares but one, in the roots; and James didn't look much brighter. Mary had an old felt hat and a new pair of 'lastic-side boots of mine on, and the boots were covered with clay, for she'd been down hustling James to get a rotten old stump out of the way by the time old Corny came round with his next furrow.

'I thought I'd make the boots easy for you, Joe,' said Mary.

'It's all right, Mary,' I said, 'I'm not going to growl.' Those boots were a bone of contention between us; but she generally got them off before I got home.

Her face fell when she saw the plough and harrow in the wagon, but I said that would be all right – we'd want a plough anyway.

'I thought you wanted old Corny to plough the ground,' she said.

'I never said so.'

'But when I sent Jim after you about the hoe to put the spuds in, you didn't say you wouldn't bring it,' she said.

I had a few days at home, and entered into the spirit of the thing. When Corny was done, James and I cross-ploughed the land, and got a stump or two, a big log, and some scrub out of the way at the upper end and added nearly an acre, and ploughed that. James was all right at most Bushwork; he'd bullock so long as the novelty lasted; he liked ploughing or fencing, or any graft he could make a show at. He didn't care for grubbing out stumps, or splitting posts and rails. We sliced the potatoes of an evening – and there was trouble between Mary and James over cutting through the 'eyes'. There was no time for the hoe – and besides it wasn't a novelty to James – so I just ran furrows and they dropped the spuds in behind me, and I turned another furrow over them, and ran the harrow over the ground. I think I hilled those spuds, too, with furrows – or a crop of Indian corn I put in later on.

It rained heavens-hard for over a week: we had regular showers all through, and it was the finest crop of potatoes ever seen in the district. I believe at first Mary used to slip down at daybreak to see if the potatoes were up; and she'd write to me about them, on the road. I forget how many bags I got but the few who had grown potatoes in the district sent them to Sydney, and spuds went up to twelve and fifteen shillings a hundredweight in that district. I made a few quid out of mine – and saved carriage too, for I could take them out on the wagon. Then Mary began to hear (through James) of a buggy that someone had for sale cheap, or a dogcart that somebody else wanted to get rid of – and let me know about it in an offhand way.

II ~ Joe Wilson's Luck

There was good grass on the selection all year. I'd picked up a small lot – about twenty head – of half-starved steers for next to nothing, and turned them on the run; they came on wonderfully, and my brother-in-law (Mary's sister's husband), who was running a butchery at Gulgong gave me a good price for them. His carts ran out twenty or thirty miles, to little bits of gold rushes that were going on th' Home Rule, Happy Valley, Guntwang, Tallawang, and Cooyal, and those places round there, and he was doing well.

Mary had heard of a light American wagonette, when the steers went – a tray-body arrangement, and she thought she'd do with that. 'It would be better than a buggy, Joe,' she said. 'There'd be more room for the children, and, besides, I could take butter and eggs to Gulgong, or Cobborah when we get a few more cows.' Then James heard of a small flock of sheep that a selector – who was about starved off his selection out Talbragar way – wanted to get rid of. James reckoned he could get them for less than half a crown a head. We'd had a heavy shower of rain, that came over the ranges and didn't seem to go beyond our boundaries. Mary said, 'It's a pity to see all that grass going to waste, Joe. Better get those sheep and try your luck with them. Leave some money with me, and I'll send James over for them. Never mind about the buggy – we'll get that when we're on our feet.'

So James rode across to Talbragar and drove a hard bargain with that unfortunate selector, and brought the sheep home. There were about two hundred, wethers and ewes, and they were young and looked a good breed too, but so poor they could scarcely travel; they soon picked up though. The drought was blazing all round and outback, and I think my corner of the ridges was the only place where there was any grass to speak of. We had another shower or two, and the grass held out. Chaps began to talk of 'Joe Wilson's luck'.

I would have liked to shear those sheep; but I hadn't time to get a shed or anything ready – along towards Christmas there was a bit of a boom in the carrying line. Wethers in wool were going as high as thirteen to fifteen shillings at the Homebush yards at Sydney, so I arranged to truck the sheep down from the river by rail, with another small lot that was going, and I started James off with them. He took the west road, and down Guntawang way a big farmer who saw James with the sheep (and who was speculating, or adding to his stock, or took a fancy to the wool) offered James as much for them as he'd reckoned I'd get in Sydney, after paying the carriage and the agents and the auctioneer. James put the sheep in a paddock and rode back to me. He was all there where riding was concerned. I told him to let the sheep go. James made a Greener shot-gun, and got his saddle one up, out of that job.

I took a couple more forty-acre blocks – one in James's name, to encourage him with the fencing. There was a good slice of land in an angle between the range and the creek, farther down, which everybody thought belonged to Wall, the squatter, but Mary got an idea, and went to the local land office, and found out that it was unoccupied Crown land, and so I took it up on pastoral lease, and got a few more sheep – I'd saved some of the best-looking ewes from the last lot.

One evening – I was going down next day for a load of fencing-wire for myself – Mary said: 'Joe! Do you know that the Matthews have got a new double buggy?'

The Matthews were a big family of cockatoos, along up the main road, and I didn't think much of them. The sons were all 'bad-eggs', though the old woman and girls were right enough.

'Well, what of that?' I said. 'They're up to their neck in debt, and camping like blackfellows in a big bark humpy. They do well to go flashing round in a double buggy.'

'But that isn't what I was going to say,' said Mary. 'They want to sell their old single buggy, James says. I'm sure you could get it for six or seven pounds; and you could have it done up.'

'I wish James to the devil!' I said. 'Can't he find anything better to do than ride round after cock-and-bull yarns about buggies?'

'Well,' said Mary, 'it was James who got the steers and sheep.'

Well, one word led to another, and we said things we didn't mean – but couldn't forget in a hurry. I remember I said something about Mary always dragging me back just when I was getting my head above water and struggling to make a home for her and the children; and that hurt her, and she spoke of the 'homes' she'd had since she was married. And that cut me deep.

It was about the worst quarrel we had. When she began to cry I got my hat and went out and walked up and down by the creek. I hated anything that looked like injustice – I was so sensitive about it that it made me unjust sometimes. I tried to think I was right, but I couldn't – it wouldn't have made me feel any better if I could have thought so. I got thinking of Mary's first year on the selection and the life she'd had since we were married.

When I went in she'd cried herself to sleep. I bent over and, 'Mary,' I whispered.

She seemed to wake up.

'Joe – Joe!' she said.

'What is it, Mary?' I said.

'I'm pretty sure that old Spot's calf isn't in the pen. Make James go at once!'

Old Spot's last calf was two years old now; so Mary was talking in her sleep, and dreaming she was back in her first year.

We both laughed when I told her about it afterwards; but I didn't feel like laughing just then.

Later on in the night she called out in her sleep: 'Joe – Joe! Put that buggy in the shed or the sun will blister the varnish!'

I wish I could say that that was the last time I ever spoke unkindly to Mary.

Next morning I got up early and fried the bacon and made the tea, and took Mary's breakfast into her – like I used to do, sometimes, when we were first married. She didn't say anything – just pulled my head down and kissed me.

When I was ready to start, Mary said: 'You'd better take the spring-cart in behind the dray, and get the tyres cut and set. They're ready to drop off, and James has been wedging them up till he's tired of it. The last time I was out with the children I had to knock one of them back with a stone; there'll be an accident yet.'

So I lashed the shafts of the cart under the tail of the wagon, and mean and ridiculous the cart looked, going along that way. It suggested a man stooping along, hand-cuffed, with his arms held out and down in front of him.

It was dull weather, and the scrubs looked extra dreary and endless – and I got thinking of old things. Everything was going all right with me, but that didn't keep me from brooding sometimes – trying to hatch out stones, like an old hen we had at home. I think, taking it all round, I used to be happier when I was mostly hard up – and more generous. When I had ten pounds I was more likely to listen to a chap who said, 'Lend me a pound note, Joe,' than when I had fifty; then I fought shy of careless chaps – and lost mates that I wanted afterwards – and got the name of being mean. When I got a good cheque I'd be miserable as a miser over the first ten pounds I spent; but when I got down to the last I'd buy things for the house. And now that I was getting on, I hated to spend a pound on anything. But then, the farther I got away from poverty the greater the fear I had of it –and besides, there was always before us all the thought of the terrible drought, with blazing runs as bare and dusty as the road, and dead stock rotting every yard, all along the barren creeks.

I had a long yarn with Mary's sister and her husband that night in Gulgong, and it brightened me up. I had a fancy that that sort of a brother-in-law made a better mate than a nearer one; Tom Tarrant had one, and he said it was sympathy. But while we were yarning, I couldn't help thinking of Mary, out there in the hut on the creek, with no one to talk to but the children, or James, who was sulky at home, or Black Mary or Black Jimmy (our black boy's father and mother), who weren't over-sentimental. Or, maybe, a selector's wife (the nearest was five miles away) who could talk only of two or three things – 'lambin'' and 'shearin'' and 'cookin' for the men', and what she said to her old man, and what he said to her – and her own ailments over and over again.

It's a wonder it didn't drive Mary mad! – I know I could never listen to that woman more than an hour. Mary's sister said: 'Now if Mary had a comfortable buggy, she could drive in with the children oftener. Then she wouldn't feel the loneliness so much.'

I said, 'Good night,' then and turned in. There was no getting away from that buggy. Whenever Mary's sister started hinting about a buggy, I reckoned it was a put-up job between them.

III ~ *The Ghost of Mary's Sacrifice*

When I got to Cudgegong I stopped at Galletly's coach shop to leave the cart. The Galletlys were good fellows: there were two brothers – one was a saddler and harness-maker. Big brown-bearded men – the biggest men in the district 'twas said.

Their old man had died lately and left them some money; they had men, and only worked in their shops when they felt inclined, or there was special work to do; they were both first-class tradesmen. I went into the painter's shop to have a look at a double-buggy that Galletly had built for a man who couldn't pay cash for it when it was finished – and Galletly wouldn't trust him.

There it stood, behind a calico screen that the coach-painters used to keep out the dust when they were varnishing. It was a first-class piece of work – pole, shafts, cushions, whip, lamps, and all complete. If you only wanted to drive one horse you could take out the pole and put in the shafts, and there you were. There was a tilt over the front seat; if you only wanted the buggy to carry two, you could fold down the back seat, and there you had a handsome, roomy, single buggy. It would go near fifty pounds.

While I was looking at it, Bill Galletly came in and slapped me on the back.

'Now there's a chance for you, Joe!' he said. 'I saw you rubbing your head round that buggy the last time you were in. You wouldn't get a better one in the colonies, and you won't see another like it in the district again in a hurry – for it doesn't pay to build 'em. Now you're a full-blown squatter, and it's time you took little Mary for a fly round in her own buggy now and then, instead of having her stuck out there in the scrub, or jolting the dust in a cart like some old Mother Flourbag.'

He called her 'little Mary' because the Galletly family had known her when she was a girl.

I rubbed my head and looked at the buggy again. It was a great temptation.

'Look here, Joe,' said Bill Galletly in a quieter tone. 'I'll tell you what I'll do. I'll let you have the buggy. You can take it out and send along a bit of a cheque when you feel you can manage it, and the rest later on – a year will do, or even two years. You've had a hard pull, and I'm not likely to be hard up in a hurry.'

They were good fellows the Galletlys, but they knew

their men. I happened to know that Bill Galletly wouldn't let the man he built the buggy for take it out of the shop without cash down, though he was a big-bug round there. But that didn't make it easier for me.

Just then Robert Galletly came into the shop. He was rather quieter than his brother, but the two were much alike.

'Look here, Bob,' said Bill; 'here's a chance for you to get rid of your harness. Joe Wilson's going to take that buggy off my hands.'

Bob Galletly put his foot up on a saw-stool, took one hand out of his pockets, rested his elbow on his knee and his chin on the palm of his hand, and bunched up his big beard with his fingers, as he always did when he was thinking. Presently he took his foot down, put his hand back in his pocket, and said to me, 'Well, Joe, I've got a double set of harness made for the man who ordered that damned buggy, and if you like I'll let you have it. I suppose when Bill there has squeezed all he can out of you I'll stand a show of getting something. He's a regular Shylock, he is.'

I pushed my hat forward and rubbed the back of my head and stared at the buggy.

'Come across to the Royal, Joe,' said Bob.

But I knew a beer would settle the business, so I said I'd get the wool up to the station first and think it over, and have a drink when I came back.

I thought it over on the way to the station, but it didn't seem good enough. I wanted to get some more sheep, and there was the new run to be fenced in, and the instalments on the selections. I wanted lots of things that I couldn't well do without. Then, again, the farther I got away from debt and hard-upedness the greater the horror I had of it. I had two horses that would do; but I'd have to get another later on, and altogether the buggy would run me nearer a hundred than fifty pounds. Supposing a dry season threw me back with that buggy on my hands. Besides, I wanted a spell. If I got the buggy it would only mean an extra turn of hard graft for me. No, I'd take Mary for a trip to Sydney, and she'd have to be satisfied with that.

I'd got it settled, and was just turning in through the big white gates to the goods-shed when young Black, the squatter, dashed past to the station in his big new wagonette, with his wife and a driver and a lot of portmanteaux and rugs and things. They were going to do the grand in Sydney over Christmas. Now it was young Black who was so shook after Mary when she was in service with the Blacks before the old man died, and if I hadn't come along – and if girls never cared for vagabonds – Mary would have been mistress of Haviland homestead, with servants to wait on her: and she was far better fitted for it than the one who was there. She would have been going to Sydney every holiday and putting up at the old Royal, with every comfort that a woman could ask for, and seeing a play every night. And I'd have been knocking around amongst the big stations outback, or maybe drinking myself to death in the shanties.

The Blacks didn't see me as I went by, ragged and dusty, and with an old, nearly black, cabbage-tree hat drawn over my eyes. I didn't care a damn for them, or anyone else, at most times, but I had moods when I felt things.

One of Black's big wool-teams was just coming away

from the shed, and the driver, a big, dark, rough fellow, with some foreign blood in him, didn't seem inclined to wheel his team an inch out of the middle of the road. I stopped my horses and waited. He looked at me and I looked at him – hard. Then he wheeled off, scowling, and swearing at his horses. I'd given him a hiding, six or seven years before, and he hadn't forgotten it. And I felt then as I wouldn't mind trying to give someone a hiding.

The goods clerks must have thought that Joe Wilson was pretty grumpy that day. I was thinking of Mary, out there in the lonely hut on a barren creek in the Bush – for it was little better – with no one to speak to except a haggard, worn-out Bushwoman or two, that came to see her on Sunday. I thought of the hardships she went through in the first year – that I haven't told you about yet; of the time she was ill, and I away, and no one to understand; of the time she was alone with James and Jim sick; and of the loneliness she fought through out there. I thought of Mary, outside in the blazing heat, with an old print dress and a felt hat, and a pair of 'lastic-siders of mine on, doing the work of a station manager as well as that of a housewife and mother. And her cheeks were getting thin, and the colour was going: I thought of the gaunt, brick-brown, saw-file voiced, hopeless and spiritless Bushwomen I knew – and some of them not much older than Mary.

When I went back into town, I had a drink with Bill Galletly at the Royal, and that settled the buggy; then Bob shouted, and I took the harness. Then I shouted, to wet the bargain. When I was going, Bob said, 'Send in that young scamp of a brother of Mary's with the horses; if the collars don't fit I'll fix up a pair of makeshifts, and alter the others.' I thought they both gripped my hand harder than usual, but that might have been the beer.

IV ~ The Buggy Comes Home

I 'whipped the cat' a bit, the first twenty miles or so, but then, I thought, what did it matter? What was the use of grinding to save money until we were too old to enjoy it. If we had to go down in the world again, we might as well fall out of a buggy as out of a dray – there'd be some talk about it, anyway, and perhaps a little sympathy. When Mary had the buggy she wouldn't be tied down so much to that wretched hole in the bush; and the Sydney trips needn't be off either. I could drive to Wallerawang on the main line, where Mary had some people, and leave the buggy and horses there, and take the train to Sydney, or go right on, by the old coach road, over the Blue Mountains; it would be a grand drive. I thought it best to tell Mary's sister at Gulgong about the buggy; I told her I'd keep it dark from Mary till the buggy came home. She entered into the spirit of the thing, and said she'd give the world to be able to go out with the buggy, if only to see Mary open her eyes when she saw it; but she couldn't go, on account of a new baby she had. I was rather glad she couldn't, for it would spoil the surprise a little, I thought. I wanted that all to myself.

I got home about sunset next day, and, after tea, when I'd finished telling Mary all the news, and a few lies as to why I didn't bring the cart back, and one or two other things, I sat with James, out on a log of the wood-heap, where we generally had our smokes and interviews, and told him all about the buggy. He whistled, then he said, 'But what do you want to make it such a Bushranging business for? Why can't you tell Mary now? It will cheer her up. She's been pretty miserable since you've been away this trip.'

'I want it to be a surprise,' I said.

'Well I've got nothing to say against a surprise, out in a hole like this; but it 'ud take a lot to surprise me. What am I to say to Mary about taking the two horses in? I'll only want one to bring the cart out, and she's sure to ask.'

'Tell her you're going to get yours shod.'

'But he had a set of slippers only the other day. She knows as much about horses as we do. I don't mind telling a lie as long as a chap has only to tell a straight lie and be done with it. But Mary asks so many questions.'

'Yes. And she'll want to know what I want with two bridles. But I'll fix her – you needn't worry.'

'And, James,' I said, 'get a chamois leather and sponge – we'll want 'em anyway – and you might give the buggy a wash down in the creek, coming home. It's sure to be covered with dust.'

'Oh! – orlright.'

'And if you can, time yourself to get here in the cool of the evening, or just about sunset.'

'What for?'

I'd thought it would be better to have the buggy there in the cool of the evening, when Mary would have time to get excited and get over it – better than in the blazing hot morning, when the sun rose as hot as at noon, and we'd have the long broiling day before us.

'What do you want me to come at sunset for?' asked James. 'Do you want me to camp out in the scrub and turn up like a blooming sundowner?'

'Oh well,' I said, 'get here at midnight if you like.'

We didn't say anything for a while – just sat and puffed at our pipes. Then I said, 'Well, what are you thinking about?'

'I'm thinking it's time you got a new hat, the sun seems to get through your old one too much,' and he got out of my reach and went to see about penning the calves. Before we turned in he said: 'Well, what am I to get out of the job, Joe?'

He had his eye on a double-barrel gun that Franca the gunsmith in Cudgegong had – one barrel shot, and the other rifle; so I said: 'How much does Franca want for that gun?'

'Five-ten; but I think he'd take my single barrel off it. Anyway, I can squeeze a couple of quid out of Phil Lambert for the single barrel.' (Phil was his bosom mate.)

'All right,' I said. 'Make the best bargain you can.'

He got his own breakfast and made an early start next morning, to get clear of any instructions or messages that Mary might have forgotten to give him overnight. He took his gun with him.

I'd always thought that a man was a fool who couldn't keep a secret from his wife – that there was something womanish about him. I found out. Those three days waiting for the buggy were about the longest I ever spent in my life. It made me scotty with everyone and everything; and poor Mary had to suffer for it. I put in the time patching up the harness and mending the stockyard and the roof, and, the third morning, I rode up the ridges to look for trees for fencing timber. I remember I hurried home that afternoon because I thought the buggy might get there before me.

At tea-time I got Mary on to the buggy business.

'What's the good of a single buggy to you, Mary?' I asked. 'There's only room for two, and what are you going to do with the children when we go out together?'

'We can put them on the floor at our feet, like other people do. I can always fold up a blanket or 'possum rug for them to sit on.'

But she didn't take half as much interest in buggy talk as she would have taken at any other time, when I didn't want her to. Women are aggravating that way. But the poor girl was tired and not very well, and both the children were cross. She did look knocked up.

'We'll give the buggy a rest, Joe,' she said. (I thought I heard it coming then.) 'It seems as far off as ever. I don't know why you want to harp on it today. Now, don't look so cross, Joe – I didn't mean to hurt you. We'll wait until we can get a double buggy, since you're set on it. There'll be plenty of time when we're better off.'

After tea, when the youngsters were in bed, and she'd washed up, we sat on the edge of the verandah floor, Mary sewing, and I smoking and watching the track up the creek.

'Why don't you talk, Joe?' asked Mary. 'You scarcely ever speak to me now; it's like drawing blood out of a stone to get a word from you. What makes you so cross, Joe?'

'Well, I've got nothing to say.'

'But you should find something. Think of me – it's very miserable for me. Have you anything on your mind? Is there any new trouble? Better tell me, no matter what it is, and not go worrying and brooding and making both our lives miserable. If you never tell one anything, how can you expect me to understand?'

I said there was nothing the matter.

'But there must be to make you so unbearable. Have you been drinking, Joe – or gambling?'

I asked her what she might accuse me of next.

'And another thing I want to speak to you about,' she went on. 'Now, don't knit up your forehead like that, Joe, and get impatient –'

'Well, what is it?'

'I wish you wouldn't swear in the hearing of the children. Now little Jim today, he was trying to fix his little go-cart, and it wouldn't run right, and – and–'

'Well, what did he say?'

'He – he (she seemed a little hysterical, trying not to laugh) – 'he said, "Damn it!"'

I had to laugh. Mary tried to keep serious but it was no use.

'Never mind, old woman,' I said, putting an arm around her, for her mouth was trembling, and she was crying more than laughing. 'It won't always be like this. Just wait till we're a bit better off.'

Just then a black boy we had (I must tell you about him some other time) came sidling along by the wall, as if he were afraid somebody was going to hit him – poor little devil! I never did.

'What is it, Harry?' said Mary.

'Buggy comin', I bin think it.'

'Where?'

He pointed up the creek.

'Sure it's a buggy?'

'Yes, missus.'

'How many horses?'

'One – two.'

We knew he could hear and see things long before we could. Mary went and perched on the wood-head, and shaded her eyes – though the sun had gone – and peered through between the eternal grey trunks of the stunted trees on the flat across the creek. Presently she jumped down and came running in.

'There's someone coming in a buggy, Joe!' she cried, excitedly. 'And both my white table-cloths are rough dry. Harry! Put two flat-irons down to the fire, quick, and put on some wood. It's lucky I kept those new sheets packed away. Get up out of that, Joe! What are you sitting grinning like that for? Go and get on another shirt. Hurry – Why, it's only James – by himself.'

She stared at me, and I sat there, grinning like a fool.

'Joe!' she said. 'Whose buggy is that?'

'Well, I suppose it's yours,' I said.

She caught her breath, and stared at the buggy, and then at me again. James drove down out of sight into the crossing, and came up close to the house.

'Oh, Joe! what have you done?' cried Mary. 'Why, it's a new double buggy.' Then she rushed at me and hugged my head. 'Why didn't you tell me, Joe? You poor boy – and I've been nagging at you all day.' And she hugged me again.

James got down and started taking the horses out – as if it was an everyday occurrence. I saw the double-barrel gun sticking out from under the seat. He'd stopped to wash the buggy, and I suppose that's what made him grumpy. Mary stood on the verandah, with her eyes twice as big as usual, and breathing hard – taking the buggy in.

James skimmed the harness off, and the horses shook themselves and went down to the dam for a drink. 'You'd better look under the seats,' growled James, as he took his gun out with great care.

Mary dived for the buggy. There was a dozen of lemonade and ginger-beer in a candle-box from Galletly – James said that Galletly's men had a gallon of beer, and they cheered him, James (I suppose he meant they cheered the buggy), as he drove off; there was a 'little bit of ham' from Pat Murphy, the storekeeper at Home Rule, that he'd 'cured himself' – it was the biggest I ever saw; there were three loaves of baker's bread, a cake, and a dozen yards of something 'to make up for the children' from Aunt Gertrude at Gulgong; there was a fresh-water cod, that long Dave Regan had caught the night before in the Macquarie River, and sent out packed in a salt box; there was a holland suit for the black boy, with red braid to trim it; and there was a jar of preserved ginger, and some lollies (sweets) ('for the lil' boy') and a rum-looking Chinese doll and a rattle ('for lil' girl') from Sun Tong Lee, our storekeeper at Gulgong – James was chummy with Sun Tong Lee, and got his powder and shot caps there on tick when he was short of money. And James said that the people would have loaded the buggy with 'rubbish' if he'd waited. They all seemed to be glad to see Joe Wilson getting on – and these things did me good.

We got the things inside, and I don't think either of us knew what we were saying or doing for the next half-hour.

Then James put his head in and said, in a very injured tone:

'What about my tea? I ain't had anything to speak of since I left Cudgegong. I want some grub.'

Then Mary pulled herself together.

'You'll have your tea directly,' she said. 'Pick up that harness at once, and hang it on the pegs in the skillion; and you, Joe, back that buggy under the end of the verandah, the dew will be on it presently – and we'll put wet bags up in front of it tomorrow, to keep the sun off. And James will have to go back to Cudgegong for the cart – we can't have that buggy to knock about in.'

'All right,' said James – 'anything! Only get me some grub.'

Mary fried the fish, in case it wouldn't keep till the morning, and rubbed over the table-cloths, now the irons were hot – James growling all the time – and got out some crockery she had packed away that had belonged to her mother, and set the table in a style that made James uncomfortable.

'I want some grub – not a blooming banquet!' he said. And he growled a lot because Mary wanted him to eat his fish without a knife, 'and that sort of tommy-rot'. When he'd finished he took his gun, and the black boy, and the dogs, and went out 'possum-shooting.

When we were alone Mary climbed into the buggy to try the seat, and made me get up alongside her. We hadn't had such a comfortable seat for years; but we soon got down, in case anyone came by, for we began to feel like a pair of fools up there.

Then we sat, side by side, on the edge of the verandah, and talked more than we'd done for years – and there was a good deal of 'Do you remember?' in it – and I think we got to understand each other better that night.

And at last Mary said, 'Do you know, Joe, why, I feel tonight just – just like I did the day we were married.'

And somehow I had that strange, shy sort of feeling too.

The Elopement of Mrs Peters

Edward Dyson

S IMON PETERS, irreverently called 'The Apostle', returned to the railway camp late on Sunday night, and found his tent topsy-turvy and his 'missus' gone. On the paling table, weighted with a piece of cheese, was a scrap of sugar-paper, on which was written in Fan's dog-leg hand: 'I'm sik. I'm goin' to cleer.'

Sim swore a muffled oath under his abundant moustache, and looked upon the unwonted disorder. The blue blanket and the rug had been stripped from their bunk; the spare, rough furniture of the big tent lay about in confusion; and amongst the grey ashes in the wide sod fireplace was a bunch of reddish hair. Peters fished this out, and examined it with as much astonishment as the phlegmatic, even-tempered navvy was capable of feeling. It was his wife's hair, and had evidently been hacked off in a hurry, regardless of effect. Piled on the bush stool against the wall were Mrs Peters's clothes. Nothing of hers that Peters could recall was missing; even the big quandong ear-rings, of which she was so proud, were thrown upon the floor. Her hat was on the bed, and her boots were under the table.

Still clutching the mop of hair in his hand, Sim backed solemnly and soberly on to a seat, and sat for a few minutes gravely weighing the evidence. Obviously Fanny had gone off clad only in a blue blanket or a 'possum rug. This was most extraordinary, even for Fanny, but there was some satisfaction in it, since it should not be difficult to trace a white woman so attired. Presently Peters arose and went forth to prosecute enquiries. On Saturday, before departing for Dunolly, he had asked Rolley's wife to keep an eye on the missus. As he approached the gaffer's tent, however, he heard a woman's voice raised in shrill vituperation, and recognised Mrs Rolley's strident contralto.

'My poor mother that's in heaven knew you, you —. She always said you was a —.'

And poor Rolley was inundated with a torrent of his own choice blasphemies. Simon Peters knew by experience that when Mrs Rolley dragged her sainted mother into little domestic differences, she was at least two days gone in drink, and quite incapable of recollecting anything beyond Rolley's shortcomings, so he turned away with a sigh, and carried his quest into the camp. Half an hour later he returned to his tent and resumed his thoughtful attitude on the stool. He had secured one piece of evidence that seemed to throw a good deal of light on the situation. Late on Saturday night someone had broken into Curly Hunter's tent and stolen therefrom a grey tweed suit, a black felt hat, and a pair of light blucher boots. Peters, putting this and that together slowly and with great mental effort, concluded that Curly Hunter and Fanny were about the same height. He recollected, too, the explanation his wife offered when he discovered her back to be seamed and lined with scars.

'Dad done it,' said Fanny. 'Por old dad, he was always lickin' me.'

'But,' gasped Peters, filled with a sudden itch to be at the throat of his deceased father-in-law, 'you don't mean to say the cowardly brute lashed you like that!'

'Didn't he?' replied she, laughing lightly. 'He used to rope me up to the cow bail an' hammer me with a horsewhip. Once when I set the grass on fire, an' burned the stable an' the dairy; another time when I broke Grasshopper's neck, ridin' him over Coleman's chock-an'-log fence; an' agen when I dressed up in Tom's clothes, took a swag, and got a job pickin'-up in M'Kinley's shed.'

Early on Monday morning Peters had an interview with Curly Hunter. Hunter was sympathetic, and readily sold Sim the stolen things at a modest valuation, promising at the same time to observe a friendly reticence in the matter; but, for all that, two hours later everybody in the camp knew that Mrs Peters had run off, and that 'The Apostle' was away hunting for her. The general opinion, freely and profanely expressed, was that Simon Peters was a superlative idiot. It was agreed that Peters would have exhibited commonsense by sitting still under the bereavement, and casually thanking Providence for the 'let off'. Since Mrs Peters started a couple of ramshackle waggons down the gradient, and nearly smashed up Ryan's gang, the camp had suddenly grown weary of her 'monkey tricks'.

Mrs Simon Peters was a woman of twenty-six, ten or twelve years younger than her husband, more comely, more decent, and more presentable in every way than the other wives of the camp. She did not get drunk in the bedroom end of Wingy Lees shanty on pay nights, did not use the picturesque idiom of the gangers in ordinary conversation, and in some respects had been a good mate to

Peters. But it must be admitted that the camp had further justification in doubting the complete sanity of Simon Peters's wife. She had an eerie expression that was quaintly accented by keen, twinkling, black eyes in combination with light red hair and rather pale brows; and she was possessed of a spirit of mischief that led her into the wildest extravagances. Her devilment was that of an ungovernable schoolboy, without his preposterous sense of humour. An uncontrollable yearning for excitement impelled her to the strangest actions. She had another peculiar characteristic, not unknown to the camp, in her apparent insensibility to physical pain. Peters had been astounded by the fact that a burn, a cut, a scald, or a blow provoked no complaining from his wife and scarcely any regard. This indifference extended to the sufferings of others. After the blasting accident in the North cutting, Fanny, of all the women in the camp, was the only one who had the nerve to approach the mangled body of poor M'Intyre, and she placidly worked over the shocking mass, still instinct with life, when the strongest men turned sick at the sight of it.

Sim made no effort to understand his wife, which was well, as he was only an average man, and she was past finding out. He concluded that her extraordinary conduct was just the natural unreasonableness and contrariness of women 'coming out strong', and made the best of the situation in which he found himself. Being an average man, Sim was a superior navvy; he only got drunk on big occasions, and, drunk or sober, treated his wife with indulgent fondness, and occasionally Fanny seemed fond of him in return; but then she had been very warmly attached to that father who used to bail her up in the cowshed and lash her with a horsewhip in the hope of converting her to sweet reasonableness.

On the Monday morning Peters first went up the road, seeking his wife, but no one at White's had seen a slim young fellow in a grey suit pass that way, so he tried down the road, with better success. Clark, at the Travellers' Rest had seen 'just sich a feller' as Sim described.

'They had a drink here Sunday, an' left, making for Moliagul, it seemed t' me,' said Clark.

'They?' queried Peters.

'Yes. There was two of 'em. The big feller shouted. A brown-faced chap, with a black moustache, an' a deep cut in his chin, here.'

Simon's grip made a dent in the pewter he held, and a grey hue crept over his cheeks and into his lips. Never before had he doubted his wife in this way; never through all her mad escapades had he had reason to question her fealty as a wife till now. Peters remembered the man distinctly; he had seen him about the camp, looking for work. The peculiar cleft chin would serve to identify him amongst ten thousand. Striding along the road the fugitives had taken, the navvy recollected hearing Fanny speaking enthusiastically of the tall, brown stranger as a fine man, and the grey in his cheek deepened to the colour of ashes, and his jaw hardened meaningly. His quest had suddenly assumed a terrible significance, and that fierce pallor and grim rigidity of the jaw never left him until its end.

Peters heard of them again in the afternoon, but got off the trail towards evening, and it was not till late on the following day that he picked up the scent. Then he talked with a farmer who had seen them.

'They slep' in an old hut up in my grass paddock las' night,' said the man, 'an' went up the road at about seven this mornin'.'

'Did both men sleep in the hut?' asked Peters.

'To be sure!'

Sim continued his journey, steadily, and with apparent unconcern, but cherishing an immovable determination to kill the brown-faced man the moment they met.

Early on the Wednesday morning Peters came up with the runaway. An old man watering a horse at a small creek told him, in answer to his enquiries: 'A tall chap, with a divided chin – name of Sandler, ain't it? He's here. I let him a bit of ringin'. That's his axe you hear up the paddock.'

Following the ring of the axe, Peters soon came upon his man; Sandler stopped working as he approached, and turned towards him, resting on the handle of his axe. Sim walked to within a couple of yards of the stranger, and threw off the light swag he carried.

'You infernal hound!' he said. 'Where is my wife?'

Sandler started up in extreme amazement. 'Keep off!' he cried. 'What the devil do I know about your wife?'

Peters rushed at him with the fury of a brute, and the two men exchanged heavy blows. Then they closed, and wrestled for a moment, but Simon's rage lent him a strength that was irresistible, and presently the other man was sent down with stunning force. As he attempted to rise, shaken and almost breathless, Peters, who had seized the axe, struck him once with the head of it, and Sandler fell back again and lay perfectly still, with a long gaping wound over his left eye, from which the blood poured through his hair upon the new chips and the yellow grass. When Peters looked up his wife stood facing him. She wore blucher boots, a pair of grey trousers, and a man's shirt, and carried an axe. She gazed composedly at the fallen man.

'What have you done, Sim?' she asked.

'You ran away with that man?' he pointed at Sandler.

She nodded her head.

'He did not know I was a woman,' she said.

Mitchell:
A Character Sketch

Henry Lawson

I T WAS A VERY MEAN STATION, and Mitchell thought he had better go himself and beard the overseer for tucker. His mates were for waiting till the overseer went out on the run, and then trying their luck with the cook; but the self-assertive and diplomatic Mitchell decided to go.

'Good day,' said Mitchell.

'Good day, ' said the manager.

'It's hot,' said Mitchell.

'I don't suppose,' said Mitchell, 'but I don't suppose you want any fencing done?'

'Naw.'

'Nor boundary riding?'

'Naw.'

'You ain't likely to want a man to knock around?'

'Naw.'

'I thought not. Things are pretty bad just now.'

'Na – yes – they are.'

'Ah, well; there's a lot to be said on the squatter's side as well as on the men's. I suppose I can get a bit of rations?'

'Ye-yes.' (Shortly) – 'Wot d'yer want?'

'Well, let's see; we want a bit of meat and flour – I think that's all. Got enough tea and sugar to carry us on.'

'All right. Cook! have you got any meat?'

'No!'

To Mitchell: 'Can you kill a sheep?'

'Rather!'

To the cook: 'Give this man a cloth and knife and steel, and let him go up to the yard and kill a sheep.' (To Mitchell): 'You can take a fore-quarter and get a bit of flour.'

Half an hour later Mitchell came back with the carcass wrapped in the cloth ...

'Here yer are: here's your sheep,' he said to the cook.

'That's all right; hang it in there. Did you take a fore-quar-ter?'

'No.'

'Well, why didn't you? The boss told you to.'

'I didn't want a forequarter. I don't like it. I took a hind-quarter.'

So he had.

The cook scratched his head; he seemed to have nothing to say. He thought about trying to think, perhaps, but gave it best. It was too hot and he was out of practice.

'Here, fill these up, will you?' said Mitchell. 'That's the tea-bag, and that's the sugar bag, and that's the flour bag.'

He had taken them from the front of his shirt.

'Don't be frightened to stretch 'em a little, old man. I've got two mates to feed.'

The cook took the flour bags mechanically and filled them well before he knew what he was doing. Mitchell talked all the time.

'Thank you,' said he – 'got a bit of baking-powder?'

'Ye – yes, here you are.'

'Thank you. Find it dull here, don't you?'

'Well, yes, pretty dull. There's a bit of cooked beef and

some bread and cake there, if you want it!'

'Thanks,' said Mitchell, sweeping the broken victuals into an old pillow-slip which he carried on his person for an emergency. 'I s'pose you find it dull round her.'

'Yes, pretty dull.'

'No one to talk to much?'

'No, not many.'

'Tongue gets rusty?'

'Ye – es sometimes.'

'Well, so long, and thank yer.'

'So long,' said the cook (he nearly added 'thank yer'.)

'Well, good day; I'll see you again.'

'Good day.'

Mitchell shouldered the spoils and left.

The cook scratched his head; he had a chat with the overseer afterwards, and they agreed that the traveller was a bit gone.

But Mitchell wasn't gone – not much; he was a Sydney jackaroo who had been round a bit – that was all.

Good-bye to the Old Home

Steele Rudd

K IT! KIT!' CALLED SARAH, standing at the back door with a saucer of milk. The kitten lay in the sun, blinked at her, and rolled over playfully, but didn't come.

'You're too well fed!' said Sarah, retreating into the kitchen. The kitten purred lazily to signify that that was so.

Everything was well fed at Shingle Hut now. A change had come. An air of prosperity was about the place. Broad-backed, upstanding draught-horses, fat and fresh, fed around contentedly; the paddock was stocked with sleek, well-bred cows and spring heifers, and four and five-year-old bullocks fit for a show; the reaper and binder in the shed was all our own, two ploughs were going, and – ye money-lenders! – the mortgage had been paid right off.

For six successive years our wheat crop had been a big success. No matter what Dad did he couldn't go wrong. Whenever he was compelled to sow late there was sure to be too much rain and early crops would run rank, or take the rust or the smut or something, while ours would come on nicely and be a success. Or else no rain at all would fall – somehow it would wait for Dad – and when Anderson's and Johnson's and all the wheat about was parched and perished, ours was a picture good to see. And Dad earned and enjoyed a reputation for long-headedness, for persistence and practical farming. People praised him and pointed to him as a pattern for the sons to follow – an example of what could be accomplished on the land by industry and a bit of brains.

Yet Dad wasn't satisfied. He talked of selling out, of taking up a thousand acres somewhere and expanding operations. But Mother opposed it; she thought we were doing well enough. Shingle Hut was good enough for her. She had worked hard and spent the best of her days in it, scraping and struggling, and all she asked now was to live the rest of her life there – to die peacefully and be buried near the house.

The rest of us agreed with Dad. We wanted a change. What the result might be we didn't consider – we only wished to shift. Ripping up the old house, rounding up the stock, camping under a dray a night or two on the way to the Promised Land, gave food for delightful speculation. We longed for it to come about.

'See anything of him?' Dad asked, as Dave rode into the yard and dismounted, after searching for a lost horse one day.

'No,' Dave said, and leant on the fence and nibbled the end of a straw. Dad leant on the other side and reflected.

A short distance off a new building was going up. Donald McIntyre, a broad-shouldered Scotsman with a passion for politics, and one McDonald, who didn't believe in governments at all, and confined his studies solely to the weather and pumpkins and profanity, were building a humpy with a shingling hammer. Donald McIntyre was on the rafters, arguing wildly and shaking the hammer menacingly at McDonald, who was on the ground.

Dad and Dave looked up.

'Come doon, ye — !' shouted McDonald, and McIntyre sprang from the rafters and pursued him round and round the humpy.

'A fight!' Dave said excitedly. 'Come on!' And he ran a few paces. But at the same moment Joe rushed to the scene out of breath.

'I fuf-fuf-found 'im, Dad!' he said excitedly.

'Where?' asked Dad eagerly.

'Bub-bub-bet y' can't gug-guess?"

'Where the devil is he, boy?'

('Look at McIntyre, after him across the ploughed ground!' – enthusiastically from Dave.)

'Down the w-w-well!'

'What?' Dad hissed, showing his teeth and punching the wind with his fist.

'Is he dead?' he added.

'Don't know that, Dad, but he s-s-smells!'

Dad groaned and walked inside and out again, then round the yard.

'Yoke up Gypsy and Tiger,' he said sternly to Dave, 'and bring them down.' Then he went off to the well by himself.

Dad peered into the well a moment and drew back and pulled a very ugly face.

Dave arrived with the horses. He went to the well to look down but ran away and spat.

Joe held the horses and chuckled.

Dave thought of the wind. It was blowing towards him. He made a wide circuit and approached the well on the other side. But when he leant forward to look down, the wind changed and he ran away again. Dad was determined. He advanced with a frown and a heavy rope, fastened one end of the latter to a sapling close by, and hurled the rest of it into the well. Then he, too, retreated.

'Now,' he said to Dave, 'go down and fasten it on 'im!'

'Me?' Dave said, backing farther away.

Joe chuckled again.

'Well, y' don't expect me to go down, do y'?' Dad snorted.

Dave grinned a sickly grin.

'It won't kill y', will it?' Then after a pause, 'Are y' going to' do it – or not?' There were shell and shrapnel in Dad's eye, and he looked ugly.

'W-w-wet y'r nose, Dave,' Joe said advisedly.

Dave hesitated, then reluctantly descended. He disappeared along the rope and was below some time. He came to the surface again, and gasped and staggered and threw himself on the grass and seemed ill. Change of air didn't do Dave much good.

Dad fastened the horses to the rope and told them to get up. The chains jerked and tightened. Gypsy and Tiger hung in their collars and strained, and tore the ground with their toes. Dad shouted and waved a big stick over them. Captain's form gradually rose till his head was in sight and his nose caught against the sleepers that lined the mouth of the well. Then he stopped.

'Gypsy ... Tiger!' Dad roared, and rattled the stick encouragingly on their hides. Gypsy and Tiger began to tire, and eased off.

'Look out!' Dave cried. 'Don't let them back!' Dad seized their heads and held on. But the dead horse gradually descended again, and was slowly dragging the live ones and Dad after it. Dad struck Gypsy on the nose with his fist to make her stand up. Gypsy reared and fell across the well and kicked desperately. Then Tiger tried to turn round in his chains and lost his footing and lay on his back, his tail hanging down the well. Dad was horror-stricken. He threw away his hat and ran in several directions in search of something. He found a sapling, lifted it, threw it down again, and ran back to the horses and held his hands above his head like a preacher.

Sal came to tell Dad he was wanted at the house, but he couldn't hear her.

'Curse it, can't y' do something?' he cried to Dave.

Then Gypsy made a big effort to rise and fell down the well and dragged Tiger's harness with her. Tiger jumped up and made off. Dad stared aghast.

'W-w-what did y' hit 'er for?' Joe asked reproachfully.

'Yah!' Dad bellowed, and sprang at Joe. Joe didn't look behind till he reached the house.

But Burton happened to come along with his bullock team, and rescued Gypsy and dragged Captain's corpse from the well. Then Dad went for a drink of water in the gully and sat down under a bush, and Sal came and spoke to him again, and when he was calm he went to the house.

The man from town who had offered us four hundred pounds for the selection was at the house waiting. They went inside.

'Well,' said the visitor, 'have you considered my offer?'

'Yes, ' Dad answered. 'I'll take it!' – and Shingle Hut was sold!

Mother clutched her knees with both hands and stared hard and silently at the fireplace till her eyes filled with tears. Sal ran out to Dave and Joe, and the three of them discussed the turn things had taken. Mother came out to them.

'It's sold?' Sal said.

'Yes,' replied Mother slowly, 'it's sold.' And again the tears came, and she sat on a sleeper beside the barn and, hiding her face in her apron, cried hard.

Sal hung her head and thought, but Dave went to Mother and sat beside her, and tried to explain the advantages of selling out and beginning afresh. The man left the house, walked to his horse, shook hands with Dad, and went away.

Then Dad paced up and down, up and down, and round about by himself a long, long time.

A cold, dull day. Heavy black clouds hung low and darkened the earth. At intervals a few drops of rain fell, a deluge threatened. No gentle winds blew, no birds whistled among the boughs. Dave was passing slowly out at the slip-rails with a dray-load of furniture and farm implements, Joe sitting astride Dad's old saddle-mare, in charge of the cows in the lane, Dad loading a second dray, Sal putting a horse in the spring-cart, the rest of us gathering knick-knacks and things about the place. We were leaving, leaving Shingle Hut, the old house we had known so long, the old home where Kate was married; where Bill and Tom and Barty were born, the home where merriment so often mocked misfortune and light hearts and hope softened the harshness of adversity.

And Anderson and Mrs Anderson came to see us off – kind-hearted people were the Andersons. And Judy Jubb came all the way from Prosperity Peak to kiss Sal.

'Goodbye, then and God bless y',' Mrs Anderson said, her large eyes swimming in tears. Mother held out her hand, but broke down and was helped into the spring-cart.

'An' I hope y' won't regret it,' Anderson said as he shook Dad's hand. Then with a last look around – a look of lingering affection – we bade farewell to Shingle Hut and started for our New Selection.

About the Authors

Barbara Baynton, 1857-1929

Much has been written about the lovable characters of the Australian outback, but Barbara Baynton observed the Australian male with a far from sentimental eye. Two of the three stories included here portray husbands who are callous to the point of heartlessness. Born in Scone, New South Wales, she met her first husband while working as a governess. He later deserted her, leaving her with three young children. Ten years later she married Dr Thomas Baynton. They lived in Sydney, where she began to contribute to the *Bulletin*. Her collection of stories, *Bush Studies*, was published in England in 1902.

Marcus Clarke, 1846-1881

Best known for his classic convict novel *For the Term of His Natural Life*, Marcus Clarke was born and educated in England. He emigrated to Australia in 1863, following family financial problems. For a while he worked on sheep stations, where he was able to observe outback life and people at firsthand. He soon began contributing to Melbourne newspapers of the day. A versatile writer, he built up a reputation for his poetry, prose and drama. The idea for his classic novel came after he was given an assignment by the Melbourne *Argus* to research convict history in Tasmania. For the *Term of His Natural Life* originally appeared as a serial in the *Australian Journal* in 1870, and was first published in book form in 1874.

Edward Dyson, 1865-1931

Dyson was an active contributor to the *Bulletin* at the same time that Henry Lawson and 'Banjo' Paterson were making their names in its pages. In fact, the *Bulletin* grouped the three together by dubbing them 'Paterdylaw and Son' because of the similarity of their names. Born in Ballarat, the son of a mining engineer, Dyson worked as a miner and factory hand before becoming a freelance writer. His knowledge of the bush and of mining communities is reflected in his short stories and poems. 'The Conquering Bush', included here, is a hauntingly evocative story which fully demonstrates his imaginative and poetic powers.

Henry Lawson, 1867-1922

Sometimes dubbed Australia's greatest short story writer, Lawson had a special gift for setting the scene and creating likeable, 'typically Australian' characters. He was also unusual in his ability to portray, with equal perception, both men and women. His short story collections include *While the Billy Boils* (1896) and *Joe Wilson and his Mates* (1901).

The son of a Norwegian immigrant, who anglicised his name from Larsen to Lawson, and a remarkable mother – writer and feminist Louisa Lawson – he was born at Grenfell, New South Wales. After moving to Sydney with his mother in 1883, he became involved in radical circles and began his long association with the *Bulletin*, to which he contributed both poems and stories. By this time he was completely deaf.

Despite the instant popularity of his writing, Lawson ended up a tragic figure. With his best work behind him, his last twenty years were spent in battling maintenance disputes, debt and alcoholism. When he died in 1922 he was given a state funeral.

A.B. ('Banjo') Paterson, 1864-1941

Paterson's passion for horses and horse racing is reflected in the two stories included here. Born near Orange, New South Wales, he spent his formative years on his family's station, where he gained a thorough knowledge of the people of the bush.

He trained as a solicitor, and began to contribute verse to the *Bulletin* under the pseudonym of 'The Banjo', the name of a racehorse at his family's property. 'The Man from Snowy River' and 'Clancy of the Overflow' had already gained widespread popularity before they were published in his first anthology *The Man from Snowy River and Other Verses*, in 1895. With the success of his verse, Paterson gave up law and embarked on a journalistic career, in the course of which he covered the Boer War and the Boxer Rebellion.

He published several other books of verse, two novels and a collection of stories. His ballad 'Waltzing Matilda' has gained the status of a national anthem.

Henry Handel Richardson (Ethel Florence Robertson), 1870-1946

Richardson's sensitive story, 'And Women Must Weep' gives a good idea of the social conventions of the times, but it is universal in its theme. Born in Melbourne, she was educated there before leaving for Germany where she studied music for three years. After deciding she was unsuited to a musical career she began writing under the pseudonym of Henry Handel Richardson. Her first two novels, *Maurice Guest*, published in 1908, and *The Getting of Wisdom* (1910), based on her Melbourne schooldays, were critically acclaimed. Richardson is best known for her trilogy *The Fortunes of Richard Mahoney*, which was published between 1917 and 1929. She spent most of her life in England where her husband, John Robertson, was professor of German literature at the University of London.

Steele Rudd (Arthur Hoey Davis), 1868-1935

Arthur Davis, the creator of two of Australia's best-loved fictional characters – Dad and Dave – was born into a large family who lived on a poor Queensland selection. After leaving school at the age of twelve, Davis took up various bush jobs before becoming a clerk. His humorous sketches about life on a poor selection first began to appear in the *Bulletin* in 1895, under the pseudonym Steele Rudd. Twenty-six of these were revised so that all the stories centred on the pioneering Rudd family, and were published in book form in *On Our Selection*, in 1899. Later collections included *Our New Selection* and *Back at Our Selection*. These endearing stories, with their laconic humour, provide a graphic account of the daily struggles of the 'cocky' farmer and his family.

– Classic –
AUSTRALIAN
VERSE

Compiled by Maggie Pinkney

Contents

BUSH SONGS & BALLADS   *405*

Early Voices

There is a Place in Distant Seas

There is a place in distant seas
Full of contrarieties:
There, beasts have mallards' bills and legs,
Have spurs like cocks, like hens lay eggs.
There parrots walk upon the ground,
And grass upon the trees is found:
On other trees, another wonder!
Leaves without upper sides or under.
There pears you'll scarce with hatchet cut;
Stones are outside the cherry put;
Swans are not white, but black as soot.
There neither leaf, nor root, nor fruit
Will any Christian palate suit,
Unless in desperate need you'd fill ye
With root of fern and stalk of lily.
There missiles to far distance sent
Come whizzing back from whence they went;
There quadrupeds go on two feet;
There birds, although they cannot fly,
In swiftness with your greyhound vie.
With equal wonder you may see
The foxes fly from tree to tree;
And what they value most, so wary,
These foxes in their pockets carry.
There the voracious ewe-sheep crams
Her paunch with flesh of tender lambs,
Instead of beef, and bread, and broth,
Men feast on many a roasted moth.

The north winds scorch, but when the breeze is
Full from the south, why then it freezes;
The sun when you to face him turn ye,
From right to left performs his journey.
Now of what place could such strange tales
Be told with truth save New South Wales?

Richard Whately, 1787-1863

The Convicts' Rum Song

Cut yer name across me backbone,
  Stretch me skin across a drum,
Iron me up on Pinchgut Island
  From to-day till Kingdom Come!

I will eat yer Norfolk dumpling
  Like a juicy Spanish plum,
Even dance the Newgate Hornpipe
  If ye'll only give me rum!

Anonymous

Botany Bay

Farewell to old England forever,
Farewell to my rum-culls as well,
Farewell to the well-known Old Bailey
Where I used to cut such a swell.

Chorus:
Singing tooral-i-ooral-i-addity,
Singing tooral-i-ooral-i-ay,
Singing tooral-i-ooral-i-addity,
We're all bound for Botany Bay.

There's the captain as is our commander,
The bosun and all the ship's crew,
The first and the second class passengers
Knows what we poor convicts goes through.

It ain't leaving old England we cares about,
T'ain't cause we misspells what we knows,
It's just that us light-fingered gentry
Hops around with a log on our toes.

It's seven long years I've been serving,
And seven long more have to stay,
For bashing a cop in our alley,
And stealing his truncheon away.

Oh, if I had the wings of a turtle-dove
I'd soar on my pinions so high,
Slap-bang to the arms of my Polly-love,
And on her sweet bosom I'd die.

Now all you young dookies and duchesses,
Take warning from what I do say,
Mind all is your own as you toucheses
Or you'll join us in Botany Bay.

Traditional

The Lass in the Female Factory

The Currency Lads may fill their glasses,
And drink the health of the Currency Lasses,
But the lass I adore, the lass for me,
Is the lass in the Female Factory.

O! Molly's her name, and her name is Molly,
Although she was tried by the name of Polly;
She was tried and sent for death at Newry,
But the judge was bribed and so were the jury.

She got 'death recorded' in Newry town
For stealing her mistress's watch and gown;
Her little boy Paddy can tell you the tale,
His father was turnkey at Newry jail.

The first time I saw the comely lass
Was at Parramatta, going to Mass:
Says I 'I'll marry you now in an hour.'
Says she: 'Well, go and fetch Father Power.'

But I got in trouble that very same night!
Being drunk in the street I got in a fight:
A constable seized me – I gave him a box –
And was put in the watch-house and then in
  the stocks.

O! It's very unaisy as I remember
To sit in the stocks in the month of November,
With the north winds so hot, and the hot sun
  right over.
O! sure and it's no place at all for a lover!

'It's worse than the treadmill,' says I, 'Mr Dunn,
To sit here all day in the heat of the sun.'
'Either that or a dollar,' says he, 'for your folly' –
But if I had a dollar I'd drink it with Molly.

But now I am out again, early and late
I sigh and I cry at the Factory gate.
'O Mrs Reordon, late Mrs Farson,
O! won't you let Molly out very soon?'

'Is it Molly McGuigan,' says she to me.
'Is it now?"' says I, for I know'd it was she.
'Is it her you mean that was put in the stocks
For beating her mistress, Mrs Cox?'

'O! yes and it is, madam, pray let me in.
I have brought her a half-pint of Cooper's best gin.
She likes it as well as she likes her own mother,
O! now let me in, madam, I am her brother.'

So the Currency Lads may fill their glasses,
And drink the health of the Currency Lasses,
But the lass I adore, the lass for me,
Is the lass in the Female Factory.

Anonymous

Jim Jones

O listen for a moment, and hear me tell my tale,
How o'er the sea from England I was compelled
   to sail.
The jury says, 'He's guilty,' and says the judge, says
   he,
'For life, Jim Jones, I'm sending you across the
   stormy sea.
'And take my tip before you ship to join the iron
   gang:
Don't get too gay at Botany Bay, or else you'll
   surely hang —
Or else you'll hang,' he says, says he, 'and after that,
   Jim Jones,
High up upon the gallows tree the crows will pick
   your bones.

'You'll have no time for mischief then, remember
   what I say:
They'll flog the poaching out of you, out there at
   Botany Bay.'

The waves were high upon the sea, the winds blew
  up in gales –
I would rather drown in misery than go to New
  South Wales.

The winds blew high upon the sea, and the pirates
  came along,
But the soldiers on our convict ship were full five
  hundred strong.
They opened fire and somehow drove that pirate
  ship away.
I'd rather have joined that pirate ship than come to
  Botany Bay.

For day and night the irons clang, and like poor
  galley-slaves
We toil and toil, and when we die must fill
  dishonoured graves.
But by and by I'll break my chain; into the bush
  I'll go,
And join the brave bushrangers there, Jack Donahue
  & Co.

And some dark night when everything is silent
  in the town
I'll kill the tyrants one and all, I'll shoot the floggers
  down:
I'll give the Law a little shock, remember what I say:
They'll yet regret they sent Jim Jones in chains to
  Botany Bay.

Traditional

Songs of the Squatters

The gum has no shade,
  And the wattle no fruit,
The parrots don't warble
  In trolls like the flute,
The cockatoo cooeth
  Not much like a dove
Yet fear not to ride
  To my station, my love;
Four hundred miles off
  Is goal of our way,
It is done in a week
  At but sixty a day;
The plains are all dusty;
  The creeks are all dried,
'Tis the fairest of weather
  To bring home my bride.
The blue vault of heaven
  Shall curtain thy form
One side of a gum tree
  The moonbeam must warm;
The whizzing mosquito
  Shall dance o'er thy head,
And the guana shall squat
  At the foot of thy bed;
The brave laughing jackass
  Shall sing thee to sleep,
And the snake o'er thy slumbers
  His vigils shall keep

Then sleep, lady, sleep,
  Without dreaming of pain,
Till the frost of the morning
  Shall wake thee again.
Our brave bridal bower
  I built not of stones.
Though, like old Doubting Castle,
  'Tis paved with bones,
The bones of sheep
  On whose flesh I have fed,
Where thy thin satin slipper
  Unshrinking may tread,
For the dogs have all polished
  Them clean with their teeth,
And they're better, believe me,
  Than what lies beneath.
My door has no hinge,
  And the window no pane,
They let out the smoke,
  But they let in the rain;
The frying pan serves us
  For table and dish,
And the tin pot of tea stands
  Still filled for your wish;
The sugar is brown,
  The milk is all done,
But the stick it is stirred with
  Is better than none.
The stockmen will swear,
  And the shepherds won't sing,

But a dog's a companion
  Enough for a king.
So fear not, fair lady,
  Your desolate way,
Your clothes will arrive
  In three months with my dray.
Then mount, lady, mount, to the wilderness fly,
My stores are laid in, and my shearing is nigh,
And our steeds, that through Sydney exultingly
wheel,
Must graze in a week on the banks of the Peel.

Robert Lowe, 1811-1892

The Kangaroo

Kangaroo, Kangaroo!
Thou spirit of Australia,
That redeems from utter failure,
From perfect desolation,
And warrants the creation
Of this fifth part of the Earth,
Which should seem an after-birth,
Not conceiv'd in the Beginning
(For God bless'd His work at first,
And saw that it was good),
But emerg'd at the first sinning,
When the ground was therefore curst;

And hence this barren wood!

Kangaroo, Kangaroo!
Tho' at first sight we should say,
In thy nature there may
Contradiction be involv'd,
It is quickly harmoniz'd.
Sphynx or mermaid realiz'd,
Or centaur unfabulous,
Would scarce be more prodigious,
Or Labrinthine Minotaur,
With which great Theseus did war,
Or Pegasus poetical.
Or hippogriff – chimera all!
But, what Nature would compile,
Nature knows how to reconcile;

And Wisdom, ever at her side,
Of all her children's justified.

She had made the squirrel fragile;
She had made the bounding hart;
But a third so strong and agile
Was beyond ev'n Nature's art.
So she join'd the former two
In thee, Kangaroo.

To describe thee, it is hard:
Converse of the camelopard,
Which beginneth camel-wise,
But endeth of the panther size,

Thy fore half, it would appear,
Had belong'd to some 'small deer'.
Such as liveth in a tree;
By the hinder, thou should'st be
A large animal of chase,
Bounding o'er the forest's space:
Join'd by some divine mistake,
None but Nature's hand can make –
Nature, in her wisdom's play,
On Creation's holiday.

For howso'er anomalous,
Thou yet are not incongruous,
Repugnant or preposterous,
Better-proportioned animal,
More graceful or ethereal,
Was never followed by the hound,
With fifty steps to thy one bound.
Thou can'st not be amended: no;
Be as thou art, thou best are so.

When sooty swans are once more rare,
And duck-moles the Museum's care,
Be still the glory of this land,
Happiest Work of finest Hand!

Barron Field, 1786-1846

Colonial Experience

When first I came to Sydney Cove
And up and down the streets did rove,
I thought such sights I ne'er did see
Since first I learnt my ABC.

Chorus:
Oh! it's broiling in the morning,
It's toiling in the morning,
It's broiling in the morning,
It's toiling all day long.

Into the park I took a stroll –
I felt just like a buttered roll.
A pretty name 'The Sunny South'
A better one 'The Land of Drouth!'

Next day into the bush I went,
On wild adventure I was bent,
Dame Nature's wonders I'd explore,
All thought of danger would ignore.

The mosquitoes and bull-dog ants
Assailed me even through my pants.
It nearly took my breath away
To hear the Jackass laugh so gay!

This lovely country, I've been told,
Abounds in silver and in gold.
You may pick it up all day,
Just as leaves in autumn lay!

Marines will chance this yarn believe,
But bluejackets you can't deceive,
Such pretty stories will not fit,
Nor can I their truth admit.

Some say there's lots of work to do,
Well, yes, but then, 'twixt me and you,
A man may toil and broil all day –
The big, fat man gets all the pay.

Mayhap such good things there may be,
But you may have them all, for me,
Instead of roaming foreign parts
I wish I'd studied the Fine Arts.

Anonymous

People
and
Places

A Midsummer Noon in the Australian Bush

Not a sound disturbs the air,
There is quiet everywhere;
Over plains and over woods
What a mighty stillness broods!

All the birds and insects keep
Where the coolest shadows sleep;
Even the busy ants are found
Resting in their pebbled mound;
Even the locusts clingeth now
Silent to the barky bough;
Over hills and over plains
Quiet, vast and slumbrous, reigns.

Only there's a drowsy humming
From yon warm lagoon slow coming;
'Tis the dragon-hornet, see!
All bedaubed resplendently,
Yellow on a tawny ground –
Each rich spot nor square nor round,
Rudely heart-shaped, as it were
The blurred and hasty empress there
Of a vermael-crusted seal
Dusted o'er with golden meal.
Only there's a droning where
Yon bright beetle shines in air.
Tracks it in its gleaming flight
With a slanting beam of light,

Rising in the sunshine higher,
Till its shards flame out like fire.

Every other thing is still,
Save the ever-wakeful rill,
Whose cool murmur only throws
Cooler comfort round repose;
Or some ripple in the sea
Of leafy boughs, where lazily,
Tired summer, in her bower
Turning with the noontide hour,
Heaves a slumbrous breath ere she
Once more slumbers peacefully.

O 'tis easeful here to lie
Hidden from noon's scorching eye,
In this grassy cool recess
Musing thus of quietness.

Charles Harpur, 1813-1868

Solitude

Where the mocking lyrebird calls
To its mate among the falls
Of the mountain streams that play,
Each adown its tortuous way,
When the dewy-fingered even'
Veils the narrow'd glimpse of Heaven:
Where the morning re-illumes
Gullies full of ferny plumes,
And a woof of radiance weaves
Through high-hanging vaults of leaves;
There, 'mid giant turpentines,
Groups of climbing, clustering vines,
Rocks that stand like sentinels,
Guarding Nature's citadels;
Lowly flowering shrubs that grace
With their beauty all the place –
There I love to wander lonely,
With my dog companion only;
There indulge unworldly moods
In the mountain solitudes;
Far from all the gilded strife
Of our boasted 'social life',
Contemplating, spirit-free,
The majestic company
Grandly marching through the ages –
Heroes, martyrs, bards and sages –
They who bravely suffered long,
By their struggles waxing strong,

For the freedom of the mind,
For the rights of humankind!
Oh, for some awakening cause,
Where we face eternal laws,
Where we dare not turn aside,
Where the souls of men are tried –
Something of the nobler strife
Which consumes the dross of life,
To unite to truer aim,
To exalt to loftier fame!
Leave behind the bats and balls,
Leave the racers in the stalls,
Leave the cards forever shuffled,
Leave the yacht on seas unruffled,
Leave the haunts of pampered ease,
Leave your dull festivities! –
Better far the savage glen,
Fitter school for earnest men!

Henry Parkes, 1815-1896

Bell-birds

By channels of coolness the echoes are calling,
And down the dim gorges I hear the creek falling;
It lives in the mountains, where moss and the sedges
Touch with their beauty the banks and the ledges:
Through breaks of the cedar and sycamore bowers
Struggles the light that is love to the flowers.
And softer than slumber, and sweeter than singing,
The notes of the bell-birds are running and ringing.

The silver-voiced bell-birds, the darlings of daytime,
They sing in September the songs of the May-time.
When shadows wax strong, and the thunder-bolts
  hurtle,
They hide with their fear in the leaves of the myrtle;
When rain and the sunbeams shine mingled togeth-
er,
They start up like fairies that follow fair weather,
And straightway the hues of the feathers unfolden
Are the green and the purple, the blue and the
  golden.

October, the maiden of bright yellow tresses,
Loiters for love in these cool wildernesses;
Loiters knee-deep in the grasses to listen,
Where dripping rocks gleam and the leafy pools
  glisten.
Then is the time when the water-moons splendid
Break with their gold, and are scattered or blended
Over the creeks, till the woodlands have warning

Of songs of the bell-bird and wings of the morning.

Welcome as water unkissed by the summers
Are the voices of bell-birds to thirsty far-comers.
When fiery December sets foot in the forest,
And the need of the wayfarer presses the sorest,
The bell-birds direct him to spring and to river,
With ring and with ripple, like runnels whose
 torrents
Are tossed by the pebbles and leaves in the currents.

Often I sit, looking back to a childhood
Mixt with the sight and the sounds of the wildwood,
Longing for power and sweetness of fashion
Lyrics with beats like heart-beats of passion –
Songs interwoven of lights and of laughters
Borrowed from bell-birds in far forest rafters;
So I might keep in the city and alleys
The beauty and strength of the deep mountain
 valleys,
Charming to slumber the pain of my losses
With glimpses of creeks and a vision of mosses.

Henry Kendall, 1839-1882

The Last of His Tribe

He crouches, and buries his face on his knees,
  And hides in the dark of his hair;
For he cannot look up to the storm-smitten trees,
  Or think of the loneliness there –
  Of the loss and the loneliness there.

The wallaroos grope through the tufts of the grass
  And turn to their coverts for fear;
But he sits in the ashes and lets them pass
  Where the boomerangs sleep with the spear –
  With the nullah, the sling and the spear.

Uloola, behold him! The thunder that breaks
  On the tops of the rocks with the rain,
And the wind which drives up with the salt of the lakes
  Have made him a hunter again –
  A hunter and fisher again.

For his eyes have been full with a smouldering
  thought;
  But he dreams of the hunts of yore,
And of foes that he sought, and of fights that he fought
  With those who will battle no more –
  Who will go to the battle no more.

It is well that the water which tumbles and fills
  Goes moaning and moaning along;
For an echo rolls out from the sides of the hills,
  And he starts at a wonderful song –

At the sound of a wonderful song.

And he sees, through the rents of the scattering fogs,
  The corroboree warlike and grim,
And the lubra who sat by the fire on the logs.
  To watch like a mourner for him –
  Like a mother and mourner for him.

Will he go in his sleep from these desolate lands,
  Like a chief, to the rest of his race,
With the honey-voiced woman who beckons and
  stands,
  And gleams like a dream in his face –
  Like a marvellous dream in his face?

Henry Kendall, 1839-1882

Are You the Cove?

'Are you the Cove?' he spoke the words
As swagmen only can;
The Squatter freezingly inquired,
'What do you mean, my man?'

'Are you the Cove?' his voice was stern,
His look was firm and keen;
Again the Squatter made reply,
'I don't know what you mean.'

'O! dash my rags! Let's have some sense –
You ain't a fool, by Jove,
Gammon you dunno what I mean:
I mean – are you the Cove?'

'Yes, I'm the Cove,' the Squatter said;
The Swagman answered, 'Right,
I thought as much: show me some place
Where I can doss tonight.'

'Tom Collins' (Joseph Furphy), 1843-1912

Tell Summer That I Died

When he was old and thin
And knew not night nor day,
He would sit up to say
Something of fire within.
How woefully his chin
Moved slowly as he tried
Some lusty words to say:
Tell Summer that I died.

When gladness sweeps the land,
And to the white sky
Cool butterflies go by,
And sheep in shadow stand;
When Love, the old command,
Turns every hate aside,
In the unstinted days
Tell Summer that I died.

John Shaw Neilson, 1872-1942

The Billy of Tea

You may talk of your whisky or talk of your beer,
I've something far better awaiting me here;
It stands on that fire beneath the gum-tree,
And you cannot lick it – a billy of tea.
So fill up your tumbler as high as you can,
You'll never persuade me it's not the best plan,
To let all the beer and the spirits go free
And stick to my darling old Billy of Tea.

I wake in the morning as soon as 'tis light,
And go to the nosebag to see it's all right,
That the ants on the sugar no mortgage have got,
And immediately sling my old billy-pot,
And while it's boiling the horses I seek,
And follow them down as far as the creek;
I take off the hobbles and let them go free,
And haste to tuck into my Billy of Tea.

And at night when I camp, if the day has been warm,
I give each of the horses their tucker of corn,
From the two in the pole to the one in the lead,
And the billy for each holds a comfortable feed;
Then the fire I start and the water I get,
And the corned beef and damper in order I set,
But I don't touch the grub, though so hungry I be,
I will wait till it's ready – the Billy of Tea.

Anonymous

The Bush

Give us from dawn to dark
  Blue of Australian skies,
Let there be none to mark
  Whither our pathway lies.

Give us when noontide comes
  Rest in the woodland free –
Fragrant breath of the gums,
  Cold, sweet scent of the sea.

Give us the wattle's gold
  And the dew-laden air,
And the loveliness bold
  Loneliest landscape wear.

These are the haunts we love,
  Glad with enchanted hours,
Bright as the heavens above,
  Fresh as the wild bush flowers.

James Lister Cuthbertson, 1851-1910

Where the Pelican Builds Her Nest

The horses were ready, the rails were down,
But the riders lingered still –
One had a parting word to say,
And one had his pipe to fill.
Then they mounted, one with a granted prayer,
And one with a grief unguessed.
'We are going,' they said as they rode away,
'Where the pelican builds her nest!'

They had told us of pastures wide and green,
To be sought past the sunset's glow;
Of rifts in the ranges by opal lit;
And gold 'neath the river's flow.
And thirst and hunger were banished words
When they spoke of that unknown West;
No drought they dreaded, no flood they feared,
Where the pelican builds her nest!

The creek at the ford was but fetlock deep
When we watched them crossing there;
The rains have replenished it thrice since then,
And thrice has the rock lain bare.
But the waters of Hope have flowed and fled,
And never from the blue hill's breast
Come back – by the sun and sands devoured –
Where the pelican builds her nest.

Mary Hannay Foott, 1846-1918

The Shearer's Wife

Before the glare o' dawn I rise
To milk the sleepy cows, an' shake
The droving dust from tired eyes,
Look round the rabbit traps, then bake
The children's bread.
There's hay to stook, an' beans to hoe,
An' ferns to cut i' th' scrub below;
Women must work, when men must go
Shearing from shed to shed.
I patch an' darn, now evening comes,
An' tired I am with labour sore,
Tired o' the bush, the cows, the gums,
Tired, but must dree for long months more
What no tongue tells.
The moon is lonely in the sky,
Lonely the bush, an' lonely I
Stare down the track no horse draws nigh
An' start at the cattle bells.

Louis Esson, 1879-1943

The Never-Never Land

By homestead, hut and shearing-shed,
  By railroad, coach and track –
By lonely graves where rest our dead,
  Up-Country and Out-back;
To where beneath the clustered stars
  The dreamy plains expand –
My home lies wide a thousand miles
  In the Never-Never Land.

It lies beyond the farming belt,
  Wide wastes of scrub and plain,
A blazing desert in the drought,
  A lake-land after rain;
To the skyline sweeps the waving grass,
  Or whirls the scorching sand –
A phantom land, a mystic realm!
  The Never-Never Land.

Where lone Mount Desolation lies,
  Mounts Dreadful and Despair –
'Tis lost beneath the rainless skies
  In hopeless deserts there.
It spreads nor'west by No-Man's Land –
  Where clouds are seldom seen –
To where the cattle stations lie
  Three hundred miles between.

The drovers of the Great Stock routes
  The strange Gulf country know –

Where, travelling from the southern droughts,
  The big lean bullocks go;
And camped by night where plains lie wide,
  Like some old ocean's bed,
. The watchmen in the starlight ride
  Round fifteen hundred head.

Lest in the city I forget
  True mateship after all,
My water-bag and billy yet
  Are hanging on the wall;
And I, to save my soul again,
  Would tramp to sunsets grand
With sad-eyed mates across the plain
  In the Never-Never Land.

Henry Lawson, 1867-1922

The Camp Fire

Reclining near his golden fire,
Alone within the silent bush,
He slowly smokes his evening briar,
And listens to the hovering hush.

The flames are points of falchion-blades,
Light-giving in their wheel and dance;
They gild the underleaf that fades
Above into a glooming trance.

The boles around rise to the night,
Ashen and grey, in solemn-wise,
Opening a heaven of starry light,
Dark violet-blue of nameless dyes.

Thoughts, many as the leaves in the woods
Touched by the first autumnal cold,
That fall and lie, in drifting floods,
Draw home with legendary gold.

Fanned from the fire a burning brand
Lights the bronzed glade with vivid glow;
On earth he whispering lays his hand:
'Mother, to thy calm rest I go.'

Barcroft Boake, 1866-1892

Clancy of the Overflow

I had written him a letter which I had, for want
of better
Knowledge, sent to where I met him down the
Lachlan years ago;
He was shearing when I knew him, so I sent the
letter to him,
Just on spec, addressed as follows, 'Clancy of the
Overflow'.

And answer came directed in a writing unexpected
(And I think the same was written with a thumb-nail
dipped in tar):
'Twas his shearing mate who wrote it, and verbatim
I will quote it:
'Clancy's gone to Queensland droving, and we don't
know where he are.'

In my wild erratic fancy visions come to me of
Clancy
Gone a-droving 'down the Cooper' where the
Western drovers go;
As the stock are slowly stringing, Clancy rides behind
them singing,
For the drover's life has pleasures that the townsfolk
never know.

And the bush has friends to meet him, and their
kindly voices greet him
In the murmur of the breezes and the river on its bars

And he sees the vision splendid of the sunlit plains
  extended,
And at night the wondrous glory of the everlasting
  stars.

I am sitting in my dingy little office, where a stingy
Ray of sunlight struggles feebly down between the
  houses tall,
And the foetid air and gritty of the dusty, dirty city,
Through the open window floating, spreads its
  foulness over all.

And in place of lowing cattle, I can hear the
  fiendish rattle
Of the tramways and the buses making hurry down
  the street;
And the language uninviting of the gutter children
  fighting
Comes fitfully and faintly through the ceaseless
  tramp of feet.

And the hurrying people daunt me, and their pallid
  faces haunt me
As they shoulder one another in their rush and
  nervous haste,
With the eager eyes and greedy, and their stunted
  forms and weedy,
For the townsfolk have no time to grow, they have
  no time to waste.

And I somehow rather fancy that I'd like to change
  with Clancy.

Like to take a turn at droving where the seasons
    come and go,
While he faced the round eternal of the cash-book
    and the journal –
But I doubt he'd suit the office, Clancy of the
    Overflow.

A.B. ('Banjo") Paterson, 1864-1941

The Blue Mountains

Above the ashes straight and tall,
  Through ferns with moisture dripping,
I climb beneath the sandstone wall,
  My feet on mosses slipping.

Like ramparts round the valley's edge
  The tinted cliffs are standing.
With many a broken wall and ledge,
  And many a rocky landing.

And round about their rugged feet
  Deep ferny dells are hidden
In shadowed depths, whence dust and heat
  Are banished and forbidden.

The stream that, crooning to itself,
  Comes down a tireless rover,
Flows calmly to the rocky shelf,
  And there leaps bravely over.

Now pouring down, now lost in spray
  When mountain breezes sally,
The water strikes the rock midway,
  And leaps into the valley.

Now in the west the colours change,
  The blue with crimson blending;
Behind the far Dividing Range,
  The sun is fast descending.

And mellowed day comes o'er the place,
  And softens ragged edges;
The rising moon's great placid face
Looks gravely o'er the ledges.

Henry Lawson, 1867-1922

Echoes of Wheels...

Echoes of wheels and singing lashes
  Wake on the morning air;
Out of the kitchen a youngster dashes,
  Giving the ducks a scare.
Three jiffs from house to gully,
  And over the bridge to the gate;
And then a panting little boy
  Climbs on the rails to wait.

For there is long-whipped cursing Bill
  With four enormous logs,

Behind a team with the white-nosed leader's
  Feet in the sucking bogs.
Oh it was grand to see them stuck
  And grand to see them strain,
Until the magical language of Bill
  Had got them out again!

I foxed them to the shoulder turn,
  I saw him work them round,
And die into the secret bush,
  Leaving only sound.

And it isn't bullocks I recall,
  Nor waggons my memory sees;
But in the scented bush a track
  Turning among the trees.

Oh track where the brown leaves fall
  In dust to our very knees!

And it isn't the wattle that I recall,
Nor the sound of the bullocky's singing lash,
When the cloven hoofs in the puddles splash;
But the rumble on an unseen load
Swallowed along the hidden road
  Turning among the trees!

'Furnely Maurice' (Frank Wilmot), 1881-1942

The Women of the West

They left the vine-wreathed cottage and the mansion
    on the Hill,
The houses in the busy streets where life is never
    still,
The pleasures of the city, and the friends they
    cherished best,
For love they faced the wilderness – the Women of
    the West.

The roar and rush and fever of the city died away,
And old-time joys and faces – they were gone for
    many a day;
In their place the lurching coach-wheel, or the
    creaking bullock chains;
Or the everlasting sameness of the never-ending
    plains.

In the slab-built, zinc-roofed homestead of some
    lately-taken run,
In the tent beside the 'bankment of a railway just
    begun,
In the huts on new selections, in the camps of man's
    unrest,
On the frontiers of the Nation, live the Women of
    the West.

The red sun robs their beauty, and, in weariness
    and pain,
The slow years steal the nameless grace that never
    comes again;
And there are hours men cannot soothe, and words

men cannot say –
The nearest woman's face may be a hundred miles
away.

The wide Bush holds the secrets of their longings
and desires,
When the white stars in reverence light their holy
altar-fires,
And silence, like the touch of God, sinks deep into
the breast –
Perchance He hears and understands the Women of
the West.

For them no trumpet sounds the call, no poet plies
his arts –
They only hear the beating of their gallant, loving
hearts,
But they have sung with silent lives the song all
songs above –
The holiness, the sacrifice, the dignity of love.

Well have we held our fathers' creed. No call has
passed us by.
We faced and fought the wilderness, we sent our
sons to die.
And we have hearts to do and dare, and yet, o'er
all the rest,
The hearts that made the Nation were the Women of
the West.

George Essex Evans, 1863-1909

Hay, Hell and Booligal

'You come and see me, boys,' he said;
'You'll find a welcome and a bed
And whisky any time you call;
Although our township hasn't got
The name of quite a lively spot –
You see, I live in Booligal.

'And people have an awful down
Upon the district and the town –
Which worse than Hell itself they call;
In fact, the saying far and wide
Along the Riverina side
Is 'Hay and Hell and Booligal'.

'No doubt it suits 'em very well
To say it's worse than Hay or Hell,
But don't you heed their talk at all;
Of course, there's heat – no one denies –
And sand and dust and stacks of flies,
And rabbits, too, at Booligal.

'But such a pleasant, quiet place,
You never see a stranger's face –
They hardly ever care to call;
The drovers mostly pass it by;
They reckon that they'd rather die
Than spend a night in Booligal.

'The big mosquitoes frighten some –
You'll lie awake to hear 'em hum –
And snakes about the township crawl;

But shearers, when they get their cheque,
They never come along and wreck
The blessed town of Booligal.

'But down in Hay the shearers come
And fill themselves with fighting rum,
And chase blue devils up the wall,
And fight the snaggers every day,
Until there is a deuce to pay –
There's none of that in Booligal.

'Of course, there isn't much to see –
The billiard table used to be
The great attraction for us all,
Until some careless, drunken curs
Got sleeping on it in their spurs,
And ruined it, in Booligal.

'Just now there is a howling drought
That pretty near has starved us out –
It never seems to rain at all;
But if there should come any rain,
You couldn't cross the black soil plain –
You'd have to stop in Booligal.'

'We'd have to stop!' *With bated breath*
We pray that both in life and death
Our fate in other lines might fall:
'Oh, send us to our just reward
In Hay or Hell, but, gracious Lord,
Deliver us from Booligal!'

A.B. ('Banjo') Paterson, 1864-1941

Bullocky Bill

As I came down Talbingo Hill
I heard a maiden cry,
'There goes old Bill the Bullocky –
He's bound for Gundagai.'

A better poor old beggar
Never cracked an honest crust,
A tougher poor old beggar
Never drug a whip through dust.

His team got bogged on the Five-Mile Creek,
Bill lashed and swore, and cried,
'If Nobbie don't get me out of this
I'll tattoo his bloody hide.'

But Nobbie strained and broke the yoke
And poked out the leader's eye,
And the dog sat on the tucker-box
Five miles from Gundagai.

Traditional

The Song of Australia

There is a land where summer skies
Are gleaming with a thousand dyes,
Blending in witching harmonies,
In harmonies.
And grassy knoll and forest height
Are flushing in the rosy light,
And all above is azure bright,
Australia, Australia, Australia.

There is a land where honey flows,
Where laughing corn luxuriant grows,
Land of the myrtle and the rose,
Land of the rose.
On hill and plain the clustering vine
Is gushing out with purple wine,
And cups are quaffed to thee and thine,
Australia, Australia, Australia.

There is a land where treasures shine
Deep in the dark unfathomed mine,
For worshippers at Mammon's shrine,
At Mammon's shrine.
Where gold lies hid, and rubies gleam,
And fabled wealth no more doth seem
The idle fancy of a dream,
Australia, Australia, Australia.

There is a land where homesteads peep
From sunny plain and woodland steep.

And love and joy bright vigils keep,
Bright vigils keep.
Where the glad voice of childish glee
Is mingled with the melody
Of nature's hidden minstrelsy,
Australia, Australia, Australia.

There is a land where floating free,
From mountain top to girdling sea.
A proud flag waves exultingly,
Exultingly.
And Freedom's sons the banner bear,
No shackled slave can breathe the air,
Fairest of Britain's daughters fair,
Australia, Australia, Australia.

Caroline Carleton, 1820-1874

Bill Brown

I met Bill Brown on Prospect Track
Astride a camel cow;
An' I said, 'I heard you had the sack,
An' where are you heading now?'

'Well, mate,' said William, 'I thought it out,
An' I sez to myself, sez I:
There's not much hope for the rouseabout,
As the rousy can testify.

'So I'll drink the honey of Freedom's Cup,
An' do as it pleases Brown;
I'll roll me swag when the sun gets up,
An' I'll camp when the sun goes down.

'I'm makin' out where the diggers go,
Where the reefs run deep an' wide;
I'll wet my whistle at Tally-ho,
An' I'll yard me a Western bride.

'She'll make me rugs with skins I get
When I'm off o' the veins of gold;
She'll strip an' thatch when the days are wet,
An' she'll stoke when the nights are cold.

'With only a fire in the trackless zone,
She'll cook like a chef, bet you;
Whatever she needs she will find alone
For her salmagundi too.

'If the tracks are barren this moke I've got
Will do with a mulga-tree,
An' the hobble-chains an' the old quart-pot
Still jangle a tune to me.'

He filled his pipe ere he said, 'So long!'
An' he rode where the sun grows red;
Where the bold are lured with a golden song
At times to a dead man's bed.

Though many ask, 'tis a nut to crack,
Where old Bill Brown is now;

He was heard of last on the Prospect Track
Astride of a camel cow.

Edward S. Sorenson, 1869-1939

My Country

The love of field and coppice,
Of green and shaded lanes,
Of ordered woods and gardens
Is running in your veins.
Strong love of grey-blue distance,
Brown streams and soft, dim skies –
I know but cannot share it,
My love is otherwise.

I love a sunburnt country,
A land of sweeping plains,
Of ragged mountain ranges,
Of droughts and flooding rains,
I love her far horizons,
I love her jewel-sea,
Her beauty and her terror –
The wide brown land for me!

The stark white ring-barked forests,
All tragic to the moon,
The sapphire-misted mountains,
The hot gold hush of noon,

Green tangle of the brushes
Where lithe lianas coil
And orchids deck the tree-tops,
And ferns the warm dark soil.

Core of my heart, my country!
Her pitiless blue sky,
When, sick at heart, around us
We see the cattle die –
But then the grey clouds gather,
And we can bless again
The drumming of an army,
The steady soaking rain.

Core of my heart, my country!
Land of the rainbow gold,
For flood and fire and famine
She pays us back threefold.
Over the thirsty paddocks,
Watch, after many days,
The filmy veil of greenness
That thickens as we gaze ...

An opal-hearted country,
A wilful, lavish land –
All you who have not loved her,
 You will not understand –
Though Earth holds many splendours,
Wherever I may die,
I know to what brown country
My homing thoughts will fly.

Dorothea Mackellar, 1885-1968

The Digger's Song

Scrape the bottom of the hole; gather up the stuff!
Fossick in the crannies, lest you leave a grain
behind!
Just another shovelful and that'll be enough –
Now we'll take it to the bank and see what we can
  find ...
Give the dish a twirl around!
Let the water swirl around!
Gently let it circulate – there's music in the swish
And the tinkle of the gravel
As the pebbles quickly travel
Around in merry circles on the bottom of the dish.

Ah, if man could wash his life – if he only could!
Panning off the evil deeds, keeping but the good:
What a mighty lot of diggers' dishes would be sold!
Though I fear the heap of tailings would be greater
  than the gold ...
Give the dish a twirl around!
Let the water swirl around!
Man's the sport of circumstances however he may
  wish.
Fortune, are you there now?
Answer to my prayer now –
Drop a half-ounce nugget in the bottom of the dish.

Gently let the water lap! Keep the corners dry!
That's about the place the gold will generally stay.
What was the bright particle that just then caught
  my eye?

I fear me by the look of things 'twas only yellow
  clay ...
Just another twirl around!
Let the water swirl around!
That's the way we rob the river of its golden fish ...
What's that ... Can't we snare one??
Bah! There's not a colour in the bottom of the dish.

Barcroft Boake, 1866-1892

Australia's on the Wallaby

Our fathers came to search for gold,
The mine has proved a duffer;
From bankers, boss and syndicate
We always had to suffer ...
They fought for freedom for themselves,
Themselves and mates to toil,
But Australia's sons are weary
And the billy's on the boil.

Australia's on the wallaby,
Just listen to the coo-ee;
For the kangaroo, he rolls his swag
And the emu shoulders bluey.
The boomerangs are whizzing round,
The dingo scratches gravel;
The possum, bear and bandicoot
Are all upon the travel.

The cuckoo calls the bats and now
The pigeon and the shag
The mallee-hen and platypus
Are rolling up their swag;
For the curlew sings a sad farewell
Beside the long lagoon,
And the brolga does his last-way waltz
To the lyrebird's mocking tune.

There's tiger-snakes and damper, boys,
And what's that on the coals?
There's droughts and floods and ragged duds
And dried-up waterholes;
There's shadeless trees and sun-scorched plains,
All asking us to toil;
But Australia's sons are weary
And the billy's on the boil.

Anonymous

The Roaring Days

The night too quickly passes
  And we are growing old,
So let us fill our glasses
  And toast the Days of Gold;
When finds of wondrous treasure
  Set all the South ablaze,
And you and I were faithful mates
  All through the Roaring Days.

Then stately ships came sailing
  From every harbour's mouth,
And sought the Land of Promise
  That beaconed in the South;
Then southward streamed their streamers
  And swelled their canvas full
To speed the wildest dreamers
  E'er borne in vessel's hull.

Their shining Eldorado
  Beneath the southern skies
Was day and night for ever
  Before their eager eyes.
The brooding bush awakened,
  Was stirred in wild unrest,
And all the year a human stream
  Went pouring to the West.

The rough bush roads re-echoed
  The bar-room's noisy din,
When troops of stalwart horsemen
  Dismounted at the inn.
And oft the hearty greetings
  And hearty clasp of hands
Would tell of sudden meetings
  Of friends from other lands.

And when the cheery camp-fire
  Explored the bush with gleams,
The camping-grounds were crowded
  With caravans of teams;

Then home the jests were driven
  And good old songs were sung,
And choruses were given
  The strength of heart and lung.

Oft when the camps were dreaming,
  And fires began to pale,
Through rugged ranges gleaming
  Swept on the Royal Mail.
Behind six foaming horses,
  And lit by flashing lamps,
Old Cobb and Co., in royal state,
  Went dashing past the camps.

Oh, who would paint a goldfield,
  And paint the picture right,
As old Adventure saw it
  In early morning's light?
The yellow mounds of mullock
  With spots of red and white,
The scattered quartz that glistened
  Like diamonds in light;

The azure line of ridges,
  The bush of darkest green,
The little homes of calico
  That dotted all the scene.
The flat straw hats, with ribands,
  That old engravings show –
The dress that still reminds us
  Of sailors long ago.

I hear the fall of timber
  From distant flats and fells,
The pealing of the anvils
  As clear as little bells,
The rattle of the cradle,
  The clack of windlass boles,
The flutter of the crimson flags
  Above the golden holes.

Ah, then their hearts were bolder,
  And if Dame Fortune frowned
Their swags they'd lightly shoulder
  And tramp to other ground.
Oh, they were lion-hearted
  Who gave our country birth!
Stout sons, of stoutest fathers born,
  From all the lands on earth!

Those golden days are vanished,
  And altered is the scene;
The diggings are deserted,
  The camping-grounds are green;
The flaunting flag of progress
  Is in the West unfurled,
The mighty Bush with iron rails
  Is tethered to the world.

Henry Lawson, 1867-1922

At the Melting of the Snow

There's a sunny Southern Land,
And it's there that I would be
Where the big hills stand
In the South Countrie!
When the wattles bloom again,
Then it's time for us to go
To the old Monaro country
At the melting of the snow.

To the East or to the West,
Or wherever you may be,
You will find no place
Like the South Countrie.
For the skies are blue above,
And the grass is green below,
In the old Monaro country
At the melting of the snow.

Now the team is in the plough,
And the thrushes start to sing,
And the pigeons on the bough
Are rejoicing at the Spring.
So come my comrades all,
Let us saddle up and go
To the old Monaro country
At the melting of the snow.

A.B.('Banjo') Paterson, 1864-1941

A Bush Girl

She's milking in the rain and dark,
  As did her mother in the past.
The wretched shed of poles and bark,
  Rent by the wind, is leaking fast.
She sees the 'home-roof' black and low,
  Where, balefully, the hut-fire gleams –
And, like her mother, long ago,
  She has her dreams; she has her dreams.

The daybreak haunts the dreary scene,
  The brooding ridge, the blue-grey bush,
The 'yard' where all her years have been
  Is ankle-deep in dung and slush;
She shivers as the hours drag on,
  Her threadbare dress of sackcloth seems;
But, like her mother, years agone,
  She has her dreams; she has her dreams.

The sullen 'breakfast' where they cut
  The blackened 'junk'. The lowering face,
As though a crime were in the hut,
  As though a curse were on the place;
The muttered question and reply,
  The tread that shakes the rotting beams,
The nagging mother, thin and dry –
  God help the girl! She has her dreams.

Then for 'th' separator' start
  Most wretched hour in all her life,

With 'horse' and harness, dress and cart,
  No Chinaman would give his wife;
Her heart is sick for light and love,
  Her face is often fair and sweet,
And her intelligence above
  The minds of all she's like to meet.

She reads, by slush-lamp, maybe,
  When she has dragged her weary round,
And dreams of cities by the sea
  (Where butter's up, so much the pound),
Of different men from those she knows,
  Of shining tides and broad bright streams;
Of theatres and city shows,
  And her release! She has her dreams.

Could I gain her a little rest,
  A little light, if but for one,
I think that it would be the best
  Of any good I may have done.
But, after all, the paths we go
  Are not so glorious as they seem,
And – if 'twill help her heart to know –
  I've had my dream. 'Twas but a dream.

Henry Lawson, 1867-1922

The Traveller

As I rode into Burrumbeet,
I met a man with funny feet;
And, when I paused to ask him why
His feet were strange, he rolled his eye
And said the rain would spoil the wheat;
So I rode on to Burrumbeet.

As I rode into Beetaloo
I met a man whose nose was blue;
And when I asked him how he got
A nose like that, he answered, 'What
Do bullocks mean when they say "Moo"?'
So I rode on to Beetaloo.

As I rode into Ballarat,
I met a man who wore no hat:
And, when I said he might take cold,
He cried 'The hills are quite as old
As yonder plains, but not so flat.'
So I rode on to Ballarat.

As I rode into Gundagai,
I met a man and passed him by
Without a nod, without a word.
He turned, and said he'd never heard
Or seen a man so wise as I,
But I rode on to Gundagai.

As I rode homeward, full of doubt,
I met a stranger riding out;

A foolish man he seemed to me;
But 'Nay, I am yourself,' said he.
'Just as you were when you rode out,'
So I rode homeward, free of doubt.

C.J. Dennis, 1876-1938

Where the Dead Men Lie

On the wastes of the Never Never –
  That's where the dead men lie!
There where the heat-waves dance forever –
  That's where the dead men lie!
That's where the Earth's loved sons are keeping
Endless Tryst; not the west wind sweeping
Feverish pinions can wake the sleeping
  Out where the dead men lie!

Where brown Summer and Death have mated –
  That's where the dead men lie!
Loving with fiery lust unsated –
  That's where the dead men lie
Out where the grinning skulls bleach whitely
Under the saltbush sparkling brightly,
Out where the wild dogs chorus nightly –
  That's where the dead men lie ...!

Deep in the yellow, flowing river –
  That's where the dead men lie!

Under the banks where the shadows quiver –
  That's where the dead men lie!
Where the platypus twists and doubles,
Leaving a train of tiny bubbles;
Rid at last of their earthly troubles –
  That's where the dead men lie!

East and backward faces turning –
  That's how the dead men lie!
Gaunt arms stretched with a violent yearning –
  That's how the dead men lie!
Oft in the fragrant hush of nooning
Hearing again their mother's crooning,
Wrapt for aye in a dreamful swooning –
  That's where the dead men lie!

Only the hand of Night can free them –
  That's when the dead men fly!
Only the frightened cattle see them –
  See the dead go by!
Cloven hoofs beating out one measure,
Bidding the stockmen know no leisure –
That's when the dead men take their pleasure!
  That's when the dead men fly!

Ask, too, the never-sleeping drover:
  He sees the dead pass by;
Hearing them call to their friends – the plover,
  Hearing the dead men cry;
Seeing their faces stealing, stealing,
Hearing their laughter, pealing, pealing,

Watching their grey forms wheeling, wheeling
Round where the cattle lie!

Strangled by thirst and fierce privation –
That's how the dead men die!
Out on Moneygrub's farthest station –
That's how the dead men die!
Hard-faced grey-beards, youngsters callow;
Some mounds cared for, some left fallow;
Some deep down, yet others shallow:
Some having but the sky.

Moneygrub, he sips his claret,
Looks with complacent eye
Down at his watch-chain, eighteen carat –
There, in his club, hard by:
Recks not that every link is stamped with
Names of men whose limbs are cramped with
Too long lying in grave-mould, camped with
Death where the dead men lie.

Barcroft Boake, 1866-1892

Shearers

No church-bell rings them from the Track
  No pulpit lights their blindness –
Tis hardship, drought, and homelessness
  That teach those Bushmen kindness:
The mateship born, in barren lands,
  Of toil and thirst and danger,
The camp-fare for the wanderer set,
  The first place to the stranger.

They do the best they can today –
  Take no thought of the morrow:
Their way is not the old-world way –
  They live to lend and borrow.
When shearing's done and cheques gone wrong,
  They call it 'time to slither!' –
They saddle up and say 'So-long!'
  And ride the Lord knows whither.

And though he may be brown or black,
  Or wrong man there, or right man,
The mate that's steadfast to his mates
  They call that man a 'white man!'
They tramp in mateship side by side –
  The Protestant and Roman –
They call no biped lord or sir,
  And touch their hat to no man.

They carry in their swags, perhaps,
  A portrait and a letter –

And, maybe, deep down in their hearts,
 The hope of 'something better'.
Where lonely miles are long to ride,
 And long, hot days recurrent,
There's lots of time to think of men
 They might have been – but weren't.

They turn their faces to the west
 And leave the world behind them
(Their drought-dry graves are seldom set
 Where even mates can find them.)
They know too little of the world
 To rise to wealth and greatness:
But in these lines I gladly pay
 My tribute to their straightness.

Henry Lawson (1867-1922)

Condamine Bells

By a forge near a hut on the Condamine River
  A blacksmith laboured at his ancient trade;
With his hammer swinging and his anvil ringing
  He fashioned bells from a crosscut blade.

And while he toiled by the Condamine River
  He sang a song for a job well done:
And the song and the clamour of his busy hammer
  Merged and mingled in a tempered tone.

And his bell rang clear from the Condamine River
  To the Gulf, to the Leeuwin, over soil and sand;
Desert eagles winging heard his stock-bells ringing
  As a first voice singing in a songless land.

The smith is lost to the Condamine River,
  Gone is the humpy where he used to dwell;
But the songs and the clamour of his busy hammer
  Ring on through the land in the Condamine Bell.

Jack Sorensen, 1907-1949

Country Fellows

When country fellows come to town,
And meet to have a chat,
They bring the news from Camperdown,
Birchip and Ballarat.
Wisely they talk of wheat and wool
From Boort and Buningyong,
From Warragul and Warrnambool,
From Junee and Geelong.

Ted tells them how the crops are now
Well up round Bullarook,
And Fred describes the champion cow
He bred at Quambatook.
'If rain comes soon 'twill be a boon,'
Says Clive of Koo-wee-rup.
'Too right,' says Nick of Nar-nar-goon;
'The grass wants fetchin' up.'

And I who have been country bred,
And love the country still,
I listen wistfully to Ted
And George and Joe and Bill.
I see again the peaceful scene,
I hear them talk of paddocks green,
At Yea and Crogan's Dam,
Koroit, Kerang and Moulamein;
Then, dreaming of the might-have-been,
I go home in a tram.

C.J. Dennis, 1876-1938

Andy's Gone with Cattle

Our Andy's gone with cattle now –
  Our hearts are out of order –
With drought he's gone to battle now
  Across the Queensland border.

He's left us in dejection now,
  Our thoughts with him are roving:
It's dull on this selection now;
  Since Andy went a-droving.

Who now shall wear the cheerful face
  In times when things are slackest?
And who shall whistle round the place
  When Fortune frowns her blackest?

Oh, who shall cheek the squatter now
  When he comes round us snarling?
His tongue is growing hotter now
  Since Andy crossed the Darling.

Oh, may the showers in torrents fall,
  And all the tanks run over;
And may the grass grow green and tall
  In pathways of the drover ...

And may good angels send the rain
  On desert stretches sandy:
And when the summer comes again
  God grant 'twill bring us Andy.

Henry Lawson, 1867-1922

Andy's Return

With pannikins all rusty,
  And billy burnt and black,
And clothes all torn and dusty,
  That scarcely hide his back;
With sun-cracked saddle-leather,
  And knotted greenhide rein,
And face burnt brown with weather,
  Our Andy's home again!

His unkempt hair is faded
  With sleeping in the wet,
He's looking old and jaded;
  But he is hearty yet.
With eyes sunk in their sockets –
  But merry as of yore;
With big cheques in his pockets,
  Our Andy's home once more!

Old Uncle's bright and cheerful;
  He wears a smiling face;
And Aunty's never tearful
  Now Andy's round the place.
Old Blucher barks for gladness;
  He broke his rusty chain,
And leapt in joyous madness
  When Andy came again.

With tales of flood and famine,
  On distant northern tracks,

And shady yarns – 'baal gammon!'
  Of dealings with the blacks,
From where the skies hang lazy
  On many a northern plain,
From regions dim and hazy
  Our Andy's home again!

His toil is nearly over;
  He'll soon enjoy his gains,
Not long he'll be a drover,
  And cross the lonely plains.
We'll happy be for ever
  When he'll no longer roam
But by some deep, cool river
  Will make us all a home.

Henry Lawson, 1867-1922

The Pannikin Poet

There's nothing here sublime,
But just a roving rhyme,
Run off to pass the time,
With naught titanic in
The theme that it supports
And, though it treats of quarts,
It's bare of golden thoughts –
It's just a pannikin.

I think it's rather hard
That each Australian bard –
Each wan poetic card –
With thoughts galvanic in
His fiery soul alight,
In wild aerial flight,
Will sit him down and write
About a pannikin.

He makes some new chum fare
From out his English lair
To hunt the native bear,
That curious mannikin;
And then when times get bad
That wand'ring English lad
Writes out a message sad
Upon his pannikin:
'Oh, mother, think of me
Beneath the wattle tree.'
(For you bet that he
Will drag the wattle in.)
'Oh, mother, here I think
That I shall have to sink
There ain't a single drink
The water bottle in.'

The dingo homeward hies
The sooty crows uprise
And caw their fierce surprise
A tone Satanic in;
And bearded bushmen tread

Around the sleeper's head –
'See here – the bloke is dead.
Now, where's his pannikin?'

They read his words and weep,
And lay him down to sleep
Where wattle branches sweep
A style mechanic in;
And, reader, that's the way
The poets of today
Spin out their little lay
About a pannikin.

A.B. ('Banjo') Paterson, 1864-1941

Middleton's Rouseabout

Tall and freckled and sandy,
　Face of a country lout;
This was the picture of Andy,
　Middleton's rouseabout.

Type of a coming nation,
　In the land of cattle and sheep,
Worked on Middleton's station,
　'Pound a week and his keep.'

On Middleton's wide dominions
　Plied the stockwhip and shears;

Hadn't any opinions,
  Hadn't any 'idears'.

Swiftly the years went over,
  Liquor and drought prevailed;
Middleton went as a drover
  After his station had failed.

Type of a careless nation,
  Men who are soon played out,
Middleton was – and his station
  Was bought by the Rouseabout.

Flourishing beard and sandy,
  Tall and solid stout;
This is the picture of Andy,
  Middleton's Rouseabout.

Now on his own dominions
  Works with his overseers:
Hasn't any opinions,
  Hasn't any idears.

Henry Lawson, 1867-1922

To a Billy

Old billy – battered, brown and black
With many days of camping,
Companion of the bulging sack,
And friend in all our tramping;
How often on the Friday night –
Your cubic measure testing –
With jam and tea we stuffed you tight
Before we started nesting!

How often in the moonlight pale,
Through gums and gullies toiling,
We've been the first the hill to scale,
The first to watch you boiling;
When at the lane the tent was spread
The silver wattle under,
And early shafts of rosy red
Cleft sea-borne mists asunder!

And so, old Billy, you recall
A host of sunburnt faces,
And bring us back again to all
The best of camping places.
True flavour of the bush you bear
Of camp and its surrounding.
Of freedom and of open air,
Of healthy life abounding

James Lister Cuthbertson, 1851-1910

How M'Ginnis Went Missing

Let us ease our idle chatter,
Let the tears bedew our cheek,
For the man from Tallangatta
Has been missing for a week.

Where the roaring, flooded Murray
Covered all the lower land,
There he started in a hurry,
With a bottle in his hand.

And his fate is hid forever,
But the public seem to think
That he slumbered by the river,
'Neath the influence of drink.

And they scarcely seem to wonder
That the river, wide and deep,
Never woke him with its thunder,
Never stirred him in his sleep.

As the crushing logs came sweeping,
And their tumult filled the air,
Then M'Ginnis murmured, sleeping,
''Tis a wake to ould Kildare.'

So the river rose and found him
Sleeping softly by the stream,
And the cruel waters drowned him
Ere he wakened from his dream.

And the blossom-tufted wattle,
  Blooming brightly on the lea
Saw M'Ginnis and the bottle
  Going drifting out to sea.

A.B. ('Banjo) Paterson, 1864-1941

The Drover's Sweetheart

An hour before the sun goes down
  Behind the ragged boughs,
I go across the little run
  To bring the dusty cows;
And once I used to sit and rest
  Beneath the fading dome,
For there was one that I loved best
  Who'd bring the cattle home.

Our yard is fixed with double bails;
  Round one the grass is green,
The Bush is growing through the rails,
  The spike is rusted in:
It was from there his freckled face
  Would turn and smile at me,
For he'd milk seven in the race
  While I was milking three.

He kissed me twice and once again
  And rode across the hill;
The pint-pots and the hobble-chain –
  I hear them jingling still.

About the hut as sunlight fails
  The fire shines through the cracks –
I climb the broken stockyard rails
  And watch the bridle-tracks.

And he is coming home again –
  He wrote from Evatt's Rock;
A flood was in the Darling then
  And foot-rot in the flock.
The sheep were falling thick and fast
  A hundred miles from town,
And when he reached the line at last
  He trucked the remnant down.

And so he'll have to stand the cost;
  His luck was always bad,
Instead of making more, he lost
  The money that he had;
And how he'll manage, heaven knows,
  (My eyes are getting dim)
He says – he says – he don't – suppose
  I'll want to – to – marry – him.

As if I wouldn't take his hand
  Without a golden glove,
Oh! Jack, you men won't understand
  How much a girl can love.
I long to see his face once more –
  Jack's dog! Thank God, it's Jack –
(I never thought I'd faint before)
  He's coming up the track.

Henry Lawson, 1867-1922

It's Grand

It's grand to be a squatter
And sit upon a post,
And watch your little ewes and lambs
A-giving up the ghost.

It's grand to be a 'cockie'
With wife and kids to keep
And find an all-wise Providence
Has mustered all your sheep.

It's grand to be a Western man,
With shovel in your hand,
To dig your little homestead out
From underneath the sand.

It's grand to be a shearer,
Along the Darling side,
And pluck the wool from stinking sheep
That some days since have died.

It's grand to be a rabbit
And breed till all is blue,
And then to die in heaps because
There's nothing left to chew.

It's grand to be a Minister
And travel like a swell,
And tell the Central District folk
To go to – Inverell.

It's grand to be a Socialist
And lead the bold array
That marches to prosperity
At seven bob a day.

It's grand to be unemployed
And lie in the Domain,
And wake up every second day
And go to sleep again.

It's grand to borrow English tin
To pay for wharves and Rocks,
And then to find it isn't in
The little money-box.

It's grand to be a Democrat
And toady to the mob,
For fear that if you told the truth
They'd hunt you for your job.
It's grand to be a lot of things
In this fair Southern land,
But if the Lord would send us rain,
That would, indeed, be grand!

A.B. ('Banjo') Paterson, 1864-1941

The Shearing Shed

'The ladies are coming,' the super says
  To the shearers sweltering there,
And 'the ladies' means in the shearing-shed:
  'Don't cut 'em too bad. Don't swear.'
The ghost of a pause in the shed's rough heart,
  And lower is bowed each head;
Then nothing is heard save a whispered word
  And the roar of the shearing-shed.

The tall, shy rouser has lost his wits;
  His limbs are all astray;
He leaves a fleece on the shearing-board
  And his broom in the shearer's way.
There's a curse in store for that jackeroo
  As down by the wall he slants –
But the ringer bends with his legs askew
  And wishes he'd 'patched them pants'.

They are girls from the city. Our hearts rebel
  As we squint at their dainty feet,
While they gush and say in a girly way
  That 'the dear little lambs' are 'sweet'.
And Bill the Ringer, who'd scorn the use
  Of a childish word like damn,
Would give a pound that his tongue were loose
  As he tackles a lively lamb.

Swift thought of home in the coastal towns –
  Or rivers and waving grass –

And a weight on our hearts that we cannot define
  That comes as the ladies pass;
But the rouser ventures a nervous dig
  With his thumb in the next man's back;
And Bogan says to his pen-mate: 'Twig
  The style of that last un, Jack.'

Jack Moonlight gives her a careless glance –
  Then catches his breath with pain;
His strong hand shakes, and the sunbeams dance
  As he bends to his work again.
But he's well disguised in a bristling beard,
  Bronzed skin, and his shearer's dress;
And whatever he knew or hoped or feared
  Was hard for his mates to guess.

Jack Moonlight, wiping his broad, white brow,
  Explains with a doleful smile,
'A stitch in the side,' and 'I'm all right now' –
  But he leans on the beam awhile,
And gazes out in the blazing noon
  On the clearing brown and bare …
She had come and gone – like a breath of June
  In December's heat and glare.

Henry Lawson, 1867-1922

The Swagman

Oh, he was old and spare;
His bushy whiskers and his hair
Were all fussed up and very grey;
He said he'd come a long, long way
And had a long, long way to go.
Each boot was broken at the toe,
And he'd a swag upon his back,
His billy-can, as black as black,
Was just the thing for making tea
At picnics, so it seemed to me.

'Twas hard to earn a bit of bread,
He told me. Then he shook his head,
All the little corks that hung
Around his hat-brim danced and swung
And bobbed about his face; and when
I laughed he made them dance again.
He said they were for keeping flies –
'The pesky varmints' – from his eyes.
He called me 'Codger' . . . 'Now you see
The best days of your life,' said he.
'But days will come to bend your back
And, when they come, keep off the track,
Keep off, young codger, if you can.'

He seemed a funny sort of man.
He told me that he wanted work,
But jobs were scarce this side of Bourke,
And he supposed he'd have to go

Another fifty miles or so.
'Nigh all my life the track I've walked,'
He said. I liked the way he talked.
And oh, the places he had seen!
I don't know where he had not been –
On every road, in every town,
All through the country, up and down.
'Young codger, shun the track,' he said.
I noticed then that his old eyes
Were very blue and very wise.
'Ay, once I was a little lad,'
He said, and seemed to grow quite sad.

I sometimes think: When I'm a man,
I'll get a good black billy-can
And hang some corks around my hat,
And lead a jolly life like that.

C. J. Dennis, 1876-1938

Days When We Went Swimming

The breezes waved the silver grass
  Waist-high along the siding,
And to the creek we ne'er could pass,
  Three boys, on bareback riding;
Beneath the she-oaks in the bend
  The waterhole was brimming –
Do you remember yet, old friend,
  The times we went in swimming?

The days we played the wag from school –
  Joys shared – but paid for singly –
The air was hot, the water cool –
  And naked boys are kingly!
With mud for soap, the sun to dry –
  A well-planned lie to stay us,
And dust well rubbed on face and neck
  Lest cleanliness betray us.

And you'll remember farmer Kutz –
  Though scarcely for his bounty –
He'd leased a forty-acre block,
  And thought he owned the county;
A farmer of the old-world school,
  That men grew hard and grim in,
He drew his water from the pool
  That we preferred to swim in.

And do you mind when down the creek
  His angry way he wended,

A greenhide cartwhip in his hand
  For our young backs intended?
Three naked boys upon the sand –
  Half-buried and half-sunning
Three startled boys without their clothes
  Across the paddock running.

We'd had some scares, but we looked blank
  When, resting there and chumming
We glanced by chance across the bank
  And saw the farmer coming!
Some home impressions linger yet
  Of cups of sorrow brimming:
I hardly think that we'll forget
  The last day we went swimming.

Henry Lawson, 1867-1922

Been There Before

There came a stranger to Walgett town,
To Walgett town, when the sun was low,
And he carried a thirst that was worth a crown,
Yet how to quench it, he did not know;
But he thought he might take those yokels down,
The guileless yokels of Walgett town.

They made him a bet in a private bar,
In a private bar when the talk was high,

And they bet him some pounds no matter how far
He could pelt a stone, yet he could not shy
A stone right over the river so brown,
The Darling River at Walgett town.

He knew that the river from bank to bank
Was fifty yards, and he smiled a smile
As he tumbled down, but his hopes they sank
For there wasn't a stone within fifty mile;
For the saltbush plain and the open down
Produce no quarries in Walgett town.

The yokels laughed at his hopes o'erthrown,
And he stood awhile like a man in a dream;
Then out of his pocket he fetched a stone,
And pelted it over the silent stream –
He had been there before. He had wandered down
On a previous visit to Walgett town.

A.B. ('Banjo') Paterson, 1864-1941

The Sundowner

I know not where this tiresome man
With his shrewd, sable billy-can
And his unwashed Democracy
His boomed-up pilgrimage began.

Sometimes he wandered far outback
On a precarious Tucker Track;

Sometimes he lacked Necessities
No gentleman would like to lack.

Tall was the grass, I understand,
When the Squatter ruled the land.
Why were the Conquerors kind to him?
Ah, the Wax Matches in his hand!

Where bullockies with oaths intense
Made of the dragged-up trees a fence,
Gambling with scorpions he rolled
His Swag, conspicuous, immense.

In the full splendour of his power
Rarely he touched a mile an hour,
Dawdling at sunset, History says,
For the Pint Pannikin of flour.

Seldom he worked; he was, I fear,
Unreasonably slow and dear:
Little he earned, and that he spent
Deliberately drinking Beer.

Cheerfully, sorefooted child of chance,
Swiftly we knew him at a glance;
Boastful and self-compassionate,
Australia's Interstate Romance

Shall he not live in Robust Rhyme,
Soliloquies and Odes Sublime?
Strictly between ourselves, he was
A rare old Humbug all the time.

In many a Book of Bushland dim
Mopokes shall give greeting grim:
The old swans pottering in the reeds
Shall pass the time of day to him.

In many a page our friend shall take
Small sticks his evening fire to make;
Shedding his waistcoat, he shall mix
On its smooth back his Johnny-Cake.

'Mid the dry leaves and silvery bark
Often at nightfall will he park
Close to a homeless creek, and hear
The Bunyip paddling in the dark.

John Shaw Neilson, 1872-1942

Five Miles from Gundagai

I'm used to punchin' bullock teams
Across the hills and plains,
I've teamed outback these forty years
In blazin' droughts and rains,
I've lived a heap of troubles down
Without a bloomin' lie,
But I can't forget what happened to me
Five miles from Gundagai.

'Twas getting dark, the team got bogged,
The axle snapped in two;
I lost me matches and me pipe,
So what was I to do?
The rain came on, 'twas bitter cold,
And hungry too was I.
And the dog sat on the tucker box
Five miles from Gundagai.

Some blokes I know has stacks o' luck,
No matter 'ow they fall,
But there was I, Lord love a duck!
No blasted luck at all.
I couldn't make a pot of tea,
Nor get me trousers dry,
And the dog sat on the tucker box
Five miles from Gundagai.

I can forgive the blinkin' team,

I can forgive the rain,
I can forgive the dark and cold,
And go through it again,
I can forgive me rotten luck,
But hang me till I die,
I can't forgive that bloody dog
Five miles from Gundagai.

Traditional

In Possum Land

In Possum Land the nights are fair,
The streams are fresh and clear;
No dust is in the moonlit air;
No traffic jars the ear.

With possums gambolling overhead,
'Neath western stars so grand,
Ah! Would that we could make our bed
Tonight in Possum Land.

Henry Lawson, 1867-1922

The Shakedown on the Floor

Set me back for twenty summers,
  For I'm tired of cities now —
Set my feet in red-soil furrows
  And my hands upon the plough,
With the two Black Brothers trudging
  On the home stretch through the loam
While along the grassy sidling
  Come the cattle grazing home.

And I finish ploughing early,
  And I hurry home to tea —
There's my black suit on the stretcher,
  And a clean white shirt for me;
There's a dance at Rocky Rises,
  And, when they can dance no more,
For a certain favoured party
  There's a shakedown on the floor.

You remember Mary Carey,
  Bushman's favourite at The Rise?
With her sweet small freckled features,
  Red-gold hair, and kind grey eyes;
Sister, daughter, to her mother,
  Mother, sister to the rest —
And of all my friends and kindred
  Mary Carey loved me best.

Far too shy, because she loved me,
  To be dancing oft with me;

(What cared I, because she loved me,
  If the world were there to see?)
But we lingered by the sliprails
  While the rest were riding home,
Ere the hour before the dawning
  Dimmed the great star-clustered dome.

Small brown hands, that spread the mattress,
  While the old folk winked to see
How she'd find an extra pillow
  And an extra sheet for me.
For a moment shyly smiling,
  She would grant me one kiss more —
Slip away and leave me happy
  By the shakedown on the floor.

Rock me hard in steerage cabins,
  Rock me soft in first saloons,
Lay me on the sandhill lonely
  Under waning Western moons;
But wherever night may find me —
  Till I rest for evermore —
I shall dream that I am happy
  In the shakedown on the floor

Henry Lawson (1867-1922)

New Life, New Love

The cool breeze ripples the river below,
  And the fleecy clouds float high,
And I mark how the dark green gum-trees match
  The bright blue vault of the sky.
The rain has been, and the grass is green
  Where the slopes were bare and brown,
And I see the things that I used to see
  In the days ere my head went down.

I have found a light in my long dark night,
  Brighter than stars or moon;
I have lost the fear of the sunset drear,
  And the sadness of afternoon.
Here let us stand while I hold your hand,
  Where the light's on the your golden head –
Oh! I feel the thrill that I used to feel
  In the days ere my heart was dead.

The storm's gone by, but my lips are dry
  And the old wrong rankles yet –
Sweetheart or wife, I must take new life
  From your red lips warm and wet!
So let it be, you my cling to me,
  There is nothing on earth to dread,
For I'll be the man that I used to be
  In the days ere my heart were dead!

Henry Lawson, (1867-1922)

A Mountain Station

I bought a run a while ago
  On country rough and ridgy,
Where wallaroos and wombats grow —
  The Upper Murrumbidgee.
The grass is rather scant, it's true,
  But this a fair exchange is,
The sheep can see a lovely view
  By climbing up the ranges.

And She-oak Flat's the station's name,
  I'm not surprised at that, sirs:
The oaks were there before I came,
  And I supplied the flat, sirs.
A man would wonder how it's done,
  The stock so soon decreases —
They sometimes stumble off the run
  And break themselves to pieces.

I've tried to make expenses meet,
  But wasted all my labours;
The sheep the dingoes didn't eat
  Were stolen by the neighbours.
They stole my pears — my native pears —
  Those thrice-convicted felons,
And ravished from me unawares
  My crop of paddy-melons.

And sometimes under sunny skies,
  Without an explanation,
The Murrumbidgee used to rise
  And overflow the station.
But this was caused (as I now know)
  When summer sunshine glowing
Had melted all Kiandra's snow
  And set the river going.

Then in the news, perhaps, you read:
  'Stock Passings. Puckawidgee,
Fat cattle: Seven hundred head
  Swept down the Murrumbidgee:
Their destination's quite obscure,
  But, somehow, there's a notion,
Unless the river falls, they're sure
  To reach the Southern Ocean.

So after that I'll give it best;
  No more with Fate I'll battle.
I'll let the river take the rest,
  For those were all my cattle.
And with one comprehensive curse
  I close my brief narration,
And advertise it in my verse –
  For Sale! A Mountain Station.'

A..B ('Banjo') Paterson (1864-1941)

Emus

My annals have it so:
A thing my mother saw,
Nigh eighty years ago,
With happiness and awe.

Along a level hill –
A clearing in wild space,
And night's last tardy chill
Yet damp on morning's face.

Sight never to forget:
Solemn against the sky
In stately silhouette
Ten emus walking by.

One after one they went
In line, and without haste:
On their unknown intent,
Ten emus grandly paced.

She, used to hedged-in fields,
Watched them go filing past
Into the great Bush Wilds
Silent and vast.

Sudden that hour she knew
That this far place was good,
This mighty land and new
For soul's hardihood.

For hearts that love the strange,
That carry wonder;
The Bush, the hills, the range,
And the dark flats under.

Mary Fullerton, 1868-1946

A Singer of the Bush

There is waving of grass in the breeze
And a song in the air,
And a murmur of myriad bees
That toil everywhere.
There is scent in the blossom and bough,
And the breath of the Spring
Is as soft as a kiss on the brow
And Springtime I sing.

There is drought on the land, and the stock
Tumble down in their tracks
Or follow – a tottering flock –
The scrub-cutter's axe.
While ever a creature survives
The axes shall swing;
We are fighting with fate for their lives –
And the combat I sing.

A. B. ('Banjo') Paterson, 1864-1941

The Teams

A cloud of dust on the long, white road,
  And teams go creeping on
Inch by inch with the weary load;
  And by the power of the greenhide goad
The distant goal is won.

With eyes half-shut to the blinding dust,
  And necks to the yokes bent low,
The beasts are pulling as bullocks must;
  And the shining tyres might almost rust
While the spokes are turning slow.

With face half-hid by a broad-brimmed hat,
  That shades from the heat's white waves,
And shouldered whip, with its greenhide plait,
  The driver plods with a gait like that
Of his weary, patient slaves.

He wipes his brow, for the day is hot,
  And spits to the left with spite;
He shouts at Bally, and flicks at Scott,
  And raises dust from the back of Spot,
And spits to the dusty right.

He'll sometimes pause as a thing of form
  In front of a settler's door,
And ask for a drink, and remark, 'It's warm,'
  Or say 'There's sign of a thunderstorm;'
But he seldom utters more.

The rains are heavy on roads like these
  And, fronting his lonely home,
For days together the settler sees
  The wagons bogged to the axletrees,
Or ploughing the sodden loam.

And then, when the roads are at their worst,
  The bushman's children hear
The cruel blows of the whips reversed
  While the bullocks pull as their hearts would burst,
And bellow with pain and fear.

And thus – with glimpses of home and rest –
  Are the long, long journeys done;
And thus – 'tis a thankless life at best! –
  Is Distance fought in the mighty West,
And the lonely battle won.

Henry Lawson, 1867-1922

Down the River

I've done with joys an' misery,
An' why should I repine?
There's no one knows the past but me
An' that ol' dog o' mine.
We camp, an' walk, an' camp an' walk,
An find it fairly good;
He can do anything but talk –
An' wouldn't, if he could.

We sits an' thinks beside the fire,
With all the stars a-shine,
An' no one knows our thoughts but me
An that there dog o' mine.
We has our Johnny-cake an' scrag,
An' finds 'em fairly good;
He can do anything but talk –
An' wouldn't if he could.

I has my smoke, he has his rest,
When sunset's getting dim;
An' if I do get drunk at times,
It's all the same to him.
So long's he's got my swag to mind,
He thinks that times is good;
He can do anything but talk –
An' wouldn't if he could.

Henry Lawson, 1867-1922

Rain in the Mountains

The valley's full of misty clouds,
Its tinted beauty drowning,
Tree-tops are veiled in fleecy shrouds,
And mountain fronts are frowning.

The mist is hanging like a pall
Above the granite ledges,
And many a silvery waterfall
Leaps o'er the valley's edges.

The sky is of a leaden grey,
Save where the north looks surly,
The driven daylight speeds away,
And night come o'er us early.

Dear Love, the rain will pass full soon,
Far sooner than my sorrow,
But in a golden afternoon
The sun may set tomorrow.

Henry Lawson, 1867-1922

The Stirrup Song

We've drunk our wine, we've kissed our girls, and
  funds are getting low,
The horses must be thinking it's a fair thing now to go.
Sling up the swags on Condamine, and strap the
  billies fast,
And stuff a bottle in the bag, and let's be off at last.

What matter if the creeks are up! – the cash, alas,
  runs down! –
A very sure and certain sign we're long enough in town;
The black man rides the 'boko' and you'd better take
  the bay,
Quartpot will do to carry me the stage we'll go today.

No grass this side the Border fence, and all the
  mulga's dead;
The horses for a day or two will have to spiel ahead;
Man never yet from Queensland brought a bullock
  or a hack
But lost condition on that God-abandoned Border track:

But once we're through the rabbit-proof, it's certain
  since the rain
There's whips of grass and water, so it's 'West-by-
North' again;
There's feed on Tyson country, we can spell the
  mokes a week
Where Bill Stevens last year trapped his brumbies on
  Bough Creek.

The Paroo may be quickly crossed – the Eulo
  Common's bare –
And anyhow it isn't wise, old man, to dally there!
Alack-a-day! far wiser men than you or I succumb
To a woman's wiles and potency of Queensland
  wayside rum!

Then over sand and spinifex and o'er range and
  plain!
The nags are fresh; besides they know they're
  westward bound again!
The brand upon old Darkie's thigh is that upon the
  hide
Of bullocks we shall muster on the Diamantina side.

We'll light our campfires while we may, and yarn
  beside the blaze,
The jingling hobble-chains shall make a music
  through the days;
And while the tucker-bags are right and we've a
  stock of weed
The swagman will be welcome to a pipeful and a feed.

So fill your pipe, and ere we mount we'll drain
  a parting nip;
Here's how that West-by-North again may prove a
  lucky trip;
Then back once more, let's trust you'll find your best
  girl's merry face,
Or, if she jilts you, may you get a better in her place.

Harry ('The Breaker') Morant, 1865-1902

Freedom on the Wallaby

Our fathers toiled for bitter bread
While idlers thrived beside them;
But food to eat and clothes to wear
Their native land deprived them.
They left their native land in spite
Of royalty's regalia,
And so they came, or if they stole,
Were sent out to Australia.

They struggled hard to make a home,
Hard grubbing 'twas and clearing.
They weren't troubled much with toffs
When they were pioneering:
And now that we have made the land
A garden full of promise,
Old greed must crook his dirty hand
And come and take if from us.

But Freedom's on the Wallaby,
She'll knock the tyrants silly,
She's going to light another fire
And boil another billy.
We'll make the tyrants feel the sting
Of those that they would throttle;
They needn't say the fault is ours
If blood should stain the wattle.

Henry Lawson, 1867-1922

The Last Sundowner

He sat upon a fallen log,
And heaved a long, deep sigh.
His gnarled hand fondling his old dog
As his gaze went to the sky.
'There goes another plane,' said he –
'A soarin', roarin' pest!'
They robs a man of privacy,
An' motor cars of rest.

'Sundownin' ain't the game it was
Since men have took to wings;
An' life grows narrer, jist because
Of planes an' cars an' things.
For the planes have pinched me private skies
An' the cars have grabbed me earth
An' all the news by wireless flies;
So what's sundownin' worth?

'Time was when I could sit me down
Where man had left no sign,
An' earth an' sky for miles aroun'
For that one hour was mine.
And I could sit an' think me thorts
An' watch the sun go west
Without no crazy ingine's snorts
To break into me rest.

'And as the afternoon grew late
I'd seek the haunts of men.

An' at some lonely homestead gate
I'd have sure welcome then;
An' tucker-bags were gladly filled
And rest found for my back,
In change for bits of news I spilled
And gossip of the track.

'But now that wireless spreads its lies
From this and other lands,
They look on me with hard, cold eyes
An' give with grudgin' hands.
It's them that has to give me news;
And when I seek some wide,
Once silent scene, planes spoil me views,
An' cars honk me aside.'

He sat upon a fallen log
And heaved a long, deep sigh,
'We're again', me and me ole dog,
An' old things have to die.
Sundownin's dead: men's minds an' ways
Is changin' with a jerk.
Seems like I'll have to end me days
Travellin', in search of work.'

C. J. Dennis, 1876-1938

Camping

O Scents from dewy grass and tree;
O fluting birds at morn,
Loud, jubilant, or broken-sweet;
O Cloudlets fleecy, torn,
Floating on the fields of azure blue
Far in the distance, low!
I think of these and raptured cry:
A-camping we will go!

With every waft from greening earth
Wet with a gentle shower;
With every moving in the trees;
With every dancing flower;
I hear a song within my breast,
Over wide spaces, and I sigh:
A-camping we will go!

By murmuring streams and fountain falls;
By ferny hills and dales;
By shadowed cleft and hidden cave,
And old forgotten trails;
By bending, perfumed lilied brake;
By waves in endless flow;
I'll sing as on the grass I lie:
A-camping we will go!

By flaming multitudes of stars,
Unvalued of most men,
Offering ephemerals purged might,

Aeries of prison-den;
By crescent moons soaring above
All beauty that I know—
A lover to the bush I'll fly:
A-camping we will go!

Barcroft Boake, 1866-1892

Progress

They've builded wooden timber tracks,
And a trolley with screaming breaks
Noses into the secret bush,
Into the birdless brooding bush,
And the tall old gums it takes.

And down the sunny valley
The snorting saw screams slow;
Oh, bush that nursed my people,
Oh, bush that cursed my people,
I weep to watch you go.

'Furnley Maurice' (Frank Wilmot) 1881-1942

Bush Songs & Ballads

The Wild Colonial Boy

'Tis of a wild colonial boy,
Jack Doolan was his name,
Of poor but honest parents
Who lived in Castlemaine,
He was his father's only hope,
His mother's pride and joy,
And dearly did his parents love
Their wild colonial boy.

Chorus:
So come all my hearties,
We'll roam the mountains high,
Together we will plunder,
Together we will ride.
We'll scour along the valleys
And gallop o'er the plains,
And scorn to live in slavery,
Bound down with chains.

He was scarcely sixteen years of age
When he left his native home,
And through Australia's sunny clime
A bushranger did roam.
He robbed those wealthy squatters,
Their stock he did destroy,
And a terror to Australia
Was the wild colonial boy.

In 'sixty-one this daring youth
Commenced his wild career,
With courage all undaunted,
No foreman did he fear.
He stuck up the Beechworth mail-coach
And robbed Judge McEvoy,
Who, trembling cold, gave up his gold,
To the wild colonial boy.

He bade the judge, 'Good morning,'
And told him to beware,
That he'd never rob a hearty chap
Who acted on the square.
And never rob a mother of
Her son and only joy,
Or else he might turn outlaw like
That wild colonial boy.

One day as he was riding
The mountainside along,
A-listening to the little birds,
Their pleasant laughing song,
Three mounted troopers rode along,
Kelly, Davis and Fitzroy,
With a warrant for the capture
Of the wild colonial boy.

'Surrender now, Jack Doolan,
You see we're three to one,
Surrender in the Queen's name,
You daring highwayman!'

He pulled a pistol from his belt
And waved the little toy,
'I'll fight but not surrender!'
Cried the wild colonial boy.

He fired at trooper Kelly,
And brought him to the ground,
But in return, from Davis,
Received his mortal wound,
All shattered through the jaw he lay,
Still firing at Fitzroy,
And that's the way they captured him,
The wild colonial boy.

Traditional

Brave Ben Hall

Come all Australian sons with me,
For a hero has been slain
And cowardly butchered in his sleep
Upon the Lachlan plain.

Pray do not stay your seemly grief,
But let a teardrop fall
For many hearts shall always mourn
The fate of bold Ben Hall.

No brand of Cain e'er stamped his brow,
No widow's curse did fall;
When tales are read, the squatters dread
The name of bold Ben Hall.

The records of this hero bold
Through Europe have been heard,
And formed a conversation
Between many an Earl and Lord.

Ever since the good old days
Of Dick Turpin and Duval,
Knights of the road were outlaws bold,
And so was bold Ben Hall.

He never robbed a needy man,
His records best will show,
Staunch and loyal to his mates,
And manly to the foe.

Until he left his trusty mates,
The cause I ne'er could hear,
The bloodhounds of the law heard this
And after him did steer.

They found his place of ambush,
And cautiously they crept,
And savagely they murdered him
While the victim slept.

Yes, savagely they murdered him,
The cowardly blue-coat imps,
Who were led onto where he slept
By informing peelers' pimps.

No more he'll mount his gallant steed,
Nor range the mountains high,
The widow's friend in poverty –
Bold Ben Hall, good-bye.

Traditional

The Streets of Forbes

Come all you Lachlan men,
A sorrowful tale I'll tell
Concerning a bold hero
Who through misfortune fell.
His name it was Ben Hall,

A man of great renown,
Who was hunted from his station
And like a dog shot down.

Three years he roamed the highway
And had a lot of fun,
A thousand pounds was on his head,
With Gilbert and John Dunn.
Ben parted from his comrades;
The outlaws did agree
To give up their bushranging
And cross the briny sea.

Ben went to Goobang Creek,
And this was his downfall;
For riddled like a sieve
Was valiant Ben Hall.
It was early in the morning
Upon the fifth of May,
When the police surrounded him
As fast asleep he lay.

Bill Dargin he was chosen
To shoot the outlaw dead;
The troopers fired madly
And filled him full of lead.
They threw him on his horse
And strapped him like a swag,
Then led him through the streets of Forbes
To show the prize they had!

Jack McGuire

The Death of Ben Hall

Ben Hall was out on the Lachlan side
With a thousand pounds on his head;
A score of troopers were scattered wide
And a hundred more were ready to ride
Wherever a rumour led.

They had followed his track from the Weddin

heights
And north by the Weelong yards
Through dazzling days and moonlit nights
They had sought him over their rifle-sights,
With their hands on their trigger-guards.

The outlaw stole like a hunted fox
Through the scrub and stunted heath,
And peered like a hawk from his eyrie rocks
Through the waving boughs of the sapling box
On the troopers riding beneath.

His clothes were rent by the clutching thorn
And his blistered feet were bare;
Ragged and torn, with his beard unshorn,
He hid in the woods like a beast forlorn,
With a padded path to his lair.

But every night when the white stars rose
He crossed by the Gunning Plain
To a stockman's hut where the Gunning flows,

And struck on the door three swift light blows,
And a hand unhooked the chain –

And the outlaw followed the lone path back
With food for another day;
And the kindly darkness covered his track
And the shadows swallowed him deep and black
Where the starlight melted away.

But his friend had read of the Big Reward,
And his soul was stirred with greed;
He fastened his door and window-board,
He saddled his horse and crossed the ford,
And spurred to the town at speed.

You may ride at a man's or a maid's behest
When honour or true love call
And steel your heart to the worst or best,
But the ride that is ta'en on a traitor's quest
Is the bitterest ride of all.

A hot wind blew from the Lachlan bank
And a curse on its shoulder came;
The pine-trees frowned at him, rank on rank,
The sun on a gathering storm-cloud sank
And flushed his cheek with shame.

He reined at the Court; and the tale began
That the rifles alone should end;
Sergeant and trooper laid their plan
To draw the net on a hunted man
At the treacherous word of a friend.

False was the hand that raised the chain
And false was the whispered word;
'The troopers have turned to the south again,
You may dare to camp on the Gunning Plain.'
And the weary outlaw heard.

He walked from the hut but a quarter-mile
Where a clump of saplings stood
In a sea of grass like a lonely isle;
And the moon came up in a little while
Like silver steeped in blood.

Ben Hall lay down on the dew-wet ground
By the side of his tiny fire;
And a night breeze woke, and he heard no sound
As the troopers drew their cordon round –
And the traitor earned his hire.

And nothing they saw in the dim grey light,
But the little glow in the trees;
And they crouched in the tall cold grass all night,
Each one ready to shoot at sight,
With his rifle cocked on his knees.

When the shadows broke and the dawn's white sword
Swung over the mountain wall,
And a little wind blew over the ford,
A sergeant sprang to his feet and roared:
'In the name of the Queen, Ben Hall!'

Haggard, the outlaw leapt from his bed
With his lean arms held on high.

'Fire!' And the word was scarcely said
When the mountains rang to a rain of lead –
And the dawn went drifting by.

They kept their word and they paid his pay
Where a clean man's hand would shrink;
And that was the traitor's master-day
As he stood by the bar on his homeward way
And called on the crowd to drink.

He banned no creed and he banned no class,
And he called to his friends by name;
But the worst would shake his head and pass
And none would drink from the bloodstained glass
And the goblet red with shame.

And I know when I hear the last grim call
And my mortal hour is spent,
When the light is hid and the curtains fall
I would rather sleep with the dead Ben Hall
Than go where that traitor went.

Anonymous

Ballad of Ben Hall's Gang

Come all you wild colonials
And listen to my tale;
A story of bushrangers' deeds

I will to you unveil.
'Tis of those gallant heroes,
Game fighters one and all;
And we'll sit and sing, 'Long live the King,
Dunn, Gilbert and Ben Hall.'

Frank Gardiner was a bushranger
Of terrible renown;
He robbed the Forbes gold escort,
And eloped with Kitty Brown,
But in the end they lagged him,
Two-and-thirty years in all.
'We must avenge the Darkie,'
Says Dunn, Gilbert and Ben Hall.

Ben Hall was a squatter
Who owned six hundred head;
A peaceful man was he until
Arrested by Sir Fred.
His home burned down, his wife cleared out;
His cattle perished all.
'They'll not take me a second time,'
Says valiant Ben Hall.

John Gilbert was a flash cove,
And John O'Meally too;
With Ben and Burke and Johnny Vane
They all were comrades true.
They rode into Canowindra
And gave a public ball.
'Roll up, roll up, and have a spree,'
Says Gilbert and Ben Hall.

They took possession of the town,
Including public houses
And treated all the cockatoos
And shouted for their spouses
They danced with all the pretty girls
And held a carnival.
'We don't hurt them who don't hurt us,'
Says Gilbert and Ben Hall.

Then Miss O'Flanagan performed
In manner quite genteelly
Upon the grand pianner
For the bushranger O'Meally.
'Roll up! Roll up! Its' just a lark
For women, kids and all;
We'll rob the rich and help the poor,'
Says Gilbert and Ben Hall.

They made a raid on Bathurst,
The pace was getting hot;
But Johnny Vane surrendered
After Micky Burke was shot.
O'Meally at Goimbla
Did like a hero fall;
'The game is getting lively,'
Says Gilbert and Ben Hall.

Then Gilbert took a holiday,
Ben Hall got new recruits;
The Old Man and Dunleavy
Shared in the plunder's fruits.

Dunleavy he surrendered
And they jugged the Old Man tall –
So Johnny Gilbert came again
To help his mate, Ben Hall.

John Dunn he was a jockey,
A-riding all the winners,
Until he joined Hall's gang to rob
The publicans and sinners;
And many a time the Royal Mail
Bailed up at John Dunn's call,
A thousand pounds is on their heads –
Dunn, Gilbert and Ben Hall.

'Hand over all your watches
And the banknotes in your purses.
All travellers must pay toll to us;
We don't care for your curses.
We are the rulers of the roads,
We've seen the troopers fall,
And we want your gold and money,'
Says Dunn, Gilbert and Ben Hall.

'Next week we'll visit Goulburn
And clean the banks out there;
So if you see the peelers,
 Just tell them to beware;
Some day to Sydney city
We mean to pay a call,
And we'll take the whole damn country,'
Says Dunn, Gilbert and Ben Hall.

Anonymous

The Bloody Field of Wheogo

The moon rides high in a starry sky,
And, through the midnight gloom,
A faery scene of woodland green
Her silver rays illume.

Dark mountains show a ridge of snow
Against the deep blue sky,
And a winding stream with sparkling gleam
Flows merrily murmuring by.

Not a sound is heard, save a bough when stirred
By the night-wind's moaning sigh,
Or, piercing and shrill, echoed back by the hill,
A curlew's mournful cry.

A twinkling bright in the shadowy night
A lonely taper shines,
And seated there is a wanton fair
Who in amorous sadness pines.

For her lord is gone, and she sits alone,
Alone in her mountain home.
For 'twas not her lord that she deplored,
For she liked to see him roam.

The joy of her heart is a bushranger smart
Who, lion-like, prowls in the night:
And with supper all spread, and a four-post bed,
She waits by the flickering light.

Equipped for fight, in trappings bright,
Came a band of warriors there,
By gallant Sir Fred right gallantly led,
The 'ranger to seize in a snare.

They spread all around, and the house they surround,
Nine men with revolver and gun;
'A reward's on his head!' cried the gallant Sir Fred,
'And we're nine to the bushranger's one!'

Still gleamed the light in the shades of night,
And still the pale moon shone;
But no 'ranger came to cheer the dame
As she sat by the window alone.

The warriors bold were freezing with cold,
And wished they were in their beds,
When the echoing beat of a horse's feet
Sent the blood in a rush to their heads!

At gentle speed on snow-white steed
And singing a joyous song
To the beckoning light in the shadowy night
The bushranger rides along.

A stalwart man was he to scan,
And flushed with ruffian pride;
In many a fray he had won the day
And the 'New Police' had defied.

Up started then Sir Fred and his men
With cocked carbines in hand

And called aloud to the 'ranger proud
On pain of death to 'stand'.

But the 'ranger proud, he laughed aloud,
And bounding rode away,
While Sir Frederick Pott shut his eye for a shot
And missed – in his usual way.

His troopers then like valiant men
With their carbines blazed away.
The whistling lead on its mission sped,
But whither, none can say.

The snow-white steed at gentle speed
Bore the 'ranger from their view
And left Sir Fred to return to bed –
There was nothing else to do.

But Sir Frederick Pott with rage was hot
As he looked at his warriors eight.
They were nine to one, with revolver and gun!
He cursed his luckless fate.

He shuddered to think how his glory would sink
When the country heard of the mess
And the tale was told of his exploit bold
In the columns of the Press.

In fury then he marched his men
To the home of the wanton fair.
With warlike din they entered in
To search and ransack there.

In slumber sound a boy they found,
And brave Sir Frederick said:
'By a flash in the pan we missed the man,
So we'll take the boy instead!'

Anonymous

The Maids of the Mountains

In the wild Weddin Mountains
There live two young dames,
Kate O'Meally, Bet Mayhew
Are their pretty names.

These maids of the mountains
Are bonny bush belles:
They ride out on horseback
Togged out like young swells.

They dressed themselves up
In their brothers' best clothes
And looked very rakish
As you may suppose
In the joy of their hearts
They chuckled with glee –
What fun if for robbers
They taken should be.

Just then the policemen,

By day and by night,
Were seeking Frank Gardiner,
The bushranger sprite.
Bold Constable Clark
Wore a terrible frown
As he thought how Sir Freddy
By Frank was done down.

They sought for the 'ranger
But of course found him not,
When suddenly Katy
And Betsy they spot.
'By Pott,' shouted Clark,
"That is Gardiner I see!
'The wretch must be taken;
Come, boys, follow me!'

'Stand!' shouted the bobbies
In accents most dread,
'Or else you will taste
Our infallibe lead!'
But the maids of the mountains
Just laughed at poor Clark,
And galloped away
To continue their lark.

The troopers pursued them,
And hot was the chase;
'Tis only at Randwick
They go such a pace.
Clark captured the pair,
Then, to show his vexation,

He lugged them both off
To the Young police station.

The maids of the mountains
The joke much enjoyed,
To see their brave captors
So sadly annoyed.
Next day they still smiled
As they stood in the dock;
Their awful position
Their nerves did not shock.

But Constable Clark
Did not look very jolly;
He had no excuse
For such absolute folly.
He admitted the girls
Were just out on a spree
And hoped that His Worship
Would set them both free.

And so the farce ended
Of Belles versus Blues,
Which caused no great harm
And did much to amuse,
But the Burrangong bobbies
Will place in the cells
No more maids of the mountains –
The bonny bush belles.

Anonymous

Frank Gardiner He is Caught at Last

Frank Gardiner he is caught at last
And now in Sydney jail —
For wounding Sergeant Middleton
And robbing the Mudgee mail,
For plundering of the escort
And Cargo mail also,
It was for gold he made so bold
And not so long ago.

His daring deeds surprised them all
Throughout the Sydney land;
He gave a call unto his friends
And quickly raised a band.
Fortune always favoured him
Until the time of late;
There was Burke, the brave O'Meally too,
Met with a dreadful fate.

Young Johnny Vane surrendered,
Ben Hall received some wounds;
And as for Johnny Gilbert,
At Binalong he was found.
Alone he was, he lost his horse,
Three troopers hove in sight;
He fought the three most manfully,
Got slaughtered in the fight.

Farewell adieu to outlawed Frank
He was the poor man's friend;
The Government has secured him,
The laws he did offend.
He boldly stood his trial
And answered in a breath
'And do what you will, you can but kill,
I have no fear of death!'

Fresh charges brought against him
From neighbours near and far
Day after day they remanded him,
Escorted from the bar.
And now it is all over
The sentence it is passed
Reprieving from the gallows cursed
This highwayman at last.

When lives you take – a warning boys –
A woman never trust;
She will turn round, I will be bound,
Queen's evidence the first.
Two and thirty years he's doomed
To slave all for the Crown;
And well may he say he cursed the day
He met old Mother Brown.

Anonymous

The Diverting History of John Gilbert

John Gilbert was a bushranger
Of terrible renown
For sticking lots of people up,
And shooting others down.

John Gilbert said unto his pals,
'Although they make a bobbery
About our tricks, we've never done
A tip-top thing in robbery.

'We've all of us a fancy for
Experiments in pillage;
But never have we seized a town,
 Or even sacked a village.

John Gilbert stated to his mates,
'Though partners we have been
In all rascality, yet we
No festal day have seen.'

John Gilbert said he thought he saw
No obstacle to hinder a
Piratical descent upon
The town of Canowindra.

So into Canowindra town
Rode Gilbert and his men

And all the Canowindra folk
Subsided there and then.

The Canowindra populace
Cried, 'Here's a lot of strangers,'
But suddenly recovered when
They found they were bushrangers.

John Gilbert and his partisans
Said, 'Don't you be afraid —
We are but old companions whom
Rank outlaws you have made.'

So Johnny Gilbert says, says he,
'We'll never hurt a hair
Of men who bravely recognise
That we are just and fair.'

The New South Welshmen said at once,
Not making any fuss,
That Johnny Gilbert after all
Was 'just but one of us.'

So Johnny Gilbert took the town
And took the public houses,
And treated all the cockatoos
And shouted for their spouses.

And Miss O'Flanagan performed
In manner quite 'ginteelly'
Upon the grand piano for
The bushranger O'Meally.

And every stranger passing by
They took, and when they'd got him,
They robbed him of his money, and
Occasionally they shot him.

And Johnny's enigmatic freak
Admits of this solution,
Bushranging is in New South Wales
A favoured institution.

So Johnny Gilbert ne'er allows
An anxious thought to fetch him,
Because he knows the Government
Don't really want to catch him.

And if such practices should be
To New South Welshmen dear,
With not the least demurring word
Ought we to interfere?

Anonymous

How Gilbert Died

There's never a stone at the sleeper's head,
There's never a fence beside,
And the wandering stock on the grave may tread
Unnoticed and undenied;
But the smallest child on the Watershed
Can tell you how Gilbert died.

For he rode at dusk with his comrade Dunn
To the hut at the Stockman's Ford;
In the waning light of the sinking sun
They peered with a fierce accord.
They were outlaws both – and on each man's head
Was a thousand pounds reward.

They had taken toll of the country round,
And the troopers came behind
With a black that tracked like a human hound
In the scrub and ranges blind;
He could run the trail where a white man's eye
No sign of a track could find.

He had hunted them out of One Tree Hill
And over the Old Man Plain,
But they wheeled their tracks with a wild beast's
skill,
And they made for the range again;
Then away to the hut where their grandsire dwelt
They rode with a loosened rein.

And their grandsire gave them a greeting bold:
'Come in and rest in peace,
No safer place does the country hold –
With the night pursuit must cease,
And we'll drink success to the roving boys,
And to hell with the black police.'

But they went to death when they entered there
In the hut at the Stockman's Ford,
For their grandsire's words were as false as fair –
They were doomed to the hangman's cord.
He had sold them both to the black police
For the sake of the big reward.

In the depth of the night there are forms that glide
As stealthy as serpents creep,
And around the hut where the outlaws hide
They plant in the shadows deep,
And they wait till the first faint flush of dawn
Shall waken their prey from sleep.

But Gilbert wakes while the night is dark –
A restless sleeper aye,
He has heard the sound of a sheep-dog's bark,
And his horse's warning neigh,
And he says to his mate 'There are hawks abroad,
And it's time we went away.'

Their rifles stood at the stretcher head,
Their bridles lay to hand;
They wakened the old man out of his bed,
When they heard the sharp command:

'In the name of the Queen, lay down your arms,
Now, Dunn and Gilbert, stand!'

Then Gilbert reached for his rifle true
That close at hand he kept;
He pointed straight at the voice, and drew,
But never a flash outleapt,
For the water ran from the rifle breech –
It was drenched while the outlaws slept.

Then he dropped the piece with a bitter oath,
And he turned to his comrade Dunn;
'We are sold,' he said, 'we are dead men both,
But there may be a chance for one;
I'll stop and fight with the pistol here,
You take to your heels and run.'

So Dunn crept out on his hands and knees
In the dim, half-dawning light,
And he made his way to a patch of trees,
And was lost in the black of night;
And the trackers hunted his tracks all day,
But they never could trace his flight.

But Gilbert walked from the open door
In a confident style and rash;
He heard at his side the rifles roar,
And he heard the bullets crash,
But he laughed as he lifted his pistol-hand,
And he fired at the rifle flash.

Then out of the shadows the troopers aimed

At his voice and the pistol sound.
With rifle flashes the darkness flamed –
He staggered and spun around,
And they riddled his body with rifle balls
As it lay on the blood-soaked ground.

There's never a stone at the sleeper's head,
There's never a fence beside,
And the wandering stock on the grave may tread
Unnoticed and undenied;
But the smallest child on the Watershed
Can tell you how Gilbert died.

A.B. ('Banjo') Paterson, 1864-1941

The Death of Morgan

Throughout Australian history
No tongue or pen can tell
Of such preconcerted treachery –
There is no parallel –
As the tragic deed of Morgan's death;
Without warning he was shot
On Peechelba station,
It will never be forgot.

I have oft-times heard of murders
In Australia's golden land,

But such an open daylight scene
Of thirty in a band.
Assembled at the dawn of day,
And then to separate,
Behind the trees, some on their knees,
Awaiting Morgan's fate.

Too busy was the servant-maid;
She trotted half the night
From Macpherson's down to Rutherford's
The tidings to recite.
A messenger was sent away
Who for his neck had no regard,
He returned with a troop of traps
In hopes of their reward.

But they were all disappointed;
Mr McQuinlan was the man
Who fired from his rifle
And shot rebellious Dan.
Concealed he stood behind a tree
Till his victim came in view,
And as Morgan passed his doom was cast –
The unhappy man he slew.

There was a rush for trophies,
Soon as the man was dead;
They cut off his beard, his ears,
And half the hair from his head,
In truth it was a hideous sight
As he struggled on the ground,

They tore the clothes from off his back
And exposed the fatal wound.

Oh, Morgan was the traveller's friend;
The squatters all rejoice
That the outlaw's life is at en end,
No more they'll hear his voice.
Success attend all highwaymen
Who do the poor some good;
But my curse attend a treacherous man
Who'd shed another's blood.

Farewell to Burke, O'Meally,
Young Gilbert and Ben Hall,
Likewise to Daniel Morgan,
Who fell by rifle-ball;
So all young men be warned
And never take up arms,
Remember this, how true it is,
Bushranging hath no charms!

Anonymous

Over the Border

Over the border to rifle and plunder,
Over the border went Morgan the bold,
Over the border, a terrible blunder,
For over the border bold Morgan lies cold.

Over the border, why, why did he wander
'Midst cold-hearted strangers all friendless to roam?
Was it that absence might make him grow fonder
Of those he had left in his own native home?

Over the border not long, did he plunder,
Swift is stern justice as slow she is here,
Bold are the men o'er the border, no wonder,
When even the women know nothing of fear.

Fiercely they hunt him the cruel marauder.
Quickly they follow him, dead on his track,
Line with their troopers the river-side border,
Over he may come, but never go back.

Never – from far and near gathering quickly,
Stern faces watch him all night through the gloom,
Nought can avail him now sympathy sickly,
Sealed is forever the murderer's doom.

Shot like a dog in the bright early morning,
Shot without mercy who mercy had none,
Like a wild beast without challenge or warning.
Soon his career of dark villainy's run.

Honour the brave hearts there over the border,
Great was the lesson they taught us that day;
Oh! that each other bushranging marauder,
Over the border would venture to stray.

Anonymous

The Man from Snowy River

There was movement at the station, for the word had
    passed around
That the colt from old Regret had got away,
And had joined the wild bush horses – he was worth
    a thousand pound,
So all the cracks had gathered to the fray.
All the tried and noted riders from the stations near
    and far
Had mustered at the homestead overnight,
For the bushmen love hard riding where the wild
    bush horses are,
And the stock-horse snuffs the battle with delight.

There was Harrison, who made his pile when Pardon
    won the cup,
The old man with his hair as white as snow;
But few could ride beside him when his blood was
    fairly up –
He would go wherever horse and man could go.
And Clancy of the Overflow came down to lend
    a hand,
No better horseman ever held the reins;
For never horse could throw him while the saddle-
    girths would stand –
He learnt to ride while droving on the plains.

And one was there, a stripling on a small and weedy
    beast;
He was something like a racehorse undersized,

With a touch of Timor pony – three parts thorough
  bred at least –
And such as are by mountain horsemen prized.
He was hard and tough and wiry – just the sort that
  won't say die—
There was courage in his quick impatient tread;
And he bore the badge of gameness in his bright
  and fiery eye,
And the proud and lofty carriage of his head.

But still so slight and weedy, one would doubt his
  power to stay,
And the old man said, 'That horse will never do
For a long and tiring gallop – lad, you'd better stop
  away,
Those hills are far too rough for such as you.'
So he waited, sad and wistful – only Clancy stood
  his friend –
'I think we ought to let him come,' he said;
'I warrant he'll be with us when he's wanted at the
  end,
For both his horse and he are mountain bred.

'He hails from Snowy River, up by Kosciusko side,
Where the hills are twice as steep and twice as
  rough;
Where a horse's hoofs strike firelight from the flint
  stones every stride,
The man that holds his own is good enough.
And the Snowy River riders on the mountains make
  their home,

Where the river runs those giant hills between;
I have seen full many horsemen since I first
  commenced to roam,
But nowhere yet such horsemen have I seen.'

So he went; they found the horses by the big
  mimosa clump,
They raced away towards the mountain's brow,
And the old man gave his orders, 'Boys, go at them
  from the jump,
No use to try for fancy riding now.
And, Clancy, you must wheel them, try and wheel
  them to the right.
For never yet was rider that could keep the mob
  in sight,
If once they gain the shelter of those hills.'

So Clancy rode to wheel them – he was racing
  on the wing
Where the best and boldest riders take their place,
And he raced his stock-horse past them, and he
  made the ranges ring
With the stockwhip, as he met them face to face.
Then they halted for a moment, while he swung the
  dreaded lash,
But they saw their well-loved mountains full in view,
And they charged beneath the stockwhip with a
  sharp and sudden dash,
And off into the mountain scrub they flew.

Then fast the horsemen followed, where the gorges
  deep and black

Resounded to the thunder of their tread,
And the stockwhips woke the echoes, and they
  fiercely answered back
From cliffs and crags that beetled overhead.
And upward, ever upward, the wild horses held
  their way,
Where mountain ash and kurrajong grew wide;
And the old man muttered fiercely, 'We may bid
  the mob good day,
No man can hold them down the other side.'

When they reached the mountain's summit, even
  Clancy took a pull –
It well might make the boldest hold their breath;
The wild hop scrub grew thickly, and the hidden
  ground was full
Of wombat holes, and any slip was death.
But the man from Snowy River let the pony have
  his head,
And he swung his stockwhip round and gave a
  cheer,
And he raced him down the mountain like a torrent
  down its bed,
While the others stood and watched in very fear.

He sent the flint stones flying, but the pony kept its
  feet,
He cleared the fallen timber in his stride,
And the man from Snowy River never shifted in his
  seat –
It was grand to see that mountain horseman ride.

Through the stringy-barks and saplings, on the rough
and broken ground,
Down the hillside at a racing pace he went;
And he never drew the bridle till he landed safe
and sound
At the bottom of that terrible descent.

He was right among the horses as they climbed the
farther hill,
And the watchers on the mountain, standing mute,
Saw him ply the stockwhip fiercely; he was right
among them still
As he raced across the clearing in pursuit.
Then they lost him for a moment, where two mountain
gullies met
In the ranges – but a final glimpse reveals
On a dim and distant hillside the wild horses racing yet,
With the man from Snowy River at their heels.

And he ran them single-handed till their sides were
white with foam;
He followed like a bloodhound on their track,
Till they halted, cowed and beaten; then he turned
their heads for home,
And alone and unassisted brought them back.
But his hardy mountain pony he could scarcely raise
a trot,
He was blood from hip to shoulder from the spur;
But his pluck was still undaunted, and his courage
fiery hot,
For never yet was mountain horse a cur.

And down by Kosciusko, where the pine-clad ridges
  raise
Their torn and rugged battlements on high,
Where the air is clear as crystal, and the white stars
  fairly blaze
At midnight in the cold and frosty sky,
And where around the Overflow the reed-beds
  sweep and sway
To the breezes, and the rolling plains are wide,
The Man from Snowy River is a household world
  today,
And the stockmen tell the story of his ride.

A.B. ('Banjo') Paterson, 1864-1941

Jim's Whip

Yes, there it hangs upon the wall
And never gives a sound,
The hand that trimmed its greenhide fall
Is hidden undergound,
There, in that patch of sally shade,
Beneath that grassy mound.

I never take it from the wall,
That whip belonged to him,
The man I singled from them all,
He was my husband, Jim;
I see him now, so straight and tall,
So long and lithe of limb.

That whip was with him, night and day
When he was on the track;
I've often heard him laugh, and say
That when they heard its crack,
After the breaking of the drought,
The cattle all came back.

And all the time that Jim was here
A-working on the run
I'd hear that whip ring sharp and clear
Just about set of sun
To let me know that he was near
And that his work was done.

I was away that afternoon,
Penning the calves, when, bang!
I heard his whip, 'twas rather soon –
A thousand echoes rang
And died away among the hills,
As toward that hut I sprang.

I made the tea and waited but,
Seized by a sudden whim,
I went and sat outside the hut
Watching the light grow dim –
I waited there till after dark,
But not a sign of Jim.

The evening air was damp with dew;
Just as the clock struck ten
His horse came riderless – I knew
What was the matter then.

Why should the Lord have singled out
My Jim from other men?

I took the horse and found him where
He lay beneath the sky
With blood all clotted on his hair;
I felt too dazed to cry –
I held him to me as I prayed
To God that I may die.

But sometimes now I seem to hear –
Just when the air grows chill –
A single whip-crack, sharp and clear,
Re-echo from the hill.
That's Jim, to let me know he's near
And thinking of me still.

Barcroft Boake, 1866-1892

The Banks of the Condamine

Oh, hark the dogs are barking, love,
I can no longer stay,
The men are all gone mustering
And it is nearly day.
And I must off by the morning light
Before the sun doth shine,
To meet the Sydney shearers
On the banks of the Condamine.

O Willie, dearest Willie,
I'll go along with you,
I'll cut off all my auburn fringe
And be a shearer too,
I'll cook and count your tally, love,
While ringer-o you shine,
And I'll wash your greasy moleskins
On the banks of the Condamine.

Oh, Nancy, dearest Nancy,
With me you cannot go,
The squatters have given orders, love,
No woman should do so;
Your delicate constitution
Is not equal unto mine,
To stand the constant tigering
On the banks of the Condomine.

Oh, Nancy, dearest Nancy,
Please do not hold me back,
Down there the boys are waiting,
And I must be on the track;
So here's a good-bye kiss, love,
Back home here I'll incline
When we've shore the last of the jumbucks
On the banks of the Condamine.

Traditional

Ballad of the Drover

Across the stony ridges,
Across the rolling plain,
Young Harry Dale, the drover,
Comes riding home again.

And well his stock-horse bears him,
And light of heart is he,
And stoutly his old packhorse
Is trotting by his knee.

Up Queensland way with cattle
He's travelled regions vast,
And many months have vanished
Since home-folks saw him last.
He hums a song of someone
He hopes to marry soon;
And hobble-chains and camp-ware
Keep jingling to the tune.

Beyond the hazy dado
Against the lower skies
And yon blue line of ranges
The station homestead lies.
And thitherward the drover
Jogs through the hazy noon,
While hobble-chains and camp-ware
Are jingling to a tune.

An hour has filled the heavens

With storm-clouds inky black;
At times the lightning trickles
Around the drover's track;
But Harry pushes onward,
His horses' strength he tries,
In hope to reach the river
Before the flood shall rise.

The thunder, pealing o'er him,
Goes rumbling down the plain;
And sweet on thirsty pastures
Beats fast the crashing rain;
Then every creek and gully
Sends forth its tribute flood –
The river runs a banker
All stained with yellow mud.

Now Harry speaks to Rover,
The best dog on the plains,
And to his hardy horses,
And strokes their shaggy manes:
'We've breasted bigger rivers
When floods were at their height,
Nor shall this gutter stop us
From getting home tonight.'

The thunder growls a warning,
The blue, forked lightnings gleam;
The drover turns his horses
To swim the fatal stream.
But, oh! the flood runs stronger

Than e'er it ran before;
The saddle-horse is failing
And only half-way o'er!

When flashes next the lightning
The flood's grey breast is blank;
A cattle-dog and packhorse
Are struggling up the bank,
But in the lonely homestead
The girl shall wait in vain –
He'll never pass the stations
In charge of stock again.

The faithful dog a moment
Lies panting on the bank,
Then plunges through the current
To where his master sank.
And round and round in circles
He fights with failing strength,
Till, gripped by wilder waters,
He fails and sinks at length.

Across the flooded lowlands
And slopes of sodden loam
The packhorse struggles bravely
To take dumb tidings home;
And mud-stained, wet, and weary,
He goes by rock and tree,
With clanging chains and tinware
All sounding eerily.

Henry Lawson, 1867-1922

A Bush Christening

On the outer Barcoo, where the churches are few,
And men of religion are scanty,
On a road never cross'd,'cept by folks that are lost,
One Michael Magee had a shanty.

Now this Mike was the dad of a ten-year-old lad,
Plump, healthy, and stoutly conditioned;
He was strong as the best, but poor Mike had no rest
For the youngster had never been christened.

And his wife used to cry, 'If the darlin' should die
Saint Peter would not recognise him.'
But by luck he survived till a preacher arrived,
Who agreed straightaway to baptise him.

Now the artful young rogue, while they held their
  collogue,
With his ear to the keyhole was listenin'
And he muttered in fright, while his features turned
  white,
'What the devil and all is this christenin'?'

He was none of your dolts – he had seen them
  brand colts,
And it seemed to his small understanding,
If the man in the frock made him one of the flock,
It must mean something like branding.

So away with a rush he set off for the bush,
While the tears in his eyelids they glistened –

''Tis outrageous,' says he, 'to brand youngsters
  like me,
I'll be dashed if I'll stop to be christened.'

Like a young native dog he ran into a log,
And his father with language uncivil,
Never heeding the 'praste', cried aloud in his haste,
'Come out and be christened, you divil!'

But he lay there as snug as a bug in a rug,
And his parents in vain might reprove him,
Till His Reverence spoke (he was fond of a joke)
'I've a notion,' says he, 'that'll move him.

'Poke a stick up the log, give the spalpeen a prog;
Poke him aisy – don't hurt him or maim him;
'Tis not long that he'll stand, I've the water at hand,
As he rushes out this end I'll name him.

'Here he comes, and for shame! ye've forgotten
  the name –
Is it Patsy or Michael of Dinnis?'
Here the youngster ran out, and the priest gave
  a shout –
'Take your chance, wid "Maginnis"!'

As the howling young cub ran away to the scrub
Where he knew that pursuit would be risky,
The priest, as he fled, flung a flask at his head
That was labelled 'Maginnis's Whisky!'

And Maginnis Magee has been made a J.P.,

And the one thing he hates more than sin is
To be asked by the folk, who have heard of the joke,
How he came to be christened Maginnis!

A.B. ('Banjo') Paterson, 1864-1941

The Squatter's Man

Come all ye lads an' list to me,
That's left your homes an' crossed the sea,
To try your fortune, bound or free,
　All in this golden land.
For twelve long months I had to pace,
Humping my swag with a cadging face,
Sleeping in the bush, like the sable race,
As in my song you'll understand.

Unto this country I did come,
A regular out-and-out new chum.
I then abhorred the sight of rum –
　Teetotal was my plan.
But soon I learned to wet one eye –
Misfortune oft-times made me sigh.
To raise fresh funds I was forced to fly,
And be a squatter's man.

Soon at the station I appeared,
I saw the squatter with his beard,
And up to him I boldly steered

With my swag and billy-can.
I said 'Kind sir, I want a job!'
Said he, 'Do you know how to snob,
Or can you break a bucking cob?'
Whilst my figure he did scan.

''Tis now I want a useful cove
To stop at home and not to rove.
The scamps go about – a regular drove –
  I suppose you're one of the clan?
But I'll give you ten bob, ten, sugar and tea:
And very soon I hope you'll be
A handy squatter's man.

'At daylight you must milk the cows,
Make butter, cheese, an' feed the sows,
Put on the kettle, the cook arouse,
  And clean the family shoes.
The stable an' sheep yard clean out,
And always answer when we shout,
With "Yes, ma'm, and No, sir," mind your mouth,
And my youngsters don't abuse.

'You must fetch wood an' water, bake an' boil.
Act as butcher when we kill;
The corn an' taters you must hill,
  Keep the garden spick and span.
You must not scruple in the rain
To take to market all the grain.
Be sure you come sober back again
To be a squatter's man.'

He sent me to an old bark hut,
Inhabited by a greyhound slut,
Who put her fangs in my poor fut,
And snarling, off she ran.
So once more I'm looking for a job,
Without a copper in my fob.
Wiith Ben Hall or Gardiner I'd rather job
Than be a squatter's man.

Anonymous

The Geebung Polo Club

It was somewhere up the country, in a land of rock
    and scrub,
That they formed an institution called the Geebung
    Polo Club.
They were long and wiry natives from the rugged
    mountainside,
And the horse was never saddled that the Geebungs
    couldn't ride;
But their style of playing polo was irregular and
    rash –
They had mighty little science, but a mighty lot of
    dash:
And they played on mountain ponies that were
    muscular and strong,
Though their coats were quite unpolished, and their
    manes and tails were long.

And they used to train those ponies wheeling cattle
  in the scrub;
They were demons, were the members of the
  Geebung Polo Club.

It was somewhere up the country, in a city's smoke
  and steam,
That a polo club existed, called the 'Cuff and Collar
  Team'.
As a social institution 'twas a marvellous success,
For the members were distinguished by exclusiveness
  and dress.
They had natty little ponies that were nice, and
  smooth, and sleek,
For their cultivated owners only rode 'em once a
  week.
So they started up the country in pursuit of sport and
  fame.
For they meant to show the Geebungs how they
  ought to play the game;
And they took their valets with them – just to give
  their boots a rub
Ere they started operations on the Geebung Polo
  Club.

Now my readers can imagine how the contest ebbed
  and flowed,
When the Geebung boys got going it was time to
  clear the road;
And the game was so terrific that ere half the time
  was gone

A spectator's leg was broken – just from merely
  looking on.
For they waddied one another till the plain was
  strewn with dead,
While the score was kept so even that they neither
  got ahead.
And the Cuff and Collar Captain, when he tumbled
  off to die
Was the last surviving player – so the game was
  called a tie.
Then the Captain of the Geebungs raised him slowly
  from the ground,
Though his wounds were mostly mortal, yet he
  fiercely gazed around;
There was no one to oppose him – all the rest were
  in a trance.
So he scrambled on his pony for his last expiring
  chance.
For he meant to make an effort to get the victory to
  his side;
So he struck at goal – and missed it – then tumbled
  off and died.

By the old Campaspe River, where the breezes shake
  the grass,
There's a row of little gravestones that the stockmen
  never pass,
For they bear a rude inscription saying, 'Stranger,
  drop a tear,
For the Cuff and Collar players and the Geebung
  boys lie here.'

And on misty moonlit evenings, while the dingoes
  howl around,
You can see their shadows flitting down the phantom
  polo ground;
You can hear the loud collisions as the flying players
  meet,
And the rattle of the mallets, and the rush of ponies'
  feet,
Till the terrified spectator rides like blazes to the
  pub –
He's been haunted by the spectres of the Geebung
  Polo Club.

A.B. ('Banjo') Paterson, 1864-1941

The Mailboy's Ride

He rode from Port Bowen bravely,
With his life held in his hands,
To carry the mail to safety
Across the wide burning sands.

Brave men who carried before him,
Blacks killed in the timber's shade;
At the first camp of the mailman,
Four graves show where they laid.

'Twas death not to reach the camp place
Ere darkness grew o'er the land,
For there had the only water

Been found on those plains of sand.

He reached the first camp in safety,
No sign of the blacks about,
So when he had eaten his supper
He tethered his horses out.

He lay down to rest in the shelter,
But long ere the break of day
He saddled his hack and pack-horse
And started once more away.

'I think I will have a smoko,'
He said, and he slackened rein,
But his horse plunged madly forward,
And he fell with a cry of pain.

He knew that his leg was broken,
And a sharp pain in his side
Told that his ribs were injured
With sixty miles to ride.

Alone on that awful desert
No hope of succour near,
He cried to God in heaven
As he fought with the rising fear.

'Oh God, Thou hast helped Thy children
Through dangers in days gone past;
Thou knowest that on this desert
Wounded and lone I'm cast.

'And now in my time of trouble,
To whom can I turn but Thee
Who rulest the earth and heavens,
The wind and the raging sea.

'Oh God of my fathers help me,'
He cried as he crawled in pain
To where the horses stood waiting,
And caught up the hanging rein.

Then slowly, with painful effort,
He mounted and rode away,
For he knew that within an hour
Would commence another day.

On as the morning brightened
He rode and he rode for life,
For over his aching body
Weakness and pain held strife.

On till the evening shadows
Steadied his fevered brain,
And in the darkness before him
A bright light shone on the plain.

The men at the station waiting
Cheered as they heard him come,
But the figure that stopped before them
Struck even the roughest dumb.

Then tenderly, kind as women,
They lifted the drooping lad,

With eyes closed tight, white faces,
And hearts all at once grown sad.

And through long weeks of fever
They watched by the sick boy's side,
And in his fevered ramblings
He told of that awful ride.

At night round the pleasant campfire
Those men still tell the tale
How across the Australian desert
The boy brought the Royal Mail.

Anonymous

The Man from Ironbark

It was the man from Ironbark who struck the Sydney
  town,
He wandered over street and park, he wandered up
  and down,
He loitered here, he loitered there, till he was like to
  drop,
Until at last in sheer despair he sought a barber's
  shop.
"'Ere! shave my beard and whiskers off, I'll be a man
  of mark,
I'll go and do the Sydney toff up home in Ironbark,'

The barber man was small and flash, as barbers
  mostly are,
He wore a strike-your-fancy sash, he smoked a huge
  cigar:
He was a humorist of note and keen at repartee,
He laid the odds and kept a 'tote', whatever that may
  be,
And when he saw our friend arrive, he whispered
  'Here's a lark!'
Just watch me catch him all alive, this man from
  Ironbark.'

There were some gilded youths that sat along the
  barber's wall.
Their eyes were dull, their heads were flat, they had
  no brains at all;
To them the barber passed the wink, his dexter eye
  lid shut,

'I'll make this bloomin' yokel think his bloomin'
    throat is cut.'
And as he soaped and rubbed it in he made a rude
    remark;
'I s'pose the flats is pretty green up there in
    Ironbark.'

A grunt was all reply he got; he shaved the
    bushman's chin,
Then made the water boiling hot and dipped the
    razor in.
He raised his hand, his brow grew black, he paused
    a while to gloat,
Then slashed the red-hot razor-back across his
    victim's throat;
Upon the newly-shaven skin it made a livid mark –
No doubt it fairly took him in – the man from
    Ironbark.

He fetched a wild up-country yell, might wake the
    dead to hear,
And though his throat, he knew full well, was cut
    from ear to ear,
He struggled gamely to his feet, and faced the
    murderous foe;
'You've done for me! you dog, I'm beat! One hit
    before I go,
I only wish I had a knife, you blessed murderous
    shark,
But you'll remember all your life the man from
    Ironbark.'

A peeler who heard the din came in to see the show;
He tried to run the bushman in, but he refused to go.
And when at last the barber spoke, and said, ''Twas
  all in fun –
'Twas just a little harmless joke, a trifle overdone.'
'A joke!' he cried. 'By George, that's fine; a lively sort
  of lark;
I'd like to catch that murdering swine some night in
  Ironbark.'

And now while round the shearing floor the listening
  shearers gape,
He tells the story o'er and o'er, and brags of his
  escape.
'Them barber chaps what keeps a tote, by George,
  I've had enough,
One tried to cut my bloomin' throat, but thank the
  Lord it's tough.'
And whether he's believed or not, there's one thing
  to remark,
That flowing beards are all the go way up in
  Ironbark.

A.B. ('Banjo') Paterson, 1864-1941

The Overlander

There's a trade you all know well –
It's bringing cattle over –
I'll tell about the time
When I became a drover.
I made up my mind to try the spec,
To the Clarence I did wander,
And brought a mob of duffers there
To begin as an overlander.

Chorus:
Pass the wine round, boys
Don't let the bottle stand there,
For tonight we'll drink the health
Of every overlander.

When the cattle were all mustered,
And the outfit ready to start,
I saw the lads all mounted,
With their swags left in the cart.
All kinds of men I had
From France, Germany and Flanders;
Lawyers, doctors, good and bad,
In the mob of overlanders.

From the road I then fed out
Where the grass was green and young;
When a squatter with curse and shout
Told me to move along.
I said, 'You're very hard;

Take care, don't raise my dander,
For I'm a regular knowing card
The Queensland overlander.'

'Tis true we pay no licence,
And our run is rather large;
'Tis not often they can catch us,
So they cannot make a charge.
They think we live on store beef,
But no, I'm not a gander;
When a good fat stranger joins the mob,
'He'll do,' says the overlander.

Traditional

The Kelly Gang

Oh, Paddy dear, and did you hear
The news that's going round,
On the head of bold Ned Kelly
They have placed two thousand pound.
And on Steve Hart, Joe Byrne and Dan,
Two thousand more they'd give,
But if the price was doubled boys,
The Kelly Gang would live.

'Tis hard to think such plucky hearts
In crime should be employed,
'Tis by police persecution
They have been much annoyed.
Revenge is sweet, and in the bush
They can defy the law,
Such sticking up and plundering
You never saw before.

'Twas in November, Seventy-eight,
When the Kelly Gang came down,
Just after shooting Kennedy,
To famed Euroa town;
To rob the bank of all its gold
Was their idea that day,
Blood-horses they were mounted on
To make their getaway.

So Kelly marched into the bank,
A cheque all in his hand,

For to have it changed to money
Of Scott he did demand.
And when that he refused him,
He, looking at him straight,
Said, 'See here, my name's Ned Kelly,
And this here man's my mate.'

With pistols pointed at his nut,
Poor Scott did stand amazed,
His stick he would have like to cut,
But he was with funk half crazed;
The poor cashier, with real fear,
Stood trembling at the knees,
But at last they both saw 'twas no use
And handed out the keys.

The safe was quickly gutted then,
The drawers turned out as well,
The Kellys being quite polite,
Like any noble swell.
With flimsies, gold and silver coin,
The threepennies and all
Amounting to two thousand pounds,
They made a glorious haul.

'Now hand out all your firearms,'
The robber boldly said,
'And all your ammunition –
Or a bullet through your head.
Now get your wife and children –
Come, man, look alive;

All jump into this buggy
And we'll take you for a drive.'

They took them to a station
About three miles away,
And kept them close imprisoned
Until the following day.
The owner of the station
And those in his employ
And a few unwary travellers
Their company did enjoy.

An Indian hawker fell in too,
As everybody knows,
He came in handy to the gang
By fitting them with clothes.
Then with their worn-out clothing
They made a few bonfires,
And then destroyed the telegraph
By cutting down the wires.

Oh, Paddy dear, do shed a tear,
I can't but sympathise,
Those Kellys are the devils,
For they've made another rise;
This time across the billabong,
On Morgan's ancient beast,
They've robbed the banks of thousands
And in safety did retreat.

The matter may be serious, Pat,
But still I can't but laugh,

To think the tales the bobbies told
Must all amount to chaff.
They said they had them hemmed in,
They could not get away,
But they turned up in New South Wales,
And made the journey pay.

They rode into Jerilderie town
At twelve o'clock at night,
Aroused the troopers from their beds,
And gave them an awful fright,
They took them in their night-shirts,
Ashamed I am to tell,
Then covered them with revolvers
And locked them in a cell.

Next morning being Sunday morn
Of course they must be good,
They dressed themselves in troopers' clothes,
And Ned, he chopped some wood.
No one there suspected them,
As troopers they did pass,
And Dan, the most religious one,
Took the sergeant's wife to Mass.

They spent the day most pleasantly,
Had plenty of good cheer,
Fried beefsteak and onions,
Tomato sauce and beer;
The ladies in attendance
Indulged in pleasant talk,

And just to ease the troopers' minds,
They took them for a walk.

On Monday morning early,
Still masters of the ground,
They took their horses to the forge
And had them shod all round;
Then back they came and mounted,
Their plans all laid so well,
In company with troopers,
They stuck up the Royal Hotel.

They bailed up all the occupants,
And placed them in a room,
Saying, 'Do as we command you,
Or death will be your doom,'
A Chinese cook, 'No savvy,' cried,
Not knowing what to fear,
But they brought him to his senses
With a lift under the ear.

All who now approached the house
Just shared a similar fate,
In hardly any time at all
The number was twenty-eight.
They shouted freely for all hands,
And paid for all they drank,
And two of them remained in charge,
And two went to the bank.

The farce was here repeated
As I've already told,

They bailed up all the banker's clerks
And robbed them of their gold.
The manager could not be found,
And Kelly, in great wrath,
Searched high and low and luckily
He found him in his bath.

The robbing o'er, they mounted then,
To make a quick retreat,
They swept away with all their loot
By Morgan's ancient beast;
And where they've gone I do not know,
If I did I wouldn't tell,
So now, until I hear from them,
I'll bid you all farewell.

Anonymous

The Fire at Ross's Farm

The squatter saw his pastures wide
  Decrease, as one by one
The farmers moving to the west
  Selected on his run;
Selectors took the water up
  And all the black-soil round;
The best grass-land the squatter had
  Was spoilt by Ross's ground.

Now many schemes to shift old Ross
  Had racked the squatter's brains,
But Sandy had the stubborn blood
  Of Scotland in his veins;
He held the land and fenced it in,
  He cleared and ploughed the soil,
And year by year a richer crop
  Repaid him for his toil.

Between the homes for many years
  The devil left his tracks:
The squatter 'pounded Ross's stock,
  And Sandy 'pounded Black's.
A well upon the lower run
  Was filled with earth and logs
And Black laid bait about the farm
  To poison Ross's dogs.

It was, indeed, a deadly feud
  Of class and creed and race
So Fate supplied a Romeo
  And a Juliet in the case;
And more than once across the flats,
  Beneath the Southern Cross,
Young Robert Black was seen to ride
  With pretty Jenny Ross.

One Christmas time, when months of drought
  Had parched the western creeks,
The bush-fires started to the north
  And travelled south for weeks.

At night along the river-side
  The scene was grand and strange –
The hill-fires looked like lighted streets
  Of cities in the range.

The cattle-tracks between the trees
  Were like long dusty aisles,
And on a sudden breeze the fire
  Would sweep along for miles;
Like sounds of distant musketry
  It crackled through the brakes,
And o'er the flat of silver grass
  It hissed like angry snakes.

It leapt across the flowing streams
  And raced the pastures through;
It climbed the trees, and lit the boughs,
  And fierce and fiercer grew.
The bees fell stifled in the smoke
  Or perished in their hives,
And with the stock the kangaroos
  Went flying for their lives.

The sun had set on Christmas Eve,
  When through the scrub-lands wide
Young Robert Black came riding home
  As only natives ride.
He galloped to the homestead door
  And gave the first alarm:
'The fire is past the granite spur,
  And close to Ross's farm.'

'Now, father, send the men at once,
　They won't be wanted here;
Poor Ross's wheat is all he has
　To pull him through the year.'
'Then let it burn,' the squatter said;
　'I'd like to see it done –
I'd bless the fire if it would clear
　Selectors from the run.

'Go if you will,' the squatter said,
　'You shall not take the men –
Go out and join your precious friends,
　But don't come here again.'
'I won't come back,' young Robert cried,
　And reckless in his ire,
He sharply turned the horse's head
　And galloped towards the fire.

And there for three long weary hours,
　Half-blind with smoke and heat,
Old Ross and Robert fought the flames
　That neared the ripened wheat.
The farmer's hand was nerved by fear
　Of danger and of loss;
And Robert fought the stubborn foe
　For love of Jenny Ross.

But serpent-like the curves and lines
　Slipped past them, and between
Until they reached the boundary where
　The old coach-road had been.
'The track is now our only hope.

There we must stand,' cried Ross.
'For naught on earth can stop the fire
  If once it gets across.

Then came a cruel gust of wind,
  And, with a fiendish rush,
The flames leapt o'er the narrow path
  And lit the fence of brush.
'The crop must burn!' the farmer cried,
  'We cannot save it now,'
And down upon the blackened ground
  He dashed his ragged bough.

But wildly, in a rush of hope,
  His heart began to beat,
For o'er the cracking of the fire he heard
  The sound of horses' feet.
'Here's help at last,' young Robert cried,
  And even as he spoke
The squatter with a dozen men
  Came racing through the smoke.

Down on the ground the stockmen jumped
  And bared each brawny arm;
They tore green branches from the trees
  And fought for Ross's farm;
And when before the gallant band
  The beaten flames gave way
Two grimy hands in friendship joined –
  And it was Christmas Day.

Henry Lawson, 1867-1922

Farewell to Greta:
A Ballad of Ned Kelly

Farewell my home in Greta,
My loved ones fare thee well;
It grieves my heart to leave you,
But here I must not dwell.
They placed a price upon my head,
My hands are stained with gore,
And I must roam the forest wild
Within the Australian shore.

But if they cross my cherished path
By all I hold on earth,
I'll give them cause to rue the day
Their mothers gave them birth.
I'll shoot them down like carrion crows
That roam our country wide,
And leave their bodies bleaching
Along some woodland side.

Oh Edward, darling brother,
Surely you would not go
So rashly to encounter
With such a mighty foe!
Now don't you know that Sydney
And Melbourne are combined,
And for your apprehension, Ned,
There are warrants duly signed?

To eastward lies great Bogong,

Towering to the sky,
From east to west and then you'll find
That's Gippsland lying by.
You know the country well, Ned,
So take your comrades there,
And profit by your knowledge of
The wombat and the bear.

And let no childish quarrelling
Cause trouble in the gang,
You're up with one another,
And guard my brother Dan.
See yonder ride four troopers,
One kiss before we part,
Now haste and join your comrades, Dan,
Joe Byrne and Stevey Hart.

Traditional

The Dying Stockman

A strapping young stockman lay dying,
His saddle supporting his head;
His two mates around him were crying
As he rose on his elbow and said:

Chorus:
'Wrap me up with my stockwhip and blanket,
And bury me deep down below,
Where the dingoes and crows can't molest me,

In the shade where the coolibahs grow.

'Oh had I the flight of the bronze-wing
Far o'er the plains I would fly,
Straight to the land of my childhood,
And there I would lay down and die.

'Then cut down a couple of saplings,
Place one at my head and my toe,
Carve on them cross, stockwhip and saddle,
To show there's a stockman below.

'Hark! There's a wail of a dingo
Watchful and weird – I must go,
For it tolls the death-knell of the stockman
From the gloom of the scrub below.

'There's tea in the battered old billy:
Place the pannikins all in a row.
And we'll drink to the next merry meeting,
In the place where all good fellows go.

'And oft in the shades of the twilight
When the soft winds are whispering low,
And the darkening shadows are falling,
Sometimes think of the stockman below.'

Traditional

Click Go the Shears

Out on the board the old shearer stands,
Grasping his shears in his long, bony hands,
Fixed is his gaze on the bare-bellied yeo,
Glory, if he gets her, won't he make the 'ringer' go!

Chorus:
Click go the shears, boys, click, click, click;
Wide is his blow and his hands move quick,
The ringer looks around and is beaten by a blow;
And curses the old snagger with the bare-bellied yeo.

In the middle of the floor, in his cane-bottomed

chair
Is the boss of the board, with eyes everywhere;
Notes well each fleece as it comes to the screen,
Paying strict attention if it's taken off clean.

The colonial experience man, he is there, of course,
With his shiny leggins, just got off his horse;
Casting round his eye, like a real connoisseur,
Whistling the old tune, 'I'm the Perfect Lure.'

The tar-boy is there, awaiting in demand,
With his blackened tar-pot, and his tarry hand,
Sees one old sheep with a cut upon its back,
Here's what he's waiting for, 'Tar here, Jack.'

Shearing is all over and we've all got our cheques.
Roll up your swags, boys, we're off on the tracks;

The first pub we come to, it's there we'll have a
  spree,
And everyone that comes along, it's 'Have a drink
  with me!'

Down by the bar the old shearer stands,
Grasping his glass in his thin bony hands;
Fixed is his gaze on a green-painted keg,
Glory, he'll get down on it, ere he stirs a peg.

There we leave him standing, shouting for all hands,
Whilst all around him, every drinker stands;
His eyes are on the cask, which is now lowering fast.
He works hard, he drinks hard, and goes to hell at
  last!

Traditional

On Kiley's Run

The roving breezes come and go
  On Kiley's Run.
The sleepy river murmurs low,
And far away one dimly sees
Beyond the stretch of forest trees –
Beyond the foothills dusk and dun –
The ranges sleeping in the sun
  On Kiley's Run.

'Tis many years since first I came
  To Kiley's run,
More years than I would care to name
Since I, a stripling, used to ride
For miles and miles at Kiley's side,
The while in stirring tones he told
The stories of the days of old
  On Kiley's Run.

I see the old bush homestead now
  On Kiley's Run,
Just nestled down beneath the brow
Of one small ridge above the sweep
Of river flat, where willows weep
And jasmine flowers and roses bloom,
The air was laden with perfume
  On Kiley's Run.

We lived the good old station life
  On Kiley's Run,
With little thought of care or strife.
Old Kiley seldom used to roam,
He liked to make the Run his home,
The swagman never turned away
With empty hand at close of day
  From Kiley's Run.

We kept a racehorse now and then
  On Kiley's Run,
And neighb'ring stations brought their men
To meetings where the sport was free,

And dainty ladies came to see
Their champions ride; with laugh and song
The old house rang the whole night long
  On Kiley's Run.

The station hands were friends I wot
  On Kiley's Run,
A reckless, merry-hearted lot –
All splendid riders, and they knew
The 'boss' was kindness through and through.
Old Kiley always stood their friend,
And so they served him to the end
  On Kiley's Run.

But droughts and losses came apace
  To Kiley's Run,
Till ruin stared him in the face;
He toiled and toiled while lived the light,
He dreamed of overdrafts at night:
At length, because he could not pay,
His bankers took his stock away
  From Kiley's Run.

Old Kiley stood and saw them go
  From Kiley's Run.
The well-bred cattle marching slow;
His stockmen, mates for many a day,
They wrung his hand and went away.
Too old to make another start,
Old Kiley died – of broken heart,
  On Kiley's Run.

The owner lives in England now
  Of Kiley's Run.
He knows a racehorse from a cow;
But that is all he knows of stock:
His chiefest care is how to dock
Expenses, and he sends from town
To cut the shearers' wages down
  On Kiley's Run.

There are no neighbours anywhere
  Near Kiley's Run.
The hospitable homes are bare,
The gardens gone; for no pretence
Must hinder cutting down expense:
The homestead that we held so dear
Contains a half-paid overseer
  On Kiley's Run.

All life and sport and hope have died
  On Kiley's Run.
No longer there the stockmen ride;
For sour-faced boundary riders creep
On mongrel horses after sheep,
Through ranges where, at racing speed,
Old Kiley used to 'wheel the lead'
  On Kiley's Run.

There runs a lane for thirty miles
  Through Kiley's Run.
On either side the herbage smiles,
But wretched trav'lling sheep must pass

Without a drink or blade of grass
Thro' that long lane of death and shame:
The weary drovers curse the name
  Of Kiley's Run.

The name itself has changed of late
  Of Kiley's Run.
The call it 'Chandos Park Estate'.
The lonely swagman through the dark
Must hump his swag past Chandos Park.
The name is English, don't you see,
The old name sweeter sounds to me
  Of 'Kiley's Run'.

I cannot guess what fate will bring
  To Kiley's Run —
For chances come and changes ring —
I scarcely think 'twill always be
Locked up to suit an absentee;
And if he lets it out in farms
His tenants soon will carry arms
  On Kiley's Run.

A.B. ('Banjo') Paterson, 1864-1941

Billy Brink

There once was a shearer by the name of Bill Brink,
A devil for work and a devil for drink.
He'd shear two hundred a day without fear,
And he'd drink without stopping two gallons of
beer.

When the pub opened up he was very first in
Roaring for whisky and howling for gin,
Saying, 'Jimmy, my boy, I'm dying of thirst,
Whatever you've got there just give to me first.'

Now Jimmy the barman who served him the rum
Hated the sight of old Billy the bum;
He came up too late, he came up too soon,
At morning, at evening, at night and at noon.

Now Jimmy the barman was cleaning the bar
With sulphuric acid locked in a jar.
He poured him a measure into a small glass,
Saying, 'After this drink you will surely say "Pass."'

'Well,' says Billy to Jimmy, 'the stuff tastes fine.
She's a new kind of liquor or whisky or wine.
Yes, that's the stuff, Jimmy, I'm strong as a Turk –
I'll break all the records today at my work.'

Well, all that day long there was Jim at the bar,
Too eager to argue, too anxious to fight,
Roaring and trembling with a terrible fear;

For he pictured the corpse of old Bill in his sight.

But early next morning there was Bill as before,
Roaring and bawling, and howling for more,
His eyeballs were singed and his whiskers deranged,
He had holes in his hide like a dog with the mange.

Said Billy to Jimmy, 'She sure was fine stuff,
It made me feel well but I ain't had enough.
It started me coughing, you know I'm no liar,
And every damn cough set my whiskers on fire!'

Traditional

Mulga Bill's Bicycle

'Twas Mulga Bill from Eaglehawk, that caught the
cycling craze;
He turned away the good old horse that served him
many days;
He dressed himself in cycling clothes, resplendent to
be seen;
He hurried off to town and bought a shining new
machine:
And as he wheeled it through the door, with air of
lordly pride,
The grinning shop assistant said, 'Excuse me, can
you ride?'

'See here, young man,' said Mulga Bill, 'from Walgett
to the sea,
From Conroy's Gap to Castlereagh, there's none can
ride like me.
I'm good all round at everything, as everybody
knows,
Although I'm not the one to talk – I hate a man that
blows.
But riding is my special gift, my chiefest, sole delight;

'Just ask a wild duck can it swim, a wild cat can it
fight.
There's nothing clothed in hair or hide, or built of
flesh or steel,

There's nothing walks or jumps or runs, on axle,
  hoof or wheel,
But what I'll sit, while hide will hold and girths and
  straps are tight;
I'll ride this here two-wheeled concern right away at
  sight.

'Twas Mulga Bill, from Eaglehawk, that sought his
  own abode,
That perched above the Dead Man's Creek, beside
  the mountain road.
He turned the cycle down the hill and mounted for
  the fray,
But ere he'd gone a dozen yards it bolted clean
  away.
It left the track, and through the trees, just like a
silver streak,
It whistled down the awful slope, towards the Dead
  Man's Creek.

It shaved a stump by half an inch, it dodged a big
  white-box;
The very wallaroos in fright went scrambling up the
  rocks,
The wombats hiding in their caves dug deeper
  underground,
As Mulga Bill, as white as chalk, sat tight to every
  bound.
It struck a stone and gave a spring that cleared a
  fallen tree,
It raced beside a precipice as close as close could be;

And then as Mulga Bill let out one last despairing
  shriek
It made a leap of twenty feet into the Dead Man's
  Creek.

'Twas Mulga Bill, from Eaglehawk, that slowly swam
  ashore;
He said, 'I've had some narrer shaves and lively rides
  before;
I've rode a wild bull round a yard to win a five
  pound bet,
But this was the most awful ride that I've
  encountered yet.
I'll give that two-wheeled outlaw best; it's shaken all
  me nerve
To feel it whistle through the air and plunge and
  buck and swerve.
It's safe at rest in Dead Man's Creek we'll leave it
  lying still;
A horse's back is good enough henceforth for Mulga
  Bill.'

A.B. ('Banjo') Paterson, 1864-1941

Stir the Wallaby Stew

Poor Daddy's got five years or more,
As everybody knows;
And now he lives in Boggo Road,
Broad arrows on his clothes.
He branded all Brown's cleanskins,
And never left a trail,
So I'll relate the family's fate,
Since Daddy went to jail.

Chorus:
So stir the wallaby stew,
Make soup with the kangaroo's tail,
I tell you things are pretty crook
Since Dad got put in jail.

Our sheep all died a month ago,
Not rot, but flaming fluke.
Our cow got boozed last Christmas Day
With my big brother Luke;
And Mother has a shearer cove
Forever within hail,
The family will have grown a bit
When Dad gets out of jail.

Our Bess got shook upon a bloke,
He's gone we don't know where.
He used to act around the sheds,
But he ain't acted square.
I've sold the buggy on my own,

The place is up for sale.
That isn't all that won't be junked
When Dad gets out of jail.

They let Dad out before his time
To give us a surprise,
He came and looked around the place,
And gently damned our eyes.
He shook hands with the shearer cove,
And said he thought things stale,
So left him there to shepherd us,
And he battled back to jail.

Traditional

The Search

I've dropped me swag in many camps
From Queensland west to Boulder,
An' struck all sorts of outback champs
An' many a title-holder.
But though I've learned the episode
By drover told, an' dogger,
I've still to meet the bloke who rode
The big white bull through Wagga.

I struck the hero out at Hay
Who beat the red-back spider

In fourteen rounds one burnin' day;
An' up along the Gwydir
There lives the man outslept the toad –
A champeen blanket-flogger –
But he is not the bloke who rode
The big white bull through Wagga.

The cove that hung the Bogan Gate
Once called me in a hurry
To buy drinks for his 'China plate',
The bloke that dug the Murray.
An' though down south of Beechworth road
I met Big Bog the Frogger,
I've still to meet the bloke who rode
The big white bull through Wagga.

The man who steered the kangaroo
From Cue to Daly Waters;
The cove who raced the emu, too
To win three squatters' daughters;
I know the fellow moved the load
That stopped the Richmond logger;
But still I want the bloke that rode
The big white bull through Wagga.

But some fine day I'll run him down,
An' stop his flamin' skitin'.
I'll punch him on his lyin' crown,
Or go down gamely fightin'.
For *I'm* the bloke to who is owed
What's paid that limelight-hogger.

I'd *love* to meet that bloke who rode
The big white bull through Wagga.

Charles Shaw

The Old Bark Hut

In an old bark hut on the mountainside
In a spot that was lone and drear
A woman whose heart was aching sat
Watching from year to year.

A small boy, Jim, her only child,
Helped her to watch and wait
But the time never came when they could go free,
Free from the bond of hate.

For McConnel was out on the mountainside
Living without a hope
And seeing nothing before him now
But death by a hangman's rope.

Hated and chased by his fellow men,
To take him alive or dead;
An outlaw banned by the world was he,
With five hundred pounds on his head.

A message had come that evening which said
'Now Jim, you mustn't wait,

If you want to save your father, or
By heaven, you'll be too late.

'He's out at Mackinnon's Crossing, they say,
The track's rough, old man,
But if any here can do it – why
It's you and old Darky can.'

And Jim knew well what the message meant,
As he brought his horse to the door!
While away through the gathering darkness came
The sound of the river's roar.

But the brave little heart never faltered as
He stooped to kiss her goodbye
And said, 'God bless you, Mother dear,
I'll save Dad tonight or I'll die.'

The old horse answered the touch of his hand
And galloped away from the door;
He seemed to know 'twas a journey for life –
Well, he'd done such journeys before.

Out from the firelight, and through the rails,
Out through the ghastly trees,
While all the time the warning roar
Of the river came back on the breeze;

Steadily down the mountainside
He rode, for his course was plain,
Though his heart was heavy, though not with fear,
But because of that brand of Cain.

The boy thinks over his mother's last words:
'I'll love him as long as I live,
He must have time for repentance on earth
But surely God will forgive.'

As he glanced back over his shoulder there
She stood by the light of the door
Trying to pierce the darkness in vain,
Thinking she'd see him no more.

Then as he looked she bowed her head
And slowly turned away,
And the boy knew that the noble wife
Had knelt by the bed to pray.

Mile after mile, hour after hour,
And then just ahead, shining white,
Was the foam of Mackinnon's Crossing –
What a jump for old Darky tonight!

And then Jim thinks of the long, lone years
And the hopes that are crushed and dead;
And a woman whose heart is as true as steel,
As true as the day she was wed.

As she loved him then in the years gone by
When the future held promise in store,
So she loved him today when the future held
Nought but death by his country's law.

Jim pressed his knees to the saddle-flap
And tightened his hold on the rein;

They had jumped the river last summertime.
How he hoped they would do it again!

Then a voice rang out through the darkness there,
'Hold, now hold, stand still!
We know you, lad, it's too late to run;
Hands up or we'll shoot to kill.'

Then he knew that the police were around him,
In the darkness they moved to and fro;
For an instant he pulled on the bridle-rein,
But he promised his mother he'd go.

And he thought of the poor, sad woman alone,
Kneeling in prayer by the bed;
So he loosened the reins on old Darky's neck
And rushed at the river ahead.

Then a volley rang out through the forest dark –
A fall in the roaring flood;
And the darkness hid from all human eyes
The form that was stained with blood.

The horse struggled hard, the waters rushed on;
He sank to rise no more.
But the boy fought the flood in silence, inch
By inch to the other shore.

Slowly and sadly, but bravely on,
Brushing away the tears;
He was leaving behind in the river's flood
His friend and companion of years.

And all of the time the blood trickled down,
O God! what a hot, burning pain!
And he knew he was doing his duty clean;
He would never come back again.

Struggling on o'er the tough, dark track,
A horrible pain with each breath;
Till he came to the hut in the ranges
Where his father was hiding from death.

Staggering through the yielding door
Into the cold dark room
Where his father lay, and the faint firelight
Showed through the ghostly gloom.

The bushranger sprang up to his feet in alarm
And levelled the gun at his head
And his loud voice demanded, 'Who are you?
Speak quick, or you are dead.'

And then a weak little voice made answer,
'It's me; Mother sends you her love,
The police are back at the crossing now,
So clear out and meet Mother above.'

Then McConnel placed his gun by the wall
And knelt on the cold, hard floor;
And somehow the tears came rushing down
As they never had before.

His arms went round the brave little lad,
He nursed his head on his breast;

He seemed to know that the end was nigh
And Jim would soon be at rest.

And the boy was speaking feebly at last,
'They shot me back at the creek,
And old Darky is dead and gone, Dad,
And oh, I'm so tired and weak.'

Then his voice fell away in a whisper soft,
So faint it could scarcely be heard,
'Oh, Dad, clear out, they are coming fast;
Tell Mother I kept my word.'

Quickly in silence the police gathered round,
They had captured the beast in his lair,
The outlaw sat with the boy in his arms,
He seemed not to heed nor to care.

He was thinking now of the seed he had sown,
He was tasting its bitter fruit,
When the sergeant stepped to the door and said,
'McConnel, bail up, or I'll shoot.'

Then the sergeant placed a lamp by the door,
The rifles gleamed out in the light,
But the outlaw said, 'Sergeant O'Grady,
Let's have no more shooting tonight.

"You can take me now to the judgement seat
As God has taken this lad;
You'd die to take my life, you men –
He died to save his dad.

'I want you to help me to dig his grave,
And perhaps you will say a prayer;
Then you can take me and hang me dead –
It's my wife, or I wouldn't care.

'Carefully now . . . Oh, thank you, men,
Lay him as best you can;
The policeman is shown by his coat, of course,
But the tears – well, they show the man.

Then the party went back to the old bark hut
As the sun was mounting the hill;
No smoke arose from the chimney cold
And all was silent and still.

The sergeant opened the creaky door,
And lifted his cap with a start,
Ah, McConnel had broken the country's laws
And broken a woman's heart.

Anonymous

The Death of Halligan

Ho, men, pile up the firewood
And let the cauldron boil
Whose bright contents will soon repay
The hardy miner's toil;
For yonder glittering treasure
Long weeks they've toiled below,
Then pile the faggots higher
And set them all aglow.

The fire is quickly kindled,
The flames leap up in sport,
And 'mid the red and lurid glare
Is seen the dark retort.
Right soon the work is finished,
The yellow gold is weighed,
It is the price for wretched souls
That Satan down hath paid.

Now Halligan has started
And left Rockhampton town
To visit the Alliance reef,
The gold to carry down.
To see him mount so stoutly
No human eye had guessed
That even now the shroud was drawn
High up upon his breast.

Alas, no dim presentiment

Passed through the rider's mind
That he would ne'er again behold
The home he left behind;
And as in pride of health and strength
He passed from out of door,
He little dreamed, as living man,
He'd enter there no more.

He got the gold, the cursed dross,
Through which he lost his life,
Through which his children orphans are
And widowed is his wife.
Then leaving Morinish behind,
To town he turned him back
And cantered speedily along
The old familiar track.

He came to where a darksome scrub
Extends along the road,
Where slimy frogs and crawling snakes
Take up their rank abode;
But far from noxious reptiles lurked
In yonder scrub that day,
Who with gloating eyes their victim watched
Come prancing on the way.

The pale assassins laid in wait
Behind a sheltering tree;
A shot was heard, the horseman reeled,
Then quickly turned to flee.
'Twas all too late, the ball had told,

His life-stream welled away,
And on the sod, a helpless clod,
The fated rider lay.

With crimsoned hands the felons clutched
The wages of their guilt;
Great heaven, to think for such a lure
His blood they foully spilt.
With blanching cheeks and trembling hearts
They anxious peered around,
Then took their ghastly burden up
And left the fatal ground.

What dastard fears were in their souls
Through all that frightful march,
Around them was the solemn bush,
Above the heavenly arch.
They only strove from human gaze
To screen their ruthless crime,
Nor cared that God's omniscient eye
Looked on them all the time.

Oh, how they started when a leaf
Was rustled by a bird,
How quailed their craven hearts when trees
The night-wind round them stirred.
And they rejoiced, I ween, to reach
That dark and swollen river,
Whose waves they fondly hoped would hide
The murdered man for ever.

And now their task was nearly done,

They stood upon the brink;
A sullen splash was faintly heard,
The corpse was seen to sink.
The eddies circled widely round
Where the pale stars seemed to quiver
And the blood-stained wretches turned in haste
And fled the darksome river.

But though, where scaly monsters roam
In yonder slimy bed
Poor Halligan, by murderous hand,
Had laid his gory head,
The swift Fitzroy refused to hold
The secret of his doom;
His corpse was found, in sacred ground
To find a Christian's tomb.

Now search, ye sharp detectives!
Hunt, bloodhounds of the law!
And from their sanguinary lairs
Those foul assassins draw;
And may their dreadful punishment
To all the world proclaim
That Queensland's justice will avenge
Such deeds of blood and shame.

Alexander Forbes, 1839-1879

The Wild Rover

Well, I've been a wild rover this many a year,
And I've spent all my money on whisky and beer.
But now I'm returning with gold in great store
And I never will play the wild rover no more;

Chorus
And it's no, nay, never,
No, nay, never, no more
Will I play the wild rover;
Nay, never no more

I went to a shanty I used to frequent
And I told the landlady my money was spent;
I asked her for credit, she answered me 'Nay!'
Such custom as yours I can get any day!'
Then I pulled from my pocket ten sovereigns bright
And the landlady's eyes opened wide with delight.
Said she, 'We have whisky and wines of the best
And the words that I told you were only in jest!'

There was Margaret and Kitty and Betsy and Sue,
And two or three more who belonged to our crew.
We'd sit up all night and make the place roar,
I've been a wild boy, but I'll be so no more.

And then as a prisoner to Cockatoo I was sent,
On a bed of cold straw for to lie and lament.
At last then I got what so long I'd looked for
And I never will play the wild rover no more.

I'll go home to my parents, confess what I've done,
And I'll ask them to pardon their prodigal son;
And if they will do so, as often before,
Then I never will play the wild rover no more.

Traditional

The Old Whim-horse

He's an old grey horse, with his head bowed sadly,
And with dim old eyes and a queer roll aft,
With the off-fore sprung and the hind screwed badly
And he bears all over the brands of graft;
And he lifts his head from the grass to wonder
Why by night and day now the whim is still,
Why the silence is, and the stampers' thunder
Sounds forth no more from the shattered mill.

In that whim he worked when the night-winds
  bellowed
On the riven summit of Giant's Hand,
And by day when prodigal Spring had yellowed
All the wide long sweep of enchanted land;
And he knew his shift, and the whistle's warning,
And he knew the calls of the boys below;
Through the years, unbidden, at night or morning,
He had taken his stand by the old whim bow.

But the whim stands still, and the wheeling swallow

In the silent shaft hangs her home of clay,
And the lizards flirt and the swift snakes follow
O'er the grass-grown brace in the summer day;
And the corn springs high in the cracks and corners
Of the forge, and down where the timber lies;
And the crows are perched like a band of mourners
On the broken hut on the Hermit's Rise.

All the hands have gone, for the rich reef paid out,
And the company waits till the calls come in;
But the old grey horse, like the claim, is played out,
And no market's near for his bones and skin.
So they let him live, and they left him grazing
By the creek, and oft in the evening dim
I have seen him stand on the rises, gazing
At the ruined brace and the rotting whim.

The floods rush high in the gully under,
And the lightnings lash at the shrinking trees,
Or the cattle down from the ranges blunder
As the fires drive by on the summer breeze.
Still the feeble horse at the right hour wanders
To the lonely ring, though the whistle's dumb,
And with hanging head by the bow he ponders
Where the whim-boy's gone – why the shifts don't
  come.

But there come a night when he sees lights glowing
In the roofless huts and the ravaged mill,
When he hears again the stampers going
Though the huts are dark and the stampers still:

When he sees the stream to the black roof clinging
As its shadows roll on the silver sands,
And he knows the voice of his driver singing,
And the knocker's clang where the braceman stands.

See the old horse take, like a creature dreaming,
On the ring once more his accustomed place;
But the moonbeams full on the ruins streaming
Show the scattered timbers and grass-grown brace.
Yet he hears the sled in the smithy falling
And the empty truck as it rattles back,
And the boy who stands by the anvil, calling:
And he turns and backs, and he takes up slack.

While the old drum creaks, and the shadows shiver
As the wind sweeps by and the hut doors close,
And the bats dip down in the shaft or quiver
In the ghostly light, round the grey horse goes;
And he feels the strain on his untouched shoulder,
Hears again the voice that was dear to him,
Sees the form he knew – and his heart grows bolder
As he works his shift by the broken whim.

He hears in the sluices the water rushing
As the buckets drain and the doors fall back:
When the early dawn in the east is blushing,
He is limping still round the old, old track.
Now he pricks his ears, with a neigh replying
To a call unspoken, with eyes aglow,
And he sways and sinks in the circle, dying;
From the ring no more will the grey horse go.

In a gully green, where a dam lies gleaming,
And the bush creeps back on a worked-out claim,
And the sleepy crows in the sun sit dreaming
On the timbers grey and a charred hut frame,
Where the legs slant down, and the hare is squatting
In the high rank grass by the dried-up course,
Nigh a shattered drum and king-post rotting
Are the bleached bones of the old grey horse.

Edward Dyson, 1865-1931

Corney's Hut

Old Corney built in Deadman's Gap,
A hut, where mountain shades grow denser,
And there he lived for many years,
A timber-getter and a fencer.
And no one knew if he'd a soul
Above long sprees or split-rail fences,
Unless, indeed, it was his dog
Who always kept his confidences.

There was a saw-pit in the range,
'Twas owned by three, and they were brothers
And visitors to Corney's hut –
'Twas seldom visited by others.
They came because, as they averred,
'Old Corney licked a gent infernal';

'His yarns,' if I might trust their word,
'Would make the fortune of a journal.'

In short, the splitter was a 'cure'
Who brightened up their lives' dull courses
And so on Sunday afternoons,
At Corney's hut they'd hang their horses.
They'd have a game of cards and smoke
And sometimes sing, which was a rum thing –
Unless, in spite of legal folk,
The splitter kept a drop of something.

If, as 'twas said, he was a swell
Before he sought these sombre ranges,
'Twixt mother's arms and coffin gear
He must have seen a world of changes.
But from his lips would never fall
A hint of home, or friends, or brothers,
And if he told his tale at all,
He must have told it as another's.

Though he was good at telling yarns,
At listening he excelled not less so,
And greatly helped the bushman's tales
With 'Yes,' 'Exactly so,' or 'Jes so.'
In short the hut became a club
Like our Assembly Legislative
Combining smokeroom hall, and pub,
Political and recreative.

Old Corney lived and Corney died,
As we will, too, on some tomorrow,

But not as Corney died, we hope,
Of heart-disease, and rum, and sorrow.
(We hope to lead a married life,
At times the cup of comfort quaffing;
And when we leave this world of strife
We trust that we may die of laughing.)

On New Year's Eve they found him dead –
For rum had made his life unstable –
They found him stretched upon his bed,
And also found, upon the table,
The coloured portrait of a girl –
Blue eyes of course. The hair was golden,
A faded letter and a curl,
And – well, we said the theme was olden.

The splitter had for days been dead
And cold before the sawyers found him,
And none had witnessed how he died
Except the dog who whimpered round him;
A noble friend, and of a kind
Who stays when other friends forsake us,
And he at last was left behind
To greet the rough bush undertakers.

This was a season when the bush
Was somewhat ruled by time and distance,
And bushmen came and tried the world,
And 'gave it best' without assistance.
Then one might die of heart-disease
And still be spared the inquest horrors,

And when the splitter laid at ease
So, also, did his sins and sorrows.

'Ole Corney's dead,' the bushmen said;
'He's gone at last, an' ne'er a blunder.'
And so they brought a horse and dray
And tools to 'tuck the old cove under',
The funeral wended through the range
And slowly round its rugged corners;
The reader will not think it strange
That Corney's dog was chief of mourners.

He must have thought the bushmen hard
And of his misery unheeding,
Because they shunned his anxious eyes
That seemed for explanation pleading.
At intervals his tongue would wipe
The jaws that seemed with anguish quaking;
As some strong hand impatiently
Might chide the tears for prison breaking.

They reached the rugged ways at last
A desolate bush cemetery,
Where now (our tale is of the past),
A thriving town its dead doth bury,
And where the bones of pioneers
Are found and thrown aside unheeded –
For later sleepers, blessed with tears
Of many friends, the graves are needed.

The funeral reached the bushmen's graves,
Where these old pioneers were sleeping,

And now while down the granite ridge
The shadow of the peak was creeping,
They dug a grave beneath the gum
And lowered the dead as gently as may be
As Corney's mother long before
Had laid him down to 'hush-a-baby'.

A bushman read the words to which
The others reverently listened,
Some bearded lips were seen to twitch,
Some shaded eyes with moisture glistened.
The boys had brought the splitter's tools,
And now they split and put together
Four panels such as Corney made,
To stand the stress of western weather.

'Old Corney's dead, he paid his bills,'
(These words upon the tree were graven),
'And oft a swagman down in luck
At Corney's mansion found a haven.'
But now the bushmen hurried on,
Lest darkness in the range should find them;
And strange to say they never saw
That Corney's dog had stayed behind them.

If one had thrown a backward glance
Along the rugged path that wended,
He might have seen a darker form
Upon the damp cold mound extended.
But soon their forms had vanished all,
And night came down the ranges faster,

BUSH SONGS & BALLADS

And no one saw the shadows fall
Upon the dog that mourned his master.

Anonymous

Widgeegoara Joe

I'm only a backblock shearer, as clearly can be seen,
I've shorn in most of the famous sheds
On the plains of the Riverine;
I've shorn at most of the famous sheds,
And I've seen big tallies done.
But somehow or other, I don't know why,
I never became a gun.

Chorus
Hooray me boys, me shears are set,
And I feel both fit and well;
Tomorrow you'll see me at my pen
When the gaffer rings the bell.
With Hayden's Patent Thumb guards fixed,
And both my blades pulled back,
Away I'll go with my sardine blow,
For a century or the sack!

I've opened up the wind-pipe straight,
I've opened behind the ear,
I've shorn in all the possible styles in which

A man can shear.
I've studied all the strokes and blows
Of the famous men I've met,
But I've never succeeded in plastering up
Those three little figures yet.

When the boss walked onto the board today,
He stopped and stared at me,
For I'd mastered Moran's great shoulder-cut
As he could plainly see.
And when he comes round tomorrow, me boys,
I'll give his nerves a shock.
When he discovers that I have mastered
Pierce's Rangtang Block.

And if I succeed as I hope to do,
Then I intend to shear
At the Wagga demonstration,
That's held there every year.
It's there I'll lower the colours,
The colours of Mitchell and Co.,
Instead of Denning you will hear
Of Widgeegoara Joe.

Traditional

The Grass Stealers

In Australia where the cattle tracks
Are two miles wide,
And run from northern Queensland
To the Great Divide,
The drover and the shearer
And the rouseabouts, alas!
They wouldn't steal a penny,
But they all steal grass.

For the neddies never wander
If the going's good and sweet,
But stick around the fire
With the hobbles on their feet.
So Alf and Bill and Bendigo
And Harry of the Pass,
They wouldn't steal a copper,
But they all steal grass.

When the overlanders gather
In the wide and dusty plain,
When tomorrow's never mentioned,
And they never speak of rain,
When the blazing sun is setting
Like a disc of shining brass,
They wouldn't steal a copper,
But they all steal grass.

They steal it from the squatter;

They steal it from his run.
They steal it from the cocky
And think it mighty fun.
They steal if from each other,
And nothing can surpass
The methods of the travellers
Who all steal grass.

It's sundown on the Darling,
There's water in the bend,
But not a blade of forage
Where the cattle musters end.
And let the horses pass!
So it's nip the squatter's wire
They'll take the track tomorrow
With their bellies full of grass.

Now stealing grass for horses
May be a horrid crime,
Especially to the squatter
With his paddocks lush and prime;
But a man who wouldn't steal
A bit of grass to feed his horse
Should be flung into the Darling
Or some other watercourse.

J. Murray Allison, 1879-1929

The Ryebuck Shearer

Well, I come from the south and my name is Field
And when my shears are properly steeled,
It's a hundred or more I have very often peeled
And of course I'm a ryebuck shearer.

Chorus:
If I don't shear a tally before I go
My shears and stones in the river I'll throw,
And I'll never open Sawbees or take another blow,
Till I prove I'm a ryebuck shearer.

There's a bloke on the board and I heard him say
That I couldn't shear a hundred sheep a day,
But one fine day, mate, I'll show him the way
I'll prove I'm a ryebuck shearer.

You ought to see our ringer, he's nothing but a farce
When the cobbler's coming up, he's always first
  to pass,
As for the shearing, he's more ass than class
And he'll never be a ryebuck shearer.

There's a swaggie down the creek, his name is Jack,
He rolled into town with a swag on his back;
He asked us for a job, said he needed a few bob
And he swears he's a ryebuck shearer.

Yes, I'll make a splash, and I won't say when,
I'll up off me arse and I'll into the pen

While the ringer's shearing eight, mate, I'll be
  shearing ten
And I'll prove I'm a ryebuck shearer.

Traditional

How the Sailor Rode the Brumby

There was an agile sailor lad
Who longed to know the bush
So with his swag and billycan
He said he'd make a push.
He left his ship in Moreton Bay
And faced the Western run,
And asked his way, ten times a day,
And steered for Bandy's Run.

Said Bandy: 'You can start, my son,
If you can ride a horse,'
For stockmen on the cattle-run
Were wanted there, of course.
Now Jack had strode the cross-bars oft
On many a bounding sea,
So reckoned he'd be safe enough
On any moke you see.

They caught him one and saddled it,
And led it from the yard,

It champed a bit and sidled round
And at the sailor sparred.
Jack towed her to him with a grin,
He eyed her fore and aft;
Then thrust his foot the gangway in
And swung aboard the craft.

The watchers tumbled off the rail,
The boss lay down and roared,
While Jack held tight by mane and tail
And rocked about on board.
But still he clung as monkeys cling
To rudder, line and flap,
Although at every bound and spring
They thought his neck must snap.

They stared to see him stick aloft
The brum bucked fierce and free,
But he had strode the cross-bars oft
On many a rolling sea.
The saddle from the rolling back
Went spinning in mid-air,
Whilst two big boots were flung off Jack
And four shoes off the mare.

The bridle broke and left her free,
He grasped her round the neck;
'We're 'mong the breakers now,' cried he,
'There's bound to be a wreck,'
The brumby struck and snorted loud,
She reared and pawed the air,

It was the grandest sight the crowd
Had ever witnessed there.

For Jack with arms and legs held tight
The brumby's neck hung round
And yelled, 'A pilot, quick as light,
Or strike me I'm aground.'
The whites and blacks climbed on the rails,
The boss stood smiling by
As Jack exclaimed, 'Away the sails!'
The brum began to fly.

She bounded first against the gate,
And Jack cried out, 'Astern!'
Then struck a whirlpool – at any rate
That was the sailor's yarn.
The brumby spun him round and round,
She reared and kicked and struck
And with alternate bump and bound
In earnest began to buck.

A tree loomed on the starboard bow,
And 'Port your helm!' cried he;
She fouled a bush and he roared 'You scow!'
And 'Keep to the open sea!'
From ear to tail he rode her hard,
From tail to ears again,
One mile beyond the cattle yard
And back across the plain.

Now high upon the pommel bumped,
Now clinging on the side,

And on behind the saddle lumped
With arms and legs flung wide,
They only laughed the louder then
When the mare began to back
Until she struck the fence at last
Then sat and looked at Jack.

He gasped, 'I'm safe in port at last,
I'll quit your bounding mane!'
Dropped off and sang, 'All danger's passed
And Jack's come home again.'
Old Jack has been a stockman now
On Bandy's farm for years
Yet memories of that morning's fun
To many still bring tears.

Anonymous

Carbine's Great Victory in the Melbourne Cup, 1890

The race is run, the Cup is won,
The great event is o'er.
The grandest horse that strode a course
Has led them home once more.

I watched with pride your sweeping stride
Before you ranged in line,

For far and near a ringing cheer
Was echoed for Carbine.

The start was made, no time delayed,
Before they got away,
Those horses great, some thirty-eight,
All eager for the fray.

No better start could human heart
To sportsmen ever show
As Watson did, each jockey bid
Get ready for to go.

With lightning speed, each gallant steed
Along the green sward tore;
Each jockey knew what he must do
To finish in the fore.

But Ramage knew his mount was true
Though he had 10-5 up,
For Musket's son had great deeds done
Before that Melbourne Cup.

No whip, nor spur, he needs to stir
A horse to greater speed;
He knew as well as man can tell
When he could take the lead.

So on he glides with even strides,
Though he is led by nine;
But Ramage knows before they close
He'll try them with Carbine.

The bend is passed; the straight at last:
He takes him to the fore.
The surging crowd with voices loud
The stud's name loudly roar.

The jockey too, he full well knew
The race was nearly o'er,
As to his mane he slacked the rein:
No need to urge him more.

Brave horse and man who led the van
On that November day!
Your records will be history still
When ye have passed away.

For such a race, for weight and pace,
Has never been put up
As that deed done by Musket's son
In the 1890 Cup.

Anonymous

Holy Dan

It was in the Queensland drought;
And over hill and dell,
No grass – the water far apart,
All dry and hot as hell.

The wretched bullock teams drew up
Beside a water-hole —
They'd struggled though dust and drought
For days to reach this goal.

And though the water rendered forth
A rank, unholy stench,
The bullocks and the bullockies
Drank deep their thirst to quench.

Two of the drivers cursed and swore
As only drivers can.
The other one, named Daniel,
Best known as Holy Dan,
Admonished them and said it was
The Lord's all-wise decree;
And if they'd only watch and wait,
A change they'd quickly see.

'Twas strange that of Dan's bullocks
Not one had gone aloft,
But this, he said, was due to prayer
And supplication oft.
At last one died but Dan was calm,
He hardly seemed to care;
He knelt beside the bullock's corpse
And offered up a prayer.

'One bullock Thou hast taken, Lord,
And so it seemeth best,
Thy will be done, but see my need
And spare to me the rest.'

A month went by. Dan's bullocks now
Were dying every day,
But still on each occasion would
The faithful fellow pray,
'Another Thou hast taken, Lord,
And so it seemeth best,
Thy will be done, but see my need,
And spare to me the rest!'

And still they camped beside the hole,
And still it never rained,
And still Dan's Bullocks died and died,
Till only one remained.
Then Dan broke down – good Holy Dan –
The man who never swore.
He knelt beside the latest corpse
And here's the prayer he prore.

'That's nineteen Thou hast taken, Lord,
And now You'll plainly see
You'd better take the bloody lot,
One's no damn good to me.'
The other riders laughed so much
They shook the sky around;
The lightning flashed, the thunder roared,
And Holy Dan was drowned.

Anonymous

Paroo River

It was a week from Christmas-time,
As near as I remember,
And half a year since, in the rear,
We'd left the Darling timber.
The track was hot and more than drear;
The day dragged out forever;
But now we knew that we were near
Our camp – the Paroo River.

With blighted eyes and blistered feet,
With stomachs out of order,
Half-mad with flies and dust and heat
We'd crossed the Queensland border.
I longed to hear a stream go by
And see the circles quiver;
I longed to lay me down and die
That night on Paroo River.

The 'nose-bags' heavy on each chest
(God Bless one kindly squatter),
With grateful weight our hearts they pressed –
We only wanted water.
The sun was setting in a spray
Of colour like a liver –
We fondly hoped to camp and stay
That night by Paroo River.

A cloud was on my mate's broad brow,

And once I heard him mutter;
'What price the good old Darling now?
God bless that grand old gutter!'
And then he stopped and slowly said
In tones that made me shiver:
'It cannot well be on ahead –
I think we've crossed the river.'

But soon we saw a strip of ground
Beside the track we followed,
No damper than the surface round
But just a little hollowed.
His brow assumed a thoughtful frown –
This speech he did deliver:
'I wonder if we'd best go down
Or up the blessed river?'

'But where,' said I 'Is the blooming stream?'
And he replied, 'We're at it!'
I stood a while, as in a dream,
'Great Scot!' I cried, 'is that it?'
Why, that is some old bridle-track!;
He chuckled, 'Well, I never!
It's plain you've never been Out Back –
This is the Paroo River!'

Henry Lawson, 1867-1922

Down the River

Hark, the sound of it drawing nearer,
Clink of hobble and brazen bell;
Mark the passage of stalwart shearer,
Bidding Monaro soil farewell.
Where is he making for? Down the river,
Down the river to seek a 'shed'.

Where is his dwelling on old Monaro?
Buckley's Crossing, or Jindaboine?
Dry Plain, is it, or sweet Bolaira?
P'raps 'tis near where the rivers join.
Where is he making for? Down the river,
When, oh when, will he turn him back?
Soft sighs follow him down the river,
Moist eyes gaze at his fading track.

See, behind him his pack-horse, ambling,
Bears the weight of his master's kit,
Oft and oft from the pathway rambling,
Crops unhampered by cruel bit.
Where is he making for? Equine rover,
Sturdy nag from the Eucumbene,
Tempted down by the thought of clover,
Springing luscious in the Riverine.

Dreams of life and its future chances,
Snatch of song to beguile the way;
Through green crannies the sunlight glances,

Silver-gilding the bright 'Jack Shay'.
'So long, mate, I can stay no longer,
So long, mate, I've no time to stop;
Pens are waiting me at Mahonga,
Bluegong, Grubben and Pullitop.

'What! You say that the river's risen?
What! That the melted snow has come?
What! That it locks and bars our prison?
Many's the mountain stream I've swum.
I must onward and cross the river,
So long, mate, for I cannot stay;
I must onward and cross the river,
Over the river there lies my way.'

One man short when the roll they're calling,
One man short at old Bobby Rand's;
Heads are drooping and tears are falling
Up on Monaro's mountain lands.
Where is he making for? Down the river,
Down the river of slimy bed;
Where is he making for? Down the river,
Down the river that bears him, dead.

Barcroft Boake, 1866-1892

The Horse in the Tree

High in the fork of a gnarled old tree
Was the skeleton of a horse
By the road that wandered to Wirrandee;
And I said to Charlie, who rode with me,
'Left there by a flood, of course.'

But Charlie answered, 'Well I must say
You fellows make me smile;
For every person that comes this way
Just thinks the same, an' he's miles astray.
Now, I'll give you the dinkum ile.

'I was on that moke when he stuck up there –
'Twas a wonder I wasn't killed;
But seein' impediments everywhere
I shifted back in the atmosphere
An' only got bumped and spilled.

'You see, I was after a brumby mob,
Which hereabouts split an' spread,
Goin' lickety-split, me an Wirrandee Bob,
An' didn't see, till I reached that knob,
The tangle o' scrub ahead.

'The only openin' was through that fork,
An' 'fore I had time to think,
Blue Streak went up like a popped-up cork,
But the game old moke was fat as pork
And jammed like a wedge in a chink.

'An' there's his bones; 'tis a wonder how
They've hung in the sun and shade;
But 'The Horse in the Tree' is a landmark now
That drovers know, an' they all allow
'Twas a dam' fine leap he made.'

Edward S. Sorenson, 1869-1940

Featherstonhaugh

Brookong station lay half asleep
Dozed in the waning western glare
('Twas before the run had been stocked with sheep
And only cattle depastured there)
As the Bluecap mob reined up at the door
And loudly saluted Featherstonhaugh.

'My saintly preacher,' the leader cried,
'I stand no nonsense, as you're aware,
I've a word for you if you'll step outside,
Just drop that pistol and have a care;
I'll trouble you, too, for the key of the store,
For we're short of tucker, friend Featherstonhaugh.'

The muscular Christian showed no fear,
Though he handed the key, with but small delay;
He never answered the ruffian's jeer
Except by a look which seemed to say –

'Beware my friend, and think twice before
You raise the devil in Featherstonhaugh . . .

Two hours after he reined his horse
Up in Urana, and straightaway went
To the barracks – the trooper was gone, of course,
Blindly nosing a week-old scent
Away in the scrub around Mount Galore.
'Confound the fellow!' quoth Featherstonhaugh.

'Will any man of you come with me
And give this Bluecap a dressing-down?'
They all regarded him silently
As he turned his horse, with a scornful frown,
'You're curs, the lot of you, to the core –
I'll go by myself,' said Featherstonhaugh

The scrub was thick on Urangeline
As he followed the tracks that twisted through
The box and dogwood and scented pine
(One of their horses had cast a shoe).
Steeped from his youth in forest lore
He could track like a black, could Featherstonhaugh.

He paused as he saw the thread of smoke
From the outlaw camp, and he marked the sound
Of a hobble check, as it sharply broke
The silence that held the scrub-land bound.
There were their horses – two, three, four –
'It's a risk, but I'll chance it!' quoth Featherstonhaugh.

He loosed the first, and it walked away,

But his comrade's silence could not be bought,
For he raised his head with a sudden neigh,
And plainly showed that he'd not be caught.
As a bullet sang from a rifle-bore –
'It's time to be moving,' quoth Featherstonhaugh.

The brittle pine, as they broke away,
Crackled like ice in a winter's ponds,
The strokes fell fast on the cones that lay
Buried beneath the withered fronds
That softly carpet the sandy floor –
Swept two on the tracks of Featherstonhaugh.

They struck the path that the stock had made,
A dustily-red, well-beaten track,
The leader opened a fusillade
Whose target was Featherston's stooping back
But his luck was out, not a bullet tore
As much as a shred from Featherstonhaugh.

Rattle 'em, rattle 'em fast on the pad,
Where the sloping shades fell dusk and dim;
The manager's heart beat high and glad
For he knew the creek was a mighty swim,
Already he heard a smothered roar –
'They're done like a dinner!' quoth
Featherstonhaugh.

It was almost dark as they neared the dam;
He struck the crossing as true as a hair:
For the space of a second the pony swam,
Then shook himself in the chill night air.

In a pine-tree shade on the further shore,
With his pistol cocked, stood Featherstonhaugh.

A splash – an oath –a rearing horse,
A thread snapped short in the fateful loom,
The tide, unaltered, swept on its course
Though a fellow creature had met his doom:
Pale and trembling, and struck with awe,
Bluecap stood opposite Featherstonhaugh.

While the creek rolled muddily in between
The eddies played with the drowned man's hat.
The stars peeped out in the summer sheen,
A night-bird chirruped across the flat –
Quoth Bluecap, 'I owe you a heavy score,
And I'll live to repay it, Featherstonhaugh.'

But he never did, for he ran his race
Before he had time to fulful his oath.
I can't think how, but, in any case,
He was hung, or drowned, or maybe both.
Whichever it was, he came no more
To trouble the peace of Featherstonhaugh.

Barcroft Boake, 1866-1892

Mad Jack's Cockatoo

There was a man that went out in the floodtime
 and drought,
By the banks of the outer Barcoo,
And they called him Mad Jack 'cause the swag
 on his back
Was the perch of an old cockatoo.

By the towns near and far, in shed, shanty and bar
Came the yarns of Mad Jack and his bird,
And this tale I relate (it was told by a mate)
Is just one of the many I've heard.

Now Jack was a bloke who could drink, holy smoke,
He could swig twenty mugs to my ten,
And that old cockatoo, it could sink quite a few,
And it drank with the rest of the men.

One day when the heat was a thing hard to beat,
Mad Jack and his old cockatoo
Came in from the West – at the old Swagman's Rest.
Jack ordered the schooners for two.

And when these had gone down he forked out half
 a crown,
And they drank till the money was spent,
Then Jack pulled out a note from his tattered old
 coat
And between them they drank every cent.

Then that old cockatoo, it swore red, black and blue,
And it knocked all the mugs off the bar,
Then it flew through the air, and it pulled at the hair
Of a bloke who was drinking Three Star.

And it jerked out the pegs from the barrels and kegs,
Knocked the bottles all down from the shelf,
With a sound like a cheer it dived into the beer,
And it finished up drowning itself.

When at last Mad Jack woke from his sleep he ne'er
  spoke,
But he cried like a lost husband's wife,
And each quick falling tear made a flood with the
  beer,
And the men had to swim for their life.

Then Mad Jack he did drown; when the waters
  went down
He was lying there stiffened and blue,
And it's told far and wide that stretched out by his
  side
Was his track mate – the old cockatoo.

Anonymous

A Bushman's Song

I'm travellin' down the Castlereagh,
And I'm a station-hand,
I'm handy with the ropin' pole,
I'm handy with the brand,
And I can ride a rowdy colt,
Or swing the axe all day,
But there's no demand for a station-hand
Along the Castlereagh.

So it's shift, boys, shift,
For there isn't the slightest doubt
That we've got to make a shift
To the stations further out,
With the packhorse runnin' after,
For he follows like a dog,
We must strike across the country
At the old jig-jog.

This old black horse I'm riding –
If you'll notice what's his brand,
He wears a crooked R, you see –
None better in the land.
He takes a lot of beatin',
And the other day we tried,
For a bit of a joke, with a racing bloke,
For twenty pounds a side.

It was shift, boys, shift,
For there wasn't the slightest doubt

That I had to make him shift,
For the money was further out;
But he cantered home a winner,
With the other one at the flog –
He's a red-hot sort to pick
With his old jig-jog.

I asked a cove for shearin' once
Along the Matthaguy:
We shear non-union here,' says he
'I call it scab,' says I.
I looked along the shearin' floor
Before I turned to go –
There were eight or ten non-union men
A-shearin' in a row.

It was shift, boys, shift,
For there wasn't the slightest doubt
It was time to make a shift
With the leprosy about.
So I saddled up my horse,
And I whistled to my dog,
And I left his scabby station
At the old jig-jog.

I went to Illawarra,
Where my brother's got a farm;
He has to ask his landlord's leave
Before he lifts his arm;
The landlord owns the countryside –
Man, woman, dog and cat,

They haven't the cheek to dare to speak
Without they touch their hat.

It was shift, boys, shift,
For their wasn't the slightest doubt
Their little landlord god and I
Would soon be falling out;
Was I to touch my hat to him? –
Was I his bloomin' dog?
So I makes for up the country
At the old jig-jog.

But it's time that I was movin',
I've a mighty way to go
Till I drink artesian water
From a thousand feet below;
Till I meet the overlanders
With the cattle coming down –
And I'll work a while till I makes a pile,
Then have a spree in town.

So it's shift, boys, shift,
For their isn't the slightest doubt
We've got to make a shift
To the stations further out;
The packhorse runs behind us,
For he follows like a dog,
And we cross a lot of country
At the old jig-jog.

A.B. ('Banjo') Paterson, 1864-1941

The Fire at Thompson's Ford

Hottest of hot December days,
Fierce and strong are the sun's keen rays,
The north wind's sulphurous breath blows strong;
Even the magpie stills his song.
Over the pools of the stagnant creek
Steaming hangs the vaporous reek.
Under the scanty she-oaks crowd
Panting cattle, breathing loud.

Slowly, out in the eastern sky,
A wreath of smoke climbs clear and high,
It sways in the air like a tangled cord –
A fire has started at Thompson's ford!

Thompson's shed is late this year,
Most of his sheep are yet to shear;
'Blackleg' labour, with half a board –
No 'truck' with the union at Thompson's ford.
The union camp breaks up today;
Horses are saddled and ready, but stay!
Thompson shears with the 'scabs'. Just so,
But a big bushfire is a common foe.

Down the gully, along the flat,
Red Bill leading with one-eyed Mat;
Past the stockyard, over the brush,
Mat now first, the rest in a crush;
Seven long miles in a blazing sun,

And yet the prelude has but begun.

The flames in mountains roar and swirl;
Dense black smoke-clouds over them curl;
Bounding, crackling, leaping higher –
Ah, strong men shrink from a big bushfire!
'A real old bender,' says Mat, 'good Lord!
But we've got to stop at Thompson's ford.'
The river at Thompson's ford runs low –
'But the homestead goes if it's crossed, you know.'

Yes, that was a battle, and, even now,
The very thought just pains my brow.
Choked with smoke, dry as a board,
With our teeth hard-set we hold the ford.
Side by side in that desperate band,
Squatter and shearer, hand to hand,
Fought like tigers for hour on hour,
Never a man was seen to cower.
The sun in the west began to sink,
When, choking, panting, gasping for drink,
We sent up a cheer, aye, how we roared –
We had stopped the fire at Thompson's ford!

Next year, Thompson's notice states:
'Shearers wanted, union rates.'

'Womba'

The Man Who Came to Burrambeit

His eyes were blue, his skin was white,
Though tanned his face to cruel brown,
He seemed so weak and limp and light
As from the coach they passed him down –
In short, he seemed in woeful plight
The man who came to Burrambeit.

The driver gravely shook his head,
'The pore young cove is green yer know,
I've 'eard 'im wish that 'e was dead
The 'orrid sun did try 'im so!
'Is parents they ain't done wot's right
In sending 'im to Burrambeit!'

For three whole days the stranger lay,
Within the pub shut out from view;
He'd sent a little note to say
The bush was all so strange and new,
He hoped that they'd forgive his plight,
The kindly folk of Burrumbeit.

And when at last quite pale and thin
The stranger showed upon the scene,
The good folk rushed to take him in
He seemed so very young and green –
To put the poor young stranger right,
Stirred every heart in Burrambeit.

He told them he had come from town

His parents – both alas! – were dead,
But he would live his troubles down
In spite of hot suns overhead;
In fact, he'd work with all his might
And win the praise of Burrambeit.

The kindly folk gave ear with pride
To all the stranger had to say,
It is a noble thing they cried,
That man should act in such a way;
In spite of luck to make a fight
Appeals to us at Burrambeit!

They made him welcome to each home,
They tended him with eager zest,
They told him he was free to roam
Just as his fancy pleased him best,
In short, they made a hero quite
Of that young man in Burrambeit.

And when the races came, they cried,
'Now to the meeting you must go,
There's no place round the countryside
Can show the sport that we can show!
The best of owners we invite
To send their gees to Burrambeit!'

The young man laughed, and cried, 'What fun!
Oh! shan't I love to see the course;
But I shall bet before I'm done,
I know I shall, upon some horse!'
His eagerness reached such a height

It made them laugh at Burrambeit.

But fate, alas! proved most unkind
Fore ere the third race had begun,
The young man soon began to find
He could not bear the blazin' sun.
'Dear friends,' he cried, 'It's hopeless quite,
I must return to Burrambeit!'

With faltering step he turned away
A teardrop gleaming in his eye,
'Oh! what would I not give to stay,'
He quavered as he waved good-bye;
'But never mind, I'll soon be right;
Don't grieve, dear friends of Burrambeit!'

Then climbing sadly on his horse
He slowly turned and rode away,
But when some distance from the course
His manner changed, I'm bound to say,
For suddenly with all his might
He galloped back to Burrambeit!

He rode until he came to where
The bank lay sleeping in the sun;
One youthful clerk alone was there,
For there was nothing to be done –
To hope for work, was useless quite
With races on at Burrambeit!

The stranger raised his hat of felt
As quietly he entered there;

Then taking something from his belt
He waved it gently in the air;
The clerk turned pink, and green, and white
For he was new to Burrambeit!

'Young man,' the stranger softly said,
'You're here alone, as I've been told,
So if you'd rather not be dead
Just hand me out your stocks of gold;
Your movements, too, pray expedite,
I think of leaving Burrambeit.'

The clerk, all trembling, turned away
And did as he was told, of course;
And all the gold, I'm grieved to say,
Was soon upon the stranger's horse;
The poor young cove who felt the sun!
But death seemed sad at Burrambeit.

The stranger once more softly cried,
'I hate to be an awful bore,
But I'm afraid you must be tied
With rope, and left upon the floor;
To find you in this sorry plight
Will soothe the wrath of Burrumbeit.'

The stranger laughed, as like a pig,
He rolled the clerk upon the floor,
Then, taking off his auburn wig,
He pinned in gaily to the door,
And underneath these words did write:
'A keepsake for dear Burrambeit!'

And this is true without a doubt
That, if you're anxious for some fun,
Just tell those gentle folk about
The poor young cove who felt the sun!
You'll find they've not forgotten quite.
And you'll remember Burrambeit!

R. Allen ('Guy Eden')

A Yarn of Lambing Flat

'Call that a yarn!' said old Tom Pugh,
'What rot! I'll lay my hat
I'll sling a yarn worth more nor two
Such pumped up yarns as that.'
And thereupon old Tommy 'slew'
A yarn of Lambing Flat.

'When Lambing Flat broke out,' he said,
' 'Mongst others there I know
A lanky, orkard, Lunnon-bred
Young chap named Johnnie Drew,
And nicknamed for his love of bed,
The Sleeping Beauty too.

'He sunk a duffer on the Flat
In comp'ny with three more,
And makin' room for this and that

They was a tidy four,
Save when the eldest, Dublin Pat,
Got drunk and raved for gore.

'This Jack at yarnin' licked a book,
And half the night he'd spout,
But when he once turn'd in, it took
Old Nick to get him out.
And that is how they came to cook
The joke I tell about.

'A duffer-rush broke out one day,
I quite forget where at –
(It doesn't matter, anyway,
It didn't feed a cat) –
And Johnnie's party said they'd say
Good-bye to Lambing Flat.

'Next morn rose Johnnie's mates to pack
And make an early shunt,
But all they could get out of Jack
Was 'All right', or a grunt,
By pourin' water down his back
And – when he turned – his front.

'The billy boiled, the tea was made,
They sat and ate their fill,
But Jack, upon his broad back laid,
Snored like a foghorn still;
"We'll save some tea to scald him," said
The peaceful Corney Bill.

'As they their beef and damper ate
And swilled their pints of tea
A bully notion all at wonst
Dawned on that roudy three.
And Dublin Pat, in frantic mirth,
Said, "Now we'll have a spree!"

'Well, arter that, I'm safe to swear,
The beggars didn't lag,
But packed their togs with haste and care,
And each one made his swag
With Johnnie's moleskins, every pair
Included in the bag.

'With nimble fingers from the pegs
They soon the string unbent,
And off its frame as sure as eggs
They drew the blessed tent,
And rolled it up and stretched their legs,
And packed the lot – and went.

'And scarcely p'raps a thing to love,
The 'Beauty' slumbered sound,
With nought but heaven's blue above
And Lambing Flat around,
Until in sight some diggers hove –
Some diggers out'ard bound.

'They sez as twelve o'clock was nigh –
We'll say for sure eleven –
When Johnnie ope'd his right-hand eye
And looked straight up to heaven:

I reckon he got more surprise
Than struck the fabled Seven.

'Clean off his bunk he made a bound,
And when he rubbed his eyes
I'm safe to swear poor Johnnie found
His dander 'gin to rise.
For there were diggers standin' round –
Their missuses likewise.

'Oh, Lor'! the joke – it warn't lost,
Though it did well nigh tear
The sides of them as came acrost
The flat to hear Jack swear.
They sez as how old Grimshaw tossed
His grey wig in the air.

'Some minutes on the ground Jack lay,
And bore their screamin' jeers,
And every bloke that passed that way
Contributed his sneers:
Jack groaned aloud, that cursed day
Seemed lengthened into years.

'Then in a fury up he sprung –
A pretty sight, you bet –
And laid about him with his tongue
Advising us to 'get'.
And praying we might all be hung
I think I hear him yet.

'Then, on a sudden, down he bent,

And grabbed a chunk of rock,
And into Grimshaw's stomach sent
The fossil, with a shock,
And Grimshaw doubled up and went
To pieces with the knock.

'And in the sun that day Jack stood
Clad only in his shirt,
And fired with stones and bits of wood,
And with his tongue threw dirt,
He fought as long as e'er he could –
But very few were hurt.

'He stooped to tear a lump of schist
Out of the clinging soil,
By thunder you should heard him jist,
And seen the way he'd coil
Upon the ground, and hug his fist,
And scratch and dig and toil!

' 'Twas very plain he'd struck it fat,
The dufferin' Lunnon Muff:
The scoff and butt of Lambing Flat
Who always got it rough,
Could strike his fortune where he sat:
The joker held the stuff.

'Well, that's the yarn, it ain't so poor:
Them golden days is o'er,
And Dublin Pat was drowned, and sure
It quenched his thirst for gore;
Old Corney Bill and Dave the Cure

I never heard no more.

'The Sleepin' Beauty's wealthy, too,
And wears a shiny hat,
But often comes to old Tom Pugh
To have a quiet chat:
I lent him pants to get him through
His fix on Lambing Flat.

Anonymous

Waltzing Matilda

Once a jolly swagman camped by a billabong
Under the shade of a coolibah tree,
And he sang as he watched
And waited till his billy boiled,
'Who'll come a-waltzing Matilda with me?
Waltzing Matilda, waltzing Matilda,
Who'll come a-waltzing Matilda with me?'
And he sang as he watched
And waited till his billy boiled,
'Who'll come a-waltzing Matilda with me?'

Down came a jumbuck to drink at that billabong;
Up jumped the swagman and grabbed him with glee.
And he sang as he shoved that jumbuck
In his tucker-bag,

'You'll come a-waltzing Matilda with me.
Waltzing Matlida, waltzing Matilda,
You'll come a-waltzing Matilda with me.'
And he sang as he shoved that jumbuck
In his tucker-bag,
'You'll come a-waltzing Matilda with me.'

Up rode the squatter, mounted on his thoroughbred;
Down came the troopers, one, two, three:
'Whose' that jolly jumbuck
You've got in your tucker-bag?
You'll come a-waltzing Matilda with me!'

Up jumped the swagman and sprang into
  the billabong:
'You'll never catch me alive!' said he;
And his ghost may be heard as you pass by
  that billabong,
'You'll come a-waltzing Matilda with me!
Waltzing Matilda, waltzing Matilda,
You'll come a-waltzing Matilda with me!'
And his ghost may be heard
As you pass by that billabong'
You'll come a-waltzing Matilda with me!'

A.B. ('Banjo') Paterson, 1864-1941

Index of Titles

Index of First Lines

Acknowledgement
'My Country' has been reproduced with the
permission of the copyright owners: the Estate of
Dorothea Mackellar, A. Coffison and S. Kruger, care of
Curtis Brown (Australia).